RUM POINT

A Baseball Novel

by Rick Wilber

McFarland & Company, Inc., Publishers

Jefferson, North Carolina, and London

LIBRARY OF CONGRESS CATALOGUING-IN-PUBLICATION DATA

Wilber, Rick, 1948–
Rum Point : a baseball novel / by Rick Wilber.
p.   cm.

ISBN 978-0-7864-4537-0
softcover : 50# alkaline paper ∞

1. Fathers and daughters— Fiction.   2. Murder—
Investigation— Fiction.   3. Baseball stories.   I. Title.
PS3573.I38796R86   2010
813'.54 — dc22   2009036777

British Library cataloguing data are available

Cover images ©2010 Shutterstock

Manufactured in the United States of America

*McFarland & Company, Inc., Publishers
Box 611, Jefferson, North Carolina 28640
www.mcfarlandpub.com*

Rum Point
A Baseball Novel

ALSO BY RICK WILBER

My Father's Game: Life, Death, Baseball
(McFarland, 2008)

This one is for Robert Smith (1923–1999),
who was both my friend and my father-in-law.
Thanks, Bob, for all the help and guidance.
We miss you.

AUTHOR'S NOTES

Rum Point is a work of fiction. Readers familiar with St. Petersburg, Florida, and residents of the Pass-a-grille area of nearby St. Pete Beach, in particular, may find themselves scratching their heads over the odd things that have happened to their town in the telling of what happened to Stu Lindsay, his daughter, his friends and his enemies, and a few assorted others.

I have, for instance, built a domed stadium (one curiously similar to Tropicana Field) on the beach at Rum Point. Readers may wonder how Ministry Field could possibly handle the parking and traffic of big-league baseball, but I can only plead that by making the traffic situation completely untenable at Ministry I have, I hope, made it look better at The Trop.

I have also given Rum Point its own small-town police department, invented a number of characters to inhabit the town, created a baseball team that is not at all similar (I hope) to the Rays, given that team a good-hearted evangelist as its owner, and generally had my way with reality in any number of fictional directions.

I have also exercised considerable literary license with Grand Cayman, most notably by moving Hell from one part of the island to another. Readers who visit the Cayman Islands will, I'm sure, find their way to Hell despite my tinkering with the local geography.

In the process of creating these people, their places, and the actions they take, I have sought the help of a number of very talented and generous people. Drs. Joe Springle and Dan Bell have been my source for medical knowledge and terminology in several books, and both were again crucial to the writing of this novel. I am also in debt to the very fine St. Pete Beach Police Department and, in particular, to Officer Kimberly Bentley who was gracious and patient with me in explaining the department's operations in useful detail.

As a friend and teammate of mine on the illustrious St. Pete Cubs (an energetic and sometimes very capable team made up of players over forty years of age), Attorney Herbert E. Gould was extremely helpful in providing background on just what a good divorce lawyer does and how one's career might go. He's also an excellent infielder and a timely hitter, though any other resemblance between my talented friend Herb and the divorce lawyer found in *Rum Point* is entirely coincidental.

A number of trusted friends read their way through the various drafts of Rum Point, providing invaluable advice on everything from infelicities of language use to major structural changes. I am deeply in debt to Christopher "Chip" Scanlan of the Poynter Institute for Media Studies, to the talented mother/daughter team of Diane and Cassidy Edwards, to my friends and colleagues Randy Miller, Larry Leslie and Jay Friedlander at the University of South Florida's School of Mass Communications, to Elaine Moreale of Niagara University, to early readers Larry Thornberry and Amelia Beamer and to many others.

I am especially indebted to my wife, daughter and son, who provided much of the inspiration for the better behaved characters in the novel, encouraged my efforts to write and rewrite and rewrite the book over a long period of time, and supported me through a challenging period of time when familial obligations to my father and mother made living with me difficult and slowed down my writing to a near standstill. Thank you Samantha, Robin and Richard Jr.

I am very appreciative of the guidance and help of my agent, the late Barbara Bova and her husband, bestselling author Ben Bova.

My father-in-law, Robert Smith (1923–1999), was important to me in several regards and I miss him deeply. In the initial explorations for this novel Bob and I visited Grand Cayman for a most enjoyable week, with Bob so delightfully involved in the research process that he took more (and far better) notes than I did and so I found myself relying on him for his support even some years after his death.

ONE

Truth was, Honker Kelsey had always been terrible at keeping things quiet and this failing had often brought him pain.

He'd first discovered the price you can pay for talking too much when, in the third grade at Holy Innocents, the nun they'd all called Sister Very Vicious got so fed up with his chatty nature that she put duct tape over his mouth one blazing hot October morning during homeroom. He could still remember the sticky taste and sickly smell of that day.

But the taping hadn't stopped him and he'd gone on being who he was: always moving, always talking, always driving the teachers and then, later, the coaches crazy and then, much later still, talking himself into one world of trouble. Now, here, swimming ashore, it was important — very, very important — that he finally keep himself really and truly quiet.

Problem was, the current was pushing him toward the inlet and danger. He knew he'd be able to swim through the tugging water easily enough if he could just take a few dozen strong strokes, but he'd tried that once already and the splash he'd made had sounded like a belly-flop in the neighborhood pool. There had been a mumbled query from the boat behind him followed by a quick look his way with the boat's searchlight. He'd slipped beneath the surface and they hadn't seen him, but he'd learned his lesson: no more free-style splashing. So here he was making do with this clumsy, half-hearted dog paddle of a breaststroke, trying to reach the beach before he got swept around into the bay or, worse, was seen by the people in the boat.

Things were going all right, otherwise. After the raucous line of thunderstorms had passed by on its way out to sea and things had calmed down, he'd been able to get quietly out of the lower bunk, slip the backpack on, pad barefoot across to the door, open it, climb up the seven wooden steps, ease over the side hanging onto the slippery aluminum ladder, and then slowly slide into the warm Gulf. All of it without a hint to anybody on board.

But this damn current. It didn't seem fair to be this close and yet have to fight the water, but Honker smiled at that thought as soon as it occurred to him. Fairness wasn't something he needed to be worrying about right now.

So he kept paddling, kept trying to keep it absolutely quiet, aware the whole time about how well sound traveled over water. The boat was behind him a couple of hundred yards but he could still hear the oddly delicate clank of the anchor chain as *Third Day* rocked on the slight swell. At least the wind was starting to pick up; that might kick up a few waves and help mask any more noise as he got closer to shore.

Ahead, the beach was almost dark. There were some hotels and the bright glow from Ministry Field up the beach to the north where the ballgame was going on, but that was a good couple of miles away. Ahead, there was nothing but dunes and darkness if he could get there. Another fifty yards, he figured.

He wondered what Samantha was doing right now. Just sitting there by the phone in his little house in West Bay, probably, waiting for him to call, waiting to hear everything was OK.

And it *would* be OK. It would be fine, it would be great. He needed to believe that. For three years he'd done a perfect job of keeping the books—the very inventive books—watching all that money flow in and out of the shell game that was the corporate world of Craig Ministries and its various Cayman-based subsidiaries. Now it was time, at last, for a little payoff.

A shape loomed up right in front of him. Shit. He splashed, backpedaling for a moment in fear before he realized it was a marker buoy for the swimming area. Damn, he'd been noisy. He was an idiot. For being involved in this in the first place. For trying to make it all come out right somehow. For sneaking away and swimming to shore with a backpack on his back. A complete, total idiot. But no one shined any lights his way and then, just beyond the buoy, his feet touched bottom. He'd made it then, could walk in through the current's pull from here, nothing to it. Maybe it was all going to work out all right. In an hour he'd have the flash drive hidden away somewhere safe. They couldn't touch him as long as he had that. He'd get his money from them, nothing too big, nothing too greedy, just enough to live on comfortably on Cayman Brac and keep the stuff with the

Kemp's ridleys going until he got it right. That'd be something, bring a whole species back from the brink. Good karma, if nothing else. He allowed himself a smile. Cayman Brac sounded good; really get away from it all.

He walked in toward the shore staying low, in a kind of crouch in the water as it got shallower and shallower, keeping underwater as much as he could while he moon-walked toward the beach, the water supporting him. Finally, ten or fifteen yards from the dry sand, he stood up. Damned if it all wasn't going to work out all right after all. And about time, too. All his wasted life nothing had ever seemed to work out like he planned, none of his great plans ever fell into place except maybe for the turtles and there was no damn money in that; that was for love. But this, maybe this was it and he could cash in at last. God knows he'd paid his dues.

There was someone coming on the beach. Shit, they were waiting for him.

No. It was just some local, out jogging on the beach for exercise; the guy said "G'evening" as he went by, the voice familiar, maybe somebody he knew from the old days growing up here.

Honker took a few steps, turned to look back at *Third Day*, its dark bulk barely visible against the faint illumination from the sliver of moon. He'd done it. Damned if he hadn't done it. He smiled, wanted to laugh out loud.

And then there was a sudden splash behind him and before he could turn a hand over his mouth, a sharp jolt against his back, a strange pinching of his stomach as he struggled, turning to look at his attacker, seeing him for a frozen moment, not surprised at who he saw while a strange calmness came, the moment stretching out and out forever as he stared into those dark eyes. He had time, plenty of time, to think about where it had gone bad, how it had come to this, how bad Mom and his brother would feel when they found out, how he'd let the turtles down after all, unable to save them. He felt sorry about all of that.

And then came a dark blurred violence toward him, something half-seen and quick now toward the side of his face, time all speeding up as wildly as it had slowed. Coming at him. Hard against his cheek, feeling the crack of bone, knowing where this was going. The beginnings of pain. A strange moment of surreal clarity, the time to think, calmly, that this is what it's like to die. Then darkness.

3

TWO

At Ministry Field, St. Petersburg Crusaders manager Stuart Lindsay stood on the dugout steps and tried to block out the clamor and fear for a moment and give some clear thought to which pinch-hitter to bring in: Macalaster or Perez?

Whichever one he chose was likely to be wrong, damn it, and then they'd lose the game and the wildcard spot with it and the whole damn season would be a waste. And maybe that wasn't a bad thing. He was tired of this season, tired of the pressure, tired of the decisions, tired of leading the double life the job required. Outside, he was calm, but inside he was in knots. Too much was going on, all of it spinning around while he tried to keep an eye on it, order it, get it organized. Win one more ball game.

All right, then, take a breath. The Porters would bring in a lefty if he pinch hit Macalaster. Sampson, out there now, would stay in and face Perez. Mac was hitting the ball on the nose lately, but had trouble against lefties. Perez, on the other hand, had been lucky in his last few at-bats, dinking a couple of soft liners into shallow right for base hits that brought his average up just over the .200 mark. What was important, though, was that both of those hits had come against guys throwing splitters, and that was Sampson's out pitch, so Perez was going to see one. So, just maybe, Perez would stay lucky one more time when the bottom dropped out on the pitch as it neared the plate.

He glanced at the computer screen perched on the table in the corner of the dugout. It wasn't telling him anything he didn't already know, but it made for a great excuse. If he followed the computer's advice and went with Macalaster the papers wouldn't rip him tomorrow, would they? No, they'd blame it on the player and not on the manager.

But Stu had a gut feeling about Perez, a feeling that Hector would make contact with the inevitable split-finger. Of course, it was likely the gut feeling was just the chicken sandwich he'd had about six P.M., which had sat there all night, a lump of nausea and tension that wouldn't go away despite his chewing on eight or ten Rolaids as the innings went by. Oh, hell, Stu hated moments like this. Stay calm. Think it through. Make a decision and live with it.

The crowd had come to its collective feet, roaring in delight with Carter Gaddis's two-out double up the gap in left and the possibilities it suddenly raised for a Crusader victory. The organist was trying to get a chant going, playing that silly theme song, but the fans were having none of that — this was time to roar.

Sure, it was a great thing to see, all this yelling and screaming that had been going on for the past few weeks. The players were loving it, feeding off it, and even the Reverend, confused as he seemed these days, was starting to get the picture, coming into the clubhouse after the games to pound some backs and shake some hands— regular happy-owner stuff. Winning will do that for you. Hell, here they were, the St. Petersburg Crusaders, playing a game on September twenty-ninth with a chance to make the post-season. Two on, two out in the bottom of the eleventh and the crowd sensed all the possibilities.

But the tension was awful, and Stu was the manager, the boss, the maker or breaker. The man. Hell. He turned to glance at the dugout. They were all looking his way, every one of them, even that sonofabitch Dickerson, who was damn lucky he could hit the ball five-hundred feet or he'd be long gone with that attitude of his.

OK, then, what did that self-help guy on TV say? Go with it, trust yourself, be a leader.

Right, use the Force, Stu.

"Hector," Stu said, waving at the slender infielder sitting at the far end of the bench, buried in a corner. "Grab a stick and get over here."

Hector Perez was going to be a helluva a ballplayer one of these days, but the kid needed a lot of talking to. He got down on himself too easily, let every little thing eat at him — that strikeout in the ninth last week had sent him into a deep, gloomy introspection that he still hadn't come out of. Stu knew that feeling and sympathized, but sharing Hector's pessimism wouldn't help anybody.

He grabbed the kid by the elbow as he walked up the dugout steps, smiled at him, took a deep breath through the nose. Time to pretend. "Smell that, Hector?"

Hector looked puzzled. His manager was famous for these little talks, these *lecciones*. But this was something new. Sniffing the air? He took a deep breath. "No, Skipper, I don't know what you mean. These are the same smells as always."

"The smell of leather? The smell of the stickum on the bats? The smell of hard work and sweat and infield clay? You smell all that?"

Hector smiled faintly. He was starting to understand. "Yes, Skipper, I smell that."

"Smells that way at home, too, right, in Santiago?"

Hector nodded. Just last year that's where he'd been, home in the Dominican, playing for Aguilas del Cibao, hitting the ball hard, making the plays in the field. Then Cristian Mendoza, the Crusaders' scout, had come with a contract and the chance to play in America. Two months in the Florida State League, then up to Raleigh at the start of this season and now, so fast he could barely breathe, Hector was with the big club here in the dome. In another month he'd be twenty years old.

"OK, Hector. Take a good sniff of that bat and then get out there and get us a base hit, all right? You know he's got that good splitter working for him. That's his out pitch. Watch for it, OK?"

Hector nodded again and then walked out toward the plate. An odd man, his skipper, Stuart Lindsay, but a spiritual man, too. Hector believed in the spiritual side of the game. He believed in Stuart Lindsay. The man was like a priest.

THREE

A slow awakening, lying on his back, his mouth underwater in a shallow tidal pool but his nose out of the water. That's why he could breathe, that's why he was still alive, just because his big damn nose, the thing that earned him his nickname, was above water. He was alive. His luck was holding, then.

His backpack was gone, but that didn't matter. The flash drive was inside a baggie and taped to his groin. He could feel it, still there, hard against his testicles. The son of a bitch who'd attacked him had missed it, must have figured it was in the pack and just grabbed that and ran.

He tried to stand and in that action, reaching down with his hands to the sandy bottom and starting to push off, to rise, he woke up the pain, a great, dull throb of it centered on his left side at first, an enormous ache that left him dizzy.

And his cheek, god, the pain there staggered him, too, this one a sharper, brighter stab. He reached up to touch his face —felt the long edge of the broken bone under the skin and wondered why that didn't hurt even more than it did. It *would* hurt more, he guessed; a lot more, and soon.

It was hard to think. He managed to sit up in the shallow water, propping himself up with his right hand in the sand, reaching down with the left to feel his side. Oh, man. He reached down. Bleeding. Lots of blood. The bastard had knifed him, left him here to die with a nasty wound in his stomach. He tried to switch hands and lean on the left one for a moment, but the left wouldn't support him, so he sat there swaying, trying to not fall over into the water.

He put the right hand back down, reached again with the left, this time to the small of the back, and there was another wound there, not bleeding as much, he thought, though it was hard to tell with all the water.

The bastard had run him through then, using that damn spear he was so proud of, the one he got that barracuda with the other day down in the Keys. So now Honker knew for sure who'd done this and, oh, hell, the guy had jammed that spear right through him, grabbed the backpack and then left him here for dead.

But he was still alive, and he still had the flash drive. There was a splash to his left as he sat there, and for a dizzy moment he thought the son of a bitch was back to do the job right this time, finish him off and find the drive. Tiredly, resigned to it, he lifted his head and looked that way.

And damned if it wasn't a sea turtle, a Kemp's ridley female, by god — could that be?—coming out of the water right next to him, no more than five feet away, ready to dig a nest and lay her eggs. Right kind of weather, with the surf starting to kick up some. Wrong time of day, but what the hell. She looked at him, her dark eyes hidden deep in the hard, triangular head.

She should have been spooked, seeing him there. She should have turned right around and headed back out to sea — too many things wrong about this— maybe come in later, when the sun was up, to lay her eggs.

But she had better things to do. She had a primitive plan that Honker Kelsey was not going to get in the way of, and while he watched she started trudging ashore and headed up the beach, reaching out with those two front flippers to dig into the sand and then pull herself along, leaving a path in the sand where she had been.

Jesus, that was a sign if there ever was one. Had to be. He could see the path, wet, with the marks alongside where the front and then the back flippers had dug in. Looked like tire tracks off some weird one-wheeled tractor. Damned if maybe some of what he'd done had been worthwhile, then, after all.

7

It was a damn miracle, he decided. A sign. That's what Samantha would say. Well, he had to get up into the dunes anyway, right? He'd just follow the Kemp's ridley up there and bury the flash drive. Then, after he'd hidden it, he would get some help for himself, get this bleeding stopped. If his luck held this could still work out all right.

He struggled for a moment with his arms, had to figure out how to get them going. Funny how they weren't paying much attention to his brain. Then, pushing mostly with his right leg, he started crawling, slowly, achingly, along the path the turtle had left.

FOUR

Officer Felicity Lindsay gave the accelerator a twist and sent the ATV scrambling to the top of the steep boardwalk that started at the parking lot and then arched over the fragile dunes and down again to the beach.

At the wide platform at the top of the boardwalk she hit the brakes, killed the engine to quiet things down, then turned the radio on so she could listen to the ball game. She hoped, for Dad's sake, that the Crusaders would pull it out.

Chip Corso, announcing the game, was getting excited; the Crusaders had a threat going in the bottom of the eleventh. Time for her to go to work, though, so she started the ATV up and headed down the ramp and onto the beach, leaving the radio on so she could catch the action from time to time and see if Dad's guys could win another one.

The evening thunderstorms had blown clear and a narrow crescent moon threw a dim path of silver toward her across the Gulf of Mexico. The wind had been calm since the squalls, but now was picking up a bit and there was a light chop out on the water. She putt-putted slowly up the beach, taking her time, her headlight lancing out ahead into the darkness, widening as it went, showing her the polite little waves of the shorebreak and the hard-packed sand that ran up to the high-tide mark.

A guy went by going the other way, tall and thin, walking fast, all elbows and knees as he emerged from the darkness huffing and puffing on the hard sand near the waterline. She caught just a glimpse of his face; sunken cheeks, a big jaw. He was focused on the beach ahead, concentrating.

She saw a lot of walkers and joggers on this beach, even when she worked the night shift. This guy was out late to avoid the daytime heat and humidity. Smart guy, given the climate. He waved to her with his right hand as he went by. In the left he carried a small bag and some kind of stick. He was shelling, then, and looking for driftwood. Good time for that, after the storm had passed and before the old folks would pick it all over early the next morning. As he hiked out of sight into the darkness, Felicity looked up the beach where he'd been. To the north, about a mile away where the town of St. Pete Beach started, the high-rise condos and hotels rose against the skyline. Another mile or so up was Ministry Field, the bright glow from inside shining through the thin dome roof with a ghostly pale luminescence.

Ministry was a nice ballpark in a lot of ways and it was good for local business, bringing all the fans out here during the season. But the field wasn't good for the turtle hatchlings; they got confused by that glow, especially when the night games ran late and well into the darkness that should, by rights, be nearly total out here by the water. Those little hatchlings needed some moonlight and no distractions if they were going to make it from their nests to the sea. The hatchlings, she thought, were one more reason that she was glad baseball was nearly done for the season.

She turned to look south, the way the guy with the bag was headed. There the darkness was nearly total, with the little business district of Rum Point paying attention to its own ordinances. She could barely see a few of the buildings set back across the old beach road, behind the dunes. About a mile beyond them the beach ended at Shell Island Pass, where the bay met the Gulf of Mexico.

Rum Point, all of one mile long and a few hundred yards wide, was quiet and calm most of the time and Felicity liked it that way. Life as a police officer here wasn't exactly a thrill a minute, but she'd seen enough action in her two years on the Detroit force to last her a lifetime. She was happy enough handing out a few speeding tickets, dealing with the likes of poor old Mrs. O'Brien who wandered off and got lost from time to time, and breaking up the occasional fight in the beach-front bars. She would be very happy, thank you, if she never saw another victim of a drive-by shooting or found another wasted junkie dying on the streets. She'd needed a change in her life and in her work and when Dad left the third-base coaching job he'd had with the Tigers to take on managing the Crusaders, she'd been happy to come along.

She smiled as she listened to Corso talk about Dad bringing in Perez to pinch-hit. Hector was hitting .190 or something and there was a lot of talk of trading him or sending him back down to Raleigh next spring. Corso was moaning about the move, and Felicity had to agree. And, of course, she'd wind up arguing with Dad about it tomorrow. He lived for the game, more so these last few years than ever before. It was the only way they could talk, the two of them, through the filter of baseball.

"Why'd you use Hector?" she'd have to ask, and he'd tell her about the pitcher's strengths and weaknesses and how they stacked up against Hector's swing. There'd be something about the psychology of the game, too, why some guys were winners and some weren't. And somewhere, buried in all the baseball, she'd be making it clear that things were all right with her lately, and he'd be saying the same thing back to her.

It was a clumsy way to talk, but things got real uncomfortable if they tried to converse any other way. There was too much history back there, too much shared pain. Pinch-hitters, sliders and fastballs, stolen bases and on-base averages—these were the codes that got them through the day, daughter and father.

Felicity understood this, realized it more than Dad did, she guessed. But it made living so near to him tough. She kept thinking it might be time to move farther away, maybe get a job over on the other coast; but then what would he do? She'd been taking care of him since Mom's death, protecting him and then, as the years went by, starting to hope that eventually he'd find someone else to fall in love with and marry. It had been eight years now and while on the outside he seemed over the horror of that time, she knew him too well: he was hurting, and confused, and depressed.

He was back to drinking again for one thing. For the past couple of months she'd been finding him sitting on that porch he liked so much; five in the morning and she'd just be getting home from her shift and she'd look over to the house as she drove down the driveway to her apartment and there he'd be, in the pre-dawn darkness, a bottle of single-malt standing empty on the table next to him, the cell phone to his ear as he talked with someone. She'd tried once or twice to talk to him about the drinking and find out who he was talking to, but the conversation hadn't gotten anywhere.

Fel thought what he really needed was someone new in his life, even as a friend or confidant, and someone who liked something other than baseball. Since Grandfather died a few years ago, Dad never talked to anyone about anything that wasn't centered on baseball. Fel didn't want to leave him alone in such a narrow world. Fel wanted to protect him, maybe even guide him. He needed her, and so that's why she lived so close, in the little one-bedroom corner apartment of the grandly named Fontainebleau Apartments, just across the shell-and-gravel driveway from his house.

She gave the ATV a little gas and headed up the hard-packed wet sand near the water. Tonight was beach patrol, which meant keeping an eye out for those baby turtles. The assignment log actually read "Beach Patrol/Lindsay/11 P.M. — 6:30 A.M.," but it was September and a lot of the baby turtles were hatching, so "Beach Patrol" meant driving by the nest sites to see if the little ones were OK. She'd spent much of the summer making sure the nests had been marked off and left alone, so she'd come to feel a certain attachment to the hatchlings. She'd seen two batches of babies making it toward the water just within the last week. It was really something to watch, the little ones working those flippers in a frenzy as they struggled through the sand and reached, at last, the warm Gulf water and their future.

She was taking her time, moving along slowly, enjoying the night, when she saw something and pulled the ATV's headlamp to the left to double-check. Sure enough, it looked like a track from a mother turtle coming in to lay eggs. This was late in the season for that — the last one before this had been three or four weeks ago — and the path was different, too; thinner, smoother at first, and then widening out later. But it was unmistakably a trail, a gouge a couple of feet wide and an inch or two deep in the sand, with flipper marks on each side, starting from the water and heading inland.

This path looked twistier than the others she'd seen; they usually arrowed right in and up the slope to the dunes. This mom must be confused or sick, that would explain why she was so late in the summer. Felicity turned the ATV to the right, gave it a little more gas in the softer sand, and followed the path up toward the dunes. There were dark splashes of water still puddled to the side of the path every few feet. That was odd, too, but it must mean that this was all fresh and that mom was still up there, digging away.

She stopped short of where the trail went between two tall sea-oat covered dunes and doused the bright headlight, turned off the engine and clicked off the little radio even though Hector was stepping into the box. She didn't want to bother the mom too much. In the sudden quiet, she could hear the scrape of flippers into the soft sand, a light screeching sound

11

as the mom dug away. Felicity smiled. The mother turtle was working hard right now, but it wouldn't be long and she'd be done and never see the babies that resulted. There was some kind of message in that somewhere.

After a minute or two the scraping stopped, which meant the mom was done digging and was now laying her eggs. Felicity relaxed; almost nothing could bother a female once she started dropping her eggs. Felicity took off her helmet, shook out her hair, which was getting way too long again. She looked good with it this long, but it was such a hassle, always needing the brush, always needing ten minutes or more with the hair dryer after she washed it.

The scraping sounds stopped and a couple of minutes later Felicity watched protectively as the mother turtle came out of the dunes, pulling herself along quickly on her front flippers, pulling her way back to the sea in what passed for a sprint for a sea turtle. It was a small miracle to watch her go, and Felicity just sat there and watched, planning on waiting until the mom was clear before going up to check out the nest and mark it off with some stakes and yellow tape so nobody would bother it.

For now, the mom heading toward the waterline, Felicity clicked the radio back on, the volume down low, and strained to hear Chip Corso, who was getting pretty excited. Hector Perez was still at the plate after the Porters' manager had visited the mound but left in his pitcher. Hector had worked the count to two-and-two and the game was on the line. The pitcher was walking around the mound, stalling, playing head games with Hector, according to Corso, trying to rattle the young hitter and not let him get comfortable in the batter's box. When the mom finally entered the water with a tiny splash, Felicity was reaching down to turn up the volume a bit and really hear how this next pitch would go when she heard, from the dunes, a groan, a muffled curse. What the hell was that?

She hopped off the scooter, pulled her flashlight from her belt but didn't click it on yet. Somebody bothering that nest full of eggs that Mom had just left? She decided not to yell, but to get closer first. If it was somebody robbing eggs she'd want to catch them in the act. Just some kids, probably, up here messing around in the dunes and then they'd had seen the turtle laying eggs and now they were going to take a look. Then there was another curse. No, not kids; a deep voice, hurt, in pain. "Shit," she heard. "Goddamnit." And then some more scraping. She flicked on the flashlight, ran up through the path between the dunes and there, in the flat space between two rows of dunes, saw the dying man.

He was on his back, lying next to the nest. His left arm was at the edge of the hole, moving like he was trying to get at the eggs. There was blood, lots of blood, and that awful iron smell of it. It had even puddled in the sand, so much of it that the sand couldn't soak it all up. He stared at her, said "Help" so weakly she could hardly hear it, and reached out that left hand toward her.

She took this all in for a long second, moving the beam of her flashlight up from his feet to his face. Swimming trunks, that's all he had on; blue ones, boxer-short style, with an orange "F" on them. He had short hair, light brown, a face that might have been handsome before somebody had clobbered him — looked like his jaw was broken on the lower left side, already swelling up. It was a wonder he could say anything at all.

For another two or three seconds she looked him over. He probably had some broken teeth and she wondered if she'd have to reach in there and keep the airway open for him. His nose was too large for his face, and bent to the right a bit from some old break. She wondered why he hadn't had that fixed. He was a big guy, over six-foot-six at least and in good shape, maybe thirty, thirty-five years old. The path led right to him; he'd dragged himself up here, bleeding all the way. There was blood, a lot more of it than the face wound could produce. She shined the light around and saw the damage around the ribs. Damn.

"I'll get help," she said to him, reaching down to hold his hand while she unclipped the radio from her belt and thumbed it on. "Charlie Three to Central, Charlie Three to Central. Copy?"

"Hi, Felicity, darlin.' What's happening? Bet ya' just had to talk to me, right? Or did you find yourself some more little turtle babies, darlin'?"

Damn Roger, always hitting on her, half joking, half serious.

"Central, I have a man down here. Send rescue. I'm in the dunes north of the Gulfway boardwalk."

Roger was suddenly very official. "10-4, Charlie Three. Man down in the dunes north of the Gulfway boardwalk. Help is on the way, Charlie Three."

"Copy, Central. Male Caucasian, mid thirties, bleeding heavily under the ribs. I'll try to stop the bleeding. Get fire-rescue here and hurry it up, Central, there's a lot of blood."

"Rescue 10-51, Charlie Three. ETA is four minutes."

"Thanks, Central," Felicity said, and set the radio down in the sand while she knelt down next to the guy. His grip was weak on her right hand.

13

Down close she could see there were actually two wounds on his left side, one in the small of his back, the other on the opposite side, under the ribs. Something had gone right through him.

"Shit," the guy said again.

"We've got help on the way," she told him. "Just hang on for a few more minutes."

Felicity had a small kit back in the ATV. She got up, ran back to it, got out the kit and tore it open to pull out two sterile dressings while she ran back. Kneeling next to the guy, she pressed the dressings firmly against the front wound. He groaned. There was an ominous rattle from his lungs, fluid in there and air struggling to bubble through it. The bleeding was slowing, but, she guessed, more from his loss of blood than anything she was doing with the pressure. He wasn't going to last long.

"Can you tell me what happened? Who did this to you?"

His eyes opened. He looked at her. "Oh, be quiet," he said. And then he smiled, a calm, satisfied smile, like he'd made some private little joke and now the pain was gone and he was at peace. "Quiet," he said again. And then his grip on her hand relaxed, and the rattle from his lungs eased and then disappeared and he was, Felicity knew, dead.

There was a lot of commotion coming down the beach, emergency vehicles running 10-18 with lights and sirens on. Through the clamor she could hear, on her little portable radio back on the ATV, Chip Corso screaming. Hector Perez had driven a line-drive up the middle. Corso was raving about it, excited, as the Porters' centerfielder chased the ball down and came up throwing while Gaddis rounded third and headed home. There was a play at the plate, a close one.

Officer Lindsay took her hand from the dead man's, laid his arm down in the sand, then stood up and waved her flashlight toward the fire-rescue people as Gaddis slid in safely past the tag and the Crusaders won.

FIVE

The clubhouse had finally cleared around midnight. Now, fifteen minutes later, only Jimmy Frazier, the Down syndrome kid who was assistant clubhouse boy, was left, rattling around straightening up the folding chairs and tidying up the lockers. Stu Lindsay knew everything would be exactly in its right place before Jimmy's disabled-services taxi showed up to take him the mile or so down the beach to his group home, where he'd get a good night's sleep. The kid had a great life in his own way. He was happy; everybody liked him; he had a great job; he had no worries and no stress.

That all sounded pretty damn good to Stu, who couldn't make the same claim about any of that as he sat in his office with the door finally shut and the sportswriters gone. He looked at the bottom right drawer in his desk and gave that a moment's thought. Damn straight, he'd earned a sip of that Macallan. Just an inch. A reminder. A little test of his will.

He opened the drawer, pulled out the glass first, wiping it clean with his shirt, then reached down to grab the Macallan by its neck and pulled it out to set it on the desk. He slowly twisted the cap to open it, and then poured an inch of it into the glass. Maybe an inch and a half. Or so.

It had a beautiful color, kind of an amber with maybe a little hint of orange. He sipped it and could taste the peaty smoke, the little tang of sherry from the casks that were used to age it. Damn good stuff.

He closed the bottle and put it back, then sat there for a few minutes with the glass, looking at it. A long sip. Another, longer, and it was done. He put the glass into the drawer with the bottle and shut it. He sat back in the chair. A little bit of peace at last. It was quiet.

First had come the half-hour of news conference stuff, sitting at the table with the microphone in front and pretending he had something important to say. Then, coming back to the office, he'd been forced to allow Nick Krusoe — the *Sports Illustrated* writer — to tag along. Krusoe was just another in a long line of overweight, over-opinionated, under-knowledged-and-never-could-play-the-game-themselves sportswriters. Like all of them, he was full of sarcasm and spit even though he couldn't hit a baseball two-hundred feet if Stu set it up for him on a tee.

But Stu had agreed to give Krusoe special access for a big profile — Brooks and the Reverend had insisted on it — and so he let him come along for a while before, finally, shooing him out and sitting in here alone for a precious ten minutes.

He took a deep breath, thought it through. Hell of a thing, all of this — having a shot at the damn pennant. Not a single sportswriter, and certainly not Krusoe, had given the Crusaders the ghost of a chance back in April and now here they were. And that, he thought, smiling, is why they play the games.

Stu just wished he was having at least a little bit of fun. Instead, the back half of the season had turned into a kind of ongoing hell. Too bad, since not all that long ago Stu had been a believer in baseball. He'd thought the game mattered. Only after Carmen's death had he found a kind of terrible wisdom, a new way of viewing reality, a new perspective on things: most of it coming from bottles a lot less expensive than the Macallan. The day she was taken from him and the lessons he'd learned from that tragedy had almost been too much to bear, had worn him down so that he hadn't even managed to be the father he should be to the precious daughter he and Carmen had produced. Felicity, his little girl, was the best thing he'd done in his life, now all grown up but still, really, the little girl who'd made his life worth getting on with after Carmen's death.

He could hardly stand thinking about them, the losses of those hard years, but eventually his daughter's patient love and the last few remnants of his career had brought him back. He'd paid more attention to his coaching. He'd faked it, at least, pretty well. Then last year he'd taken the chance of moving down to St. Petersburg from Detroit, taking Felicity away from the people and places she knew and asking her to start over here in the heat and sunshine. Bless her heart, she'd said yes. It had been a risk, coming here, and he still couldn't decide if it had been the right thing to do. The Tigers had been good to him during those hard times, and he'd been set as their third-base coach, showing up every day and getting the job done. It was safe, secure work, or at least as close as you got to that in baseball. And then, out of nowhere, had come the chance to manage in St. Pete, the Reverend himself calling him up on the phone to offer the job and a pile of money and how do you turn that down? Not the money, that was easy to pass on. But the job; it was the brass ring and you had to grab it, especially when you thought all of that kind of dreaming was long gone.

And maybe it *was* gone, maybe this was all too much. He'd gotten himself into quite a mess here, winning all these games in August and September and now the Crusaders had won tonight's damn game and were two up on the Porters for that wild-card spot with just three left to play. Win one of them and they'd have it, these young kids and the few veterans. Stu wondered if he could take it should they win one more. Playoff baseball? It sounded hellish. It sounded like enough to make him explode. It sounded like for sure they'd figure him out, the sportswriters and the fans: they'd suddenly realize that Stu Lindsay was living a lie.

His cell phone went classical on him from where he'd left it in the desk drawer before the game started; the ringer set on a snippet from Beethoven's Ninth. There were only a handful of people who had this number, and just one or two who'd be calling at this time of day.

He flipped it open, looked at the number. It was his father. Damn.

He put the phone to his ear. "Hello, Father."

"They've just announced the Nobel for physics in Stockholm, son. Did you see who they named?"

"Hey, we won, Father, thanks for asking. One more win and we're into the post season."

"My old friend, Lewandowski. He won it for work he did twenty years ago at Chicago, with the Fermi lab."

Stu gave up. His father had always ignored baseball utterly, was disappointed that his son had taken up a worthless sport for his life's work. "That's great, Father. His work on superstrings, yes?"

"Yes, yes, of course," the old man was grumpy that his son would say such a thing, as if Lewandowski had worked on any other theory for the past twenty years. "And it's crap, you know; the whole thing is crap. He'll be discredited within the next two or three years, you watch."

Stu's father had been a vocal critic of string theory for years. And of Lewandowski. And the University of Chicago, for that matter. Only the great minds at Cornell — and his great mind, in particular — really understood a thing when it came to life, the universe and everything.

There were voices out in the clubhouse. Stu looked up to see Cassidy Craig chatting with Jimmy, both of them grinning and then high-fiving as they walked Stu's way. Jimmy was on his cell phone at the same time. Stu had been surprised that Jimmy could use the cell phone; talking to him you wouldn't have guessed he could handle the complications of the thing, but he seemed to do just fine with it and was talking on it all the time. Just goes to show.

"Father, can we talk about this later? I've got a little press conference coming up."

"You're at that baseball arena? You had a match tonight?"

"It's a park, Father; that's what they call it — a baseball park. And, yes, I'm here and we just won a pretty big game."

There was a sigh at the other end. "Son, I understand how much you care about sports, though for someone with such a good mind, you know I've always felt..."

Stu cut him off. "I know, Father, I know; it's all a terrible waste. But

17

really, I have to go just now. Maybe we can talk tomorrow about Lewandowski and the prize, all right?"

He could hear his father's peremptory sniff. "Fine then, some other time, *son*," he said, emphasizing the last word to make the point about filial respect. "Goodbye then," and he hung up.

Jesus, the old man was difficult. He'd always been difficult in the past. He would always be difficult in the future. That's the way life was, and it was depressing to think about it.

But then the world brightened as Jimmy led the way into Stu's office, closing his cell phone and shoving it into his pocket as he came up to give his favorite manager a major-league hug. "You a winner!" he shouted, "and a great man! I be very proud for you."

Short and stocky, with a round face that usually wore a happy smile, Jimmy was a lovable guy. He worked hard to keep the lockers straight and the shoes shined for the players, and the fact that he was a little slow didn't bother most of the players, who seemed to really like him. There were times—like right now—that Stu thought Jimmy had it all figured out pretty good.

Cassidy was right behind Jimmy, carrying her briefcase, dressed in a business suit and wearing those herringbone glasses that announced firmly that she was definitely not your archetypal ditzy blond.

"Who was that on the phone?" she wanted to know.

"My father," Stu said, "complaining, as usual."

Cassidy looked puzzled.

"Something bothering you, Cassidy?"

She smiled, waved it off. "No, no, not really." She looked at the notes in her hand, something she'd printed out from her laptop. "So, Lucky Lindsay, did you know that since mid–July, Hector Perez is hitting .330 against right-handed pitching after the seventh inning with men in scoring position?"

"You know what, Cassidy. It's almost twelve-thirty."

"I'll bet you didn't know that. Further, I'll bet you used Hector because you 'had a hunch,' or 'felt like he was due' or something like that." She shook her head. "You know the sportswriters will have a field day with this: 'Lucky Lindsay Wins Another Miracle.'"

"Coffee?" Stu stood up and walked over to where his little drip coffee maker was keeping some strong, dark chicory coffee warm. He'd started it going a half-hour ago, just part of the pretense.

"No, it would keep me up. And Macalaster is hitting just .247 with men in scoring position after the seventh over the same time span. I'll bet you didn't know that, either."

"You bring me those fielding numbers you talked about yesterday, Cassidy?"

"Oh, and for both players the numbers I just gave you are for home games. Hector's slightly worse on the road, Macalaster about fifteen points better, unless he's in St. Louis, where he's thirty points worse, Lord knows why."

"Like your father says, the Lord knows, Cassidy, that's for sure."

She reached into her briefcase and pulled out another sheet of paper. "I'm not sure where you get your nerve, but like I've said a thousand times, wouldn't it be great to have some statistics to back up all the courage? Here's the fielding numbers, but they won't make any sense to you."

He took the sheet from her, looked at it for a long thirty seconds. "It's not courage, Cassidy, it's baseball." He waved the paper in the air. "So you're saying Garn is having trouble going in the hole. A lot of shortstops have trouble going in the hole, and some of them a lot better with the glove than Ron Garn."

"No, it's more complicated than that, Stu. Look," and she pulled her laptop out of the briefcase, opened it up, and tapped her nails on the scratched and worn surface of Stu's desk, the one he'd brought with him from Detroit, while the computer booted up.

Stu sighed. He appreciated just how good Cassidy was with numbers. As assistant comptroller for the Crusaders she was, no doubt, a legitimate whiz no matter who her father was. But what had started as a little bit of information about his players and the opponents a few months ago had grown into some kind of statistics monster. She was in to see him daily, had even come along on the last two road trips with the team, and was filled with numbers, so many they all blurred together on him. And she gave him constant grief about this courage thing, which was, Stu guessed, a nice word for guessing.

"Look," she said again, pulling him over toward the screen. The outline of an infield filled the small screen and a tiny figure stood at shortstop. "See the red areas? Those are base hits up the middle. Now watch what happens if we move Garn one step to his left." She pushed her finger around on the metal touchpad for the mouse and the red blotch on the screen narrowed considerably.

19

Stu took a sip of his coffee. It tasted terrible. "What do we give up on the third-base side?"

"Statistically insignificant. If it's a problem with a particular hitter I can compensate for that and move him back for those instances. He's better going right for some reason."

"Yeah, throws across his body pretty good."

"Exactly. Stu," she clicked again, moving the tiny Ron Garn on the screen back to his right so the red blotch grew. "Look, you're always talking about defensive strength up the middle, how that's what wins games. Well..."

Stu nodded. All right, all right. "Thanks, Cassidy. Thanks a lot. This is really helpful. I'll talk to Garn about, and to Quent. We'll try it out during batting practice, hit him some grounders up the middle, see how it works."

She smiled, satisfied. "That's great, Stu, really. I knew you'd see what this information could do." She reached over, took his coffee from his hand, and sipped from it, grimaced, handed it back, closed the lid of the laptop. Then she turned to look at him, their faces no more than three feet apart. "And there's one more thing, too. Daddy asked me to tell you. There's a group of French doctors coming to the next game. Their plane gets in about eight-thirty, so they'll get here about the fifth inning or so and watch the rest of it from in the skybox. Daddy wanted to know if you'd stop by after the game and say hello to them, shake a few hands."

"Daddy" was the Reverend Morrel Craig, who owned the Crusaders, who also personally hired Stu, and who, twice now, had coughed up the money for expensive free agents—so there was no question about whether Stu would show up after the game or not. Cassidy knew it. Stu knew it. Still, it was nice to be asked.

"Of course, Cassidy. I'll be there about a half hour after the game."

"About a half hour after we win the game."

He smiled. "Sure, after we win it."

Her smile widened. "You're such a pessimist. We're a couple of games in front, Stu! Hey, with your courage and my statistics, we'll go all the way, right?"

He nodded. Sure, nothing to it, he could guess them all the way. "Right. The World Series, Cassidy."

She laughed, "And you need to get home and get some sleep, Stu. You look tired."

"I'll get some. Sleep like a baby after a win like this." Which was a lie, of course. He'd lie there for an hour or more before finally dozing off into a light sleep, everything running through his mind, all the baseball crap, the potential for wins and losses, who was swinging the bat and who wasn't, whose arm looked good and who needed some extra work in the field and what to do about Sonny Dickerson and all the rest of it, the great swirl of complexity that roiled around him every hour of every day.

And on a good night that would be it, just the baseball wrestling match, as he thought of it. On a bad night—and let's hope this wasn't one of those—there would be a full load of all the other things eating at him, all of his weaknesses and failings coming out to beg him to have a drink, just the one, so they could scuttle back under the bed and he could, maybe, get a little sleep.

Cassidy reached out to touch his face, her hand for a moment across his cheek, lightly, just a quick brush. "Sure you will," she said. "You'll sleep for a few hours and be back here by eight." She paused, looked him in the eyes for a moment. "You need to take better care of yourself, Stu." And then she shoved the laptop back into the briefcase as he ran his own hand across his face, touching the cheek then rubbing his eyes. He was tired.

And then she was gone, waving at him as she left, tugging the door shut behind her, the room suddenly quiet and empty, like there'd been a crowd and they'd all just gone home.

He walked back around behind his desk, sat down and leaned back against his chair, putting his feet up on the desktop. She was nearly twenty years younger than him, had to have a flock of boyfriends around. And Stu was in a pennant race here, trying to win one more crucial game and sneak into the playoffs with this team of damn-near children and one bad-attitude veteran with a good stick. The last thing he needed was to be thinking about some woman, about the boss' daughter, at that. Jesus. He opened his desk drawer, stared at the Macallan for a moment, then proved something to himself by shutting the drawer and pulling out a line-up card, thinking of getting a head start on roughing it out for tomorrow night's game.

From his pocket his cell phone got classical again, violins sawing away energetically at Beethoven. His father again? Damn.

He didn't much want to, but pulled the phone out and took a look at the front screen. The call—thank god—was from Felicity, not his father. She was probably just checking up on him to make sure he'd get home at a decent hour and get some of that sleep.

But when he answered it turned out that she was calling in from the police station to say she'd be getting home late. She was filling out paperwork and talking to some homicide detective from the Sheriff's Department. There'd been a murder on the beach and she was the one who'd found the victim.

SIX

The little girl was a bashful, wide-eyed cutie; hiding behind Mommy's legs and not saying a word. And her brother — oh my, what a wonderful, big smile that boy wore, and quite the talker, rattling on about last night's Crusader game and what a great hitter Hector Perez was.

Morrel Craig reached down to ruffle the hair of the twins, two of the sweetest little ten-year-olds you could imagine, and said to the smiling parents, "God love them, Mr. and Mrs.—" he'd forgotten their names.

"Whitby," the mother offered with a smile.

"Whitby," the Reverend said, adding "God love you for bringing them up so well. They're wonderful, wonderful children. You must be very proud of them."

The parents blushed, smiled shyly, and managed a happy nod. They were, indeed, proud of their twins and overwhelmed to get a chance to show them off to the Reverend Craig himself. The Whitbys had known there was a chance that they would get to meet the Reverend when they came to St. Petersburg; it was one of the reasons they'd chosen this part of Florida for their vacation. But watching the Reverend's *Crusader Hour* on cable television back in Mankato, Minnesota, was one thing, and actually standing in the presence of the great man, after only an hour or so of waiting in the cool lobby of the Crusader Cathedral's office annex on Baypoint Drive in St. Pete — well, that was another thing entirely.

It wasn't as if you could make reservations. No, they'd come here today with muted hopes, joining the dozen other families with similar ambitions to see the Reverend. And surely, the Whitbys had thought when they'd seen the crowd in the lobby, he couldn't meet with them all personally. But now, to their amazement, he *was* meeting them, giving each family two or three minutes, time enough for a quick hello, a strong handshake with the father, a gentlemanly hug for Mom, a quick lift and a hug and that famously huge, warm smile for each child.

The Whitbys were the last, but it was well worth the wait. The Reverend was an amazing person, they thought as they left, just as impressive in person as he was on the show. And an honest man, too, one who did some real good in the world with his missions in Africa and Asia and Central America. There were no false promises from the Reverend, no laying on of the hands for a sham cure, no claims for miracles, no trying to be president of the whole country.

And no constant requests for money, either. The Reverend Morrel Craig wasn't like that, wasn't like the others. He was too spiritual, too good, too warm for that. He was, as far as the Whitbys were concerned, the only preacher around who really cared about his flock and their spiritual welfare, and didn't beg for their money all the time so he could spend it on himself. There were no mansions, no private jets, no lavish offices. The Reverend felt it was wrong to be asking for money from his followers, and said so every day. Just send what you can when you can, he always said, and that will do. God will provide.

And God did provide. You could see it in the videotapes on the *Crusader Hour* that showed people being fed in Somalia and the Sahel and Cambodia and Indonesia; showed people being cared for in those hospitals, the kids with full tummies going to school.

The Whitbys loved this man. They loved him because despite his fame as an evangelist, despite the power of his Word, he seemed to still be, at heart, a humble, unassuming preacher.

The Reverend, the Whitbys knew, always flew coach.

And it was all true. Morrel Craig, closing the door behind the Whitbys as they left, was proud of that, proud of the truth of who he was, the honesty behind what he said. It allowed him to believe in himself, and he needed that, especially now, with things in turmoil.

This memory problem was getting worse, that was one thing. He seemed to remember some things just fine, but forgot others in a heartbeat. He knew what that might mean at his age, had already talked to Joe Springler, his personal physician, about it over the phone. Springler was a young guy — he couldn't be more than forty — but had the unflappable calm of an older man and the Reverend liked that about him. He'd said he thought it was probably nothing serious, that all sorts of things could lead to a little

23

memory loss. On the phone he'd chuckled and said it was probably just a urinary tract infection and a round of antibiotics would clear it right up.

Thing was, the only reason the Reverend could recall the conversation at all was that he'd written it down, a lengthy note on it, in fact, and there it was, in his handwriting, right in the middle of the desk: "Two P.M. Monday at Springler. Might be urinary infection. Antibiotics will clear up. Don't forget!!!!"

He didn't remember writing it, but there it was, in his handwriting, and every time he saw it there on the desk he remembered the appointment, so that was something. An infection? Lord, let it be that simple, please. And if it wasn't? If it was something worse? Well, he'd get through it, Lord willing.

There was another note, a memo, with his daughter's name on it, so she'd written it. "Finances," it read across the top, and then as he opened it up and started to read he remembered what that was about, too. The new financial backers that Brooks brought in with him a couple of years ago had seemed fine at first, but they were already past the investment mark from the stock transfer agreement, said Cassidy, and still the money was coming in, a lot of it in securities and bonds. And worse, where was the money going? These investments that Cassidy said were in the financial report, what in God's name were they all about? Her memo finished with a list of the investments and a brief question about each one. The Reverend set the memo in the center of the desk, where he was sure to see it when he needed it. He intended to get some answers.

He walked over toward the picture window that looked out over Tampa Bay, sparkling in the summer heat, a line of thunderstorms in the far distance, inland. He kept Brooks on his mind, tried to think it through. He'd brought the man in to heal the wounds of the ministry; he remembered that well enough. And, sure enough, the man had done it. Even the huge, insane gamble of buying the baseball team — a team that would have left town or even gone out of business if the ministry hadn't bought it, renamed it, then spent the millions more to revive it here in St. Petersburg — even that had worked out. The Crusaders were making money. But Brooks was secretive about how and where all the money flowed, Cassidy's memo said, and the Reverend had to make sure it was all clean, respectable.

Well, he sure agreed with his daughter on that score. Morrel Craig was not like so many of his brethren; he would never be touched by scandal. He would lose everything, would throw it all way, before he would lose his self-respect.

He loved the view from here: to the right the little private airport's runways ran right up to the water; straight ahead in the distance two sailboats headed across the bay toward Tampa. Closer, St. Pete's big pier jutted out into the bay; to the left, the old, classic deco Augustine Hotel and its new condo units marked the end of downtown. It was a beautiful place.

He sighed, turned, and walked back toward his desk, sat down. Now, what was on the schedule? He hit the voice button on the intercom. "Alice, what do I have scheduled for today?"

"Your meeting with George Brooks in a few minutes, Reverend. You asked him to come by."

"And what was that on?"

"There's a report from Cassidy, Reverend, that has the details. I'll come in there and find it for you if you like," Alice said.

He looked at his desk and there it was, bold as brass. How could he have failed to notice that? Oh, Lord. He keyed the intercom again. "I have it, Alice, thank you."

But Alice was already coming in the office door, a slight, worried smile on her face. She walked over, reached down and picked up the memo, handed it to him.

"Thank you, Alice, thanks very much," he said, and held it in his left hand as she smiled again and walked back out through the door to her outer office.

He looked at it and realized it looked familiar. Cassidy had highlighted the parts of it she must have found important. There were plenty of those highlights.

He stood, then walked over to the mirror that backed his office door and assessed his five-foot-four, one-hundred-twenty pound frame. Cassidy, he recalled, said he was getting too thin for his own good. His flock wanted him to look healthy, she said, and needed him to look fit and industrious— not so thin that they'd worry about him. That was weeks ago that she'd said that, and he wondered why he could recall it. She'd said he needed to put ten or fifteen pounds back on.

He liked to listen to his daughter's advice. She'd come along pretty late in life for him, so he treasured her all the more. She was every bit as smart as her mother had been, and Lord he missed Emily. Strange how the Lord had wanted Emily while she was still young.

Cassidy, growing through those years without a mother, had seen her

25

share of problems, but those were behind her now. She'd turned things around after some trouble at her college; some problems with drugs, some bad company. But now she was home again and she seemed fine. He ought to see about getting her back to school, maybe at the university right here in town, where he could keep an eye on her as she kept making progress. How long had she been home now? He couldn't recall exactly, but surely it had been a month or two. He was proud of her, proud of how she'd saved herself from her own troubles. He decided, right there on the spot, that he was going to bring her into the ministry on the accounting side, get her involved as part of getting back in school. That was a great idea; he'd have to write it down.

His intercom bleeped. "Reverend," Alice said, "Mr. Brooks is here. You asked him to come by after the *Family Hour*?"

Had he said that, had he asked Brooks to come by? He could hear the distaste in Alice's voice. She didn't like Brooks a bit. He couldn't blame her; George Brooks wasn't all that pleasant a man.

He smiled just to think of Alice, who'd been with him since the old days, back when he'd first started the ministry. She'd seen it all, from the tents in places like Pine Mountain, Georgia, to the satellite broadcasts of a global ministry and the successes, the real impact, the real help, that the ministry had given over the years. He recalled sitting at the wheel of that old Chevrolet, driving through the red clay of Georgia with Alice over in the other seat planning the next revival and counting up the successes— the souls saved as well as the money earned—as they drove along toward Umatilla or Milledgeville. A few years later, when he'd met and married Emily, just eighteen to his thirty-five, Alice had moved into the back seat without a bit of complaint and they'd all prospered. Those has been wonderful days of hard work and sweat and toil for the Lord.

He was lost in thought, standing next to the his simple desk and the famously small chair he'd had since seminary — the simple piece of furniture, unpainted, with just a new coat of varnish every few years; the hard, wooden seat meant to remind him of who he'd been, how far he'd come — when the door opened and George Brooks walked through. What was he doing here? Why didn't Alice buzz him to let him know Brooks was coming? Did he have an appointment? He must have.

Brooks was just under six feet tall, prosperously overweight — he'd be fat in a few more years if he didn't watch out, the Reverend thought — and sharply dressed in a gray suit, light blue dress shirt and a broad, splashy tie

26

with the Crusader symbol — a knight with crossed baseball bats on his shield astride a sturdy horse; ready to battle the devil himself for the pennant. And Brooks was smiling — always that smile.

Brooks coughed, cleared his throat. "Hello, Reverend. I understand you wanted to see me this morning? Quite a game last night, wasn't it?"

A game last night? Wanted to see him? Well, there was nothing for it but to get through it, assume he'd asked for the meeting, assume there'd been a game last night.

"Yes, George, yes. A great game, and thank you for coming in, I know how busy you are these days."

Brooks walked over to the corner of the office where the four stuffed chairs were gathered around the small table. He sat. The Reverend walked to his chair behind the desk and sat down himself, and there, thank the Lord, was a memo from Cassidy. All right, then. He grabbed the memo, stood, and walked over to sit across the table from Brooks.

He glanced at the memo and things started coming back. The ministry. The accounting. Cassidy. He leaned forward and thought about how to phrase this. Gently, then, ease into it: "George, I'm a bit uncomfortable with how things are going lately with the ministry's finances. I feel like I'm not getting enough information. I'm losing track of things, and I thought we should talk about it."

"Delighted to talk things over, Reverend, of course."

"Well that's fine, George, just fine. The Lord knows you've been doing wonders." He glanced the memo's checklist on page one, "But what concerns me is I understand we've made some new investments." He glanced again at the list, "including this trust company in Sarasota, for one. Can we afford that? Should we be buying up other companies? All these new firms we've bought here and there, George, they seem to have nothing at all to do with our work, our real work."

The Reverend held out his daughter's memorandum. "Cassidy made this list for me, George, of our recent acquisitions." He read from the list. "A mutual fund administrator? A mortgage firm? A commodities brokerage? A bank? George, what do these kinds of companies have to do with the Ministry?"

Brooks smiled, sat back in his chair, coughed again, covering his mouth with his left hand, patient with the questions. "We talked about this a few days ago, Reverend, and it's consistent with the growth plans we agreed to last year and our desire to handle our own transactions as often as we can.

You brought me in to turn things around financially and I've done it. The positive cash flow from the Crusaders has helped, and our new subsidiaries have all been profitable right from the start."

Brooks was warming to it as he spoke, moving up in his chair, then sitting on the front edge. "Even the offshore opportunities have worked out well, though the capital expenditures there were higher than we wanted. But Crusader Bank and Crusader Retreat on Grand Cayman have done well, Reverend, and let's not forget that the Retreat was your idea, remember? We knew it would be expensive to build and support. We put nearly three million into that building and its staffing; but when it opens in a few months you'll see results right away, Reverend. It's going to cost us nearly half-a-million a year to operate and, frankly, it may be years before it comes out of the red for us, but the promotional aspects are worth millions—it will be the top spiritual resort of its type in the world."

He coughed again, hard and looser this time, some phlegm rattling around in there. The man needed to see Joe Springler, the Reverend thought, that cough sounded awful. But what was he going on about? Something about a resort?

"Point is, Reverend, you wanted to do this and we've done it. And these other investments? Not only are they good for the Ministry, we need to do more of them, especially if we're going to operate places like Crusader Retreat."

The Reverend looked at Cassidy's report again, held the piece of paper in his hand as he stood up and walked away, his back to Brooks as he looked at the notes and read from a line near the bottom of the first page. "George, Cassidy says this looks like a textbook way to overexpand before we're fully capitalized and ready for that kind of growth. She thinks we should be slowing down all this growth."

Brooks sat back again in his chair, the cough under control for now, smiling calmly as the Reverend turned to face him. "Reverend, we're all very proud of Cassidy now that she has her life back in order and she's back in school and all. Working toward that master's degree in finance over at the university is terrific. But this is the real world, not some college class being taught by a professor who's never actually run a business as big and complex as Craig Ministries. I think you're going to have to trust me that things are going along well. The Ministry is in good financial shape and getting better all the time." He leaned forward, looked the Reverend steadily in the eye. "This is what you have me here for, Reverend, to save the ministry. Trust me to do my job."

The Reverend sighed. Yes, trust. "George, of course, we're all appreciative of what you've done. But I have a responsibility to millions of the faithful, and to myself. I worry when I find out about these things after they're
done. I mean, George, at the very least I should be kept fully informed."

Brooks nodded. "Of course, Reverend. Fully informed."

The Reverend looked at his notes again, read the comment underlined
at the top of the page. "And from now on I would really appreciate weekly
updates, George, and from you personally. Does that sound all right?" That
sounded like pleading, he realized, and he needed to be more firm with
George, more in control. But it was hard. Certainly the man had his faults,
was too secretive, mainly. But hadn't he done a wonderful job for the ministry? Hadn't he brought it back from financial ruin? The Reverend thought
he remembered that being so.

He walked back over to where Brooks sat, still smiling. He could smell
the man's cologne, mixed with the stale odor of too many cigarettes. A stray
strand of hair stood out on the back of Brooks' head, fighting the spray that
held the rest of the hair in place, combed over the bald spot that spread back
from the forehead. What an odd thing to suddenly notice. He almost mentioned it, but caught himself. What was he wanted to say? Ah, yes, there,
the very last line on Cassidy's memo.

"We need you, George, heaven knows, but as your friend and as the
chairman of the board, I'm asking you to try and slow things down a little,
and to keep me better informed. All right?"

Brooks stood, broadened his smile. "Of course, Reverend. Absolutely.
I'll have you a complete breakdown on recent activity by this afternoon, and
I'll keep you informed weekly from here on. That sound all right?"

"That'd be fine, George. Thanks so much for taking the time to bring
me up to date on all this."

Brooks coughed, a hard one, his shoulders shaking with it. "Sure, Reverend. Absolutely. We all have the same goals here. I'm sure you'll feel more
comfortable once you see how well these new acquisitions are doing for
us."

Brooks rose, heading for the door, coughing hard again, his fist to his
mouth to block it some.

"George," the Reverend said, his voice suddenly so firm that Brooks
stopped and turned around, a hint of anger in his face.

"George, I want you to get that cough looked at. Have Alice call Joe
Springler for you on your way out, all right?"

Brooks smiled, coughed, then chuckled. "Sure Reverend. I'll have her call him and then I'll see him tomorrow."

The Reverend smiled back, some small bit of control exercised. "Thank you, George. Some antibiotics will probably do you wonders."

Brooks left, and the Reverend walked over to the window, looked out at the sailboats and St. Petersburg's long pier jutting out into the bay. He still held the notes from Cassidy in his hand and looked at the piece of paper for a few seconds before turning again toward the window and the wonder of God's nature; fluffy white clouds floating out over the blue waters of Tampa Bay.

SEVEN

Brooks loved the Jaguar; the subtle rumble of the engine, the comfort and smell of the leather seats, the soft hiss of the air conditioning as it battled the midday heat and pulled away the smoke from his cigarette. He'd worked hard to get to this point in life, rolling down the friggin' Bayway in this big, comfortable Jag, heading toward a quick meeting with Mackie and then a couple of quiet hours later in the afternoon, sitting on the second-floor deck of his beach home with that terrific goddamn view of the beach and the Gulf of Mexico.

He coughed, cleared that phlegm out of his throat, pushing down the button for the window long enough to spit the gunk out and then get the window back up before too much heat got in. He was tired of the damn cough, all the allergies he'd had in Guatemala years ago coming back to get him again here. So what the hell, he'd go see that doc of the Reverend's and get something to clear this up—should've done that long ago, really.

He smiled. In Guatemala, the last time he'd had this kind of cough, he'd been living miserably, working for the friggin' agency. Here, cough or not, allergies or not, he was, by god, living right. A little tickle in the throat was nothing now. He'd paid his dues for this. He'd earned it.

Only problem was that between the screw-up with Honker Kelsey and this new hassle with the stupid Reverend and his daughter the whole thing was a little shaky, so that had to be fixed, and quick.

He'd really kind of liked Honker Kelsey at first, and the kid had looked all right and had the right credentials. Before deciding to let him handle the books in Grand Cayman, Brooks had even had his old agency contacts check Kelsey out completely. The kid had come up clean: he'd lived abroad for a few years playing basketball, spoke French and Italian, had a degree in accounting, and seemed smart enough to do the work and smart enough to keep his mouth shut. Perfect.

Then it all went sour when the son-of-a-bitch turned out to be a greedy bastard, so they had to go to all the trouble of setting him up to see who else was in on it. Jesus, a whole lot of friggin' work went into all that and it wasn't settled yet and wouldn't be until they recovered that flash drive.

And now it was starting to look like the Reverend and his daughter would just have to be dealt with one way or another, too. Tricky business there, of course. It would have to be done very carefully; a clear accident, no suspicions of anything else, no investigations. A plane crash maybe, or a bad wreck in that stupid old Ford the Reverend drove. A house fire? Something like that. Mackie would know how to take care of it.

But then he frowned at that. Was it time to worry about Robert Mackie, too? He loved the guy. Hell, they had a history, the two of them, that was for sure; but this latest thing was sloppy work. Kelsey died just a couple of hundred yards away from Brooks' own damn house, which was way too friggin' close. That was stupid, and not like Robert's work at all. And somehow he didn't wind up with the flash drive. They'd have to talk about that, and about the Reverend and Cassidy, at this little noon meeting. Then later this afternoon he could sit down with a drink or two and plan things out a bit. Sergei, working out of Prague now, was sending a guy over to Grand Cayman next week for a routine little discussion on how things were coming along. Brooks wanted to be ready for that meeting.

But first, Mackie. Brooks coughed again, caught it before it got too hard, then forced the cough back under control as he eased the Jag along toward Rum Point and a nice quiet lunch with Robert Mackie.

EIGHT

It was nearly noon when Felicity woke up. It had been six A.M. before she'd gotten home this morning after spending the rest of her shift last night on automatic, getting the job done. First, she'd chatted with the detective who was running the case, Kimberly Bentley, from the County Sheriff's Department. Then she helped set the perimeter of the crime scene, taping it off. Finally, after forensics got there and started trying to find something, anything, in the sand that might serve as evidence, Felicity went back to the report room at the station, sat down behind the battered old desk they all shared — a desk that she guessed had been there since Rum Point first incorporated in 1935 — and filled out her incident report.

She'd hoped that doing that, writing short phrases in small spaces on the form, would turn the guy's death into something routine, something ordinary. Instead, when she got to the narrative, describing those few minutes, she'd wished for better skills as a writer, wished there was a way to describe with more truth how weird it all was, with the turtle eggs right there beside the guy as he died.

She'd seen plenty of violence in her two years in Detroit, but seeing this guy die right in front of her, watching him bleed away from deep inside as she tried to talk to him — that was a first, an ugly first.

When she finally got home to her apartment she could see her father waiting for her as she drove up the shell driveway that led to both places, his house and her apartment building. He sat out on the back porch of his house, enjoying the relative cool of the morning, reading the newspaper. Her place — a two-story building with four apartments in it — and her dad's house shared an alleyway in back. She could see him sitting there talking on his cell phone as she drove the little Honda down the alley. He waved at her. She waved back, sighed, and walked over to him after parking her car.

He closed up the phone and shook his head as she walked up. "Murder? In Rum Point?"

She shrugged. "Guy on the beach, Dad. I was the one who found him. He was still alive when I got there."

"I'm sorry, sweetie."

She sat on the other chair, one of those PVC pipe and plastic-weave contraptions that everyone used here, comfortable enough, she supposed, until the salt ate away at the strapping and the cushion fell through to the floor. "He didn't last long. He lost a lot of blood."

"I'm sorry," he said again.

"Tough decision, putting in Hector?" she asked him.

"I don't know. Tell you the truth, I was guessing and I got lucky."

She'd nodded at that and then the two of them sat there, quiet, for

32

another few minutes before she rose, said she had to go get some sleep, and walked over to her place for a few hours of sleep.

There'd been a dream, the usual bad one. It had been a few months since the last time her subconscious conjured those surreal memories of the night of Mom's death, the way the car in painful slow motion started spinning and then caught the low wooden rail at the side of the old road and rolled over once, twice and then again, tumbling down the riverbank until it landed on its roof in the cold, shallow bed of the Black River, breaking through the thin ice and stopping there, finally, top down in just three feet of water. Just enough water.

Now, slowly sitting up in bed, she glanced out the window to see the heat rising off the asphalt of Beach Road as it angled over to the parking lot and the boardwalk that led to the beach. It was blazing out there, and cool in here, her air conditioner cranked all the way. She wanted to stay in bed, but if she was going to find out anything about last night's murder she'd need to do it now, before too much time passed, hot weather or not. It wouldn't lead anywhere, she knew, the case was out of her hands now and she was just another spectator; but the first murder in ten years in Rum Point had her curious, that was for sure. Involved or not, she wanted to know about it. So, reluctantly, she got her feet onto the floor and stood up, determined to face the heat.

NINE

He sat opposite Robert Mackie at a little table on the outdoor deck at Woody's seafood shack, drinking iced tea. Summer, high noon, and even under the shade from the big umbrella that hovered over the table it was blazing hot, but in friggin' Florida you couldn't smoke indoors. There were no other patrons stupid enough to sit outside so they had the wooden deck to themselves. Dressed in a business suit, sweating away, he smoked Winstons and fought the damn cough while Mackie waved away the cigarette smoke.

"I told you," said Mackie quietly, "there was nothing on him. It all went just like it was supposed to. He figured he'd made a clean escape. He should've had the flash drive with him, but it wasn't there. I checked the body before that girl cop got in the way. I took the bag and we checked that, too. There was nothing."

Brooks took a drag on his cigarette, blew the smoke toward the umbrella. "We have to find that little flash drive, Robert, no way around it. A lot depends on this, for both of us. You check up his butt? Son-of-a-bitch might have used that old mule trick."

Mackie laughed, a single sharp bark of humor. "Yeah, that'd be about right for Kelsey, shove it right up his ass. Just the kind of thing he'd do." Then he waved away a cloud of smoke, admitted, "No, I didn't get a chance to check his asshole. I whacked him, then gave the body a quick pat-down. But that girl cop was heading my way on that little scooter. I had to get going. Shit, Brooks, I figured the flash drive was in the backpack, anyway."

"You know they found the body up in the dunes?"

Mackie hadn't thought that through. "Shit, yes. I read that. Look, I killed him right at the water, ankle-deep."

"How'd the body get up there?"

"No fucking idea."

Brooks shook his head. "Worse and worse, Robert. He must have crawled up there, must have been alive when you left him."

Mackie just sat there, face blank for a moment. Slowly, he shook his head. "I popped him one in the jaw to shut him up, then I ran him through with the diving spear, popped the heart wide open. No way he was alive."

"But he must have been alive when you left him or he couldn't have made that crawl. What if he said something to the girl cop?"

Mackie gave him a tight smile. "He didn't say nothing. I broke his jaw. Shattered it. I heard the bones breaking. He wasn't saying nothing, even if he was alive."

"You're sure of that?"

"Hell, yes. Dead or alive, he couldn't have said a thing."

"Well I hope you're friggin' right."

Brooks paused, took a long, thoughtful drag on the Winston, then stubbed it out. "Robert, we've been working together a long time, you and me. I've always taken care of you. Good pay. Good benefits."

Mackie nodded, all the smiles gone.

"And you've always come through for me. Every single damn time."

Another nod.

"This was your idea, setting Kelsey up so he'd lead us to whoever he was working with."

34

"And you liked it," Mackie reminded him. "You said it was a hell of a good idea."

"I did, Robert, I did. And it was. But it didn't work out, did it?"

Mackie just stared at him.

"All right, then, I know you'll come through this time, too, Robert. We have to have that friggin' flash drive. Here's what we'll do. I'll go back and check the beach, see if it fell out when he crawled up there, see if it's in the sand somewhere. I'll find it if it's there."

"And me?"

"You go to the morgue. You find the body. You check out the anal cavity, Robert."

"Anal cavity. Right." He nodded, lips tight. "Sure. If it's in there, I'll get it. Be a pleasure, checking for it. One final message for that fucking Kelsey."

Brooks smiled. Only Robert Mackie could find pleasure in that kind of work. "Just do it cleanly, all right? We don't want anyone knowing the body was checked for anything."

Mackie was playing with a salt shaker, tapping it on the wooden slats of the table-top. "Brooks. Remember the look in that slope's eyes the first time, in the Nam?"

Where was this coming from, Brooks wondered? Jesus, thirty-five friggin' years ago, the first time they'd worked together, couple of young kids trying to earn their way. "At the door of that slick. Yeah, Robert, I remember."

"Just before I shoved him out, he looked at me straight. Hard, you know. Fucker believed in himself, you know?"

"Yeah, Robert, I saw that. And the guy watching, he saw it, too, started talking in a hurry, remember that?"

Mackie nodded, thoughtful for a second. "Kelsey had that look last night. I'll give the son-of-a-bitch that. He had that look. Yeah, I'll do it carefully, Brooks. Real professional."

"And I'll do the beach," Brooks said, and then smiled. "Now get going. I'm going to have another cup of this coffee and one more cigarette."

It was a little joke between the two of them. "You know, I've told you a thousand times, Brooks, those things'll kill you."

Brooks nodded. "Right," he said, "they're gonna kill me." He lit up, took a deep drag and blew the smoke toward the ceiling. This was not something he was worried about.

35

TEN

At six A.M. he'd watched his daughter leave, looking back at him as she was turning the corner past the azalea hedge that escorted the sidewalk to her apartment. She'd waved. He'd waved back and she'd disappeared.

She was one terrific girl, so at least he'd done one good thing in his life. How had Jimmy, the Down's clubhouse boy, put it the other day? "I love you and I like you," he'd said to Stu as he gave him a big hug after that disastrous loss to the Cardinals just one week ago.

That's how Stu felt about his daughter. He loved her, sure, the way a father can love a daughter, so fiercely and protectively that he'd give anything, his own life if he had to, to make the world safe for her. But he liked her, too. She was a good person who'd had to face some really nasty realities and yet she'd found a way to bounce back, come back to life and kept things moving forward. She'd done a lot better job of that than he'd done, that was certain.

He'd rubbed his eyes. There was a ring of darkness creeping around the edges of his sight again. It happened the first time after a four-game losing streak on the road. He'd been sitting on the plane when he'd felt it coming on, darkness at the edge slowly closing in his vision. He'd written it off to stress, or to being so damn tired he could hardly think, or maybe just that bad bourbon from the hotel minibar the night before in Chicago. He'd put his seat back that first time and napped for a half-hour or so on the flight home and when he awakened it was gone. He forgot about it.

Until it happened again, a little worse. And then again. And now, here it was, starting this time with some blurry gray blobs that were floating around his peripheral vision, slowly coming together and merging and growing and darkening bit by bit.

It was probably a stroke. Or a heart attack. Or cancer. Or Parkinson's. Or he was going blind.

Shit. He got up, maneuvered his way to the kitchen using the narrowing corridor of sight. Found the bottle of Macallan he was working on. Poured himself a good one, drank it, then poured another before staggering back to the chair and collapsing into it. He should read the paper. Or look over his notes, or think some about the lineup. Or not. He could shut his eyes for a few minutes, relax, deep calm breathing, pushing the black away, maybe a few minutes sleep would do it. Or maybe kill the black with alcohol. He took another sip, that was good, and then finished it off and poured another. At some point soon his father would be calling him to give him hell about one thing or another to do with how he'd thrown his life away for a silly game. But for now the phone was quiet and it was early morning in Rum Point and he could taste the peat as he sipped on the Macallan.

He'd pulled out the cell phone, turned it to off, then set it on the lamp table next to the chair. Another sip. That felt good.

ELEVEN

Felicity slid into some shorts and a t-shirt but stayed barefoot, then loaded up the coffee-maker and walked outside to get the newspaper off the driveway. The heat was blistering. Two steps on the black asphalt of the driveway and she could feel the burn on her soles, had to hop off the pavement and onto the rough grass at the side. Months of this summer heat and she still hadn't learned all her lessons.

A quick two-step out and back and she had the newspaper and headed inside to the air conditioning. She read the paper pretty closely, keeping an eye on things locally but also thumbing through the national and international news — most of it bad most of the time — and then, the last thing she looked at every day, the sports pages. Today, thank god, was her day off and she could just sit, relax, and read it through, maybe even take the time to do both crosswords and the sudoku.

There the story was, front page. She learned some things in reading it. Turned out the victim had been a basketball player at the University of Florida ten years before; a real star.

"Gator Player Murdered," said the story, and the subhead added "Gator Star Kelsey Found Slain on Beach."

Thomas "Honker" Kelsey led the Gators to the NCAA tournament twice. They hadn't gone far, not like the team from a couple of years ago that won the whole thing; but they'd played pretty good ball. A perimeter player and a good one, he'd had a great outside shot, the paper said, winning some big games with that three-pointer. Then he'd finished school and slowly faded from view, lasting one season on the bench for the Magic in the NBA before going to Europe for a few years to play. He'd done all right there, but had been a journeyman. He wasn't really quick enough or tall enough or tough enough, the stories seemed to imply, to be the star that some people had thought he'd be.

There were photographs of him, a good-looking guy with a nice smile, that prominent nose. Action shots showed him playing for the Gators. One of the photographs was of him hugging his mother and brother after the Gators won some NCAA tournament game. He was grinning. Such joy on his face.

But all Felicity could picture of that face was the way the broken jaw, already swelling, had hung loose on the left side, and then the strange look of peace at the last moment. And all she could see in her mind of that athletic body was the blood and the sand that was stuck to him from the hard crawl up to the dunes, that terrible wound in his side.

It was an ugly way to die.

Two cups of coffee and a day-old doughnut from Krispy Kreme later she shoved her little cell phone, her ID, and her sidearm, a little baby Glock, into a belly pack that she clipped around her waist before leaving the apartment to start walking up the beach to the place behind the dunes where it had all happened. She went alone. Her father was long gone, she knew, at the ballpark by mid-morning, no matter how late he'd been up the night before.

It was muggy even near the beach, so hot and still she broke a sweat just walking down the shadowy path, lined by palms, sea oats and Brazilian pepper trees. Then, when she walked out from the shaded path and out onto the beach the real heat kicked in, the sun blaring off the white sand, the only relief a slight sea breeze.

Still, there were a few people here and there in the water cooling off, and a few tourists, probably Brits, actually lying there on towels blistering in the sun. This was Felicity's first Florida summer and now she understood why the locals who could afford it left each summer for the Carolina mountains. Anything to dodge this heat. It was twelve-thirty or so and the sea-breeze was building up the thunderheads a few miles inland. Another two or three hours and those storm clouds would drift to the coast and let 'er rip. It would pour down rain, one of those windy, blinding showers that she was slowly getting used to. That would clear away the beachgoers and wipe out the crime scene, which was why if she was going to go back and take a look at things, she had to do it now.

She had no reason to be there, really; the homicide detectives would come to her with questions when they felt the need. But she'd watched that Kelsey guy die from a nasty wound right in front of her eyes and that wasn't something she saw every day. She wanted to go back there, see it all in the daylight, talk to forensics or whoever else might be there at the site. She wanted a better feel for it.

Ankle-deep in the warm Gulf water, she dodged the occasional little kids and their sand castles, and every now and then kicked up the water and sand to scare off the stingrays that liked to rest there, just under the sand. Step on one of those and its stinger would whip into your ankle, bringing a day or two of pain. Twice this summer she'd helped someone who'd stepped on one, and it didn't look like fun.

There was a quiet splash about thirty yards out, and she turned to look. A pod of porpoises went by, five or six of them, the dorsal fins rolling up out of the water and then back in. Two of them were obvious youngsters, smaller and bobbing up to get air at twice the rate of the adults. A couple of moments later the tourists noticed and suddenly there was a lot of shouting and staring from the people on the shore and the few swimmers got out that way.

She'd read somewhere that the porpoises in this area didn't roam much; instead, they lived here like any other locals. She liked that idea, liked thinking that the porpoises she was watching out there right now were the same ones she'd seen a few days before, and the week before that. The thought of them hanging out by her beach added a certain consistency, a pattern, to her life that she liked. She'd spent her childhood traveling from city to city with her dad as he got traded or, later, switched coaching jobs. Major-league towns and minor-league, she'd lived in a lot of them: Boston, St. Louis, Cincy, Louisville, Albuquerque, Spokane, Buffalo. The only constant through all of that had been Spring Training in Florida, something she'd looked forward to each winter. All the way through all those different elementary schools her parents had taken her out of class and down to Florida for a few weeks each winter; Mom home-schooled out of textbooks while she was here. It was quite a way to grow up.

Finally, by eighth grade they'd settled on Detroit, and Dad's career had finally seemed stable there, coaching with the Tigers. Mom's career had taken off, too, with the long, late-blooming climb from law school leading to the assistant prosecuting attorney job. Later, in the first case where she'd been lead prosecutor, they'd finally put a local drug lord away. Mom got a lot of ink for that, the lawyer-wife of the Tigers' third-base coach putting the bad guys in prison. And that was just the first of a half-dozen of those scum that she'd nailed over the next few years. Those had been good times, those Tiger years, until Mom's death.

She still thought of that death too often, and not just in nightmares but in the hard light of the day. Certain kinds of pain, she'd discovered, never truly go away. Those bright lights behind them on the old, two-lane road. The first bump, another one even harder, that corner near the little stone bridge, Mom cursing and screaming and then the car that had done it to them going by as they spun completely around once, twice, before going over the low railing and rolling down the riverbank. Felicity, in the middle of that chaos, had seen the driver of the other car, got one good look at his face — a big jaw, high cheekbones, thick and dark eyebrows, a vicious smile — as his car went by, and then heard her mother say, in a final, wild moment of calm just as the car started to roll over, "I love you, Felicity."

Later, Fel woke up in the hospital with Mom gone. An accident, manslaughter, murder? No one knew, no one was ever arrested, there was never a likely suspect, despite Felicity's description, despite the paint scrapes, the tire marks on the road.

It was all a long time ago, ten years, and she was getting better with it. There were times now that a day would go by without her thinking about it, without picturing that face. It was just that this murder here had reminded her of it, that was all.

She reached the crime scene up in the dunes, yellow tape strung atop a series of wooden stakes outlined the spot and a path from there down to the water. It was high tide now, and a good twenty feet of the path was underwater, erased. Later, when the rains came, the rest of the path and the scene itself up in the dunes, would be erased, too; gone, as if the whole thing never happened.

It turned out no one was there. The forensics people must have gotten what they needed in a couple of hours last night, working away under those floodlights and then maybe finishing up this morning in the sunlight. They were done, and in an hour or two the tape would be gone. But Felicity wasn't done; she wanted to see the spot one more time, clear, in the daylight, with the tape that she'd strung last night still there defining things.

It was quiet on this part of the beach. The concession stand and the three-story expanse of the Hurricane Restaurant was a half-mile away to the south. Hotel row started a good half-mile to the north. This middle stretch was almost deserted. Maybe, Felicity thought, that was why it had happened here, maybe Kelsey had been in the water from some boat, and had come in this way, away from the bar and hotel lights, a quiet place where he could get ashore and walk away from trouble.

That might have been it, but it sure hadn't worked for him. Someone had been waiting for him, had known he was coming ashore here and attacked him as soon as he waded in from the water.

She looked out toward the Gulf. There'd been lights out there last night, a long line of distant ones from the freighters waiting their chance to enter Flagler Bay, and one set of closer ones, from a boat a half-mile out or so. She'd put that into her report and told Detective Bentley. Couldn't see much of the boat, though, just a rough outline, some sort of expensively big yacht, she thought.

And that guy walking, the big guy. She looked up and down the beach. He might have been the murderer, that guy. Could have done it a few seconds before she'd seen him. She'd written that up in her report, too, of course, and told Bentley.

So, OK, that was who and how. But why? Why kill the guy? Some drug deal gone bad? Something domestic, somebody cheating on somebody?

Later, she planned to give Bentley a call just to see if she needed any help. There weren't many murders—hell, there weren't any until this basketball star—in calm, little Rum Point. They had an agreement with the Pinellas County Sheriff's Department for homicide cases, which was how Bentley got the call. That was good; Felicity liked Kim Bentley and knew she wouldn't mind getting a call on it, though it would be days before the forensics investigators got around to having much to say about what they'd found.

She bent down to pick up a sand dollar, the flat little round shells with the pretty design. They were supposed to bring good luck. This one was half buried in the sand, and when she tried to pull it free from the wet sand it snapped, then fell into pieces, little angel-shaped bits of shell tumbling out of it. Was that good luck? Bad? She couldn't remember the local story, something about angel's wings and Christ on the cross.

There was a shout from behind her, up in the dunes, maybe twenty yards north of the crime scene. What the hell was going on up there? She took a few steps that way, thought about zipping open her belly pack and getting the baby Glock and her badge out, just in case, but didn't do it, not yet. Instead, she hustled up toward the nearest opening between the dunes, finding it tough going once she hit the soft sand above the waterline.

A man came charging out of the dunes, looking back toward whatever was after him, running hard, sand spraying out as he clumsily rounded the corner between the opening. She had no time to get out of his way. "Hey!" she yelled, but he'd barely turned his head to see her there when they collided and he ran her over, the two of them tumbling backward into the sand, all arms and legs flying, falling right on top of the yellow-taped trail left by the mother turtle and the murdered man the night before. Felicity wound up face down in the gritty sand.

"Damn," she heard the guy who'd run her over say in a voice that sounded familiar somehow. He was struggling to get off her.

And then came another voice; calmer, deeper. "All right, just stop right there, both of you. Just freeze. I have a weapon and I'm aiming it."

Felicity froze, and could feel the guy next to her on the beach do the same.

"Look, buddy," the guy next to her said, without looking up. "I don't know what's got you so upset. I was just checking out that nesting site, and..."

"Shut up," the deep voice said. "And just get up and turn around, slowly, so I can see you. Both of you."

Felicity climbed to her knees, then stood and turned.

The guy with the deep voice was medium height, pudgy, dressed in shorts and knit shirt, light blue. He wore thick sunglasses and a Gator baseball cap so his face was hard to see clearly. He had a .38, an old classic police special, in his right hand, but not pointed toward them.

She held out her hands, palms up. "I'm a police officer," she said, "with the Rum Point department. I found the victim last night. Came to take a look at things today."

"Sure you did," the guy said, looking her over.

"Who are you?" Felicity asked.

"We'll get to that in a minute. I don't suppose you have any ID on you, officer, do you?"

Felicity, carefully, zipped open her belly pack and held up her badge. The guy nodded and lowered the gun. Then he looked at the tall, gangly guy standing next to Felicity, "And who the hell are you?"

"Michael Kelsey," the guy said, standing taller, trying to look like he knew what he was doing, like he belonged there. "I'm a marine biologist, with the university. I track sea turtles, and there's a nest site up there; a very, very unusual nest site. Look," and he knelt down to point at the tracks from the turtle the night before. "These tracks here? I think they're from a Kemp's ridley. If there are eggs in there, they were laid by a Kemp's ridley turtle. That would be, well, astounding."

"Yeah," the guy said, "I bet. Astounding."

And then the name clicked. "Kelsey? Like the victim? You're related?"

Kelsey nodded, and then Felicity saw his whole frame collapse a bit with the admission, the false front and bravado giving way to grief.

"Yeah," he said. "I mean, yes. He was my brother. My only brother."

"My god," Felicity said, turning to face him, seeing the anguish on his face. "I'm sorry."

The pudgy guy was sliding his .38 into its holster. "Yeah," he added, "I'm real sorry, too, pal. But you shouldn't be here."

"I had to come," Michael said. "I had to see the place. I work here, I'm on this stretch of beach a lot. And to think that Honker died here..."

Felicity turned to the pudgy guy. "I'm Felicity Lindsay. I was first on the scene last night and came back to take a look. Now, do you have some ID? Who are you with?"

He smiled, and there was a grim malevolence behind that smile that she wasn't used to seeing. He was getting off on this, she realized.

He reached into a back pocket to pull out a wallet. From that he took out an ID card and handed it to her.

Felicity took a look at it. "Drug Enforcement Agency? What is the DEA doing here, Special Agent"— she looked again at the ID —"D'Amico?"

"I'm afraid I can't tell you that right now, officer. I'll give you a call, though, later this evening, at your little department down there," and he smiled again and waved in the general direction of the department's five-room house at the tip of the beach town, right on the pass.

"For now, why don't we call this a wash, OK? You two get going, I'm going to take a look around a bit, and then we'll touch base later, you and me. All right, Officer Lindsay?"

She nodded. It was probably best that she get Michael Kelsey away from here right now, anyway. And she could always come back in an hour or so and try to take her own look at things before the daily rain showers hit.

She turned to look at Michael Kelsey, offered him a smile. "C'mon, Mr. Kelsey. Let's take a little walk up the beach, OK? I'll answer any questions I can."

"It's Michael," he said, running his hand through his light brown hair,

43

"And, yeah. I suppose that's best. I've got some questions, you know, about how it was."

Felicity turned to say something to D'Amico, but he was already gone, back up into the dunes. She turned back to Kelsey. "OK, Michael," she said, "let's talk. You can tell me all about these Kemp's ridleys turtles." And the two of them headed up the beach. Behind them, in the dunes, D'Amico took his look around.

TWELVE

Stu woke up with a hell of a headache, still sitting in that damn uncomfortable rattan chair, his head slumped forward. He struggled up, noticed that he could see, the darkness was gone for now. He stood there for a moment to get his bearings then walked back through the sliding glass doors and into the living room, through there and into the kitchen and the cabinet over the sink, where he kept some ibuprofen. He shook out three of them, threw them into his mouth, leaned over the sink to get a mouthful of water to wash them down with, then headed for the bathroom. It was nearly eleven A.M.

His cell phone rang, off in the distance somewhere. Damn, he'd thought he'd left it turned off. He could ignore it, but then the old man would just keep calling. Thing was, where the hell had he left it?

It kept ringing and so he tracked it down, stumbling some, his head hurting, the ibuprofen a long way from kicking in. There it was on the little lamp table next to the chair. Had he set it there last night as he had those couple of drinks? Must have.

He picked it up, looked at the front screen then flipped it open. "Hello, Father."

"Things a little ragged this morning, Son? You're later than usual getting up."

"I had a couple of drinks last night, Father, if that's what you're hinting at."

"You know it doesn't have to be this way, Stuart."

"What doesn't have to be this way, Father?"

"Your life."

The goddamn old man, always looking to dig at him. "Father," he said, "I'm the manager of a major-league baseball team. I'm well-paid. My team wins more than it loses. Some people like me. Some might even envy me."

"When you were fifteen and you took the SAT; do you remember that."

"Let's not go there again, Father, all right?"

"A perfect score in math, Son. At fifteen! You could have gone anywhere. Done anything."

"Been a physicist, Father? Like you?"

"Caltech, MIT, Chicago: they all wanted Stuart Lindsay."

"And I wanted to play baseball, Father, which I was pretty damn good at."

"And you wanted to play baseball. You wanted to throw and catch and run and swing bats. And now you're sitting there, Son, hungover. Again."

Stu shook his head, knowing his father couldn't see it. "It's been a rough few years, Father. Very rough, OK?"

"You would have made a real contribution to the field, Stuart, I'm certain of it. Instead. Well..."

"Instead I've had too much to drink, Father. I know it. I'm sorry."

His father had been a heavy drinker himself, but had given it up when his wife's cancer was found. Too late, as it turned out, to make things better between them.

"You know we can do better, Stuart, right?"

"Do what better, Father?"

"Me. You. You know it could be different, even now. You could coach at some good college, do some teaching on the side, put that master's of yours to work some, maybe go back and get the doctorate after all." He paused. "That fine mind of yours. The things you still might do, the contribution you still might make."

"Father, I have to go. I have to get to the ballpark."

"Oh, hell, Son; you weren't listening to me, were you? You never listened to me. Ever." His voice was louder. He was angry. "You're just a thick-headed old jock," he said, loud and firm, and then he hung up.

He was not an easy man. Never had been. Ever. Stu closed the cell phone and sat back in the chair. Damn.

A few minutes later Stu was back at the sink, took two more ibuprofen and wondered what it would take to overdose on them as he washed them down. Then, slowly feeling a little better, somewhere between still a little buzzed and already into a receding hangover, he walked through the living

45

room, up the staircase to the second floor and into his bedroom. He got dressed in slacks and a nice knit Crusaders shirt in case someone saw him before he got into the clubhouse at the ballpark, and then he headed out to the garage, and the Honda and the short drive up Gulf Drive to the park.

By the time he got to the park, parked the car and walked through the green door and into the long concrete corridor that led to the clubhouse he was feeling better. Not great, but better. Hell, he was all right. He was fine. Just paying for it a little bit, that was all. He tugged open the door of the clubhouse and walked in. Jimmy was there, smiling like always as he swept the floor and straightened up and organized around the lockers. He was on the cell phone as he swept, talking with the left hand holding the cell while he pushed the broom with the right hand. Stu smiled at the kid, told him hi, and walked to the office, opened the door and got in there as Jimmy, in the background, promised someone on the phone that he'd take care of something, ending with an "I promise you," and then a goodbye as Stu shut the door, walked over to the desk, sat down, and took a deep breath.

It was peaceful there for the moment. Jimmy had Stu's uniform hanging in his locker ready for him. Somebody, Cassidy no doubt, had left a little stack of papers on his desk with baseball-diamond charts on page after page. The charts were filled in with all sorts of pretty colors. Great.

He sat down and looked at the charts, thinking he really needed the headache to finally disappear entirely if he was going to make any sense of them. It was lunchtime, so maybe a ham sandwich would help. Or not, since despite the time of day he didn't feel all that hungry.

But there was one good way to help the headache, he thought. He opened the bottom drawer and pulled out the glass tumbler and the Macallan. One little glass of that peaty burn would do the trick, warm all the way down, clearing the head, straighten things right up. He unscrewed the cap and poured.

THIRTEEN

Felicity didn't quite know what to make of Michael Kelsey. It was two-thirty in the afternoon and they sat at one of the Hurricane Restaurant's outdoor tables as he took a rare bite of his fried grouper sandwich, the house specialty. Fel had ordered a cheeseburger and it was long gone, but all Michael did was take a little bite every now and then of his grouper, and so the sandwich and fries mostly sat there, barely eaten, as he rambled on and on about the Kemp's ridley sea turtles and about how rare the species was, about how it might go extinct, about its reproduction habits and its strange travels in the Gulf Stream, about how one even showed up on the coast of France, about the myths that surrounded the turtle, beginning with Native American tales and coming right up to date with a sneaky effort by some biologists to convince shrimpers and fishermen that the Kemp's ridley was bad luck, that capturing or killing one would bring you a bad catch, so it was best to throw it back overboard, alive, if one got tangled in your nets.

It was all very interesting, of course, but watching him speak while she took a sip of her iced tea, Felicity began to wonder, after awhile, if he'd forgotten somehow about his brother's murder the night before, about the tragedy of that, the horror of it.

Then, while he went into more depth than she thought she'd ever need to know about that one Mexican beach where all the poor Kemp's ridleys nested, she began to hear it in his voice, hear the pain of the terrible thing he was going through. This, she began to understand, was how he could deal with it, the unreal shock of murder. By talking about the thing he loved most, by pretending that his life was still normal, full of the normal concerns, normal worries, he could avoid the pain.

Well, she had news for Michael Kelsey. You can't avoid it for long. Life would never be the same. Never. From now on he would know his brother had been murdered, had died an ugly, stupid death at the hands of some monster, some sick demon who could kill another human being in cold blood. From now on, Michael Kelsey would always have that hanging around, always in the background. Always. She shook her head, thinking of that.

"What's the matter?" he asked.

"Nothing. It's just that..."

She couldn't say it, couldn't tell him. She wanted to, wanted to tell this guy she'd only known for the past hour or two that she knew what murder was like, that her mother had been killed and the murderer never found, and that she, Felicity, didn't have any damn turtles to hide behind and had to face the knowing of that every day. It was years later now, and she was still thinking about who'd done it, thinking about Mom. "No," she said. "Maybe later."

And he went on some more about endangered turtles and extinction. "Did you know," he asked her, "that the earliest known sea turtle fossils go back one-hundred-fifty million years? Imagine that, and now we may wipe them out. After all this time, wipe them out: gone, extinct."

The irony was, she thought, that his brother was gone now. Species Honker Kelsey gone completely, and all Michael could talk about was how the turtles he loved so much looked like they were on the way out, too. She sympathized. It was too bad, really, but what was Felicity supposed to do about it? She'd spent all summer protecting mother turtles and their nests, she felt a lot of sympathy for them whether they were leatherbacks or greens or Kemp's ridleys or anything else. But after more than two hours of hearing about them, after listening to Michael talk about them while they walked on the beach, after listening some more after she stopped him long enough to call in the information about the D'Amico guy and check on the guy's background with Bentley up in St. Pete Beach, after listening still more here at the restaurant — well, she'd about had it. She wondered when he would finally get to the real stuff.

Suddenly, without thinking about it, just doing what felt like the right thing to do after staring deep into those pained brown eyes, Felicity spoke up. "What was your brother doing out there? He must have come in off that boat I told you about, Michael."

Michael stopped in mid-sentence, looked at her. She could see the anger in his eyes for a moment, the flash of passion. This was the second time she'd seen this already, this heat from him. He came across as an academic type, calm and dispassionate; but there was something down in there that was hard and angry.

He took quick control of himself, sat back in his chair, took a sip of his soft drink. "I don't know. Isn't that what you're supposed to find out?"

"Me? I'm just a local cop, Michael. Officer Felicity Lindsay, that's me. I drive an ATV on the beach. I was looking for turtle hatchlings and just found your brother, that's all."

"You know what I mean. All of you, the police, aren't you supposed to be the ones who find out what was going on, why he was killed, who did it? Not me. I don't know anything about what he was doing." He shook his head. "Honker and I didn't talk much, you know, these last few years. To tell you the truth, we just didn't seem to have much to say to each other

anymore. He was headed in one direction, and I was going the other way."
He paused for a second, added, "Jesus, that sounds like such a cliché."

"But it's true?"

"Yeah. It's true. I was worried about job things, about getting my journal articles published so I can get tenure and make associate professor, things like that. I was getting deeper and deeper into my work, trying to figure out ways to save these turtles and my career at the same time. I was busy all the time and he didn't give a shit about any of that. He thought it was all just bullshit, part of a game he didn't want to play. So he opted out, you know? He wasn't around much. There were times he disappeared for months."

She nodded, said nothing.

He waited for her to speak, and when she didn't, he went on. "Look, don't get me wrong, he was a great guy, everybody loved him. Honker Kelsey, Mr. Jump Shot, you know? But that was years ago and people start to forget. He couldn't stand that, I think. He still wanted to be a star."

"I read that he never really made it in the NBA."

"Oh, he had a few good years in pro ball — he liked it over in Italy and France when he played there. But, yeah, he wasn't the big star like he'd been at Florida."

Michael looked out the window of the restaurant. Outside it was blazing hot, temperature in the low nineties, high humidity. There were still people walking the beach, though, sweating with every step. Felicity heard a rumble of thunder from the storms that were drifting slowly seaward. The patch of sky they could see out the window was blue right now, but it wouldn't be long now and it would be black with rain, the hard-driving summer showers that renewed this place every day in the summer months, washing it clean, including the crime scene.

"You know," Michael was saying as another roll of thunder rattled the windowpanes, "he was more complex than that. I want you to know that. He was plenty smart; got his bachelor's in business from UF and always talked about going back for an MBA. And part of Honker always wanted to do the right thing, too. He was always into helping out with the Special Olympics back when he was playing, spent a lot of times with those kids, showing them how to shoot. Hell, I watched him spend an hour with one kid, teaching him how to dribble the ball up and down a couple of times."

Felicity nodded.

"And he liked to help me. He was the one who got me started on the

49

turtles. He's been an amateur sea turtle biologist since high school, studying them, worrying about them."

Michael shook his head as he remembered it. "He was a sophomore in Gainesville when I was a high-school senior. He was already a big star, pre-season All-American, that sort of stuff. And yet, when I was doing a term paper for my honors class on sea turtle reproduction, he came down and spent every weekend he could with me, studying the nests, tagging the hatchlings. He had a real thing for them, the hatchlings, loved to watch them come boiling out of the nests and head for the water."

Felicity nodded. "You know you'll have to tell all this to the homicide detective who's running the case. Her name's Kim Bentley."

"Yeah, I figured she'd contact me today sometime. There's probably a message on my machine at home."

Felicity reached for a napkin, pulled a crayon out of the little bin next to the napkins where the kids could grab them, started writing down Bentley's number.

"Here. You call her, Michael. She'll need to know all this. She's good, she's very good. She'll find the guy who did this."

"Sure," he said, not believing that but reaching over to take the napkin, fold it carefully and put it into the front pocket of his shorts. "I'll call her. Might as well."

Felicity watched him do that, thinking about the dead brother. Sure, he'd been a nice guy, that was the good news about Honker Kelsey. She wondered what the bad news would be. Drugs? Was he a junkie? A smuggler? Then it hit her. "Wait a minute," she said. "He was interested in turtles, too?"

"Yeah. But for him it got to be like a hobby, you know, something to do when he wasn't getting into trouble."

"What kind of turtles? The Kemp's ridleys?"

"I don't know. Maybe. What are you getting at?"

"Michael," she said — it was the first time she'd used his name — "maybe this connects up somehow. Maybe that sea turtle and your brother were there together for some reason."

"I don't know. Maybe. But it doesn't make much sense to me. Why would he be on this beach watching a mother turtle? Did she have a radio tag, maybe, and he'd been tracking her? And why... why..." He shivered once, hard. "I mean, Jesus, why would someone kill him like that?"

"I don't know, Michael. I didn't see anything on the mother turtle, but

50

it was dark. And we're working on it, OK? We'll find the guy who did it, we'll find out why."

"Sure," he said. "Sure you will." And then, abruptly, he stood up, kicking his chair back, almost shaking with the pain of what had happened to his brother. She could see him losing it, getting angry and near tears at the same time.

"Look," he said, "I've got to go, OK. It's been great talking to you and all, but I've got to go, I've got to get back to work. And there's funeral plans. And Mom, I mean, someone's got to spend time with Mom."

Felicity nodded, tried to calm him down a bit. "Sure. Listen, you need anything you stop by or give me a call, OK? Here's my address and my phone number." She used the crayon again to jot the information down on a napkin and shove it into his shirt pocket. "I live right around the corner from here. Just come on by, or call me, OK? I'll be glad to help."

"Yeah," he said, almost shaking now, struggling with it, trying to get his control back, trying to freeze away the thought of his brother's murder. "Sure," he said hurriedly. "I'll call. Maybe we can talk again sometime. About turtles. About the Kemp's ridleys."

She smiled. "That'd be nice, Michael. That'd be fine. You just give me a call when you can."

He left, walking away quickly. She thought maybe she saw his shoulders shake, like he was crying.

Oh, hell, she didn't even know if he had a car parked around here somewhere or lived here or was taking the bus or what. She ought to go after him, offer him a ride or something.

Her cell phone jingled at her from her pocket. She grabbed it, opened it up and said hello.

"Fel? It's Kim Bentley."

"Yeah, Kim, what'd you find out about this D'Amico guy?"

"Listen, Fel, I ran that name through the computer link and came up with something interesting. You ready for this?"

"Yeah, Kim, sure, tell me."

"OK, Fel, this is it. D'Amico's been dead for two years. Killed in a car crash in Virginia, ran off a mountain road in the snow."

"What? He's dead? Then..."

"The guy you met today is no DEA agent, Fel. He's something else, someone else."

"Someone else, and using this alias."

51

"That's right."

"Why?"

"I don't know, Fel. Listen, I called DEA as soon as I found out about this. Got some friends there, and when I told them about this they got real serious on me right away and passed me on to another guy, and I got passed on again from there. All very spook, you know? A guy finally called me a few minutes ago and said I should ignore the problem, that it was a case being worked. He asked me to let it go. Said I didn't want to know more. Whoever he is, we're supposed to back off, Fel."

"Jesus, Kim. Who is this guy?"

"I don't know. And now I officially do not care. You hear me on this?"

"Yeah, I hear you, Kim, back off. Well, hell, all right, back off it is."

"OK, Fel. Take care of yourself. Let me know if there's anything else. Oh, and tell your Dad I said hi."

She smiled. Kim Bentley was always looking for free tickets to the Crusaders games.

"I'll do that, Kim. I'll see if I can get you a pair of box seats for tonight's game, all right? Pay you back for checking on this for me."

She could almost hear Bentley's grin over the static of the bad connection before she thanked her and hung up.

Well. So the guy was some kind of spook, maybe, or tied to the Feds some other way — a protected witness or something. My, that was interesting. But this wasn't the kind of trouble she was looking for. She was happy to get out of the way, thank you very much. Back off? Hell, yes, no question about it, those guys played for keeps. He probably wouldn't contact her again, despite what he'd said. That had just been to get her to walk away. Which was fine. Walk far away from that, in fact.

Felicity pulled a twenty out of her purse and left it on the table, that added up to a good tip on top of the sixteen bucks for the food and drink.

Then she rose, headed for the door. Her dad's house and her own apartment were just a few blocks down the beach from here, an easy fifteen-minute walk. She could get home, clean up a bit, and then head over to the ballpark to see how her Dad was doing, maybe spend a few minutes with him in his office and get Bentley some tickets and then wander up to the stands to watch batting practice before tonight's game. It was nice having a day off here in paradise.

52

Fourteen

Robert Mackie watched as she left, then he threw a ten down on the bar to cover the two beers and followed her.

It had been simplicity itself getting into the morgue. There wasn't a lot of security there and the one guy he had to get past had glanced at the DEA ID and waved him through.

But the body had been clean, nothing in there. And right then, with his finger up in there checking for the goddamn flash drive, was when it dawned on him who else had been there when the guy got hit. That girl cop; the young one who'd come up the beach just a few minutes after he'd whacked Kelsey.

It was a small town, with a real Keystone Kops police force with its offices in what looked like an old guesthouse. Eight or ten cops on the whole goddamn force, maybe. He looked the place over, then went to a payphone to make a secure call to an old friend in Langley. Three minutes and he knew that Rum Point had just one girl cop, so that was her. And now he knew where she lived.

He went there and saw her place was a little apartment in a two-story building just back from the beach. It was a snap to get into. She wasn't there, so he did a job on the place, searched it everywhere, tore it the fuck apart. No flash drive. Then he decided to go looking for her, and found her, in just the third try, eating lunch with some guy. That might have been tricky, but then the guy left, so it was just her alone. And she would know where the flash drive was.

She was walking home, he was sure of it. Following her, taking his time, he began to think it through. He wouldn't be able to wait, she'd freak when she saw what he'd done to the place as he searched. No, he'd have to get in right behind her and get her quieted down right away; then he could ask some questions and get some answers. He smiled, confident. He was very good at that, at getting answers, and he enjoyed the work, too. She'd tell him, and then he'd whack her. Simple.

FIFTEEN

Stu had, as usual, his right foot on the top wooden step of the dugout, looking every bit the knowledgeable manager keeping an eye on his ballplayers. He glanced one more time at his watch.

A couple of quick shots of the Macallan had helped. The headache had eased and his stomach had settled down. He'd even gotten some paperwork done and then he'd felt up to having a sandwich in his office.

He'd thought about driving home for a quick nap after that, which would have helped, but then one thing led to another along with a few quick sips of Macallan here and there and all of a sudden it was time to start thinking about tonight's game with its early starting time and about two problems: Sonny Dickerson and Pete Macalaster.

He looked at his watch again. It was four-thirty now, and Dickerson and Macalaster still weren't at the ballpark. The rest of the Crusaders were out taking batting practice. The guys who weren't starters were about done taking their swings and the starters were standing around the cage talking. There was a satisfying crack and then a happy little yell as a long flyball to left just cleared the fence for a batting practice homer. The Crusaders seemed happy today. Hell, they ought to be happy, a couple in front with three to play. They were playing well, the defense was solid up the middle, the pitching was holding up and the bats were hot.

And then there was Sonny Dickerson, and now Pete Macalaster, too. Jesus, it was a hell of a thing, how guys like that could be unhappy at a time like this. Dickerson was around the .340 mark, with eighty-six ribbies and thirty-two dingers. You'd think he'd be showing up early and spreading good cheer. But no, he was in another one of those moods, showing up late and pushing Stu hard, rubbing up against his manager like he wanted nothing but damn trouble. And now he was getting Macalaster in on it, too. Pete had been a starter earlier in the season and had the tools to be back in the starting line-up again at some point if Dickerson didn't ruin him.

There was the clatter of spikes on the wooden slats of the clubhouse tunnel. Stu didn't turn to look, but stared instead out toward the batting cage, where Ron Garn was stepping into the cage to try and jack one out. Stu shook his head, a few more batting practice dingers would probably ruin Garn's swing.

"Hi, Skip," said Pete Macalaster, coming up to him from behind and then scrambling up the dugout steps, stumbling a bit on the top one.

"Hold it, Pete." Stu turned to look at him, stared him in the eyes. "You're late."

"Well, yeah, we got caught in traffic, Skip. The drawbridge over the pass was stuck and everybody had to turn around and come back through the other way, through the Bayway. Sorry about that. Sonny knew you'd be pissed, but there wasn't anything we could do."

Stu shook his head. "Pete, you want to get back into the starting line-up, you got to take your swings at batting practice, and you missed your chance by half-an-hour, son."

Macalaster was a big kid, six-two and around two-hundred pounds. But he had a baby face, with the innocent, wide-eyed farm-boy look you'd expect from a nice kid from Nebraska. The sportswriters loved him for that look, but right now Stu was getting real tired of seeing it, especially when it offered nothing but excuses.

"Skip, I'm really sorry. It won't happen again, OK?"

"Yeah, Stu, it won't happen again," said Sonny Dickerson, coming up the tunnel. "It was just one of those things, you know?"

"Pete, get out there and shag a few. Then sit, you're watching this one tonight. Sonny, I'd appreciate it if you'd hang around here a minute."

Stu watched Macalaster trot out toward center. The kid seemed too damn smiley, come to think of it. Drunk? Maybe, but hell, some coffee and some ibuprofen could fix that up. But something else? Cocaine or something? Maybe that, too, and that was something a pot of coffee wouldn't fix, not in the long run. Damn shame, the way it went these days; these young kids with all this money. He turned to face Sonny Dickerson.

"That kid has a lot of talent, Sonny. He's going to make a hell of a big leaguer someday if things go right for him."

"Yeah, Stu, sure."

"I don't want you messing him up, Sonny. I know you like to drive down your own road and all that, and you get away with it because you can hit like a son-of-a-bitch, but don't mess up that kid or I'll fine your ass and sit you down. If I think you're messing him up I'll trade you, Sonny. Hell, I'll give you away."

Dickerson just smiled. "Sure, Stu, you'll bench me here in this pennant race. Look, don't worry about it; Pete's a big boy. He's old enough to know what he wants."

55

"Oh, Christ, Sonny, even you know better than that. He's a damn kid, and you're screwing with his life here."

"OK, Stu, OK. Look, I'll make sure he doesn't get into any real trouble, all right? And I'll make sure he's here when he's supposed to be, too. Fair enough?"

Stu frowned. This was probably as good as he was going to get from Dickerson. "Yeah, Sonny, sure. Hell, get out there and hit a few," and he waved his star hitter toward the batting cage. He wanted to crack down on the guy, but you can get away with a lot when you're hitting .340 in late September.

Stu watched Dickerson amble toward the batting cage, then took the last step up from the dugout himself and walked onto the field, into the strange light of the dome. He looked up at the high, light gray of the roof. It was tough material, but not quite opaque, so an odd half-light came through during day games. Now, later in the day, it threw weird, thin shadows across the field, five of them for every player.

The lighting always made the first few innings of a night-game tough on the outfielders, who had to stare into that roof and pick the ball out of the general grayness before it got fully dark outside. First time he'd come into the dome, Stu had thought about having the Reverend paint that roof. Then, in the second game of the season, Bryan Love, the Cardinal's new centerfield phenom, had lost one in that tough lighting and the Crusaders had scored two runs on the error. The dome had stayed gray.

Strange place, Ministry Field. Strange owner. Strange team for that matter.

But Stu Lindsay was manager of it, headache and a little nervous stomach notwithstanding. And here they were, still in it, this odd brew of bought talent, promising newcomers and over-the-hill pitchers; within one win of the wild-card spot.

As he thought about that, allowing himself a moment's satisfaction despite all his insecurities, a sharp drive came off Dickerson's bat and headed toward the gap in right center. Pete Macalaster, awfully energetic for batting practice, got on his horse and ran it down, snagging it in the webbing of his Rawlings while running full-tilt toward the warning track.

Macalaster celebrated the catch with quick snap of the wrist, a little showboating for the early fans, and then fired a hard shot into second to add a final flourish on the play. A stupid play, really, since he hadn't loosened up yet.

But he got away with it, grinning out there as he trotted back toward center. Heckuva talent, that kid. He had a future, maybe, if things didn't go wrong.

Stu turned to walk back down the dugout steps and into the clubhouse tunnel. Time to sit in the office for a minute, sip on a little of that Macallan maybe and pull together tonight's line-up. It sure would be nice, it would be wonderful, to win another one tonight against the Porters and clinch the wild-card.

He rounded the corner from the tunnel, shoved on the door into the clubhouse and walked in, heading past the long row of lockers on his left as he aimed at his office.

Garn, Godinez, Leon, Gaddis, Holman, O'Connor, Perez, Waterson, Alec, S. Martinez, H. Martinez — the names on the lockers made him think of what an odd assortment they were and yet how well they were doing.

Macalaster's locker showed how hastily the kid had dressed. Clothes were strewn over the bench and folding chair in front, and his sport coat had fallen onto the floor. Jimmy was out in the dugout watching batting practice. He'd left the place spotless before going out there, but now Macalaster had messed it up.

Stu shook his head, leaned over to pick the coat up and at least hang it on the hook in the locker. There was the crinkle of plastic from the left side pocket and small packet fell onto the carpeted floor.

Stu stared at it for a long few seconds. A white powder in a little plastic baggie. Oh shit, Mac had a pocketful of cocaine. Oh, Christ. What now? He turned to look at Dickerson's locker, where the street clothes were hung neatly on wide, wooden hangers. No, Sonny was too damn smart for that.

Quickly, half afraid he'd find more of the shit or that someone, maybe Jimmy or one of the players or coaches, would walk into the room, he searched the other pockets. Nothing.

He picked up the little baggie, held the shit in his hand, staring at it. Stu was the wrong generation for this kind of crap, booze had always been plenty enough for him to deal with, so he wasn't really sure if the stuff was what he thought it was. But what else could it be, heroin or something? Well, goddamn it, he was going to have to report this to someone, to the team and to the league, and there would be all kinds of hell to pay. He shook his head and started to stand when he heard a voice from behind him.

"Hello, Stu. What's going on?"

Lindsay turned, and it was George Brooks, the Reverend's right-hand man, director of baseball operations, the real power behind the throne. Stu kept trying to avoid Brooks, though he knew he had to cultivate that friendship if he wanted to stay on as manager. Problem was, the guy came on with a smile and had always acted decently; but underneath you could feel it, there was something vicious, something really mean and low, and Stu wanted as little to do with it as possible.

"Hello, George. I'm glad you're here. I've just come across a little problem, something I found in Pete Macalaster's coat pocket."

He held up the baggie and Brooks' eyes widened. He coughed; a deep, loose hack that took him a moment to get through. Then, in a change so abrupt that Stu couldn't help but feel a chill, the eyes tightened and a slight, narrow grin emerged from Brooks' puffy face. "Why don't you give that to me, Stu, and I'll take care of it."

"I don't know, George, I think it's best if I just hang onto it for now. We'll have to do a urinalysis on him, you know, and if he comes up positive he'll be suspended and into rehab. It's the league rules. There's nothing we can do about that."

Brooks coughed again, got it under control. "Stu, there *is* something we can do about it. Just give me that baggie and let Macalaster know I'd like to see him up in my office in ten minutes, all right? I'll take care of it from there."

This put Stu in a bad spot. It certainly looked like Brooks was going to let Macalaster off with a reprimand and a warning. If Stu let it go at that, then he'd become part of the problem. Damn, there were legal liabilities he guessed, not to mention the moral ones. He'd hate to see the damn kid lose his way over this. He wanted to help him while there was still a chance. "Tell you what, George, I'll hand this over and send Macalaster up to your office. But I have to let the Reverend know about this, too, and my coaches. We're the ones who are going to have to deal with it if it's more than just Pete."

Brooks nodded. "Of course, Stu. You tell the Reverend. In fact, I'll set up a meeting for tomorrow or the next day with you, me and the Reverend and we'll talk the whole thing over, all right? Until then, though, why don't you keep it quiet with the coaches? No sense in stirring things up until we know if there's a real problem or if this is just a one-time incident."

That looked like a way out, like Brooks was offering Stu a chance to keep it honest and still keep the clubhouse from blowing up over this. It was a pennant race, after all, and who knew, with any luck it might not even be cocaine in there. Stu nodded, handed over the baggy. "I've got to get in and figure out my line-up. I'll send Pete up your way in a few minutes."

"Good, Stu, and you've done the right thing here. This is something I'd like to handle in-house if we can." He coughed again.

Stu tried being friendlier. "Yeah, me, too," he said, adding, "You ought to get that cough looked at, George. Maybe get some antibiotics for it."

Brooks smiled. "Yeah, going to see the doc tomorrow, as a matter of fact." He shoved the baggie into his pants pocket, patted it once, and smiled. "We'll do what we have to do, Stu, right? You just keep the Crusaders winning and I'll take care of this little problem. That's my job, Stu. Boil it all down, that's what I do for the Reverend. I take care of little problems."

And he chuckled at that, patting Stu on the back as the Crusader manager, thinking about how Cassidy talked about his courage all the time and wondering exactly how this reality fit into that, headed toward his office and tonight's line-up and the pennant race. Before he could sit down, his cell phone started ringing. Had to be his father and he'd be full of advice on how to handle this crisis. How did the old man know about these things? It was a mystery.

But what the hell. He flipped open the phone and said hello.

SIXTEEN

Instead of the heat and humidity she expected, Felicity felt a down-draft of cool air as she walked outside through the door of the restaurant. The front edge of the thunderstorm was on them and sheets of rain would be pouring down in a minute or two. She'd have to hustle to get home without getting soaked.

She started walking down Gulf Drive toward her apartment. It was only six blocks, but when she cleared the restaurant's porch overhang and looked up all she could see was a deep blue-gray swirl of cloud. Might as well be six miles— she was going to get wet. A drop, a huge one, splattered at her feet, then another. She started walking faster. She'd hated these storms at first, back in June when they'd started up. There was always a lot of lightning and crashing thunder, and she wasn't used to that. But they cooled things off, she discovered, and they were usually over as fast as they arrived.

They were spotty, too, sometimes surprisingly so. There were times when she was out on the beach and she could see the shower coming, marching right up the surf line. Behind it there'd be bright sunshine, ahead of it the same, but right in the middle it would be dark as night, with a blast of cold, wet rain and wind that could lift you off your feet.

She crossed the intersection at Third Avenue and thought for a minute she might make it home dry. She was only three blocks away now and it was still the fat, single drops splashing down. But then she looked toward her dad's house and her own little apartment off to the side and there, right on top of them, was the squall line. She started running, but it caught her just a few seconds later, a downpour so thick you could hardly see where you were headed. She was soaked in an instant.

There was a bright bolt of lighting — too damn close — and an almost instantaneous crack of thunder. She thought about stopping in the bus shelter there at the corner for a few minutes to let the rain pass, but she was only a block away now, and was already soaked, so she kept going, slowing down to a walk, giving up on it, really, trying to enjoy the cool rain after all the summer heat she put up with.

She was thinking about Michael Kelsey and about the sea turtle connection and how this squall would wipe out any clues still there at the murder site, as she made it to the yard, opened the little gate and walked down the brick sidewalk to the apartment, fishing around in her shorts pocket for her key as she rounded the corner and headed for the door. She stood there, under the overhang and so out of the worst of the rain for a second as she got her key into the lock, turned it and started opening the door.

All hell broke loose. It started with an odd pressure on her left shoulder. It was only there for an instant, but it felt longer as that pressure grew. Then there was another pressure point, at the top of her right arm. That one came and went and then suddenly there was a huge hand over her face and she was being shoved through her door and into her apartment, all of this happening so fast — and yet so deadly slow at the same time, like every moment was an hour — that she had no time to react.

She could hear a deep grunt of exertion, nothing more, and then a wooden kick followed by the door slamming shut and then they were inside, in the dark gloom of the storm despite the curtains being open on the windows.

Her mind was catching up to it all — strange what you can notice —

and she felt a moment's slightening of the pressure on her face as she was shoved farther into the room.

No time to think about it, she kicked back with her right leg, felt her heel hit a shin, had a brief, fleeting thought that she hoped his shin hurt as much from that as her heel did, and then she was twisting down and away, getting away from the guy and then, stumbling over things on the floor, she backed away in a crouch, all those hours of training in the gym paying off.

The room's darkness felt absolute, no lights on and that storm outside. She reached down to zip open the belly pack and pull out the Glock. She'd never fired it at anyone in her life.

"I'm armed," she said to the darkness. "I have my weapon out."

She could hear him breathing, tried to still her own breathing but found it hard. Part of her wanted to scream, part wanted to run. Why wouldn't he answer? It occurred to her that he was probably armed, too, so things might get very nasty very fast here. Damn.

"I'm going to turn on the lights," she said. "You stay right where you are or I'll fire."

"No, you're not," a voice said; deep, resonant, rumbling. "If you move I'll kill you. Right now. Here."

She could start shooting, aiming at the sound of his breathing. But that was a stupid idea. What if she missed? He'd be shooting back and that would be that. Oh, hell, what was she going to do?

The phone. She thought of that, but there was just the one landline phone in her bedroom and the one out here, in the kitchen nook, behind where the guy was. She couldn't get to either one. The cell then, but as soon as she opened it and said a word he'd likely start shooting.

She needed to find cover. She edged left, stumbled again over something on the floor, an overturned drawer from the old rolltop. He'd trashed the place before she ever got in here, she realized. She could see him now as her eyes adjusted, at least see the huge hulking shape of him there against the thin gray light from the front window. He was crouching, probably trying to see her, but she wasn't outlined against the window like he was. The squall line was starting to pass over. He was a big guy; part of her mind, the trained part, catalogued that. OK, she raised the Glock.

"I can see you. I'm aiming at your chest. I'm going to count to three. I want to see those hands go up. Slowly."

And she thought she saw that happening, thought she saw him raising both hands, then a sudden frenzy of motion, something hitting her hard in the chest, throwing her back, sending her onto the floor, into the furniture and drawers and clothes and kicked-over chairs that comprised her once-neat little apartment. Damn. The Glock was gone, flying off into the darkness when she fell and hit the legs of a chair, hard, right in the ribs.

"I'm coming," he said. "I want you to know that. I'm coming for you right now."

She looked up but he wasn't outlined against the window anymore. She edged left again, reached down, trying to find something to use against him. And felt the handle of her softball bat, the one that was supposed to be sitting upright in the corner with her ball and glove. She'd bought it when she joined the police team. Dad had been happy about that, but the new bat hadn't done her much good; she had a hard time making any contact at all during the games. So maybe today was the day, she could make some damn contact right here, right now. "Weapon of opportunity," that's what they'd said in her self-defense training class. You find what you can and you make it work.

She wrapped her right hand around it, pulled it loose from the mess on the floor. Grabbed it with both hands. This was the best it had ever felt in her hands. She raised it, breathing harder, angry and nervous and scared to death and ready to swing and kill the bastard. And she heard a deep chuckle. "Ah, you little bitch, there you are," a voice said, and the shape moved toward her.

The head? The chest? The legs? The head would be the most effective, but that was a hard target and god knows she wasn't great with this bat. But anywhere else might not even slow him down.

The shape moved toward again, another chuckle. He was only seven or eight feet away now. Then five. She screamed, and leaped forward and swung, all at once, putting everything she had into it.

And felt the impact, solid, like hitting a melon might feel. The bat vibrated in her hands, the huge dark shape staggered, almost fell, then caught itself and roared. He was hurt now. He'd try to kill her for sure. She swung again, made contact with a shoulder. There was another roar of pain and anger.

And the front door opened.

"Felicity?"

It was Michael.

She started to scream at him, tell him to get away, get help, but before she could get the first word out the huge shape, still staggering slightly, turned and ran toward the open door, howling like some wounded beast, shoving Michael aside and stumbling into the little hallway and then, suddenly, there was only the hiss of rain on the concrete outside, a burst of distant lightning and Michael, briefly lit by its flash, walking toward her, reaching out to her, trying to help.

SEVENTEEN

Sitting in his special chair in the MinistryOne Skybox high above home plate, the Reverend was studying page one of the financial report, looking it over again, trying to make sense of it. What he really wanted to do, he admitted to himself with a sigh as he re-read the first column of figures, was just sit back and watch out the huge open window in front of him as the Crusaders took the field to start tonight's game against the Porters. After all, this was it, Cassidy had explained just a minute ago. A win tonight clinched that wild-card spot, but lose this one and they were one up with two to go against the Infernal Porters.

He laughed at himself. "Infernal Porters," indeed. Sixty years he'd been in the ministry and never once had he called someone or something "Infernal" except for the Devil himself. And now here he'd done it with this group of perfectly innocent baseball players. My.

He tried to read the report again. He wanted to understand it — render unto Caesar — but he couldn't seem to concentrate. He turned in his seat, looked back up toward the sofa chair on the second deck of the Skybox, and smiled at Cassidy. "Are you all right, dear?"

"Fine, Daddy, just fine. Are you going to be able to put that report down long enough for the national anthem? You know we're on national TV. I asked Holly to sing it tonight."

Holly? The Reverend turned to look toward home plate and it clicked. Sure enough, Holly Day was walking briskly out toward the pitcher's mound. Holly's newest single, "He's My Man," was the crossover hit of the year so far for Morrel Ministries. For a white girl who was singing blue-eyed gospel in a tiny Baptist church in Nashville two years ago, Holly was doing well these days, and she had the Reverend and his music division to thank for it.

63

The Reverend stood and took Cassidy's hand as she walked down to join him. The scoreboard's huge electronic flag flew in a gusty electronic wind, then withstood a flurry of electronic explosions as Holly hustled through the song. As she hit that last high note on "the land of the free," the Reverend looked back at his daughter and smiled. Thank the Lord for Cassidy. The Reverend didn't know if he could deal with any of this without her. She was the silver lining the Lord had given him around the deep, dark cloud of Emily's death all those years ago. That evil cancer, the wasting away. It had tried him, tested him, it surely had.

But out of that had come at last this good and lasting relationship with his daughter. The two, father and daughter, were closer now than they'd been in many years— maybe ever. Now, feeling himself go, fearing what was to come, he was counting on her even more.

Eighteen

Stu Lindsay had thought old, worn-out Pat Jerome had pretty good stuff when he'd watched him warm-up down in the bullpen. Darned if his fastball didn't seem to have a little pop on it and the curveball seemed to be snapping. It would be great if Jerome could get into the fifth or sixth before Stu had to go to the bullpen.

Now, as if to prove him right, Jerome got the first guy, Jorge Dominica, with a fastball low and away for a called strike three. The pitch, up in the mid eighties, froze Dominica, who was looking breaking ball all the way. It was a hell of a pitch, and one that Dominica obviously didn't expect to see from Jerome. Stu chuckled as Dominica headed back toward the dugout.

"Pat's really got it tonight, Stu." It was Del Quentin, the hitting coach for the Crusaders. Stu had brought him over from Raleigh, where he'd done a good job with the younger kids. If you can't do it yourself, get someone who can, was Stu's philosophy. Quent's job was to work with the old-timers who had a lifetime of bad habits and then to teach the youngsters with no habits at all. Damned if he hadn't done well at it. He'd be somebody's manager in the big leagues someday soon.

The usual call from his father had gone about as expected at first, lots of talk about alcohol and baseball and ruining his mind and what a terrible waste and all that. Stu had agreed with his father right down the line: a waste, for sure, and too much of that soothing Macallan, and too much worrying over baseball, which was, let's face it, just a game where they happened to pay you a lot of money if you could do certain things well about half the time.

So he'd promised the old man he'd read the new book from Ashketar at Penn State on quantum bouncing and multiverses, and he'd consider any college coaching and teaching jobs that came along. Sure, sure, sure: anything to get the conversation to end. Which it finally did, though Father tossed in an enigmatic "Take very good care of that granddaughter of mine, Stuart. She's the best thing you've ever done." And then he'd hung up.

Well, Stu wouldn't argue with that sentiment, Felicity was everything to him. But right now he had a pennant to think about, too, which brought him back to the conversation at hand. "Yeah, Del. When's the last time Pat started a game with five straight fastballs?"

Quentin chuckled. "About fifteen years ago? Hell, it won't last, Stu, but it's fun for right now. Like everyone else around here, he's juiced up over nailing down this wild-card spot."

"It's not nailed down quite yet, Del," Stu said, but then the ump called another strike and damned if things weren't going pretty good for the Crusaders. Momentum was a wonderful thing, and Jerome got Stauffer to ground out to Leon at second, and then worked Hodge to a full count before coming in with a straight change that Hodge just did manage to get a piece of for a pop-up to Dickerson at first. Three up, three down. An easy top of the first.

"C'mon guys, let's go get 'em early now, all right?" Stu clapped his hands energetically and shouted encouragement to the Crusaders as they came in from the field. A run or two right now, with Jerome pitching like this, and the Crusaders could get the momentum in this game before the Porters had a chance to wake up.

Stefan Leon led off and slapped a single right up the middle on the first pitch. The damn kid still didn't have any discipline at the plate, but as long as his batting average hovered around the .280 mark and he kept stealing bases, Stu and Quent weren't going to say too much about it.

Bobby Martinez, hitting from the left side, took the first three pitches and worked his way to a two-and-one count while trying to give Stefan a chance to steal. Then, when Stefan finally paid attention to the signs and broke for second on the fourth pitch, Martinez turned on a slider that came in high and sent it screaming toward the right field wall.

Leon rounded second and was halfway to third by the time the ball came off the wall, but Marty Grabien, the Porters' rightfielder, played it perfectly, taking the ball on the first big rebound hop off the warning track. Grabien turned, took one step and fired toward home as Leon rounded third and sprinted for the plate.

The whole thing caught the fans by surprise, a play this exciting coming in the first inning. But as it occurred to everyone that the ball was on its way toward the plate and Leon was coming in hard at the same time, the crowd reacted, got on its feet and roared. Andy Bernes, the Porters' catcher, had the plate blocked, but the throw was just off his line, up toward first a bit, and he had to take two steps up and a step over to get it. Leon, seeing the catcher move, angled a bit to his right, and then threw himself into a spectacular hook slide while Bernes caught the ball on the first hop, turned and dived back toward the plate, trying to tag the runner out before that left foot caught the plate.

It was close, but from the Crusader dugout perfectly obvious that Leon's foot had crossed the corner of the plate entirely before Bernes made the tag high up on Leon's left shoulder.

Larry Leslie, the home plate ump, saw it differently. After starting to signal safe, he seemed to change his mind and with a huge, dramatic flourish thumbed Leon out.

Stu was out of the dugout in a heartbeat, running toward Leslie and screaming about the call. "Oh, Christ, Larry! Jesus, what the hell are you looking at out here! Jesus, his foot was there, damnit. Hell, his foot was all the way across the damn plate!"

Leslie stood there, impassive, arms folded, expecting this.

Stu was chest to chest with him in another few steps, his face contorted in anger. For the moment, this play stood for the whole pennant race. Hell, if they couldn't get an obvious call like that then they didn't have a chance in this thing. Leon was safe, absolutely safe.

But Leslie just stood there.

After a minute's anger, Stu's common sense kicked in, the outrage ebbing, though not before he kicked some dirt over Leslie's too-damn-shiny black shoes.

But it wouldn't make much sense to get thrown out in the first. This game meant too much for that, and both Lindsay and Leslie knew it. So Stu resorted to just staring at Leslie for a minute, holding the long moment.

"OK, Stu," Leslie finally said calmly, "You made your point, now get back to the dugout before I have to throw you out of here."

"Damnit, Larry, you blew this one. You know that, don't you, that you blew it?"

Leslie just looked him in the eye.

Hell. Stu turned to walk back to the dugout, thinking his point was made, at least. Maybe this would fire everybody up, get them going for this game. Might be a good thing.

Quent was up out of the dugout, walking toward his manager, a worried look on his face. "Stu. I've got bad news for you. Something's happened to Felicity."

That took a moment, two more steps toward the dugout, before it sunk in. Felicity? Oh my god, he'd heard that kind of talk before, that "something's happened" phrase that led directly to places he didn't want to go again, ever. He felt dizzy, stopped to grab the rail by the top step of the dugout. He looked at Quent, squeezed out the question: "How bad?"

"She'll be OK, but they won't tell me more than that. She was attacked, in her apartment, an hour or two ago. She's at Baypoint Medical right now. They said for you to get there right away. I got Jack Crevalle to drive. He'll have a car around by the clubhouse door. C'mon, I'll get you to the car."

She was alive, then, and maybe, he prayed, not in too much danger, but he had to get to her, and now. Doctors lie, trying to be nice. He remembered that awful feeling from eight years back, when serious turned into dead. Thinking back on that, his memory filled with the pain of that day when Carmen died and Felicity watched it happen. He followed Quent's lead as they walked down into the dugout, through the tunnel to the clubhouse, and out that door. He remembered the pain of this kind of thing, the shock. All he could think was not again, not again, not again, not again.

NINETEEN

In the MinistryOne Skybox, Morrel Craig was watching Stu be led away by Del Quentin as he heard the news about Felicity Lindsay from Cassidy, who was on the phone.

He turned to watch his daughter, who was repeating what she was hearing from a team official down in the clubhouse, saying it loud enough for the Reverend to hear. "She was attacked? In her own apartment?" She nodded. "Yes, yes. I got it. She's at Baypoint."

She hung up, turned to her father. "Stu's daughter. You heard that, right?" The Reverend nodded. "She's not critical but they're still checking her over. Some young guy, a friend of hers, broke it up, just in time apparently. That's all we know right now, Daddy. What a terrible thing."

The door to the skybox opened and George Brooks walked through, coughing some and shaking his head. "These are terrible times," he said, "terrible, terrible times."

For a brief, dizzy moment, the Reverend wondered what Brooks meant. What was so terrible? Had something horrible happened, an earthquake, a hurricane, a bomb? Then the Reverend realized Brooks was talking about Felicity Lindsay. "Yes, yes, Brooks. Terrible thing, terrible thing." He shook his head. "Just a terrible thing." But what was it that was so terrible, the Reverend wondered? He couldn't seem to focus tonight, everyone talking to him and all it going right through him, like a sieve.

Brooks almost seemed to smile for a moment, then took on a somber note. "You and Cassidy should go there and see her, Reverend. I'll stay here and guard the fort."

"Yes, yes, that's a good idea, Brooks. Cassidy and I will go to the hospital. I'll take these with me," and he grabbed the financial report. "It's important work we're doing, Brooks, important work."

"Right," said Brooks. "Important work."

The Reverend and Cassidy walked toward the door of the skybox. "Have Richard bring the car around for us, would you, Brooks? And then take care of the press if they come up there to ask any questions, all right?"

As the door was closing Brooks coughed, bent over for a second with the effort before saying, "Right, Reverend. I'll be here. You want me to come along to the hospital later?" But the Reverend was gone and there was no answer to that.

This must be Mackie's work, the friggin' idiot. Brooks was worried about him; he was getting out of control, attacking that girl. Didn't he have any idea of how this could screw things up? Brooks wondered, for a moment, if it was time to do something about Robert Mackie. This was two screw-ups in as many days, and the friggin' operation couldn't afford those kinds of mistakes. Something would have to be done, and soon, if Mackie couldn't get it done right. It was all very strange, really. Mackie had been the best in the business for as long as he'd known him, for decades. He'd always loved the way the guy worked: clean, quick, no mistakes. And now this.

There was a knock at the door. That, Brooks thought, would be the press, probably that pretty little blonde reporter from Channel 12. Brooks took a deep breath, tried to calm down the rattle in his chest that had him coughing so much. Tomorrow, maybe, the Reverend's doc would give him something for it. He thought compassionate thoughts, and opened the door.

TWENTY

Michael Kelsey stood next to Felicity's bed. She was talking to the doctor in charge, a young resident with a condescending bedside manner who just smiled at her, patted her on the head and turned away to look at one of the monitors even as she was saying, "Look, I'm fine, all right? Just let me go home now."

For Michael, a sense of reality was really returning after a couple of hours of almost out-of-body weirdness. It started when he'd gone to his car after talking with Felicity in the restaurant. He'd actually started driving home, heading up Gulf Drive toward Pasadena Avenue, when he realized what an asshole he must have sounded like when he was leaving the restaurant. He'd looked at the scrap of paper she'd written her address on, driven back to her place in the driving rain and walked up to her apartment to knock on her door and apologize. He'd heard muffled shouts from inside, opened the door and then, out of the darkness, this huge guy came at him and suddenly Michael found himself in the middle of some kung-fu movie.

He'd thought, at first, that he was being attacked, and there'd been a quick tangle of arms and legs as he'd struggled against the guy. But the guy had shoved him out of the way like that was all he'd ever wanted to do, and then ran into the rain and darkness.

It took Michael a few seconds to recover from that and figure out that Felicity might be in real trouble. She might be dead, in fact.

"Felicity?" he'd said into the dark cavern of an apartment. He'd been terrified, afraid to stay if the guy came back, afraid to leave if she was hurt. "Felicity? Officer Lindsay?"

He'd heard a groan, a weak, gasping "Michael. Help."

And it was all even more of a blur from there. He'd checked on Felicity, seen she was hurt and dazed, but he couldn't find any major wounds or anything that looked broken. Then he'd tried the phone but it was dead. He'd left his cell phone in his car and Felicity had one, but he couldn't find it in the dark and got panicky after just a few seconds of searching for it on his hands and knees, reaching around under chairs and an overturned table. So he gave up on that, ran outside and down the street to where he'd parked the car. He grabbed the cell phone from the cup holder in the center console where he'd left and started dialing 911 even as he ran back toward Felicity's apartment. He got back inside, found his way in the darkness to her, and that's where he was, kneeling over her, not letting her move, a few long minutes later when the cops, the parameds, the fire department and everyone else showed up, almost all at once. There must have been half-a-dozen emergency vehicles out in the driveway, lights flashing, radios crackling, people walking around looking busy. It had been dizzying.

Now, a couple of hours later here in the hospital it was getting pretty clear that she wasn't too badly hurt. Bruised ribs, the doc said. No apparent sexual assault. Some bruises on the throat area. She was one tough girl, Michael thought. And now she wanted out.

"Felicity," Michael said. "Look, they're going to keep you overnight, just for observation, OK? I don't think they'll let you go until the morning."

"Let me go?" she asked. "Michael. I'm a big girl, all right. If I want to go, I'll go."

And she would, too, he figured, though every time she moved he could see the pain in her face. Bruised ribs really hurt.

Felicity was wondering if the x-rays had it right about her ribs. They sure hurt like they were broken, not just bruised.

She heard a polite tap on the jamb of the open door. It was her father, talking on the cell phone with someone telling them about his daughter's troubles as he stood there. He was still wearing his baseball uniform, with one of those lightweight pullovers with Crusaders in script written across it over his game jersey. At least he'd taken his ballcap off. Tom Klinger, a Rum Point cop, held a hand on his chest to stop him from coming in, then dropped it in amazement as Stu shut the cell phone and said to Klinger, "I'm her father."

"Let him in, Tom, please," Felicity said, and Klinger stepped aside.

"Sweetheart," Stu said, and walked over to his daughter. He leaned over

70

to hug her and Felicity started to return it, but then gasped in pain and her father let go.

The quick, sharp stab was a reminder of what she'd gone through just a couple of hours before. She sat back onto her pillows and forced a calm smile for her embarrassed father.

"Oh my god, I'm so sorry, Fel..."

But she waved off the apology. "I'm the one who's sorry, Daddy. I'm fine, really, and they shouldn't have called you. You're in the middle of a pretty big game."

He just shook his head. "Don't be silly, Fel. Quent's got the game under control. I had to come. Jesus, I was scared to death." They both knew what he meant by that.

He reached down to touch her hair and smiled. "Your grandfather gives his best wishes. He said he broke a rib once during the Korean War and that it was no damn fun at all. But that young doctor told me you were going to be all right, Fel. He said your ribs were going to be pretty damn sore. I can see he's right."

Grandfather? Felicity wondered for a second what the hell that was about: both her grandfathers had been dead for years. Who the hell had her father been talking to? Was this another damn sign of how things were falling apart for her dad? The drinking, and now imaginary phone calls? God, how awful, and yet more proof about how badly he needed her. He'd never really gotten over the murder, even years later.

"Daddy," she started to say, thinking she could pin him down on that call. But then he leaned over to kiss her on the cheek and she could see the worry in his eyes. This was no time to pin him down on his failings, god knows. The quiz on phone calls from a dead grandfather could wait until tomorrow, she supposed. She'd put that on her lengthy mental to-do list for her father. Instead, she said "Daddy, really, nothing happened. I had a fight with this guy, and then Michael came and broke it up. You go ahead and get back to your game."

"Who's Michael?" her dad asked.

Michael walked over from the other side of the bed to shake hands and it was obviously the first time that Stu realized there was someone else in the room; a tall, thin, gawky young guy wearing glasses, a sports shirt, baggy shorts, flip-flops on his feet. This guy broke up a fight?

"Michael Kelsey, sir. I met your daughter today, um, at the beach."

"Michael's the brother of the man who was murdered, Daddy. We met

71

at the place where it happened." She paused, wanting to say more, to somehow define Michael better for her father, but it all seemed too formal, like introductions at some business meeting. And she was, as she thought about it, very tired.

"Yes. Honker was my brother. He was... I was..."

There was a long, strained silence. Stu broke it up. "I'm awfully sorry, Michael. It's a terrible thing that's happened. We know, me and Felicity, we know what it's like."

Michael frowned, not knowing what that meant but too polite to ask.

"Michael is a marine scientist, Daddy. We wound up talking about sea turtles at the Hurricane for a while, and then he left. I walked home and that's where the guy attacked me."

"I came back to apologize to her for the way I left, sir," said Michael. "I was pretty shook up. I came back and knocked on her door and it swung open and..."

"Michael saved my life, Daddy."

"Oh, Fel," said her father. "Oh, sweetie. My god." He took her hand in his and she grimaced as he tugged on her. He didn't notice. "They'll catch the guy, I'm sure," he said. "I heard on the way over that they're searching everywhere, trying for fingerprints at your place, checking local hotels; the works."

"Sure, Dad, the works," she said, to placate him. But the truth was, she wanted to be in on that, she wanted to find the guy herself. She had a score to settle.

Michael stood there, thinking. Saved her life, she'd said. Had he done that? Yeah, maybe he had. The thought hadn't occurred to him before, but maybe that's what he'd done, just by being there.

Michael didn't think of himself as a lucky guy, or an important one. He was just a crummy assistant professor, too busy with his research to play all the right academic games, never the athlete his brother had been, not the brilliant genius he'd once hoped to be. He was a drudge, really. Nobody important, nobody big, nobody having any impact. Nothing interesting had ever happened in his life or seemed likely to. Until now. A horrible thing, his brother's murder. And now this. It was way, way too much to process. There was a huge hole in his heart somewhere, a kind of unbearable pain that was everywhere and hidden away at the same time: too big, too huge to deal with.

"Michael," Felicity was trying to change the subject to something less

72

painful, "tell my father about the sea turtles, about the Kemp's ridleys. I've forgotten the details."

Michael smiled. This, at least, was something he was used to, something he knew. He could try. "They're an endangered species, sir. Historically, they all nest at just one site, and..."

Felicity settled back, trying to relax. This was all stuff she'd heard before, so maybe now she'd get a few moments peace and just zone out.

There was another knock on the door, a hesitant, cautious tap. Cassidy Craig stuck her head around the corner. Tom Klinger, the Rum Point cop, was standing watchfully next to her. "Felicity, the Reverend and I came to see you. Can we come in?"

Felicity hardly knew the Reverend or anyone else having to do with the Crusaders for that matter. She'd tried to stay away from that, wary of the publicity she'd draw if she was around the field much. Still, she'd been introduced to the Reverend a couple of times since Dad had come down here to manage the Crusaders, and the man clearly never remembered who she was from one time to the next. He was pretty dotty, she figured. Cassidy, though, she knew a bit better, and she liked her. Cassidy had been to her dad's house a few times when Felicity had been there. Turned out she was quite the whiz with her laptop, always coming up with statistics to forecast which relief pitcher to bring in for a given situation, or who to pinch-hit or when to try and steal a base.

Felicity had heard that Cassidy had been through rehab after some drug problem when she was in college. But, truth was, Cassidy seemed to have her head on pretty straight now, really, despite her famous father and his television ministry. Fel figured that sooner or later she and Cassidy might wind up friends. She also thought that maybe there was some potential for a little romance between Cassidy and her dad. Frankly, Dad could use a bit of that; it might help him cut down on the drinking if he found a woman he liked. But Fel figured he was so caught up in the baseball team that he didn't have time or interest in anything else, except that damn Scotch.

Right now, for instance, he was standing here by her bedside, the archetypal caring father; but at the same time he was sure keeping one eye on the little television that sat on that high shelf in the corner of the room. The Crusader game was on there, and tied at two all in the third inning. Well, hell, at least he wasn't on the phone talking to his long-dead father. That was spooky.

73

"Sure, Cassidy, c'mon in," Felicity said. She wanted to sound cheery, but her voice came out strained and tired instead.

Her dad took over, "Hi, Cassidy. Hello, Reverend. It's really nice of you two to stop by."

Cassidy carried a large floral arrangement, the "Get Well" basket from the hospital's flower shop. Michael, to make himself look useful, took it from her hands and set it atop the small dresser next to the room's window.

Stu tried to handle the introductions. "Reverend, Cassidy, this is Michael, Michael..."

"Kelsey, Dad," Felicity said, "Michael Kelsey." She turned to smile at Cassidy and the Reverend. "Michael helped me during the fight."

"What a terrible attack!" Cassidy said. "And to think it happened in quiet little Rum Point. That sort of thing's not supposed to happen here."

"Murders don't happen here, either," Felicity said with a tired smile. "The place is getting real interesting lately."

"I'll go check on things with the nurses, if that's all right," Michael said, heading for the door. Felicity smiled at him and nodded. This was all too damn much for him, the Reverend and his daughter and the manager of the Crusaders all here in this one small room and now the reminder again of his brother's death. The poor shy guy had his own deep troubles and didn't seem interested in being sociable. She couldn't blame him.

"A murder?" the Reverend asked. "Someone was murdered in Rum Point?"

"Yes, Daddy, you must have read about it in the *Times* this morning," Cassidy said. "A guy was murdered on the beach last night."

"And Felicity was the officer who found the victim," Stu added.

"Murder? In Rum Point?" the Reverend asked again. He didn't seem to be able to quite grasp the idea.

"Yes, Dad, murder. And now this terrible attack on Felicity."

"I'm all right. Really, I'm all right," said Felicity. "It wasn't all that terrible. I really think it's all being overplayed."

"Murder?"

"Reverend," said Stu, "why don't you have a seat over here and relax for a minute. Stu gave Cassidy a quizzical look. What the hell was going on with the Reverend? Cassidy just shook her head slightly and shrugged her shoulders. She turned to smile at Felicity. "Felicity, what can we do to help?"

"Yes," said the Reverend, "Yes, of course. What can we do? Just ask, dear."

Fel, her hand in her father's as he stood there next to her, felt a sudden pressure as he squeezed her's tight. On the little television in the corner, Sonny Dickerson had just caught a hanging curve and sent a towering drive deep to left center. As she watched, the ball dropped into the tenth row, where kids and adults scrambled for it crazily before the camera switched back to Dickerson rounding second in his home-run trot. There, the Crusaders were ahead 3–2.

Michael came back into the room.

"The doctor says Felicity needs to rest," Michael said, almost reading her mind. "And the nurse said we all ought to clear out. Except for Mr. Lindsay, that is."

"I'll just sit here by the bed a bit, if that's all right, Fel," said Stu.

She smiled at her father, who obviously wanted to keep an eye on the game as much as he wanted to sit by the bed and hold his injured daughter's hand. He'd been through a lot in his life, some really tough times with his whole baseball career, always never turning out to be the star everyone thought he'd be. And then the horror of Mom's murder. She shook her head slightly in wonder. Her dad had earned his successes. Together, the two of them, daughter and father, had gotten through all those bad times, had made it to here, where things were better, really. Dad was finally a big-league manager, finally had his brass ring and the team was winning and life was calming down, getting better for the both of them. Until tonight. Why was all this happening to her? She didn't have an answer. Not yet.

The others were leaving as the nurse came in to firmly shoo them out, Michael with a shy smile, Cassidy and the Reverend with looks of concern.

Michael waved as the door closed. His hand was the last thing she saw. He was a nice guy, this Michael Kelsey. Another guy facing the horror of murder. She'd seen too much of that, had Felicity Lindsay. She was wandering, drowsy. Maybe spending the night wasn't such a bad idea, after all. Just get a few hours of sleep, that was all. Her father took her hand again and looked at her. She returned the gaze, smiled, and as she was drifting off to sleep managed a soft "I love you, Daddy."

He loved her back. Later, maybe, he'd sneak out for a quick drink and at some point soon his father would probably call him on the cell phone again. But right now he was staying right here with his daughter. There was nothing, almost nothing, more important than that.

TWENTY-ONE

Robert Mackie hurt, and he hated hurting. His head throbbed where a huge knot had built up from where she'd clobbered him, and his shoulder ached with the promise of more pain and stiffness to come. He rubbed the side of his head where the bat had connected. Shit. He probably had a concussion, but couldn't go anywhere to get it taken care of. Jesus, things really went wrong. He didn't think she'd be fighting back like that, and what the hell kind of luck was it that she had a fucking baseball bat in there where she could reach it? Hell, he'd seen the damn bat, too, when he'd ransacked the place, and he just left it sitting there. That was stupid.

It was stupid to run, too, but he couldn't think for all the pain in his head and he'd gotten rattled when someone showed up at the door. Christ, should've just pulled out the fucking Glock and wasted them both. Instead, he'd panicked — it wasn't easy admitting that — and cleared out, getting tangled up some at the door before shoving the guy out of the way and getting clear. Then, when he got back to his car, the nice Buick that Brooks got him, he'd shoved it into drive and ran it into the goddamn seawall that ran along the water there. He was lucky some cop hadn't seen that happen, for Christ's sake.

Dizzy with pain, he'd managed to get the Buick back across the Bayway Bridge before the crushed radiator finally blew steam at him and the engine started bitching and moaning. He'd ditched the damn thing in a mangrove swamp back behind a ritzy subdivision and then boosted a Porsche to get out of that neighborhood and get back here to his room. Now, a lot of hours later, he lay on his back on the motel room bed, still trying to get his mind in gear, trying to think it through carefully despite the throbbing in his shoulder and the sharp pains behind his eyes.

He had the phone jack unplugged and had the place as dark as it could get, lights out and the shades drawn tight to block out the morning light. It wasn't helping all that much. The ice in the washcloth pressed against the knot on the side of his head, the fucking ibuprofen, the darkness and the cold air from the laboring air conditioner: none of it helped all that much. Jesus, it had been years since he'd been hit that hard.

At least he'd gotten away clean, neither one of them had a good look at his face there in the dark. Still, Brooks would be pissed as hell. This hadn't been part of their arrangement. As soon as Brooks heard the news he must have started calling, ready to scream at him. He groaned, rolled over and shoved the jack back into the phone and went ahead and turned his cell phone on. Then he rolled back and tried for more sleep. He needed the goddamn sleep.

It wasn't ten minutes, though, before the cell phone rang, jangling and rattling right through his roaring headache. He groaned again, rolled to his left and grabbed it off the lamp stand. "Yeah?"

"Mackie? Jesus, what the friggin' hell are you doing? I been trying to reach you the whole goddamn night."

"Yeah, Brooks, thanks for asking. I'm going to be all right. Christ, she clobbered me a good one, the little bitch."

"What are you talking about, you idiot? She clobbered you? She's in the hospital right now, along with most of the friggin' media in this town. This is not what we needed, Mackie."

"She's in the hospital? Really?" That was good, he was glad to hear it. Maybe he'd cracked a rib or two when he'd pounded her in the chest.

"Mackie, do you even know who she is, this lady cop of yours? She's the daughter of the manager of the friggin' Crusaders, that's who. You tried to whack the little girl of a local celebrity who connects up to me. Plus, we got a lot of history with that girl and her father, Mackie. Jesus, what were you thinking? Damn it!"

The manager's daughter, that's who she was? Oh, hell, Mackie thought, that did complicate things.

"Listen, Mackie, we have to talk. Where are you, at your room?"

"Yeah."

"Stay there, all right? I'll get there within the hour. She didn't see your face, right?"

Now that hurt his feelings. "I'm a professional, Brooks. No, she did not see my face. The boyfriend didn't either, when he showed up."

"Some boyfriend was there? Good god, it just gets worse and worse."

"They didn't see me, I tell you. Don't worry about it."

"You're sure?"

"Yeah, I'm fucking sure."

"Oh, and I take it you didn't find that flash drive."

"No. It wasn't up Kelsey's ass, and then it came to me that she'd been there so I figured I'd check it out. It wasn't in her apartment, that's for sure. I planned to get her to tell me where it was. That's what the little wrestling match was all about."

"So that's why you were there?" There was a long pause. "Don't you think that if she had it, she'd have turned it in as evidence, Mackie?"

He hadn't thought of that. Stupid, stupid. What the hell was wrong with him?

He thought fast. "Yeah, of course. But I figured it couldn't hurt to check it out. What if he talked to her before he died? What if she knows what that's worth? She coulda' kept it then, trying to make some money, right?"

Another pause, Brooks thinking it through. "Yeah, yeah, it's possible it could have gone that way. Not friggin' likely, but possible. But then it didn't work out the way you wanted it to, did it?"

"No. It didn't work out." The son of a bitch. Mackie had just about had it with Brooks and his fucking sarcasm.

"All right. Well, we still need to find that friggin' flash drive. And you know what, Mackie? I think maybe you're right. I think maybe she knows where it is, her and that boyfriend of hers."

"So I tail them? Let them lead us to it?" So maybe this whole headache thing wasn't completely a waste of time and effort and goddamn pain.

"Yeah. Maybe that's not a bad idea. All right, then, Mackie." Brooks was suddenly all business. "You just wait for me there and when I get there we'll talk it through, put together a little plan. I think we can still make this whole thing work if we can stay calm, all right? We've got bigger fish to fry than these people here. This is the big one, Mackie, let's not mess it up. Just stay right there, stay low, OK?"

"Yeah, sure. All right. I'll wait here."

There was a click, then a dial tone. Mackie was so tired he almost couldn't get the phone back on the cradle. He put a lot of effort into it, managed to roll to his left just enough to reach over and slap it into place, then lay back again with a sigh. He was tired, a nap would help, a nice little hour or two of sleep.

In seconds he was out, dreamless, just lying there.

Twenty-Two

Felicity didn't feel like she'd slept at all. First there'd been Dad watching the game, which seemed to take forever before the Porters went ahead in the ninth and the Crusaders couldn't rally. Then, even after Dad had cursed quietly and turned off the TV, there'd been too many things rolling around in her mind and too much pain when she tried to move into a more comfortable position. Dad had left the room for a while and she thought with some relief that maybe he'd gone home. But no, then he'd come back stumbling around some, so he'd probably been drinking somewhere at two in the morning and that couldn't be good.

Fel just lay there, faking that she was asleep, not really having the energy to get into it with her father right then about the drinking but knowing that conversation was going to have to happen soon.

And then it got worse. Her dad had made himself as comfortable as he could in the chair and fallen asleep, snoring like a champ. Then, five minutes later, he'd come awake with a start and fumbled around in his pocket for his cell phone. Felicity hadn't heard it ring, but he was sure enough answering it, and then talking to his dead father again. Just listening to him talking sent cold chills right up Fel's spine. Dad was losing it, no question; he really thought he was talking to grandpa. God, it felt like the whole world was weighing down on her all of a sudden: the murder, the fight, Dad's drinking and these phone calls.

All these things rolled around in her head even as Dad finished his weird call, hung and up, and went back to sleep. And to snoring, loudly.

Finally, maybe four or four-thirty A.M., he rolled over on his side, the snores stopped and Felicity finally found a few hours of restless sleep. Now, at seven A.M., she was bored, cranky, stiff and sore, and ready to get out of the hospital and back to her life. When she hadn't been thinking about her dad she'd been wrestling with a cycle of analysis, trying to piece all the action together on the murder and the fight. The more she thought about it, the more it seemed obvious that her getting mugged was part of the same puzzle as the murder on the beach. But why?

The murderer must figure she knew something and was trying to shut her up, so the mugging was probably meant to be a murder — she shuddered when that thought came to her. But why trash the place first? He must have been looking for something and must not have found it. But what did she have that the guy could possibly want? Something from the murder scene, she guessed, but that was as far as she could go with it.

There was one guy she could call for some help on it, a lawyer friend she'd met in a cops and lawyers softball game when she'd first come to Rum Point — Len Gold, a one-time defense attorney who now made his money on divorce cases. More money, less work, he'd explained to her when she'd asked why he'd changed. She sometimes wondered if that was really why. Divorce seemed so damn depressing, with none of the emotional payoffs that came from being a good defense attorney.

Len, she bet, would still be connected some to the word on the street; god knows he'd defended enough scum and got them off or treated lightly, to have a few chits out there he could call in. And she got along with Len, easily putting off his joking efforts to romance her. He was a good guy, middle-aged but still playing baseball for some old-guys team he loved. He'd help her find out if there were rumors going around about this whole damn mess and then maybe she could start doing a little detective work on her own and figure this thing out.

But first she had to get out of the hospital, sore ribs or not. She felt fine if she was breathing lightly, but anything, a deep breath, a cough, a laugh (she guessed at that, since there hadn't been much cause for laughing lately) — god forbid a sneeze, and her ribcage screamed at her with a pain that left her limp.

But that was just pain, that's all. Part of the deal. All right, then, it was time to wake Dad, get checked out of here, call Len and try and make some things happen here.

"Dad," she said, lightly at first. Then, "Dad. Dad!" louder, though it hurt to raise her voice. Then, frustrated, wanting to say it even louder but not being able to, she got it as loud as she could: "Dad! Wake up!"

And his eyes finally opened.

"Dad, I've got to get out of here, this place is driving me nuts."

"What?" He rubbed his eyes. "Out of here? Fel, wait a minute, give me a minute." And he stood up, walked into the tiny bathroom. Felicity could hear the water running, heard the toilet flush, and then he came walking back out with a towel, wiping his tired face. "Now, what's this about leaving the hospital? You know we have to wait for the doctor to take a look at you before we leave, Fel."

"Daddy, I hardly got any sleep at all in this place, all these people running around all night, and just, you know, the general thing, being in a hospital."

He did know. The last time they'd spent the night in a hospital, the two of them, had been the night of Carmen's death, when Felicity had escaped that horrible crash with a broken leg, some cuts and bruises, and not much

80

else in terms of physical damage. But Carmen; poor, dear Carmen. He didn't want to think too much about it, even now. That had been the worst night of his life, waiting to hear if his wife would pull through, finding out when the doctor walked in, that look on his face, that she hadn't made it. "I know, sweetie," he said now, "but they probably won't let you go until somebody takes a look at you."

"Then let's get somebody." And she reached up to her headboard, grabbed the call button and started squeezing. A nurse was there in under a minute. She was a tall, thin black woman, all professional smiles and niceness. Behind her, as she came in, was Nan Violante, the Rum Point cop who'd come in a couple of hours ago to take over when Tom Klinger ended his shift. Nan smiled at Felicity and waved hi, then shut the door.

The nurse was professionally friendly. "Good morning, Felicity, Mr. Lindsay. How do those ribs feel this morning, dear? A little sore?"

"Not too bad, really," Felicity lied. Truth was, they seemed to be getting worse and she wondered if an ice wrap on them would help. But otherwise she felt all right, the enormous tiredness of last night, when she felt like she was about to lose consciousness at any time, had eased. "Look, I'd like to check out of here as soon as possible. Can you help me with that?"

"I'll certainly ask right away, Felicity. Oh, and Mr. Lindsay, I'll bring you in a paper if you like. I'm sorry the Crusaders lost last night. They missed you, I think."

"Yeah, sure, a paper would be nice. And a cup of coffee."

"Two cups," Felicity added, and the nurse smiled. "And then, Daddy, I need a little help. I have to pee in the worst way, and that bathroom looks like a million miles away from here. Can you give me a hand?"

Together, they managed, Stu gently easing her up into a sitting position, then helping her cautiously stand, then gently supporting her as she walked slowly over to the bathroom. There he helped her sit, but the rest, she insisted, she could manage on her own. It all embarrassed Felicity no end but reminded Stu so much of his daughter as a toddler that he just smiled, happy to be needed again like he'd been in those better days, back when Carmen and Fel had been his two girls, the joys of his life.

By the time they got back to the bed the coffee was there, along with some toast and a scrambled eggs and the morning *St. Petersburg Times*. Stu turned right to the sports page and started looking at the baseball situation; but Felicity, sitting up now, sipping on her coffee, checked the front page of the metro section to see what it said about her. Nothing. Then, wondering why the story didn't get in at all, she turned idly to the front page of section A, where the really important news was, and there she was, in full color, smiling, in uniform, a picture from a feature story the paper had done on her months back, the daughter of the Crusaders' manager.

"Manager's daughter assaulted," the headline read, which would have brought a laugh from her if one wouldn't have hurt so much. Great. Manager's daughter. The story didn't tell her anything she didn't know until she got to the end, where it mentioned she'd been put on administrative sick leave for the next two weeks. "We want to give Officer Lindsay a chance to recover from this vicious attack while we expend every possible resource to find the attacker," was how Chief Bohnenstiel put it.

She smiled at that, too. She got along all right with the chief, but there was no question he used her for all the good publicity he could get. If a gesture like that would make him look good, then he'd do it, and in a hurry. She'd have to call him later this morning and say thanks but no thanks, she'd be back at work in a couple of days, let these ribs heal up a bit and then right back into the saddle. Hell, she'd be safer at work than just about anywhere else, even if it had been a murder attempt, which was something the story, or the chief, didn't even hint at.

"I wonder how these guys are going to react to this kind of pressure, Fel," her Dad said, reading the paper. "Look at what Steve Plasher is saying in his column. He says it's too much damn pressure for these kids, that they'll fold. Damn it, these sportswriters don't know their asses from their elbows." He threw the sports page across the room, took a deep breath, and then forced a smile as he turned to look at his daughter.

She smiled back patiently. "Win tonight and win it all, Dad," she said. "Come on, nothing to it."

"Right," he said, smiling again, "nothing to it, sweetie."

Then the doctor came in, looking at her chart and, thank god, smiling. She was cleared to go, but warned she'd be hurting for a while, those ribs would take two or three weeks, maybe longer, before they'd heal up enough that she'd be ready for work, the doc said. Sure, two or three weeks. She just smiled, and planned on a day or two, no matter what the doctor, or the chief, was trying to say about it.

It took awhile to make the great escape, filling out forms, arguing with the doctor, waiting for decisions to be made. At least that gave her time to call Len and chat with him for a minute or two about what was happening. It felt good just to get that process started. Finally, more than an hour later

82

her dad struggled with the wheelchair they made her leave in, trying to ease it down the ramp that led to the circular drive at the front of the hospital. Felicity was in pain, but mostly from trying to hold in her laughter at her dad's inability to maneuver the clumsy chair around corners, in and out of elevators, and through doors. For a graceful, if aging, athlete he sure could be clumsy at times. Felicity doubted they'd have made it out alive if Nan Violante hadn't stuck around to help.

But they finally made it out to the drive, where her dad left her sitting there in the wheelchair with Violante at her side while he walked across the street to the parking garage. Sitting there, thankful for the clouds that were already building up and slowing down the sun's effort at the usual late summer brutality, Felicity watched her father trot across the street and into the darkness of the parking garage.

She'd seen the way he looked at Cassidy Craig last night. He obviously liked her, which would be fine except that she was the boss' daughter. God knows Felicity had tried to fix her dad up from time to time over the past few years, and with some good women, too. One, a really beautiful woman of about forty, had owned her own business, some accounting company. She'd been a big baseball fan, but it hadn't clicked. Another was a lawyer, like Mom had been, but that hadn't lasted past the first date. He liked them both, he told Felicity, but he was so busy with baseball that he didn't have time for something else in his life.

Right. Of course she was in no particular shape to say much herself. She dated now and then, but hadn't had more than two dates with any guy in — what? — maybe six years now? There'd been no one, really, since Tyler. Something about being a cop, and being the manager's daughter, seemed to scare them off. That and the fact that most of them were worthless. She managed a laugh at that, and it hurt her ribs but felt good anyway.

"Something funny?" she heard from behind and then a shadow came over as someone grabbed the back of the wheelchair and started to turn her around.

It was Michael Kelsey.

Michael was smiling, but it sure looked forced. "I came to see how you were doing and they told me that you'd checked out of this luxury hotel," he said. "Glad I caught you here before you left."

"Hi, Michael." She gave him a smile. "I just had to get out of here, it was driving me nuts. I think I'm going to stay at Dad's place until I can get my apartment cleaned up."

"Well, I had to come see you. Things are driving me nuts, too."

She smiled at him, poor guy, the murder was only now really starting to sink in. God, it would hurt him for months, for years. Forever. "I know how hard it must be for you," she said.

"Yeah, well, it *is* hard. And now there's more. Now there's this."

He held up an opened letter.

"A letter?"

"Yeah," he said, "a letter, in my mailbox this morning. I want you to read it, Felicity. It's from Honker. Here, take a look."

It was handwritten, in a large, loopy scrawl that she could barely figure out, and on a piece of white paper, no lines. The letterhead at the top showed a sea turtle from a top view, and it read "Cayman Turtle Farm, Grand Cayman, BWI."

Dear Mikey,

I know it's been a long time since we talked, little brother, but I'm sort of in a tough spot here and I need your help. Mikey, this is important, and it has to do with the Kemp's ridleys. I'd just call you and tell you, but it's a little difficult for me to get to a clean phone line right now (look, it's a long story, all right?).

Thing is, I'm caught up in something that's gotten a little out of hand (don't tell Mom) and you're the only guy who can help. So I'm counting on you, little brother.

I'm going to try and set it up so that you can't get into any real danger (yeah, it's that sort of trouble. Getting kind of scary, to tell you the truth), but that will only work if you don't know too much, so just do exactly what I say and no more. No more than that, you hear me?!

If we do this right we can help save the K-r's, and that's what matters to me the most right now.

So. OK. Here's what you do:

Go to George Town, on Grand Cayman, and see a girl named Samantha who works at Parrot Landing. Sam and I are good friends (OK, more than good friends). She'll take you from there. I don't know whether I'll be able to see you while you're on the island or not. Depends on things. If I can, Sam will know where and when.

Mikey, this may require a little tricky work on your part on your way back to the States. Just wanted to warn you about that.

I love you, little brother. Tell Mom I said hi.

Honker

Felicity folded the letter carefully and gently slid it into the small envelope.

"So, what are you going to do? Are you going down there?"

Michael's eyes were red. Just watching Felicity read the letter had clearly torn him up. The first time he read it, a ghost letter, must have been painful as hell. "Yeah, I guess I have to. I already called the Center and took a couple of more days off. I have to see this Samantha, this girlfriend of Honker's. She may not even know he's dead. And then, if this thing with the Kemp's ridleys is still possible, I have to do it. I have to."

"Michael, it sounds like he wants you to smuggle something back, turtle eggs or something, maybe. You could get into real trouble doing that."

"Look, Felicity, I have to go there and find out. You can see that."

"Yes, sure I can. But you don't have to go alone."

She'd made up her mind as she read the letter. A few days in the Caymans might be good for her anyway, get away from Dad and this whole mess. Dad could get back to being a baseball manager and she could spend some time lying in the sun on some perfect beach, maybe letting a hot tub nozzle play on her sore ribs, drinking something sweet and alcoholic while some steel drum music played in the background. It sounded good.

And she could keep an eye on poor Michael, too, make sure he didn't get into trouble. God knows what he might do down there. If she came along she could help him get his brother's stuff in order, bring things back to the States, meet this Samantha girl and help Michael break the news to her.

There was an almost polite squeal of tires as her father turned his Jeep Cherokee onto the circular drive, heading toward them. She could see him smiling as he noticed Michael. Dad liked the guy. That was good.

"Michael," she said, handing him back the envelope. "I think you're right, you need to go down there."

She smiled at him, placed her hands on the sidebars of the wheelchair to push off and stand, a symbolic gesture despite how much it hurt her to do it. "And I'm going to come along, too."

TWENTY-THREE

The windshield wipers couldn't really keep up with the rain. Damn town got this kind of downpour every day all summer long. Might as well be back in El Salvador or Guatemala.

Guatemala. George Brooks smiled — now those had been the days. You could do what you needed to do and not have to worry about it all the time. Like this situation with Stu Lindsay's daughter. He was going to have to be careful about this, handle it just right, be delicate. Nice, nice, nice all the way until the problem was solved. Worst case, if it came to that, it would have to look like an accident.

In the old days, with the agency, he'd have had them both gone, shipped home to the States or, if they knew too much, have them whacked. Clean as a whistle that way. Done and over. And, god love him, Robert Mackie had been great at getting that kind of work done for all these many years. Quick and quiet and nobody to raise any red flags over the how and whys if some priest died or a few people went missing here and there. It had been a great way to work.

But of course they'd always been broke in those days, too, watching millions float by and not really able to touch most of it, spending it instead on AK-47s or Stingers or tree-top flying Cessnas that made the coke runs that helped fund the various operations. Millions, and for all those years he'd been a good boy, just doing his job and watching all the damn money flow right on by.

Well, not any longer. George friggin' Brooks had his shot at the money now, and he was very close to making it all happen, working all three ends against the middle so he would end up both clean and very, very wealthy. There were some problems right at the moment, sure, and a little tension between the money guys in Bogotá and the money guys in Prague; but it was nothing he couldn't handle, or, locally, have Mackie handle for him. As long as they didn't hear about this recent crap everything would stay smooth, and he didn't figure they would. The guy from Prague was flying over next week, but he was coming into Grand Cayman, not here in St. Pete. And he was just coming on a routine visit, just a look-see on how the new businesses were doing. Brooks would fly down for a day or two, show him the new corporate structure and dazzle him with the possibilities of the Reverend's new Retreat House, which had storage space coming out the ass and a friggin' dock that could handle anything, even that pie-in-the-sky submarine the boys in Bogotá said was about built. What a friggin' hoot that was.

The rain suddenly stopped. In the space of one block it went from a blinding downpour to bright, hard sunshine. Amazing thing, the way these thunderstorms could be so isolated. He turned off the wipers and cranked the Jag's air conditioner up some to combat the heat. You could see the steam rising up off the pavement.

So, there were several things that had to be done here. First, he had to make sure Mackie was OK. If the guy was in seriously bad shape, they'd need a doctor to look at him. That would complicate things. Would the Reverend's doc take a look and be smart enough to stay quiet about it? If not, they'd have to make sure he stayed quiet. Then he still had to find that friggin' flash drive. If they found the flash drive then everything was OK. If they didn't find it and no one else did, he was still OK, just worried. If someone else found it, and knew what they'd found, then the shit hit the fan and more people would have to die.

Goddamn Honker Kelsey, the cause of all this trouble. He'd had everything going for him, the stupid fuck. Brooks had been thinking about promoting Kelsey to running the whole courier operation. And then this, trying to rip him off. Imagine. Greed, that's what it was.

And, oh yeah, another thing. He had to keep a lid on Stu Lindsay and his daughter. Here the Crusaders were about to nail down the wild-card spot in the playoffs and Lindsay was worried about a little cocaine in the clubhouse. Jesus, what a baby; like everyone else around the league didn't use it, right? And the daughter, sticking her nose in where it didn't belong and now look at all this crap.

Brooks shook his head and made the final turn into the Hot Top Motel on U.S. 19. The daughter was a problem. He'd had her backing away after that scene on the beach and a couple of phone calls. But now she had a choice; she could still walk away from all this and stay alive. Or she could get pissed about it and try to figure things out, in which case she'd be dead in a day or two.

As far as her father went, he could always fire the guy, but that would look pretty stupid unless he had a reason, some kind of scandal or something. You couldn't fire a winning manager right at the big moment of the pennant race unless there was a reason. Lindsay was an alcoholic, that was for sure; but this was baseball and firing a successful manager for drinking too much expensive Scotch wouldn't work.

Drugs, though. Drugs would work. That was it. The guy's had a long history with booze and that would just make the next step seem natural. So, come to think of it, he needed to start setting up the thing now, make it look like he was into the nose candy. It'd be easy enough to do, get the situation ready so he could come right to it if he needed to get rid of the guy. He was thinking about it as he headed for the far corner of the parking lot, around where the last unit was, the one by the trees, where Mackie was holed up. It would be a damn shame if all this shit messed up the season. Brooks was as big a fan as anyone else. Go Crusaders. He grinned. He did get a kick out of watching these guys play.

And then his grin faded. He rounded the corner and there was a cop car, lights flashing, sitting in front of that last unit, where Mackie stayed. Why in Christ's name he wanted to live there instead of some nice house on the beach, or at least a friggin' condo, Brooks had no idea. The door was open and a couple of St. Pete cops were standing there, talking things over. Shit. He had to get out of there and had to do it without drawing any suspicion. He eased into a spot in front of the unit at this end of the building. He sat there for a second, thinking it through. Yeah, make it look good.

He got out, walked up to the door, knocked, hoped there'd be no answer. The cops were watching him, not recognizing him at this distance but keeping an eye on him for sure. He knocked again, making it look real. There were noises from inside, some shuffling feet. Shit. A bolt turned, the latch was unhooked and the door opened a crack. He could barely see the guy in the darkness, the shades pulled tight. An older guy, maybe sixty, fat, and there back behind him on the bed was a young girl, had to be a hooker, sitting up, lighting a cigarette and smiling, not worried at all.

"Yeah?"

"Is, uh, Pete Seals in there? I need to see him."

"You got the wrong room, pal. No Pete in here."

"Yeah, OK, the note said," he looked at the door, "room forty-seven. Must have been wrong. Sorry."

"Yeah, sure." The door shut.

Brooks nodded, as if he'd heard something sensible from the guy, gotten his message or something, and then walked calmly back to the Jag, opened the door and climbed in, started her up, backed out and drove slowly away. He was back on U.S. 19 before he took a breath. That was too fucking close. Now he had to get back to the ballpark, look as normal as possible while he figured out where Mackie was and what the fuck was going on.

TWENTY-FOUR

Robert Mackie was thinking about how lucky he'd been. He hated being lucky. You always got to have it under control, know what's going on, who's where and what all the possibilities are. Know your exits. Have a plan. Damn, have a fucking plan.

Well, hell, he hadn't been thinking clearly, that was it, starting with that girl. It all started with her. Fuck. His mind was wandering. Concentrate. Fucking concentrate.

OK. He was sitting in a back booth at the Red Tide restaurant, which was attached to the Sunshine Inn, which was a beat-up old place across U.S. 19 from the Hot Top Motel, which was where the cops, right now, were surrounding his room and coming in to get him for boosting that car. He'd been out buying a six pack of Bud at the Circle K at the corner — pure luck or they'd have him right now, and then everything, the whole house of cards, would be tumbling down, starting with him and then going on through Brooks and the Reverend and who knew where else, all the way on up the ladder to the asshole Russians in Prague or the beaners down in Bogotá. The Whole Fucking Deal could collapse, and all the money and security that came with it, just because of that goddamn girl cop.

Think. Think.

He popped open a Bud and took a long pull at it, feeling the cold go past his throat and spread right down his chest — it was so damn hot in this town. The waitress, the only person in the whole place, watched him, maybe thinking she'd have to come over and make him throw it away or something. He'd bought the beer and was walking back to the motel when he saw the cop cars pull in, two of them, no lights flashing, just sneaking up on him. And it had to be the boosted car that gave him away. Shit. After the girl had hit him he'd needed to get away from her, from the whole deal, and in a hurry. He'd cracked up the Buick and managed to get it into that subdivision before it gave out on him. The Porsche had just been sitting there in a driveway, unlocked, no alarm set, so he'd staggered into it, ripped out the wires from under that bottom panel, yanked them together with the wire from the column and that was what, he was gone. Maybe a minute all told and he was clear, driving away from all the trouble.

Then he got stupid. Instead of ditching it and taking a taxi to the motel room, or even changing it for another boosted car, something less expensive and obvious, he drove it right to the motel, left it out for God and the whole world to see, and then staggered into his room and that huge headache and those hours of sleep. He'd forgotten entirely that the stolen Porsche was sitting right there in front of the door to his room. Eventually someone had put two and two together, some cop driving by no doubt, seeing the blue color of the Porsche first and then coming close, reading the tags, and then calling for backup and then there they were. He'd been incredibly lucky to not be in the room.

He laughed to himself, took another sip of the Bud and thought there was a bright side to this. It was some kind of sign, a good omen, that he'd finally come awake and felt good enough to go for a little walk, buy some beer. If he hadn't been out for that walk...

And, hell, he'd taken his money belt with him, and everything that ID'd him, or the real him, was in it. He had his money, a few passports, everything that mattered. All the stuff in the room was garbage. Sure, they'd get a bunch of fingerprints, but Brooks had taken care of that years ago. His fingerprints were tied to a guy who'd been dead for years, an ex agent. He sat back, allowed himself a little smile.

The waitress came by. "I get you something?"

"No, I'm fine, thanks."

"You're really supposed to buy something if you're sittin' here. And I shouldn't let you drink that beer you brought in."

She said that with a little smile, making it clear she was going to let him get away with it, that he owed her for the favor. That was OK, being safe in here was worth it. He'd owe her. He watched her look outside. Across the street it was raining, but on this side it was dry and sunny.

"Funny, ain't it," she said, "this summer weather around here. Three years I been down here and I'm still not used to it."

"Where you from?"

"Buffalo. I liked it just fine where I was, had a decent job, you know; but there was this guy, and he was down here working construction. You know how it goes."

He nodded. Sure, he knew.

"And then that didn't work out and I said, 'What the hell, I'm stayin,'" and I been here since, doin' what I have to do, you know, to keep body and soul together."

She wasn't bad looking at all, a little thin, maybe, but with nice-sized tits. Not much in the face to look at, but, hell, he wasn't all that great a prize himself right now, all bruised up and all. And she had nice legs, and those big tits. He liked them like that, liked burying his face in there, and then stickin' ol' Henry in there, too, between them. He was getting a hard-on just thinking about the possibilities.

"You down visiting?" she wanted to know.

"No," he said, "No. It's work. Been here awhile now."

She sat down across from him. "Look," she said. "I get off in about an hour. I know this guy can get us a few rocks for maybe twenty bucks. Good shit, you know. We could do some smoke, maybe go for a ride later, see the sunset, do the beach thing, then get back to my place."

She reached over and grabbed his Bud, took a long slug from it, smiled. Her hands were shaking some. Crackhead? Hell, she didn't look it, not yet anyway. He'd seen some of them, all wasted and thin. Stupid fucking thing to do to yourself, smoke it all up like that, everything down a big fucking hole and then you're gone. So maybe she was early on with it, not too far gone yet. But begging for it, right here. He wanted to laugh at her, she'd be on the streets hooking in another month or two, and probably dead a few months after that, way things went with that shit.

"You got a car?" he asked. "Mine's sort of in the shop right now."

"Yeah," she said, "out back. It ain't great, got a few miles on it, an old Toyota. But it goes, you know?" She paused for a second, took another long drink from his Bud, killing it, then setting it down nice and easy on the tabletop. "Look, you got some cash we could have a good time."

He pulled another Bud out of the paper sack, popped the top, took a long pull on it, handed it over to her. "I thought I couldn't drink this beer in here."

She took a good long pull on the Bud, "You can't," she said, "but we just closed." And she smiled.

Twenty-Five

Leonard Gold, attorney at law, stood behind his desk, feet spread apart, and gripped the taped handle of his official Louisville Slugger aluminum baseball bat, The Thumper model. Concentrating, he centered his eyes on an imaginary pitcher sixty feet-six inches away and waited for that fantasy fastball to come at him again. Patient, patient, and there it was, out over the plate and waist high, fat, begging to be hit. Len started into his swing, turning the hips and then bringing the shoulders through, rolling the wrists. In his mind, a whole long way from reality, he connected and the ball jumped off the bat, rocketing out toward right, sailing over the 375 mark, a dinger, roundtrip, the yard, homerun. It felt good. It felt great. The phone rang.

"Mim," he said, "I thought I said to hold the calls for a few minutes. Whoever it is, I'll call 'em back."

"You did, Mr. Gold, but it's Felicity Lindsay on the phone, calling from the hospital. She says it will only take a few minutes."

Felicity? Well, hell, that was worth losing an at-bat, poor girl. He punched the speaker-phone. "Fel," he said, "I read about you in the morning paper, planned to come by and say hi later this morning. How are you feeling?"

"I'm pretty beat up, Len, but there's nothing really serious. I'm on my way out of here now."

"That's great, Fel," Len said and set the bat down on the desk, "but what a terrible thing. You have any idea who did this, or why?"

"That's why I called, Len. I thought maybe you could help me find out a few things. You know, check around a little and see what the word is on the street."

He laughed. "The street? Been a long time since I've known much about the word on the street, Fel."

There was a pause, a sigh from Felicity. She didn't sound good. "Well, I know you've been working divorce cases for awhile now, Len, but I thought there might still be someone you could talk to from the old days. This thing has gotten kind of personal for me."

"Of course it has." He thought quickly. Hell, he had to try something for this girl, she was a real sweetheart. He'd kind of taken her under his wing, helped her get to know Pinellas County and its own peculiar brand of law enforcement. "Look, Fel, I'll see what I can find out for you, all right? I'll ask around a bit, make a couple of calls. But I don't know if I'll be able to turn up much. I don't want to mislead you."

"But you will try for me, Len?"

"Absolutely. And who knows, maybe something interesting will turn up."

"Thanks, Len. Thanks a million." Then her voice lightened a bit. "How'd that game go last night for you?"

Len frowned. He played first base for a baseball team of guys forty years and older. They were pretty damn awful, but, hey, it was fun and it was hard-ball, the real thing, none of that sissy slow-pitch softball. "Tell you the truth, we got pounded again. It's a good thing you didn't come watch us. They thumped us, twelve to six."

She laughed, maybe her first laugh of the day, Len thought. "Have you guys won a game yet this season?" she asked.

"Hell, yes," he said in mock seriousness, "and I resent the tone of that question. We've won four games, thank you very much. And only lost eight. Give us a break here, Fel."

She laughed again. "And how'd you do last night yourself?"

"Had a basehit in the second; a line-drive up the middle, a shot."

"A bleeder, I bet," she said. Then her voice tired again. "Len, the nurse is here with some forms for me to sign if I want to get out of this prison. I have to go."

"Sure, Fel. Listen, you take it easy. I'll call you or leave a message on your machine if I find anything, all right?"

"That'd be great, Len. And thanks." And she hung up.

Len sat down behind the old antique desk. All right, then, he'd said he'd help her, but who could he call? Then it came to him. There was that case from seven or eight years ago, that drug smuggling thing that ended oddly. Who the hell was that guy? And when was that damn case? He vaguely recalled it; was it simple possession or was there a sale involved? He couldn't recall, but it didn't involve trafficking or he'd recall that.

Lawyers remember facts, not names. Len sat down at the computer and brought up the felony file in his documents, started flipping through the cases. Nothing rang a bell. The computer, a fancy Dell model, only went back maybe five years, so the case was before then. Len got up from behind the desk. Like him, the desk was a little beat-up here and there but, damnit, had a lot of character. His grandfather, the family's first lawyer, bought the desk in Brooklyn and installed it in his office there in 1929, about a week before the big crash. A year later, he'd pooled what was left of his money with some friends and they bought several apartment buildings on the block for back taxes. A new factory went into the neighborhood the next year and suddenly the apartments were full; that was how Grandpa dodged the worst of the Depression. He died in his late eighties. The Golds had been dodging big trouble and living long lives ever since. Dad fought in Korea and should've died three different times but lived through it all untouched. He was eighty now himself, and doing fine in The Fountains, that assisted-living home out by the beach in Treasure Island.

And Len himself had been in 'Nam, during the last year of American action there, and lived to tell that tale, too. He'd been pulled out of a firefight once by a slick, had been jumping through a paddy and just managed to grab the bottom sled when the pilot took it straight up and then out. Len wrapped first one arm and then the other around that sled and hung on for dear life. It was bumpy as hell, and he was soaked from the damn muck, and finally he could feel himself starting to lose the grip, starting to go as the guys in the chopper yelled and screamed for him to climb up, tried to reach down to help him while they yelled. The pilot was trying to wrestle it back down, a mile away from the action, but the sled was so damn slippery and Len had been so damn tired and so finally, a couple of minutes later, a couple of years later, he did let go and thought he was falling to his death. But they were down to twenty or thirty feet up, and it was over another paddy, and he fell flat on his back into the same shitty muck, sinking so deep it covered him up so that he thought for a moment he might drown, or suffocate, or whatever you did when half-water, half-mud covered your face.

But he lived through all that. Came home in one piece, went back to law school ready to fix the world's ills. That was two wives ago now, but this one had been with him for eight years and they had two great little girls—they played soccer instead of baseball, but what the hell. Len walked into the back room, over to the twin file cabinets. What year? '99 maybe? He flipped through the yellow files. Again, nothing rang a bell. 2000? Same result. 2001 then? And there it was. Roberto Delgado. A pilot, a good one, but caught on the ground on a small dirt runway in Imperial County after an emergency landing. The plane was empty after Roberto had turned the bales into square grouper, but there was some flake hidden under the passenger seat, cut into eight balls, and so they got him for that.

Yeah, Len remembered the case now. Court appointed as the defense attorney, Len had hoped they could plea bargain it down to two years in the state prison, followed by three years probation. If they went to trial Roberto might get five years for this second offense. The plea seemed reasonable. Then the assistant state attorney came in with an offer that was under state guidelines, so there was an agreement to deviate from minimum mandatory and Roberto got two years DOC probation and no time at all incarcerated. Basically, he walked.

Damndest thing. It didn't make a lot of sense, unless the police blew the investigation somewhere along the line, but it was too good a deal to walk away from and Len took it, happy to have the four grand he made from the case and let it go. Here was Delgado's phone number, damn near ten years old now. Well, hell, worth a shot. Len walked back to his desk, picked up the phone, punched out the number. A woman's voice answered. "Digame."

"Habla Ingles?" Len asked.

"Yes. What do you want?"

"I'm looking for Roberto Delgado."

"Mierda. Who are you? What do you want with 'berto? He doesn't live here anymore." This woman was used to getting occasional calls about Roberto, you could tell from the tone of her voice.

"He's not in any trouble. I was his lawyer in a case a few years back, name is Leonard Gold. I just want to talk with him, that's all."

"What is your number?"

He told her.

"OK. Maybe he'll call you, OK?"

"OK, you tell him it's important, all right?"

"Si, sure, it's muy importante. No problem."

And the line went dead.

Len shrugged, got up, walked back to the filing cabinets and slipped the file folder back into the drawer, shut it. Strange case, he remembered it fine now. Looking back on it, the guy must have been working for the local cops or the DEA maybe. That's why he got off. Len walked back into the front room and smiled at Miriam, who was living proof that older women were better damn secretaries and receptionists than younger ones. "Mim, I'm heading out for lunch, be back about twelve-thirty. If you get a call from a Roberto Delgado, you give him my cell phone number, OK? I'll leave my phone on."

Miriam nodded. "Sure thing. Don't forget you have a one o'clock with Mrs. Standiford."

The soon-to-be ex–Mrs. Standiford, Len thought. And her husband was going to be paying for the rest of his days for his inability to keep his pants on. It wasn't exactly exciting, divorce work; not like the old days, when he'd been on both sides of the adjudication fence, first as an assistant DA and then as a defense attorney. But divorce work paid pretty damn good, and he wasn't getting any death threats anymore — been six or seven years since the last of those. You get married, get older and settled, get a couple of sweet kids, and your view of things changes. You start to think about safety and security a little more and excitement a little less. He liked it that way, most of the time, he really did.

A half-hour later he was sitting alone at a table for two at La Teresita on 66th Street, working his way through the back half of a Cuban sandwich and some black beans and rice with a little chopped onion on the top, when the cell phone chimed at him with that cute little University of Florida fight song. He flipped the phone open. "Hello?"

"Hey, lawyer man."

"Roberto?"

"Yeah, man, it's me. Been a long time. What's up with you?"

"Roberto, thanks for calling. How are things going for you these days?"

"Just fine, man. Great. Rolling in the money, women everywhere. Clean and sober, too, man, you know? Life is good, lawyer man, life is good."

Len laughed. "Should I ask what business you're in, Roberto? Still flying?"

"Yeah, still a pilot. Self-employed now, man. Listen, life is short, you know? What can I do for you?"

"Roberto, I got a question or two about a murder case. A friend of mine is involved in this and she wants to know a few things?"

"The guy on the beach, yes? And this friend, is she the girl cop?"

"You sound pretty tuned in, Roberto."

"Tuned in? Tuned in? Where you get that from, lawyer, some old movie? Nah, I don't know a thing, man, just bits and pieces I hear from friends, that's all. Little shit. Mierda, you know?"

"Like what?"

"I'll meet you, man, and we'll talk a little, OK?"

He couldn't just tell him over the cell phone? Damn, there must be something to all this, then. So, "Yeah, Roberto. Where do you want to meet?"

"You know The Wharf? The one in Rum Point?"

"Sure, on the bay side. Nice view of the mansions across the water."

"That's the one, man. I meet you there tonight, about ten, ten-thirty, OK?"

"Yeah, Roberto, that sounds fine. I'll be there."

"Good man, see you then."

There was a pause, Len was about to hang up, then, "Listen, lawyer."

"Yeah?"

"You tell your girlfriend cop to keep her mouth shut, keep her head down for now, you know?"

"I hear you, Roberto."

"She's in the hospital, right? Cops all around protecting her? She's lucky to be there, man. You know what I mean? We'll talk, man. I see you there."

The line went dead. Len set the phone down and stared at the rest of the sandwich and the black beans and rice. He wasn't really very hungry anymore. There was a knot in his stomach, one that hadn't been there for years. Hell, he could back out now, just walk away, call Felicity and say he couldn't find out anything, then call that number back and cancel the meeting with Roberto. End it right now. Or he could meet with Roberto, find out the details, see where this thing was going. He sipped on his diet cola, thinking that phone call through. Keep her head down. Well, hell, he had to at least pass that message onto her, and once he did there was no goddamn turning back. Jesus, so much for the calm life, so much for safety and security. He picked up the cell phone and dialed Felicity. Waiting for the call to go through he tried another spoonful of the rice and beans. They tasted like cardboard.

Twenty-Six

The tension in the clubhouse was like a fog Stu waded through on the way to his office, everyone putting on the warm-ups to head out for batting practice, tying their spikes, pounding a hand into a glove pocket, staring at the floor in concentration. They didn't look at him. He felt guilty as hell. He'd done the right thing, staying with Felicity, no question about that. But they'd needed him last night and he hadn't been here for them.

He walked into the office, shutting the door behind him, and sat down to look at the stack of papers on his desk. Same stuff. Line-ups, computer printouts, charts. The book. Play it by the book.

Last night's loss hurt. Now, one in front of the damn Porters with two to go. Win tonight and clinch it, lose it and go into the final game all tied up. That'd be like handing the Porters the wild-card spot on a tray, all the momentum on their side. Lose tonight and lose tomorrow and that doesn't bear thinking about. The clubhouse was too quiet. Even Jimmy boy was somber, and he was always cheerful, with that smile on his face and happy hugs and pats on the back.

And, Stu thought, his daughter had nearly been killed, had spent the night in the hospital recovering. It was a hell of a life, that was for sure.

He opened the drawer on the right and pulled up the Macallan. He needed it. Just the one, to steady things. He poured a good one, drank it clean. That helped. He poured and drank another. The warmth of it helped. He stood up and walked over to the locker to start changing, thinking it all through as he took off the street clothes and putting on the uniform. At least his father hadn't called him in the last few hours.

The clubhouse was too damn quiet. He paused to give that some thought. Like a lot of clubhouses, this one wasn't always happy. There were too many egos, too much money, too much pressure for everyone to get along. The fantasy of a happy team of underdog Crusaders having a lot of fun while they battled for the pennant was an invention of George Brooks and his public relations flacks. The truth of the matter was that there were enough troublemakers in this clubhouse to ruin any team, and that Stu had worked hard all season to keep a lid on that, to keep them focused on the game, on winning, on what mattered.

Dickerson was the focal point of most of the problems — no surprise there. Like he'd done his whole damn career, he was always spoiling for a fight. If it weren't for Dickerson and his attitude, in fact, the Crusaders might actually have a pretty close-knit team. This latest stuff with the cocaine was just another example — a big one — of how disruptive the guy was, like he was on self-destruct and wanted to take a few people down with him.

But the thing was, if it weren't for Sonny Dickerson and his hitting, that happier team would be somewhere under .500 and not worried at all about the pressure of a pennant race. Stu thought about that trade-off as he walked past Dickerson's locker. The guy was late again. Always pushing it, always on the verge of getting suspended. Stu wondered briefly what kind of life Dickerson must have had as a kid to turn out to be such a jerk as an adult. Would the Crusaders be better off if Stu benched Dickerson as a disciplinary measure for being late again today after yesterday's warning? Maybe. Damnit, if the cocaine Stu found yesterday in Macalaster's coat was Dickerson's doing, Stu would drop him from the team like a rock, and the hell with his damn batting average.

At least Macalaster was here on time today, and it was Stu who was a little late after taking Felicity back to the house and getting her situated there, with another of the Rum Point cops stationed out front to keep an eye on things while at the house. The Michael Kelsey kid had come along, too, and promised to take care of Fel — get her some lunch and help her move around some with those sore ribs.

He got his socks and pants on and was pulling on his sweatshirt when there was a knock at the door. "Come on in," he said.

Stefan Leon opened the door and stood there. "Hey, Skip, your kid OK?" he wanted to know.

"Yeah, she's all right, Stefan. The docs say it's just some bruised ribs."

"Hell of a thing, Skip, sorry to hear about it. Some of the guys asked me to come and check with you on that." He turned to walk back out the door. "You did the right think, Skip, staying with your kid. We're cool with that, you know."

Stu smiled. "Thanks, Stefan. It was a tough call for me to make."

"You made the right one, Skip. My dad was a New York City cop until he retired a few years ago. He got into a couple of scrapes, too, over the years. It's a tough job. The guys, we're with you, OK?"

He nodded. "OK, Stefan. Thanks again."

Stu finished getting dressed for the field and walked outside his office. Things were quiet, the players sitting or standing, all of them looking his way. OK, time to talk to these guys. He took a deep breath.

There was a sudden bang as the clubhouse door opened and Sonny Dickerson walked through, not saying anything, just moving through to his locker and starting to unbutton his shirt as he went. He stumbled as he neared his chair, grinned sloppily and then fell into the chair. Jesus, the guy was drunk, or stoned, or both.

Stu didn't say anything to Dickerson, just gave him a few seconds to settle in and then started talking.

'I know you all heard about my daughter getting roughed up by some guy in her apartment. Well, the good news is that she's OK, a little bruised up but otherwise fine. The bad news is that they haven't found the guy yet, but they're looking. Important thing is, though, that Felicity is going to be fine."

He took another breath, forced out a big smile. "So that takes a big load off my mind. I'm just thinking one thing right now, and that's this game. I'm not worrying about my family. I'm not worrying about tomorrow's game. All I'm thinking about is tonight's game."

The clubhouse was eerie it was so quiet as he spoke. He dropped his tone down to something more conversational. "Look, guys. You've done a hell of a job getting to this point. Let's just take 'em one at a time now. Stay focused right here, right now and we can win this thing. Pressure's on them, the way I see it. Nobody figured we'd be here for this and they've been talking post-season the whole damn year. Now here we are with a chance to put things away. We can do it. Here. Tonight. All right?"

There were a few general murmurs of assent.

"All right, line-up will be posted in five minutes. Just a couple of changes. Macalaster, you're hitting seventh tonight. Garn, you're hitting fifth. Oh, and Dickerson, you're sitting this one out. Perez, you're on first, hitting sixth. Gaddis, you're cleanup. Everybody got it? All right, let's go get 'em, guys," and he clapped his hands hard and made two tight fists like his hands were on a bat. There were some shouts of approval and a general clatter of spikes and bats as the Crusaders headed for the tunnel to the dugout. Stu watched them go. Sonny Dickerson, in his street clothes, just watched them quietly, and then turned to look at his manager.

"What the fuck is this all about, Lindsay?"

Stu looked at him. "I warned you yesterday, Sonny about being late. You're late. And you're drunk."

"I had a couple drinks, Lindsay. I'm not goddamn drunk. And then the traffic was murder out there with this big crowd. I didn't think it would be that bad."

"Everyone else got here in plenty of time, Sonny. It's a damn pennant race. You're sitting this one out. You're lucky you're not getting fined, too."

Dickerson rose from his chair, stood there angrily. "Yeah, Lindsay, like you said, it's a fucking pennant race. You need me in there. We need to win this goddamn game."

"You're sitting this one out, Sonny. That's it."

Dickerson shook his head, then opened his hands, clenched them once, took a deep breath. "All right, all right. You made your point. But I'm a goddamn team player, Lindsay, I always have been. I'll be ready to pinch hit when you need me."

"You're not going to pinch hit, Sonny. You're not going to pinch run, you're not coming in to relieve. You are sitting this one out," Stu said, emphasizing each word slowly in the last sentence, and then adding "Sitting it out. Got it?"

Dickerson's face reddened as he fought for control of his anger. "You're

100

making a big fucking mistake, Lindsay. I'm telling you, a big mistake. The news guys'll be all over your ass. Not to mention Brooks and the fucking Reverend."

"That's my worry, Sonny. That's what they pay me for, to take the heat when I make a decision. Now put your uniform on and get out to the dugout and show the rest of the team that you want to win as much as they do. Pay your dues, Sonny, and you'll be back in the line-up tomorrow night."

Dickerson, trembling with anger as he stood there, arguing with his manager, looked for a moment as if he was going to stride across the room and start throwing punches at Stu. Then, instead, he took a breath, nodded his head, decision made, and said "Fuck that, Lindsay. I'm outta here. Screw you." And he threw his mitt into the locker, stood there for a second, kicked hard at the folding chair in front he'd been sitting on, sending it flying toward Stu, and then angrily stalked out. The door banged hard behind him as he left.

There was the clatter of spikes on the concrete floor of the dugout tunnel and then the door swung open and Del Quentin walked into the clubhouse. He looked at the door that led outside.

"I heard the door slam. Dickerson?"

"Gone," said Stu. "I believe the quote was 'I'm outta here. Screw you.'"

"You had to do it, Stu. The guys will back you up on it all the way. Dickerson's a jerk and they all know it."

"Baseball's full of jerks, Del. But he's a jerk who can hit."

"Sure, but there's so much damn tension around here already that his attitude was getting to be a serious factor, Stu. The guys will understand, even Macalaster will back you up, I bet."

"Great." Stu shook his head slowly from side to side. "Damn it, Quent, all I want us to do is play ball, you know? All the other bullshit just gets in the way. If we stay focused..."

"We'll win it, Stu. Take this one tonight and tomorrow won't matter."

Stu pulled off his Crusaders baseball cap; dragged his fingers through his thinning hair, put the cap back on. "We can win it, Quent. These guys have the tools if we can get rid of all this other crap that's going on and just play ball, just play the damn game the way I know we can."

Quentin nodded. "Brooks will shit over this, of course. He loves Sonny. And Brooks'll take his bitching right to the Reverend."

Stu looked at his coach, nodded. "Yeah, Brooks was the one who convinced the Reverend to part with the $2.6 mil to get Sonny, did you know that?" was all he said.

"Figured it." Quentin laughed. "Hell, Stu, just being able to yank Brooks' chain this hard is reason enough to suspend Dickerson right there."

Stu smiled, nodded. Yeah, it was at that. "OK, Quent, you get out there and tell the guys what's happened. I'll deal with the press. Dickerson is suspended until he returns and we talk it over. Don't know how long, don't know what kind of fine. We'll figure all that out after tonight's game. And keep it simple with the guys, right? Try to keep them focused out there. I'll be out in five minutes. I've got to call upstairs and tell Brooks and the Reverend."

"You got it, Stu." Quent turned to leave, stopped, turned back around. "You did the right thing, Stu. This has been building for a while and the guys know it. I think this will help clear the air. I bet the guys play great tonight."

"Sure, it'll help them," said Stu. And then, as Quent walked back through the tunnel to the dugout, Stu walked over to his office and his office phone. It was the right thing, he was confident of that. The team would be better for it. But he knew Brooks wouldn't see it that way. Just how angry would the guy get over this?

He sat down at his desk and was about to pick up the desk phone and dial upstairs when the cell phone rang. He glanced at the phone's front screen: it was his father, of course. He shouldn't answer it. Wasn't it time to end all that with the old man? Tell him like a man that he needed to shut up and leave his son alone?

But Stu knew he wouldn't do that. For now, the best he could manage would be to apologize again for not living up to his potential and then hang up. Then he had to call upstairs and let Jay Freed, the general manager, know and then call Brooks and the Reverend to tell them, too, what he'd done. None of that would be any damn fun at all.

The cell phone chimed again. Stu opened the desk drawer and pulled out the Macallan and the empty glass. One of these days he'd summon up the courage to have it out with the old man and see if he could end this harassment. One of these days. For sure. And he flipped the phone open to answer the call. And poured an inch of that peat and smoke from Scotland into the glass. And said hello to his father.

TWENTY-SEVEN

The Wharf is a weatherbeaten, wooden shack of a restaurant on the bay side of Rum Point's narrow peninsula. The building was used to process the local commercial fishing catch for the first fifty years of its life. For the last five it had been a bar and restaurant. Len Gold had been there twice in the past, both times after baseball games with the Jawbones. It was just the right kind of place for a bunch of childish men sweaty from playing baseball to eat some grouper nuggets and drink beer. But the place's lack of air conditioning had convinced him not to come back for a third try; all the wide open windows on planet Earth can't compensate for summer's heat and humidity in Rum Point. So for the meeting with Roberto he came in shorts and a St. Pete Crusaders t-shirt, expecting things to be hot.

Instead, he nearly froze, sitting at the bar waiting for Delgado. The Wharf had a new air-conditioning system and was, by god, determined to prove it worked. Gold ordered a cup of coffee from the bartender, took a sip, and then kept one eye on the door and the other on the TV screen over the bar, where the Crusader game was on. The game was in the third, and the Crusaders were down a couple of runs already to the Porters. Sonny Dickerson, Chip Corso was saying, had been benched by Stu Lindsay, just to add some extra craziness to the proceedings. Jesus, that took some balls, benching your best hitter.

Corso talked, too, about Lindsay's daughter being roughed up in a burglary at her apartment. She was out of the hospital and said to be OK, Corso said, but that had to be an extra burden for the Crusaders' manager to carry into this crucial game. Gold had called Felicity, warned her to back away from this case, and got her to promise she wouldn't do anything else — no more phone calls, no damn sniffing around — until Len got back to her after his meeting with Roberto. But she'd added that she wasn't about to just let it be. She was involved, she said, and she wasn't about to just disappear.

Hearing Corso talk about her on TV reminded him just how public this case was, how high profile. In some ways that was good, it would slow down the bad guys, make them think, anyway. In other ways it was very, very bad. There was no hiding on this one, no way to just fade into the woodwork and let it slide by. He sighed, took another sip of coffee, and kept an eye on the TV screen, hoping the camera would scan the box seats out behind first base, where his season tickets were. He'd be sitting there right now instead of in this freezing dive of a bar if he had any damn sense. He figured he'd get over there after he talked with Roberto, see the back half of the game, at least. He took a sip of the coffee and shook his head; awful stuff, hours old. Jesus.

He felt a hand on his shoulder.

"Hey, lawyer man, you drinking coffee at night now? That's a bad sign, man. Next thing you know you'll be in rehab." Roberto sat down on the next stool over and waved at the bartender for a beer. "So, man, long time no see."

Roberto looked downright respectable; thin, wiry, dark-skinned as much from the sun as from his genes. He was wearing a short-sleeved white shirt and a tie. Same scraggly, unkempt hair, though, and the same silly, thin mustache.

"Yeah, Roberto, it's been a while. You staying out of trouble?"

"Me? I'm never in trouble anymore, man, you know that. I learned my lesson back when you got me off. Straight and narrow ever since."

Gold smiled. "Sure, Roberto. Listen, this friend of mine, this police officer, she figures this thing has gotten personal, you know? She wants to make things happen on this case. You know some people she can talk to?"

Roberto frowned, took the glass of beer from the bartender and waited for her to walk away before saying, "Yeah, I know, she got beat up pretty good. But you got to listen to me, lawyer man. I'm doing you a favor here, a personal favor because of how you helped me back then. Here it is. Tell the girl to forget the whole thing. Let the detectives work the murder case, you know? Don't get no closer herself, don't ask too many questions."

"Roberto, she's a cop. That's what she does, she asks questions."

"She gives out traffic tickets and breaks up bar fights, lawyer man. She don't want to mess with this murder, it goes way too fucking deep for her, man."

"Too deep?"

Roberto leaned forward, looked around once to make sure they wouldn't be overheard, lowered his voice another notch. "The guy who died, he was trying to turn on his employers, you know? They're in the import business and he was going to sell some information he had about them, man. That's a bad idea. That's what the dead guy found out, just how bad an idea it was."

"Who are these people, Roberto, the ones he was going to turn in?"

"Oh, man, don't ask me that. They big, that's all. One or two of them,

they right here in town, holy as all hell, you know. Clean and holy business-
men."

"Holy?"

Roberto just looked at him for a moment. "Madre de Dios, lawyer
man. Yeah, holy."

Gold nodded. "OK, Roberto, I'm going to run a couple of names by
you, and you don't have to answer or anything. Just look at me, all right?"

Roberto smiled, nodded, this was a game he'd played before.

"The Reverend Morrel Craig."

Roberto frowned, shook his head. "No, man, that's way too simple.
You got to think past that."

"OK, then, how about the Fortunato brothers?"

Roberto shook his head again. "Way past them, man, way past them."

Past the Fortunato brothers? Who, then?

"Some local politician, Roberto? Franklin, or James? Maybe the gov-
ernor?"

More head shakes. But if not the Reverend, then who? Maybe the Reverend's right-hand man, the director of baseball operations, the fat guy, the
chain-smoker. What the hell was his name? Ah, yeah.

"Brooks, George Brooks."

Roberto took a sip of his beer. "You know, I do some work for the ball-
club. Fly people around, drive a limo sometimes. I get to know people; visitors from out of town, even some of the ballplayers, the people in the
clubhouse. It's interesting work."

"So it's Brooks?"

Roberto just smiled.

That was it, then. Brooks. Damnation. All right, that was a start. "Any
one else, Roberto, you want me to guess some more?"

"No, man, I think you did fine," Roberto said, and took a long pull
on his beer. "Just remember this. This local guy, he ain't even the top of the
food chain, you know? He got bosses, and those bosses got bosses. It just
gets bigger and bigger, man. It gets into some things you don't want to know
about. I don't know where it ends."

Great, thought Gold, a conspiracy theory from a junkie. How much
of all this was true, he wondered?

"Roberto, you don't have anything else, someplace to start looking for
a paper trail, maybe?"

Roberto laughed nervously, pointed his beer bottle at Gold. "You not listening to me, man. I tell you any more names and the wrong people find out and we're both dead, you know? Anybody finds out about today, about this right here, and we're dead. You got that? Hell no, no more names, no fucking paper trail. Do the smart thing, lawyer man, and tell the girl cop to back off or get ready to duck, you know what I mean? These guys, they play hardball. They play for keeps, no screwing around."

Gold nodded. "Sure, I know what you mean, Roberto." He turned toward the bartender, raised his empty coffee cup, signaling for another. "You want another beer, Roberto?" he asked. There was no answer. He turned back to ask him again, but Roberto was gone. On the TV screen, some Porters hitter was jogging around the basepaths after a homerun. Well, that was great, just fucking great, thought Gold. Roberto drops a bomb on me and the Porters take the lead, all in ten seconds' time.

He took another sip of the black, awful coffee and then sat there for a minute, thinking it over. Across the bay, lights twinkling, sat the homes of the wealthy. Gold pulled his cell phone from his shorts pocket and placed a call to Felicity.

TWENTY-EIGHT

The French doctors were sipping on Pass-a-Grille pale ale and warily looking over a tray of Ministry Field hotdogs while watching the Crusaders take the field. The Reverend and George Brooks had promised the doctors an All-American evening, complete with hotdogs, peanuts, beer and baseball, and by god, that was what they were getting. They all planned to watch the first few innings of tonight's game, then move back into the meeting room to discuss the Sahel proposal and drink a decent glass of Bordeaux merlot.

The Reverend stood momentarily alone at the big picture window overlooking the diamond. In his hands he held a file folder labeled "SAHEL/ FRENCH." He'd just read the two-page synopsis inside it and now he couldn't remember any of it, not a blessed thing. He wanted to cry. He heard Brooks come up from behind, the heavy tread of the man's shoes on the carpet and the raspy sound of his troubled breathing making it obvious

106

who it was. Up close, Brooks always smelled of cigarettes. He wondered if Brooks knew how annoying it was to others. Maybe so.

"It's another perfect evening for baseball, Reverend," said Brooks.

"Yes, it is, George, at least inside the dome." Outside, another thunderstorm was ripping through town.

"Reverend, by the way, Island National needed some decisions made on the architectural drawings for the Retreat House in Grand Cayman. I chose the proposal with the redundant roofline supports and the extra supports on the wharf area, so the House would meet hurricane shelter standards. It's only another hundred thousand, and I thought it would make for good public relations for us."

The Reverend nodded. Retreat House? What in God's name was that? He needed Cassidy here to help him through this. He seemed to need her around all the time, he thought, and if this was what he thought it was, he'd just get worse and worse over the months and years ahead. The poor girl, what a terrible, selfish, thing to inflict on her, laying his troubles at her feet. "Good decision, George," the Reverend said, hoping that was the right answer. "Roof supports, though?" There, that should be safe enough.

"The extra hundred thousand seemed like a no-brainer to me, Reverend. The local government went for it and zipped us right through the permits and procedures process mostly because we did it this way. Made them happy, so they made us happy."

Brooks paused, looked out toward the diamond where the Crusaders were throwing the ball around the infield one last time. "Look, Reverend, I understand how you feel about this, I really do. You want to keep an eye on things more, and that's fine. But I came into this organization to get things done. My backers have put a lot of money into this effort, Reverend, and they expect me to turn things around. Well, I've done that, and I haven't bothered you with the details. Like I said in your office, Reverend, you let me handle these things and I'll give you regular updates, all right? You want to make changes, all you got to do is ask."

Brooks reached into his coat pocket and pulled out a pack of Winstons. The Reverend frowned. Brooks smiled, and put the cigarettes back. "Look, Reverend, we're doing fine. We'll finish the fiscal year in the black and that means we can start repaying the loans and you can continue to plow money into efforts like this thing with the French doctors."

That was it, the Reverend thought, that was exactly what he had in mind, things like this effort with the French doctors. Where was it? Africa somewhere, that was it. And what was it they were doing? He couldn't remember. The Reverend went silent for a minute, looking out toward the field as the public address system announced the singing of the national anthem. What was it about this game? Something important about it. Oh, yes: "Win this and we clinch the wild card spot. That's a miracle, don't you think, George? A real blessing."

"A miracle, Reverend, like you say. If Dickerson stays hot with the bat, these guys might go pretty deep into the post-season. That'd be something, wouldn't it? Being in the World Series?" Saying that, Brooks looked out toward first, where Hector Perez stood there in place of Sonny Dickerson.

Brooks frowned. "Hey, what the hell ... Sonny's not on first, Reverend. I wonder what happened?"

The phone on the desk behind them beeped politely, and Brooks turned to answer it.

"Brooks here."

There was a long pause.

"Goddamn it, Lindsay, you can't..."

Brooks noticed the look on the Reverend's face, reacting to both the volume and the language Brooks was using. He calmed it down, took a deep breath, spoke more quietly.

"Lindsay, you can't suspend Sonny Dickerson, especially now. I don't care that you've cleared it with Jay Freed — he's just the general friggin' manager and he works for me. You got that? And so do you, goddamnit. You can't do something like this without clearing it first. The press is going to love jumping all over us for this."

The Reverend came up to Brooks, said nothing, just reached out quietly and took the phone from Brooks' hand. "Stu? What's this about?" He listened, nodded. "I understand." He nodded again, seemed energized by the discussion with Stu Lindsay. "All right, Stu. There's no real harm that's been done yet. A one-game suspension is not a disaster, especially if we win, right?" Another pause, another nod. "I agree, Stu. I'll pass that on to George right now. We'll take it from here, Stu. You just worry about tonight's game, all right? Let's win this one, Stu." Another brief listen, then the Reverend put the phone back in its cradle, turned to face Brooks.

"It seems reasonable to me, George. Stu says that Sonny came into the clubhouse drunk, so he's sitting him down."

Brooks seemed to struggle for control. "Look, Reverend, it's the last two games of the season and we want to win that wild-card spot. The newspaper and radio sports guys will jump all over Lindsay, all over us, for this."

"Will they? Stu doesn't seem to think so. He points out that Dickerson has a history of this kind of behavior."

"Of course he does, but Lindsay said he could handle him, right? He promised us he could get Dickerson to 'live up to his potential,' I think that's what he said back last December when we spent all those millions on Dickerson."

"Did he say that? I don't recall. But we all knew that Dickerson could be a liability, too." The Reverend turned away from him and looked over toward Cassidy, who'd just walked in and was standing across the room chatting with some men — oh, the French doctors, that was who they were.

The Reverend turned back to chat some more with George Brooks but the man was leaving, and without saying goodbye, at that. What had they been talking about? Some argument? He couldn't recall. But there was Cassidy and she'd know. He started to walk her way.

Jesus Christ. Brooks had wanted to say something, wanted to friggin' scream about all this stupidity. But he kept his mouth shut for the moment and turned to walk away. There was no use arguing with this doddering old fool, and besides, the French doctors were standing around over there with Cassidy Craig wondering what the hell the arguing was all about. Brooks didn't want to look bad in front of them. He had plans for the French doctors, for their planes when they started that work in the Sahel.

He was smiling as he crossed the room and reached the nearest of the French doctors, reaching out to shake the guy's hand. It would work out fine, Brooks thought. One way or a friggin' another, this whole goddamn thing would work out fine.

TWENTY-NINE

After Stu left for the ballpark, Felicity and Michael had talked through the implications of Honker's letter. Michael was convinced he had to go to Grand Cayman, and right away. Felicity, so sore she could hardly move without pain, kept insisting that she come with him. They were too new to each

109

other to argue, but the discussion was going nowhere fast until Cassidy Craig arrived with a solution.

Cassidy, carrying a picnic hamper full of soups and salads, had come to wish Felicity well and see how she was holding up. In minutes, after listening to the two of them discuss the letter, she had the answer they all needed. "Look, you two. Michael has to go, that seems clear. And Felicity wants to go, that's clear, too. But, Felicity, what you should be doing is relaxing and healing. Well, I have the perfect solution for all of this. You two can fly down there and stay at our place."

"Your place?"

"It's a little three-bedroom bungalow, up in West Bay, north of Seven-Mile Beach. Dad goes down there once or twice a year to relax for a few days, and George Brooks gets there once a month or so, working on the Ministry's Caribbean initiative. There's a maid service that goes by twice a week, so it will be ready for us when we arrive."

Felicity just looked at her "We?"

Cassidy smiled. "You need the help. I love going down there anyway. Why not? I have to go talk to some people at the ballpark for about an hour, and then I'll swing by and get you two and we'll take the nine P.M. flight on Cayman Air." She laughed. "Hey, I'm a preferred customer so I can get us upgrades to first class. Couple of hours of comfortable seats and then we're there."

Michael nodded his head. "It'll be expensive, but I have to go, so this would work fine as long as you don't mind putting us up. Felicity, you could just relax on the beach while I check out a few things, and then you'll be there for me to talk it all through with once I find something out."

Felicity was too tired to argue, and a little R&R didn't sound that bad anyway. Michael, standing next to her, was in too much of a hurry to worry about it much longer. He wanted to get there, and soon. Cassidy, smiling, figured she had it all under control. So three hours later, when the Cayman Air Boeing 737 taxied away from airside D and headed for the main north-south runway at Tampa International, all three were on it, sitting up front.

Felicity hurt. Her ribs ached constantly, with an occasional sharp pain when she moved wrong, like someone was sticking a knife into her chest. She hadn't felt this sore since the day of the accident that had killed her mother. The doc at the hospital had given her a prescription for Lortab, but she wanted a clear head and so stuck with ibuprofen to take the edge off the pain. For the moment, sitting calmly in a nice, wide seat for a couple of hours and drinking something icy and filled with rum was working all right. When they got down there, she thought, she'd try and use the cell phone to call her dad and clue him in on where they were. If the cell phone didn't work from there, she'd use the phone at the Craigs' place. Then she could call Len Gold, too, and see what he'd learned, maybe start putting things together and making some damn sense out of all this. Carefully, cautiously, she moved her shoulders around, got as comfortable as she could in her aisle seat with Michael next to her in the window seat.

"You all right?" he asked.

"Just sore," she said. "I'll get over it."

"You shouldn't have come."

"You're probably right." But she smiled as the nose of the 737 rose up off the runway and they headed out over Tampa Bay and then aimed south. She had the airline magazine open and could see the route they'd take: past Key West, over Cuba's Bay of Pigs and then down to Grand Cayman. Should be fun.

Michael just shook his head and then sat back, took a deep breath, and wondered what this Samantha girl would be like in George Town.

In row 32, seat D, back in coach because first-class was sold out, Robert Mackie felt beat-up and used up and crummy. He looked out the window at Tampa Bay below and wondered what the waitress would look like in a few days when somebody found her body.

They'd bought her a couple of rocks off a scraggly teenager at a street corner in south St. Pete and then gone to her place, a little beat-up apartment in a rough part of town. She'd grabbed a little glass pipe, offered him a smoke and when he'd said no thanks to her she'd happily dropped one rock and then another into her little pipe and lit up, him watching from the chair and she sitting on the side of her unmade bed. There had been a good half-hour of nodding then, a squishy, soft smile about all she could manage past those droopy eyelids while he sat on the battered chair in her two-room apartment and thought about how sore he felt and how much his head hurt while he watched her. Then she'd woke up enough to really see him, had stood up from the bed, come over to take his hand, brought him back to the bed, had him stand there while she slowly pulled down the zipper on his pants, pulled him out, smiled at him and then taken him in her mouth and brought him off.

111

It went pretty well then for a while; he even forgot the headache while they screwed. She made all the right noises, doing him with her mouth then pushing him back on the bed and getting on top of him, then asking for it from behind. It had been a while, to be honest, since it had been that good. Brooks was always reminding him that he couldn't get into any trouble here, had to keep himself clean if the whole thing was going to work for the both of them. That was what the hookers in the Caymans were for if he needed some sex. That was why they got up to New Orleans every couple of months for a few days. But not in St. Pete, that was dangerous.

But it was, goddamn it, pretty good. He was actually feeling a little better, even thinking of maybe arranging something with her, keep her supplied with her crack and then have a steady thing on the side with her, that sort of thing, when she finished blowing him for the second time, looked up at him, swallowing with a wicked little grin, and said something stupid.

"Wait 'til I tell Licia about you."

"Licia?"

"She's a friend, really into having fun. We talk all the time."

"All the time, huh."

"Licia started hooking a few months ago, just to make a few bucks on the side, you know? She figured she was doing it all the time for fun, anyway, she might as well get paid while she was at it."

The bitch was rattling on, unstoppable now as she sat back on the bed and reached over to grab a Marlboro out of a pack of cigarettes in her purse. She lit it, inhaled long enough to get a deep drag and then blew it out toward the ceiling. "Anyway, the trouble is there's so many real assholes out there, you know? Not everybody's as nice as you. I can just tell you're one of the nice ones, the way you make love tells me that. Someone's been treating you mean, you got that nasty bruise there on the side of your face and your shoulder's all banged up."

She reached out to touch him on the head bruise, gave it a little butterfly flick with her fingers, then leaned over and kissed him there, like a mommy would. "You deserve better than that, sweetheart. I'm very sensitive to those things, to the little things, you know? The way you touch the other person, the way you were just stroking my hair while I did you just then? Those sorts of things. I can tell you're a good man that's just had some bad things happen, that's all."

She took another drag, had a sudden, serious expression on her face. "You know, I don't even know your name. Isn't that dumb?" She shook her

112

head at her own stupidity. "I don't know your name, or what you do or anything, and I can just tell that this isn't just a one-time thing, you know? We could, like, get to know each other a little better, right?"

So. She wanted to know more about him, was going to brag about him to her friend Licia. Women. Shit.

So he reached over and grabbed her by the hair, pulled her brutally toward him, saw that quick look of fear and then outright terror in her face, and then wrestled with her for a minute before snapping her neck and watching her eyes go blank. It was, he thought with a certain pride, a very professional job. He just left the body where it was on the bed, taking his time to clean up the place, got rid of the fingerprints, the cigarette butts, the glasses and everything else — playing maid there for a half-hour or so before he was able to stop and think it through, figure out what was next.

And this was what was next. Down to the Caymans and the place the Reverend had there, where he stayed when he did the courier runs. He'd just been there last week, in fact, when all the trouble with fucking Honker Kelsey got started.

He'd get down there, get settled down a bit, and then call Brooks, figure out what was next, let things cool off for a bit, maybe even take a walk on the beach.

Too bad about the waitress.

He took a last look out the window as the south side of St. Pete slipped back behind the plane and the open Gulf yawned wide. Too bad about her, but he was, goddamn it, a professional, so he did what he had to do with her. He was tired, and tugged down the plastic blind over the window, sat back into his seat and closed his eyes. At least the sex was great. He thought about that and smiled.

THIRTY

Michael watched out the window as the Florida Keys disappeared behind them, clear in the thin moonlight, dots of land stepping off into the blue Gulf Stream. He'd been to the Keys plenty of times, but had never seen them quite like this. Everything was happening so damn fast. He wasn't used to that. He'd always been the cautious one, the careful one. Honker, poor

Honker, had always taken the risks, and look what it had gotten him. And now here Michael found himself on a plane heading toward trouble in the tropics, no doubt about it. But he had to do it, no doubt about that, either. He had to go find this Samantha, talk to her, find out what had been going on in Honker's life, put that all to rest.

He shook his head. He was no hero, had never thought of himself as having the courage in the family. He was a plodder; never a brilliant student, never a great athlete. Too tall, too skinny, too clumsy, he'd always been out of the loop in school and with friends. Now, here he was in adulthood, just another mediocre researcher who plugged away at his field, staying out of trouble, getting through it all with a minimum of ripples. Until now.

"You look worried, Michael."

He turned away from the window to look at Felicity. Next to her, Cassidy looked like she was sleeping, head into a pillow pushed up against the far edge of her seat. "Yeah, of course I'm worried. I don't know if I'll even find this girl. And if I do, I don't know what'll happen from there."

"But we have to follow it through, don't we?"

"I do, sure. I'm just not sure why you two came along. I mean, don't get me wrong, I'm glad you're here. But this is my problem. He was my brother, and somebody killed him over something. I just want to find out who, and why."

He felt Felicity's hand cover his on the armrest their two seats shared. "Hey, somebody tried to kill me, too. I'm as deep into this as you are now, pal. We're in it together until we get it settled, all right?"

She was right, of course. He knew that. Funny how sharing this whole damn tragedy was difficult for him. He smiled at her. "Thanks, Fel," he said simply. It was the first time he'd called her by her nickname. She didn't seem to mind.

He turned away from her to stare out the tiny, scratched window again, thinking about Honker, the Golden Boy, the guy who had it all going for him once and now was lying, still, in the St. Pete city morgue. In four days there'd be the funeral service and he'd have to be home for that, which didn't leave him much time to find anything out in the Caymans. It was, he knew, probably all just a stupid wild-goose chase coming down here, finding this girlfriend of Honker's, doing what Honker asked him to do. Honker, for sure, didn't need it anymore.

Later, the captain came on the P.A. to tell them that was Cuba below, and the huge, half-moon bay passing underneath them was the Bay of Pigs.

Michael looked down at it, visible in the nearly full moon. He remembered from his high-school Florida history class about how Castro had come to power and the CIA had helped some counter-revolutionaries try to overthrow him and the whole plan fell apart right down there. The teacher had talked about a popular uprising that didn't take place, and there was something about poor planning.

They landed some forty minutes later, circling over tiny Grand Cayman, its bright lights a sharp contrast against the huge expanse of dark water around it. On the approach they came in over the harbor and the compact mass of George Town, which looked bigger, taller, than Michael had expected. Plenty of newer buildings, a lot of them several stories tall. He'd forgotten this was a banking center, had been thinking of it as just another dot in the Caribbean.

He'd been to the Keys and the Dry Tortugas on several survey teams, tagging and counting turtles, mostly greenbacks and loggerheads. He'd been to the British Virgins two or three times doing the same thing. But that was it; most of his work was done on Florida's coasts. He'd never been down to the Leewards and never over here to the Caymans, either. In better circumstances he'd be excited about it. This whole island's history was based on sea turtles. In the early days the few people who lived here were mostly turtle fishermen, he knew, and the emblem on the big tail of the Cayman Air jet they were on was a stylized sea turtle. So it all rang true for him. He belonged here in a way. The turtles, the history of the place. And Honker, damn Honker. What had he found here that had cost him so much?

The grandiose title of Owen Roberts International Airport didn't mean that the place had jetways or very many gates. Their jet parked near one of the two gates and the ground personnel rolled up a ramp and then the passengers got off, walking down the steps and then across the tarmac toward the customs area. The heat was the same as in St. Pete, maybe even more humid, if that was possible. It was late enough at night that it should have cooled off some, but Michael started to sweat in just the short walk over to the customs building. He welcomed the air conditioning once they got inside.

He stood in line for passport control behind Felicity. The guy behind the desk was getting people through in a hurry, being tourist friendly. Fel, Michael and Cassidy had stopped and picked up their passports and packed a few things before getting to the airport, so they sailed through it all. Michael, tired and bored, looked back over the rest of the passengers as they all waited in line. There, toward the back of the line, was a tall, thin guy who looked like he'd just been in a hell of a fight, the area around his right eye bruised purple, the top of his forehead above that eye swollen with a bump the size of a golf ball. A car accident, maybe, and the guy had hit the windshield. He was cleaned up, but it sure looked painful. And then the guy looked at him, the left eye icily clear, staring at Michael, something deeply cold in that look. He held it for a moment, then nodded, one passenger recognizing another, and looked away.

Some damn pirate or something, a smuggler or dope dealer or a hit man or something, here in the Caymans to launder his money. Michael, looking away, too, thought for a moment that he might know the guy, then laughed at himself for having the thought — the Michael Kelseys of the world didn't know people like that.

They breezed through customs, no one checking any of their bags, and then they walked outside the small terminal building, down a sidewalk and over to the Cico car rental, still open this late, where they rented a little Daihatsu jeep, steering wheel on the right side, of course, since the Caymans drove on the left. Inside of fifteen minutes from leaving the plane they were in the car — a strange mauve-colored thing that brought the three of them their first laughter in awhile — and on their way.

Felicity wanted to drive and was arguing with Cassidy about it, but Michael wouldn't let either one. Truth was, he wanted to give it a try. He climbed behind the wheel after first walking around to the wrong side of the car and opening the wrong door. Then he struggled with the stick shift and hit the windshield wipers when he thought was hitting the turn signals. It was all pretty funny, but he did manage to get them through town and out toward Seven-Mile Beach and then north to West End, where the Reverend's house was and they could all get a good night's sleep.

Felicity was getting a head start on that as they drove. After all her griping about not being able to do the driving, she fell asleep within a few minutes of their leaving the rental place. Michael, wrestling with the steering and listening to Cassidy's directions, got them there, heading out Crewe Road, turning right on Eastern Avenue, and then picking up West Bay, which ran along the beach. The place looked a lot like Rum Point, thought Michael. Put a Ministry Field up here somewhere and he could be home. You wouldn't think a little island like this would be this built up, but the place was packed with high-rise hotels and condos.

They stopped for a few minutes on the way, Michael staying in the car with Felicity while Cassidy went into a little supermarket that was open late and bought them a couple of bags of groceries. Then they drove on, Michael still following Cassidy's directions until after another four or five miles they left the high-rises behind and pulled into an area of individual homes on both sides of the road. One of them, a nice little place set back from the beach in a stand of pine trees, had a circular drive in front of it that came in from the street. Cassidy pointed them that way and Michael pulled in.

"Home, sweet home," said Michael softly as Felicity opened her eyes, yawned and turned to smile at him. Michael got out, walked to the back of the little jeep and grabbed the two bags of groceries, and then walked toward the door. There were two large hibiscus to the left of the front door, and a thick, low palm to the right. He stood there, waiting for Cassidy to walk up with the key, when he heard a rustling behind the palms.

A raccoon or something? There was another rustle, more definite, and coming his way. He set the bags down, turned and raised his open hand to stop Cassidy and, behind her, groggy, Felicity, and then looked around for something to use as a weapon; a stick at least would be handy.

And from the darkness a figure emerged, someone on hands and knees. There was a moan, and as Michael bent over to see who it was, what was happening, the figure collapsed, then looked up, her eyes opening, unfocused, exhausted before shutting again. He could see her face in the thin light of the single lamp that was next to the front door. It was a girl, in her twenties, dark hair in snarls and tangles, a pretty face bruised now on the left side, her cheek red and scratched. He reached down to help her as Felicity came up from behind. The girl's eyes opened again, seemed to find focus, and saw him reaching down to help. "Help," she said, and then again, "Help me," and then she collapsed.

THIRTY-ONE

While Stu Lindsay watched from the top step of the Crusader dugout, face impassive, calm on the outside in the middle of the panic and fear on the inside, Hector Perez fouled another one off, keeping the count at two and two against Marcelo Vera, the Porters pitcher. It hadn't been a good night for Hector, filling in for the suspended Sonny Dickerson. He was hitless against two different Porters pitchers, and now here he was in the bottom of the ninth, down by a run with a man on second and a chance to tie the game or win it, and his last swing looked awful, a stab with the bat that just managed to catch a bit of a good, hard slider away and bounce it down the first-base line, foul.

The fans moaned at the foul ball. Hector was a crowd favorite most nights. He worked hard out\there and had a good attitude on and off the field. He made rookie mistakes, sure, but he was young enough and new enough to the big leagues that he still played like it mattered, like he cared. But the fans didn't love him tonight, not with Sonny Dickerson not even in the ballpark when he ought to be up at the plate with a chance to win it. Dickerson, for all the problems he brought to the team, had a penchant for the big hit, the line drive when it counted most, the late-inning homerun that won the game.

Either one of those would be nice here, Stu thought, and took a deep breath. C'mon, Hector. Vera came in with a good, low fastball over the plate but maybe a bit low. The crowd moaned again, but then Larry Leslie, the home plate ump, slowly raised his left hand. Ball three.

"C'mon, Hector. Keep your head in there," Stu yelled, clapping his hands. Behind him, the Crusaders had their rally caps on, the Crusader blue caps turned backwards. Stu wondered briefly what the Reverend thought of that, wasn't superstitious stuff like that anti–Christian or something?

Vera stood on the mound, dug his right foot into the dirt in front of the pitching rubber, went into the stretch, paused, looked back at Ron Garn on second, and then came in with the next pitch, another vicious slider, this one starting in at Hector's belly and then coming across the inside corner of the plate down low. It was a hell of a pitch, and the Porters sure had the book on poor Hector, who had a lot of trouble handling things inside and down. Stu started to shake his head, game over, all tied in the standings with one game left. But Hector, still on a roll maybe from the game-winner of a couple of nights before, fought the slider off, dropping his right shoulder, bringing those wrists through like Quent was always showing him, and hitting the ball off the handle for a looping liner into short right-center.

Ron Garn, running on the full count, never hesitated, pumping hard toward third where third-base coach Harry Regis windmilled him toward home as Garn rounded the bag in full stride and then, right foot pushing off, headed toward the plate and the tie score. In center, Terry Mackie fielded the ball on the second hop and came up throwing, all in one smooth motion. The throw looked too damn accurate. Garn was maybe fifteen feet away when Porters catcher Andy Bernes came off the line a bit toward first to catch the ball on the first hop, then turned and dove toward home to make the tag.

The crowd was on its feet roaring as the play came together, all diving and colliding bodies and that small little baseball tucked tightly into the catcher's mitt while forty-seven thousand voices all screamed for the call, wanting Garn to be safe, willing it to be so. But Leslie, behind the plate, was in the perfect spot to make the call and though Garn got his hand across the plate, Bernes had been there, reaching with the glove to brush it against Garn's hip and then winding up in a sitting position with the ball still tucked tightly away in his catcher's mitt. Out.

Not again. Oh, Christ, another play at the plate and another goddamn bad call. Stu was out of the dugout and on his way to the plate to argue the call as the Porters came running in from the field and the dugout to mob Bernes, who stood up and then held the ball up high, smiling while his teammates surrounded him, patting him on the back, yelling their joy at him.

Stu's argument didn't last long and the crowd's vocal disappointment faded just as fast. He was out, no matter how hard one wanted to believe otherwise, and that was that. Ministry Field started to empty. Tied now with the Porters for the damn wild-card spot. Jesus. Stu was the last man off the field and into the clubhouse, trailing his players through the long tunnel from the dugout. He was not, by nature, a screamer, not like some managers. And there was really nothing to scream about here. Hector did his job, Garn did his. The Porters just did theirs better, that was all.

But he *wanted* to kick something and scream. That was probably the wild-card spot out there, that one play. After a whole long season of struggle and improbable wins, it had come down to that one play. Jesus, he was depressed. He stopped at the clubhouse door from the tunnel, looked around the quiet clubhouse where players slowly stripped off their uniforms. In a few minutes the sportswriters would come in and want to know the hows and whys and what-nows of all this and then they'd all be gathering in the interview room for the TV reporters after that and Stu would have to say something cogent in response to the usual inane questions. For now, Stu had a few minutes to tell his team something useful. What the hell could you say? He waved to the guard at the door to keep it shut.

"All right, guys. Listen up. This one hurt, no question. But, damn it, there's another one tomorrow night. That's where your heads have to be right now — tomorrow night."

He stopped, took off his cap, rubbed his head in thought for a moment or two. "Hector, hell of hit, guy, way to fight him off. Garn, nice job, it took a great throw and a great tag to get you. Guys, you played like champions out there. You played like winners. It just didn't work out that way tonight, that's all. That's the way baseball is."

He smiled. "And here's the way it is, too. You get a second chance. Win tomorrow night and you're in the playoffs. That simple. You just got to stay focused, guys. Stay focused on it, one game at a time." He waved at them, smiled. "Now say nice things to our friends from the media."

Stu walked toward his office as the door opened and the sportswriters walked in, Nick Krusoe at the head of the pack, way across the room but certainly heading Stu's way while a lot of the other writers cornered various of the players. Stu had successfully avoided Krusoe for a couple of days now, but there'd be no avoiding him tonight, not with things the way they were. All the national writers were here, mixed in with the local reporters now that the Crusaders were fighting for that last spot. The clubhouse babble rose as he reached his office.

Stu sat down behind his desk and watched through his clubhouse window for a minute as the writers wandered through, picking their prey. Perez and Garn had a little gathering each, of course, and a couple were talking to Macalaster, no doubt about what really had happened to his friend Sonny Dickerson.

Stu wanted a drink and who could blame him, after that call? He opened the drawer, pulled out the Macallan and poured a good, long, warm sip. It felt good, but that was all that felt good: he wondered how many of the Crusaders still believed in their chances after that game-ender. He wondered what would have happened if Sonny Dickerson had been in the game. He wondered what his players were saying right now to the press about that very topic. Oh, hell.

Krusoe walked through the door, a couple of other writers behind him. Did the writers know how the players felt about them, he wondered? Did they know the players— especially the veterans who'd been burned a few times— despised most of the writers but never really admitted it? That they couldn't stand the smart-ass sarcasm of the writers and the know-it-all bullshit that most of them fed the gullible fans? Sportswriters: fat, out of shape, ignorant of what the game was really like, what it was really about, yet sarcastic and mean with their opinions. And powerful as hell in their own way. It was a hell of a mix.

Oh, well, time to think of something to say, starting with Dickerson and ending with your basic managerial cautious optimism. We'll just have to play them one at a time. We're still in this thing. We still have a shot. It would all be harmless enough. He just wondered if he believed that himself as he said, "Hi, Nick. Hi, guys. Have a seat."

"Hi, Stu," Krusoe said, smiling and then easing his bulk into a solid wooden chair that sat on the far side of the manager's desk. He took out his narrow reporter's notepad — it looked tiny in his meaty left hand — then hauled out a small digital recorder, switched it on and set it on top of the desk. "I heard an ugly rumor today, something about drugs in the clubhouse. Any truth to that?"

Stu could only stare at him for the moment before trying to come up with something to say. Damned if it all wasn't about to fall apart.

THIRTY-TWO

Sonny Dickerson was angry and wired. Brooks didn't like what he was seeing, and didn't need the grief. Mainly, he wanted to hear from Robert Mackie and get that cleared up. He'd checked with his sources downtown and the police hadn't picked anybody up when they found the stolen car at the Hot Top Motel, so Mackie had avoided that, at least. But where the hell was the guy? Instead of finding out, Brooks was stuck behind his desk watching Sonny Dickerson pace back and forth.

"They lost. They lost and I would've won it, Brooks, I would have goddamn won it. Base hit," he brought his fists together into a quick batting grip, snapped the wrists over in a mock swing, "just like that. Double off the wall. We win. Simple as goddamn that, you know? One swing. Bingo. Double."

Brooks just watched him. This was the last thing he wanted to deal with. All this shit coming down, and now Dickerson, the fuck-up, was in his office pissing and moaning about his poor miserable life. Dickerson was getting to be more trouble than he was worth. When Brooks had first arranged the trade with the Yankees he'd known about the drug problem, of course; everyone in the league knew about it. But Brooks had figured he could control the drugs— hell, he'd had plenty of practice with that over the years— and get a good year out of Dickerson. And it had worked out great until recently. Hell, it was the one single damn thing that Brooks had done all season long that was really just for baseball, for the Crusaders, trying to turn this friggin' team into a winner. So he'd kept Dickerson supplied with coke, free of charge, but put a tight limit on it. They'd agreed on that the first time they'd talked about it. A tight limit. A gram a week and no more. Now, watching the son-of-a-bitch walk nervously around the room, wearing a path in some very expensive carpet, he wondered how much more Dickerson was getting from elsewhere to supplement the weekly ration.

"I'm not surprised he canned you, Sonny. You friggin' forced him to do it. I think this is your own damn fault."

"My fault? Are you nuts? The guy's only got to win one goddamn game and he suspends his best hitter. He's an idiot. He deserved to lose."

"The team lost, Sonny. You know, the Crusaders? That's who lost, not Stu Lindsay. And you weren't there."

"Whose side are you on, anyway, Brooks? Goddamn it, you brought me in here to hit, not to be a fucking Boy Scout, and I've done that, I've hit a ton. I'm third in the league in ribbies, I'm fourth in extra base hits, I'm seventh in batting average, I'm..."

Brooks waved his hand, trying to slow down both the walking and the tirade. "I know, I know, Sonny. You've done a great job at the plate. But you know what?— he wanted to say you friggin' idiot, but held back — you gotta' make amends on this. Your team needs you to do that, Sonny."

Dickerson finally stopped his pacing. Looked right at Brooks, staring hard. "No goddamn way, Brooks. You want me to go in there and kiss his ass and beg to get back on the team for this last goddamn game, so we can make it into post-season play and make you and the Reverend a ton of money. Well, no way."

Brooks was out of patience. "Let me put it this way to you, Sonny. You need to apologize to Lindsay and your teammates, say you had a headache or something, beg for forgiveness, talk about what a team player you are and how much you want the team to win. You need to do all that or it's over, I'll quit covering for you. All the drug stuff will come out, I'll goddamn make sure it comes out, and you'll be done with baseball. This'll be your third time, Sonny, and you're getting up there, you're thirty-five years old. They'll kick you out of the game and make it stick. You'll be gone. Maybe, after a few years, they'll let you come back as a commentator, do color for some independent club. You'll love spring in St. Paul."

Dickerson just stared, saying nothing.

"You listening to me, Sonny? You got it? Play the game the way I want it played here or it's over."

Dickerson's face reddened. He looked like he might have a heart attack right there in the office, and, shit, wouldn't that be ruination? Jesus.

"If you try and bring me down, Brooks," he finally managed to spit out, slowly, choosing his words, "you'll goddamn go down with me. I'll tell the league, the press guys, everyone. And you'll go right down with me."

Brooks smiled, an icy, practiced upturn of the lips. "You've never quite realized just what you're involved in, Sonny, just how deep this goes. Say one word, one word, about this to anyone and you're a dead man."

He slowly stood up, pointed his finger at Dickerson. "A dead man, Sonny. A bullet to the head, your tongue ripped out and shoved into your friggin' pants as a little message."

Dickerson paled. "You don't scare me, Brooks," he said. But, in fact, he did scare him, a lot. Sonny Dickerson was terrified, which, Brooks thought, might keep the son-of-a-bitch alive a little longer.

"Now get out of here, Sonny. Go dry out and calm down. Tomorrow morning, nine A.M., you and me will meet with Lindsay and see if we can smooth this over. Here, in my office. Got it?"

Dickerson nodded.

"Now get your friggin' ass out of my office while I figure out how we'll get past the drug test the league is going to want."

Dickerson left, closing the door gently as he went, a gentle click a bit of an indicator of how scared the guy really was. Good.

Now, one friggin' problem solved, what was next? He opened the bottom right drawer of his desk and the light on that private-line phone, the one with no ringer, was blinking. A call had come in while he'd been dealing with Dickerson.

He hit the button for the message. "Brooks," the cautious voice of Robert Mackie said. "It's Mackie. I've got something you want to know about. Give me a call at 809-949-8755. Room 230." And he hung up.

Oh, hell, 809 area code was down in the Caymans. What the hell was Mackie doing down there? And the number wasn't the Reverend's house down there, either, so it was some hotel or something. What the hell? Brooks shook his head. Mackie had always been good. Over the years, the guy had always done the job, done it right, no problems. He'd always loved him for that. But now, Jesus, one bad move after another. Shit. He dialed the number and it was the Sand Dune on Seven Mile Beach. He asked for Room 230. Mackie picked it up on the second ring.

"Yeah?" The voice sounded dopey. Maybe the guy was asleep.

"It's Brooks."

"Oh. Yeah. Just a second." Brooks could hear some rustling, maybe getting up from under the sheets, sitting up on the side of the bed. He wouldn't have a woman in there, that would be way too stupid even for Mackie, even the way he'd been going lately. "OK. Sorry. Yeah, listen, I'm down in Grand Cayman."

"I know that, Mackie, I dialed the number."

"Oh, yeah. Listen, I ran into a little trouble up there, you know? The cops came by my place. They fuckin' almost got me, Brooks. It was seconds, that's all, just seconds, or they'd a got me."

"You stole that damn car, Mackie, and then left it parked in front of your motel room. I went by there and the place was swarming with cops."

"Well, yeah. But that was after the girl hit me with that fucking baseball bat. Jesus, I wasn't thinking so straight." He didn't think now to ask how Brooks could know that, either. "Anyway, I got out of there, hid out a bit, then decided to catch the evening plane down here, stay cool for a couple of days, then come back up when you say it's OK."

Made sense. "Yeah, that's all right, Mackie. Just relax for a couple of days, get yourself better, get patched up, and then we'll figure it out from there."

"Yeah, but it ain't that simple, Brooks. There's complications."

"Complications?"

"On the plane, on the way down, was the girl cop and her boyfriend."

"No shit?" Jesus, that couldn't be good. What did they know? "What the hell were they doing on the plane?"

"It gets worse. They were with Cassidy, the Reverend's daughter, flying first class while I sat in the back with a huge fucking headache. Anyway, I figured I'd follow them, see what they were up to."

"And?" Brooks humored him, but Cassidy made things better. If they were with her they probably didn't know a thing, they were just going down to the condo for a few days to rest up. That would be fine, they'd be out of the way down there. Hell, they could stay down there for a week, a friggin' month, all year.

"It gets worse, Brooks. When they got to the Reverend's place the fucking girl was there, hiding out in the bushes, the one that was the best friend of that Samantha chick, Kelsey's girlfriend."

Brooks paused. Goddamn Mackie. "I thought I told you to get her taken care of, Mackie. You were the one who said she might have heard too much from Kelsey's girl and you said you'd handle it. That was three friggin' days ago."

"Yeah, well, my people here said they'd do it, Brooks, and they never let me down before. I figured her for barracuda bait by now. She scubas, so I guessed it would be like her regulator had fucked up and that would be that."

"But it isn't."

"No. It isn't. She was beat up some, looked like to me, but I couldn't tell much from where I was. She was definitely alive. They helped her inside. She's probably talking to them right now."

"You should have had Kelly Ennis take care of her, Mackie, instead of your guy down there, the one hooked in with the beaners." Jesus, this was awful. "How much do you think she knows?"

"If that Samantha girlfriend told her anything before we took care of her, than it could be fucking everything. Hell, they could be calling the cops right now, game over."

Brooks thought furiously. "You and Kelly down there did take care of that Samantha bitch, right?"

"Yeah, no question. Kelly did that one herself. Ten miles offshore and she dropped the body in a trench that goes down two-thousand fucking feet. She ain't never coming up."

That, at least, was good. But this other girl? How much did she know? "When did all this happen with the girl?"

"Couple of hours ago."

"And no cops showed up at the house yet?"

"I don't think so. I watched for over an hour and figured nothing was happening so I got back here."

OK, then, either they didn't know anything or they weren't calling the cops anyway — maybe because Cassidy knew how deep the Reverend was in and how it would all come crashing down — all those starving children in Africa wouldn't get fed — if she called the cops. Still, Brooks realized, thinking it through, he had to get down there and handle this in person.

"Mackie. I'm flying down. Tonight. I'll be there in a few hours. I don't think they'll do anything until the morning now. Wait for me there, in your room, and then we'll take care of it when I get there. Got that?"

"Got it. Sit tight. Tell you the fucking truth, that sounds like a good idea. My head's hurting again. Bad. I got to get some aspirin or something and then lie down for a few minutes."

"Yeah, you do that. Lie down right there and wait for me. I'll have it planned by the time I get there and we'll stop this thing now, while we still can. And I'll get Kelly in on this, too. We'll meet in your room."

They hung up, and Brooks stood, walked over to the window that overlooked the bay, thinking it all through one more time. All right, he had the night to play with. If he could take care of this before dawn he'd probably be fine.

But, hell, it was going to be messy. The girl cop and her boyfriend. And this girl who'd been Kelsey's girl's best pal. And Cassidy Craig; Jesus, the Reverend's own goddamn daughter. How could he make this work? A fire maybe, with pipes and crack around so it looked like a drug thing? Maybe. It might work.

Or just break in, do it, and get out, let it ride as a burglary murder.

Anyway, something had to be done, and tonight. No waiting around for a morning flight. He picked up the phone and called the one guy in town he knew he could count on for something like this, Roberto Delgado. Roberto was upscale now, flying corporate jets like a big shot. Well, Roberto owed him a favor or two from a few years back, when a twelve-year sentence for smuggling had turned itself magically into probation. Time to call in that debt and get down to the Caymans. And there, time to take care of business.

THIRTY-THREE

She wasn't Samantha, Honker's girlfriend. They got that much from her after they got her inside and calmed down. She was Samantha's roommate and best friend, and hadn't heard from Samantha in days. She thought Samantha had either left the island or was dead.

And she wasn't hurt much, either, just scared and scratched up and hungry, with a bad rash around her neck and on her hands. She'd been hiding in the bushes around the house for two days—eating and drinking what she could find while waiting for someone to show up, doing what Samantha had told her to do that last day the two of them had been together.

Her name was Robin, and Felicity suspected she was a pretty girl when she wasn't in this kind of shape. But now, even after a hot shower and two bowls of turtle soup with what must have been a loaf's worth of bread, she looked pretty ragged, her red hair clean now, but still a tangled mess; her face, arms and legs scratched.

Felicity had called Stu's home phone and left a message saying where she was. Then she'd started calling the local cops, but the girl begged her not to make that call, and so, for now at least, Fel had hung up the phone and decided to listen, not telling the girl yet that she was a cop and would get the locals out here in a hurry if she needed to.

"Sam said I could get some help here," Robin said between spoonfuls of the turtle soup. "She said someone comes here at least once a week, and they'd help me if I told them I was her roommate.

"So when these guys knocked on the door and I looked through the peephole and saw them, I knew I had to get out of there, so I just left, didn't take my purse or any clothes or anything, I just ran, out the back door and down the steps and ran like hell with nothing on but my shorts and a t-shirt and these sandals. It was midnight, maybe later, and the apartment's a mile or two from here is all, so when I got so tired I couldn't move another step I realized I wasn't far from here so I came and I've been hiding out here and waiting since. It's been a couple of days of hiding and sneaking around."

It had all poured out in one long breathless frenzy, and then the girl stopped, took a deep breath, another sip of her ice water. Felicity nodded, supportive. She and Michael and Cassidy didn't know what this was all about yet, but the other two had, without talking about it, known right away that Felicity was the obvious one to take the lead on this.

Fel reached out and put her hand on the girl's shoulder. "So, OK, we're here. Why don't you let us just call the local police for you, so you can tell them your whole story?"

"Are you insane? Why do you think I didn't call them at first? I'm no good at acting, they'd find out everything right away. They'd be able to tell how nervous I was, and then I'd spill it all."

Felicity smiled. "Sure, we can't let them find out everything, right?"

"That's right." She sat back from her bowl of turtle soup, slumped in her chair, exhausted now that she felt safe. "Can we talk about this more later? Do you guys think I could, like, take a nap, get some sleep or something for a few hours? I mean, like, thanks for the soup and the shower, I really owe you. But just a few hours sleep would really help, you know? Then we can, like, talk it all over, OK?"

She was too tired to argue with, so Felicity and Cassidy walked her to one of the guest bedrooms and let her collapse on the bed. She was asleep in a minute. Cassidy pulled a sheet over her and the two of them left, shutting the door behind them and walking back toward the living room, where Michael sat waiting.

"So," he said, "What the hell is she all about?"

Felicity sat next to him on the couch, put her hand on his knee. "She ties into it all, Michael, that much is obvious. And she's scared." She gave him a thin smile. "Most importantly, she thinks we already know everything, so I think that maybe in the morning, if we don't scare her off, we can just let her talk and get the whole picture from her."

Cassidy sat down in a chair on the other side of a small coffee table from the couch. "Hey, you two, I came into this late. What the hell are you talking about? Believe her about what?"

Felicity looked at her then shrugged her shoulders. "That's just it, we don't know. You know about as much as we do—somehow this ties into the murder of Michael's brother."

Michael shook his head. "First thing in the morning, after we talk to this girl, I'm going on over to Parrot's Landing and see what they say about this Samantha."

Felicity nodded. "I'll go with you. Cassidy can stay here with the girl. We'll keep checking in by phone. If her story holds up we'll know from what they tell us there, and come right back here."

"She may sleep until noon, you know," Cassidy added. "Anyway, I want to get some work done with the computer here, so I'm happy to stay behind with her."

Michael was pretending to want to go it alone, but Felicity could see he wanted her along, too. She smiled at him, patted his knee. He was a sweet, warm guy, trying hard to be something he wasn't, trying hard to be some kind of avenging warrior here, out to solve his brother's murder and get even all at once. But it just wasn't in him; he wasn't trained for it, and she didn't know how he'd react if he really found himself in a tough spot. The little thing at her apartment had all happened in a second. What if there was a real confrontation here on this island with some legitimately dangerous

128

people? He'd probably try to *talk* them into surrendering. He needed her. She was trained for this kind of work. She'd been there, knew what she was doing, and she could take care of him in a crunch. She didn't like going it alone out here, without any backup, without even having the authorities in on it, but she could change that with one quick phone call once they knew something solid, and that ought to be by some time tomorrow.

All right, then. Felicity rose slowly, her ribs aching. Michael stood alongside her, helping her up, and the two of them headed for the bedrooms that Cassidy had said were theirs at the end of the long hall. Felicity was happy to have Michael assist her into bed, she ached now, the sharp pains spreading out and dulling as she started to heal. Breathing was still a bit tricky, she had to consciously try to keep her breathing shallow and slow or it hurt like hell.

With a little help from Michael she managed to splash some soap and water on her face, run a toothbrush through her mouth and get back to the bed, where she sat. Then he helped her take off her blouse, coming around behind her to undo her bra strap and then handing her a nightshirt from her bag, reaching around in front, careful not to stare, trying to be a gentleman.

But, she thought, he was there. It wasn't Cassidy helping her, it was Michael. And she liked it that way. As he helped her ease the t-shirt over her up-stretched arms she half-turned to him, smiled, and said thanks. His face was red, and he stammered "You're welcome." He was really too sweet to be true, she thought, and then she reached out to take his hand. "Thank you, Michael. For everything."

"You're, you're welcome. For everything, Felicity. Listen. I..."

"Yes?"

"I'm really, um. Listen, when this is over? When it's settled? I'd like to take you out to dinner or something. I mean, I understand if you don't want to. I know you're just being nice to me and this is your job and everything."

"This is not my job, Michael. My job is back in Florida, in Rum Point. Instead of being at my job I'm here, with you. And sure, I'd love to go out for dinner."

"Well, OK." He took a quick breath, bounced up off the bed and headed for the door. He stopped there for a second, turned to look back at her as she eased back onto the propped up pillows on the bed, and smiled. Felicity, suddenly realizing just how tired she was but spinning just the same over all this from him, smiled back, and then, as he brought the door shut, she closed her eyes and waited for some sleep.

It had been a good three months since Cassidy had been in the house. That time, on a weekend visit with her father, she'd used the computer in the Reverend's office to tweak some stats for Stu Lindsay, trying to figure out which of his right-handed middle relievers would work best against the Cubs. This time, all she wanted to do was send some e-mail, which should take just a few minutes.

But the computer, an old Dell Optiplex from a good six or seven years ago — an antique in computer terms — wouldn't come online. They were on a broadband cable modem and she should have been right into her account, but nothing came up on the computer screen except complaints from the software, a window opening up to tell her there was bad news with her pop3 server. She wondered if it was a problem with the cable line or with this particular computer. It was probably the latter, but there'd be no harm in checking, she could just go out to the guesthouse office and try to get online on one of the computers out there.

She grabbed the keys to the guesthouse from the kitchen drawer where they were kept and headed out to the small, tin-roofed house built to resemble — at least on the outside — an old Caymanian cookrum, the detached kitchens the islanders had used to keep the kitchen's heat and danger of fire away from their main homes.

The guesthouse was some twenty yards from the back door of the main house, down a winding flagstone path that ambled through a garden edged with casuarina trees and filled with pink and red hibiscus and jacaranda, anchored in the middle by three large coconut palms. It was a beautiful, peaceful little secret, this garden, with a small wooden picnic table set at the halfway point, under the thin shade of the palms. Not quite two years ago Cassidy and her father had been enjoying a lunch of island meat patties and iced raspberry tea when they'd been bombed from above as a pair of coconuts came crashing down right into the middle of the table, flattening two of the patties and sending the raspberry tea flying from both their cups.

The Reverend had laughed it off with a grin, calling it an act of God, a sure sign from above that they ought to stay away from those meat pies. That moment in the garden had been the start of their renewed relationship; the first time they'd laughed together in a long, long time. After ten years of being lost in a kind of personal wilderness of drugs and parties, Cassidy had come back to reconcile with her father and that lunch had been a big part of the success of her efforts. They'd been too far apart for far too

130

long, he'd said. And then he'd taken the blame for it, said he'd been the one to drive the wedge between them, hadn't been understanding enough of her life and its complications. That had been a lie, of course, and she'd known it. Her messed up life was her own damn fault — heading in all the wrong directions with all the wrong damn people, most especially David with his baby-faced smile and brutal dark side.

But she'd taken the lie for what it was, a father reaching out to the prodigal daughter, inviting her home for a fatted calf. And so home she had come, home at last. It hadn't been easy, but the changes had done her nothing but good. She was a better person; she liked herself now, liked who she was and who she could still be. She hadn't felt that way in the old days.

The key turned the big deadbolt smoothly and she walked inside the guesthouse, turning on the lights. It wasn't a place she came into often. They all called it the guesthouse, and for the first year or two after they'd built it they'd actually used it for that. But over time it had ended up being used mostly for storage and office space. With the Crusader Retreat program getting started, Brooks and his staff were in Grand Cayman often, using the guesthouse to get their work done. If nothing else, it offered some privacy, away from the main house. She hadn't been in it in more than a year.

There was just one computer inside, a nice new one with all the bells and whistles. It sat on a computer table in the front room, a comfortable chair wheeled up to it. The way things were set up, it looked like it got a lot of use, and whoever was working on it was a big-time Florida Gator fan. There was a Gator calendar, a Gator pennant, a Gator coffee cup and on the wall behind the computer's monitor a picture of a Gator basketball player, arm raised in joy, being held up by his teammates after what must have been some big victory. She chuckled at the Gator shrine, out of place down here in the Caymans but otherwise exactly what she'd come to expect from the vocal Gator alums she'd met since she'd moved to Florida. In a plastic box to the side of the computer's monitor there were half-a-dozen high-end flash drives in their little plastic cases. You could plug one of those into the computer's USB slot and download — she tugged one out of the slot to look at it — up to twenty gigabytes of memory.

She sat down and booted up the computer. In a minute or two it was ready — an underwater scene with a turtle swimming through it was the wallpaper that glimmered there while she tried to log onto the cable network. Like the computer in the main house, this one wouldn't connect through the cable modem, so that meant there was something wrong with the network, for sure, and not with the computers. But she was here, and the machine was on, and as she thought about that she came to the conclusion that maybe there'd be something in here that would help her understand the books she'd been looking at back up in St. Pete. She clicked on the QuickBooks icon.

And, my, what an interesting world opened up before her very curious eyes.

First she had to get past the passwords. The first one was easy — the system was password protected but whoever had used it last had taken advantage of the Windows password shortcut and then forgotten to unmark it. With a click of the mouse she was into a folder called "Babbling." She tried to open that and another password window popped up. She spent a minute or two trying the obvious ones, "pass" and "password" then, in a flash of intuition, looking around at all the University of Florida things surrounding the desk, she tried "Gators," and got nothing and then "Go-Gators" and, sure enough, the system opened up. She had in front of her now a whole list of subfolders. She started at the top, with "Accounts" and then worked her way down, glancing at things to get a feel for what was in there. Most of it seemed pretty ordinary, routine accounting material for everything from household expenses to a long list of files on the Crusader Retreat being built over near the tiny village of East End on the far side of the island.

Then she opened up a folder called "Trust Me," and things got a lot more interesting, indeed. First, there were Word documents that explained, at length, about investments in the Cayman Islands. Chapter by chapter it ran through Incorporation Requirements, Partnerships, Establishing Trusts and Banks, Mutual Funds, Taxation and Duties, Establishing an Office in the Caymans Islands and on and on. Whoever had been working here and had done some schooling on matters Caymanian, no question about that.

She glanced at one or two of the files. "There are no taxes on companies or individuals and no inheritance taxes or estate duties," one of them read. "Government revenues are principally derived from import duties on virtually all imported goods, stamp duties, registration and license fees. This absence of direct taxation means there are no double taxation treaties and hence no disclosure of information clauses on taxation matters with other territories."

She found another: "Audited financial statements need not be filed with the Monetary Authority. If the financial statements are not filed, the officers must provide a written statement that the accounts have been prepared in accordance with generally accepted accounting principles."

She kept scrolling, opening folders and then files at random. In the folder "Limited Life Companies," the names of the corporations and their officers didn't make any sense; "Huey," "Dewey," "Louie," "Cinderella," for four of the couple of dozen companies, for instance, and officers with names like Tim Smith, Robert Smith, James Smith, Thom Smith and on and on. She found an income statement in the Limited Life folder and that didn't make any damn sense, either. The Net Sales, the Cost of Goods Sold, the Gross Profit, all if it was in some kind of code, the figures alphanumeric instead of numbers. She found the same code — or something close to it — being used in the balance sheet file. It was weird and pretty much unfathomable without the code. Even the organization of things in the balance sheet was all screwed up — purposefully so, she assumed. Normally you'd organize a balance sheet by order of liquidity — the length of time it takes to convert items to cash. So cash itself should be first on the list, and then accounts receivable, and then probably inventories and then all the way down to stockholders' equity. But it was all over the place on this sheet, which meant the names were faked, the order faked, everything twisted and changed around so she couldn't tell a thing. Except that something was up, something big, or the books wouldn't be coded like this. Come to think of it, that was why it had been so easy to get past the password firewall — the code kept you from understanding anything even when you were into the books. Without the key to the code you couldn't know much beyond the fact that something, something huge and ugly, was going on. She kept at it, seeing more and more that had to be awful, stuff that would bring her father to tears if he had any inkling something this huge was going on — there had to be millions involved, maybe tens of millions, maybe more than that. But she couldn't pin it down, not without the code.

She wound up spending another hour searching the desk and the single file cabinet next to it for something that would break the code, but if it was there she couldn't understand it for what it was. Eventually she had to give it up. When she looked at the clock hours had passed and it was nearly three in the morning. She had to get some sleep, and then she'd have to call her father and in the morning and tell him what she'd found. That wouldn't be an easy phone call. In the top left drawer of the desk there were blank back-up flash drives. She tore the shrink-wrap off one, shoved it into the drive and copied everything. Then, dead tired, she dropped the flash drive into her pocket, shut down the computer, turned off the lights and walked back through the darkness to the main house where the fold-out sofa bed waited for her. A few minutes later, some water splashed on her face, her teeth brushed, her mind somewhere between furious worry and complete exhaustion, she opened up the bed, threw a sheet over the thin mattress and a comforter over that, and climbed in. A few hours of peace and quiet would be nice.

She was almost asleep when she heard one of the bedroom doors open and quietly close, and then, a few seconds later, another door did the same. Dreamily, she figured one of them was up to use the bathroom. Was it Felicity? Should she help her? Groggy, she sat up and there, in the shadows, she saw a tall, thin form go by. Had to be Michael. She lay back and in a few seconds finally found sleep.

THIRTY-FOUR

Michael had been lying on his back on the too-soft bed for hours, occasionally dozing off for a few minutes, but never managing to really drop into a deep sleep. When the light went on in the guesthouse he could see it shining through the open window of his room. He stood, walked over to the window and looked out there, thinking that would have to be Cassidy and maybe he'd go out there and talk with her — there was no use trying to sleep anymore, he had way too much on his mind for that.

But he didn't want to burden her with his problems, not the way he'd already burdened Felicity. Tomorrow, maybe, he'd get some answers. For now, he stood there at the window and watched awhile longer, then finally went back to the bed, thinking it all through, trying to fit it together. He wondered if Felicity was OK, if her ribs were keeping her awake. She was something, was Officer Felicity Lindsay. He ought to check on her, just to make sure she was OK.

Felicity heard the doorknob turn and opened her eyes as the light from the hallway spilled into the bedroom.

"Felicity?"

"Hi, Michael."

"Hey, I was awake and then just sort of wondered how you were doing. Your ribs hurting a lot?"

"Come here, Michael."

She waited until he sat on the bed, then reached out slowly to touch his shoulder, his arm, tracing the length of the arm with her finger. It hurt to move quickly, her ribs shouting at her, so she took her time, slowly pulling him toward her, bringing his face toward hers until they were inches apart. With that same finger, then, she reached up to touch his lips.

Still, he didn't move the final inches. She smiled, reached cautiously behind his neck and brought him gently closer until their lips met, lightly, she just touching his lips with hers at first, then stronger, lips opening, her tongue darting in as he finally committed fully to this, kissed her back, reached down toward her face, holding it in his hands as the kiss went on.

Finally, it ended. Michael sat on the bed, shook his head in wonderment. "Do you know how long I've been thinking about that?"

She smiled. "Me, too," and she reached up to the top of his shirt and began unbuttoning the top button. "Let's take it very easy, OK, I'm still awfully sore."

"Easy," he said wonderingly, his eyes locked on her hers as the top button came loose, the next one, the one after that. "Sure, yes, we'll take it very, very easy," and he eased out of his shirt, then reached down to help raise her into a sitting position where she slowly raised her arms so he could slip off the t-shirt they'd worked so hard to get on not long before.

He felt out of his own body, dizzy with this, watching himself do this thing he wanted so much with her. He was not a womanizer, had made clumsy love just twice in his life to girlfriends who'd been as clumsy as he.

Now, in the faint light from the hallway, looking at her as she reached out to touch his chest, then brought her face to that chest, lightly tongued one of his nipples, kissed higher on his chest, his neck and then again on his lips, he lost himself in it, became someone new, some higher sort of being, transcendent in this moment.

They were, for the next few minutes, very careful of her sore ribs. And then, too-soon later, he protected them in his sleep, his arm around her, his leg over hers, too, as he half-slept, a part of his mind still tumbling this all around while he drifted, occasionally moving his face over to hers where, in wonder, he kissed her time and again, lightly, on the cheek as she slept, and dreamed of turtles in a bright, blue sea.

Nothing, he thought, could disturb them from this perfection.

135

THIRTY-FIVE

She was restless, not trusting all this, unable to stay asleep for more than an hour or two before waking up, fitful, heart pounding. She'd never wanted to be involved in anything like this. She'd come to the islands to get away from a boring life in small-town British Columbia, but this was a whole lot more than an Okanogan girl from Kalona had bargained for.

She was terrified. Each time she woke up she tried to calm herself. She was safe here, relax, get some sleep, safe. The third time it happened she thought she knew what to do, took a few deep breaths, trying to calm it down, whispering a little mantra to herself, "Safe. Safe. Safe. Safe."

There was a rustle, a slight scraping, at her window, where light from a nearly full moon poured through. She froze. It was just the wind, surely, some local rain shower stirring things up, palm fronds against her window, that was all. Then again, a scraping, like somebody trying to open the window from the outside.

Oh my god. She was suddenly terror stricken, heart racing, afraid to sit up in the bed, afraid to even turn and look, just lying there in the bed hoping it was all some dream, hoping it would go away if she just lay there long enough. And then scraping again, a muffled sound of pushing. She had to sit up, knew she had to get up, get out of there before whatever it was, whoever it was, came through that window, before it opened and they crawled through it and that would be that for her; dead, horribly dead.

OK, then. She took a quick, deep breath, than edged away to the far side of the bed, the side away from the window, and eased her legs ever so slowly over the side, first the left and then the right until they both touched the floor. Good, then she slipped from under the covers down onto the floor completely, hearing another scrape, and then another. Oh, Jesus. She started crawling around the corner of the bed. From there it was maybe ten feet to the door to escape from this. She decided she'd make a dash for it and so, half crawling, half running she made for the closed door. The window behind her rattled then, somebody trying to get it up, somebody frustrated that it wouldn't budge.

She reached the door, panicked, and couldn't turn the handle. The knob just wouldn't turn, her hands, palms wet with sweat, sliding around it. Then, finally, she squeezed it hard and it turned.

Behind her the glass shattered. Not wanting to but not being able to help it, she turned and looked there as she opened the door.

There were two faces, a man and woman. The man was monstrous in the half-light from the moon, all dark shadows over heavy brows and a huge jaw. Oh, god, she knew that face from before, she knew that hateful stare. Behind him the woman, something raised in her hands, a piece of coral she'd broken the window with.

The girl knew in her soul that they'd kill her if they could, knew they were trying to do exactly that. But then alarms started hooting and lights flashed and she pulled herself through the doorway, slammed the door behind her, and ran down the hall screaming for help.

THIRTY-SIX

Kelly Ennis was fucking insane. Since she'd first showed up, more than two years ago, Mackie had been complaining to Brooks that Ennis had no discipline, that she couldn't be trusted, that she might go flying off the handle at any time. Like he kept telling Brooks, she was unprofessional.

Brooks, of course, saw it differently. Maybe all he could see was her tits and that sweet ass, Mackie figured, and in some ways he couldn't blame the guy for that.

Now, tugging on her, taking her back to the car so they could get out of there before the local cops showed up, he was kicking himself for not having done something about her long before and for listening to her tonight and driving up here to do this stupid fucking break-in. Really, what he wanted to do was kill her, just whack her and be done with it, but that would just add to his problems; so, instead, he dragged her along, bitching all the way, back to the car, shoved her halfway in the driver's side, stopped, cursed at remembering they drove on the left here and so he yanked her back out, walked her around to the other side of her little Daihatsu, shoved her into that seat, walked back around himself—all of this taking way too much fucking time—and then, finally, drove off, driving nice and easy, innocent as a lamb while she sat there, sullen.

Ten minutes later they were in the clear, back in the hotel parking lot. Jesus, that was too close, and all because she couldn't keep it calm and professional, had to go nuts all the time. She was sitting there to his left, quiet, her long, black hair that she usually had tied up had fallen loose so that it fell across the side of her face. He couldn't see her eyes as she stared straight ahead at the row of palm trees that stood between the lot and the Caribbean, the hotel to their left.

"Look," he said, "Kelly, I'm sorry, all right? But, Christ Almighty, you lost it in there."

"I lost it? Who the hell\panicked and split? Another minute and I'd have been in there and killed her and the others and it would be over, Mackie. But no, you got to panic and start running, yanking me along like some goddamn kid. I'm telling you, I had it under control. And you're especially fucking lucky I didn't break your goddamn arm when you grabbed me."

She had it under control? Right. He looked straight out through the windshield. "I told you to ease that window up an inch or two, then I could've cut the wire and we're in, no alarms. But no, the girl starts to roll over in bed and you hit the shit button and start breaking glass and the alarm goes off." He shook his head. "Christ. Kelly, you got all the tools, you know? You could be good at this. But you got to learn to keep it controlled."

She slumped in her seat, rubbed her right shoulder where he'd been gripping her hard as he shoved her into the car, "Mackie. Look, I got excited, that's all. And I thought we could get it done and get out of there. It just seemed to make sense at the time." And then she looked over at him and smiled, and reached over and gently squeezed his knee and Robert Mackie was reminded one more time why he hadn't done something about Kelly Ennis a long time ago. "Look," she said, "You go in and get some sleep. I'll come by in the morning and we'll get some breakfast and figure out how to take care of this little problem. It's too late now to do anything else tonight, and you need the rest."

He nodded. She was, in fact, a beautiful thing, that dark hair all tumbling down the side of her neck like that, those wide-set eyes over that broad nose, those tiny, perfect breasts. He'd imagine sucking on them a hundred times, biting the nipples, watching them come erect, then climbing on her and getting it done. But he hadn't touched her in the two years they'd been working together, because that wouldn't be professional. God knew he wanted to; hell, she had to know he wanted to and she played off that, always touching him like this, showing off that hair or those titties in those tiny swimsuits she wore all the time. But he was a professional. He opened his door, got out, looked back at her there in the dim moonlight. Beautiful fucking woman, no question.

"Yeah, in the morning then," he said. "Don't forget Brooks is getting here in the morning, too, probably on that first Cayman Air flight. Gets in at eight-thirty. Let's meet him at the airport."

She nodded. "I'll pick you up at eight. We'll get him, go somewhere and talk, figure out what to do about that girl."

He stood there in the lot as she drove off, heading back to her little apartment down by Smith Cove. She'd never asked him to stay there, and he'd never pushed it. Hell, Brooks would shit if he thought the two of them were doing something, and he was in enough trouble with Brooks right now anyway.

He thought about that as he walked up the outside stairs to the second floor of the hotel and then walked down the long hallway to Room 230. Brooks was going to be really pissed about this latest fuck-up, another in the list of recent mistakes. Mackie had hoped to have it all over with by the time Brooks showed up — the girl dead, along with the Rev's daughter and the girl cop and her boyfriend, too. He figured on getting in quietly, whacking the girl, then whacking the Reverend's daughter, and then, at the end, taking care of the girl cop and her boyfriend, making their deaths as slow and painful as he had time for. He owed them both, big time.

Anyway, after Kelly had called him he'd talked it all through with her and they'd gone to the house and waited until everybody settled down — the Reverend's daughter the main problem, out doing something in the guest-house and not coming back to the main house until the wee fucking hours. No problem, though, and eventually everything was going fine until Kelly lost it and started breaking glass. Too bad. Too fucking bad.

He reached his room and froze. Four o'clock in the goddamn morning and the door was open a couple of inches and there was a light on. He pulled out the Glock from where he had it tucked into his pants in back, held it in his right hand, barrel up and pointing forward, and eased open the door.

THIRTY-SEVEN

Stu was dog-tired. He'd lost track of the time but it was two or three in the morning and he was just getting home, pulling into the driveway in

Rum Point. First he'd wrestled conversationally with Nick Krusoe, trying to lie about the cocaine but not lie at the same time. The effort gave him a new appreciation for the team's public relations people while he talked about it — it couldn't be easy doing that kind of lying for a living.

He hadn't fooled Krusoe for a second, though; the guy wasn't that stupid and he'd heard a lot of PR bullshit over the years. But Stu had at least made it clear that whatever the truth was, Krusoe wasn't going to get it from him right then and there and eventually Nick gave up on it. By then Stu had let in the other sportswriters, a whole big pack of them, and answered the more common questions with the usual answers: Yes, he thought the Crusaders would come back from this and win the final game against the Porters. No, he wasn't worried about the Sonny Dickerson situation and yes, the team would bounce back from that. No, he wasn't feeling any pressure from the Reverend or George Brooks about his job. Yes, he was...

It had gone on like that for more than an hour; all if it pretty much lies, really. He thought about that — about how well he'd learned to lie to sportswriters, as anyone with any sense always did — as he hit the button on the garage door opener and sat there waiting for the door to lift so he could pull the Pathfinder in and finally be home, safe, away from all the craziness. Truth was, he didn't know if these guys *could* come back and win it, especially with the Dickerson thing all tangled up in it, too. Stu didn't want Dickerson in the clubhouse anymore, was glad to be rid of him and that attitude and the constant stress level he brought along as part of his damn baggage. But, hell, the guy could hit. With him in there tonight they might well have won the game.

And his cell phone rang: his father calling. He pulled the Pathfinder into the garage, hit the button to close the door behind him, and then answered the insistent ring.

"Hello, Father," he said, simply, after opening up the phone.

"How's Felicity?"

Good question, Stu thought. He hadn't talked to her in hours. Hadn't talked to his father in hours, either. Hadn't worried about it. Hadn't thought about anything but baseball, in fact. But "She's fine, father," seemed like the right thing to say.

"Are you sure? I'm worried about her, son."

"She's fine, father. She's a little banged up and sore, but the docs say she'll heal, and the police are keeping an eye on her to make sure the guy doesn't try it again."

"Do you know where she is, Stu?"

"Asleep, I'm sure, and I'm not going to wake her with a phone call checking up on her, father, so don't even ask."

"All right, son, but I think you're in for a surprise."

Now what the hell did the old man mean by that?

"You must be feeling the pressure, son, from all this baseball silliness. That would explain why you're still there in Rum Point."

"Father, what the hell is that supposed to mean?"

"It means you're worrying about that Sonny Dickerson player and your baseball matches and your coaching job, when you should be worrying about your daughter. Please, son, think about who you are, who you could be. And think about that wonderful girl of yours. All right? That's all I ask."

"Sure, Father, I'll be thinking of her. Honest. I think about her all the time, you know."

"Except during the baseball matches, apparently."

"Games, Father. They're called games."

"Yes, games. They certainly are games," came the response, and then a slight click and silence. His father had hung up on him.

Well, hell. He hated it when the old man was right. Could Stu lose his job? Sure, this was baseball and logic didn't always figure in when it came to owners and their hired hands. He didn't need to talk to Brooks to know that, he knew the slimy guy well enough to realize that Brooks liked Sonny Dickerson a lot more than he liked Stu Lindsay. And the Reverend, bless his heart, wasn't about to step in and do anything about it.

Stu sighed, finally turned off the engine and shook his head as he did that, thinking that letting the car run in the closed garage might solve some problems for him, but sure wouldn't help Fel.

He got out, walked into the laundry room that connected the garage to the house, hit the light and then reached over to tap in his code on the burglar alarm to disarm it. Then he walked into the kitchen, grabbed a tumbler and reached into the cabinet for the bottle of Macallan he'd been working on. He poured himself a very necessary glass full and started to walk out toward the porch for a quiet sit, but on the way he walked by the phone and there were six messages on the answering machine.

He took a long pull on the Scotch and then another pull as he listened. The first four were from media types who thought of themselves as friends, wanting to get a few quotes. The fifth was from Krusoe, who just wouldn't let go and was trying one last time to get Stu on the record about the drugs.

He hit the erase button for each one without bothering to listen. The last one was from Felicity, from ten-thirty.

"Hi, Daddy," she said, "Listen, I didn't want to bother you on the cell phone about this, but we're down in the Cayman Islands, at the Reverend's place with Cassidy. Address here, so you have it, is 4542 West Bay Drive. Cassidy offered and we took her up on it, staying here. We flew down this evening. Everything's fine. I'm going to be here a few days, just relax and get better, and then come on back up there, OK? I'll call you tomorrow. Love you." And she hung up.

The Caymans? Why the hell would she do that? Oh, hell, he was too tired to deal with it. She sounded safe and happy. It was probably a good thing, down there with Cassidy, relax for a couple of days, heal up some.

Man, he had to quit worrying about all this. Fel was a big girl, damn it, and she was doing fine. The Crusaders would do fine. Everything was fine. He took another long sip on the Scotch, sat down and put his feet up on the coffee table and tried to relax, wind down a bit. God knows he needed a good, long sleep. Maybe he could stay in the sack in the morning until nine or so and then head over to the field and try to figure out a way to beat the damn Porters. One game, that was all he had to worry about now, just that one game. Win it, and then worry about the NL pennant and the World Series and all the rest. For right now, stay focused on this one game.

He thought about the TV, but decided no. Made the same decision about the radio or CD player, and, instead, just sat there, staring into space, trying to will himself to relax, finishing off the glass of Macallan and pouring one more, just one more. One game, that was all. Just one more. He was exhausted, from all the stress mostly, he guessed. He leaned back against the couch, started to drift off, some part of his mind noticing that and feeling good about finally getting some sleep. After a bit, he woke up enough to get up slowly, walk into the bedroom, unbuttoning his shirt on the way, slipping out of his shoes, reaching the bed, stepping out of his pants. He sat on the bed, fell back, didn't even pound the pillow, too tired to bother.

And thought about the alarm. Oh, hell, he hadn't set it after turning it off. Had he at least locked the door? He couldn't remember. No, everything was fine, just relax, just relax, just close those eyes and relax. And, finally, it worked, he drifted off, working his way into a dream where the Crusaders won it all, swept the Blue Jays in four, world champions and all was good and calm and right with the world.

The cell phone rang. Groggy, he heard it at a distance at first, wondered what that clatter was. Then he came awake enough to realize it was the cell. His father again? Some demand from dear old dad? Something about the faults of superstring theory at four in the goddamn morning?

Damn it all to hell. He got up, walked over to where he'd thrown his trousers, fumbled into the left front pocket and got the cell, opened it and brought it to his ear. "Hello?"

"Daddy? It's me."

Felicity. Oh, god. Felicity. Even through sleep he knew she wouldn't be calling unless it was serious. Adrenaline pumped and he came awake, heart pounding, "Fel? Are you in Grand Cayman? What's the matter, sweetie? Are you OK?"

"I'm fine, Daddy. Everything is fine. Yes, we're here in Grand Cayman. Listen, no one's been hurt, but there was a break-in here and I thought I'd call you first thing and tell you before some reporter found out and woke you up with the news."

"What happened? A break-in, at the Reverend's place down there?" All he could seem to do was ask questions. He took a deep breath, tried again. "So. Someone broke in. Did you see them?"

"Are you awake, Daddy? I'm really sorry to wake you up, but I thought you should hear this from me, you know?"

"Sure, sweetie, sure. Thanks for calling me. Now tell me what happened."

And she did, starting with the flight down and the girl on the front step. She mentioned Michael, said he was with them, staying in another guest room. "He's a really nice guy, Dad," she added.

And then told him the rest. How she woke up when it happened, someone breaking the window in the girl's bedroom, trying to get in. The alarms going off and the person running away. That simple. The police were there now, and a guy was putting some plywood over the broken window and that was that.

"Were they out to get this girl, then, Fel?"

"I don't know, Daddy. Either that or they followed me here and they thought it was me in that bed. Maybe I'm just totally paranoid, but that seems like it could be, too. But how'd they get here? And why would they want to do that?"

This was his daughter, and she sounded lost. Stu was wide-awake now, thinking clearly. "Just stay put for now, Fel. Are they leaving an officer there for a while?"

"There'll be one out front in a squad car, Daddy. I told them what happened in St. Pete and they said they'd take care of it for tonight but then I'd have to get the U.S. authorities in on it somehow, or just fly home to deal with it."

"Flying home sounds like a great idea to me, Fel. Why don't you just get back on the morning flight. I'll meet you here at the airport."

"I can't, Daddy. We have some things to do there tomorrow, and maybe the next day, and then we'll be back."

"Things?"

"For Michael. For the murder of his brother. I think I need to stay and help, Daddy. I am a cop, you know, and a damn good one."

"But this isn't your case, Fel, and that's a foreign country down there. And you're hurt already and can't get around much." He paused, took a break, threw his best pitch at her: "And people are breaking into homes to get at you."

"*Maybe* at me, Daddy. And maybe not. And they're trying to get at me up there, too, whoever they are, so coming home won't help. No, I'm staying, Daddy. Just for another day or two."

"Sweetheart, if you came home you could stay here with me, and we could hire some help, you know? Even if you want to stay with Cassidy we can protect you better here."

"I'll protect me, Daddy. Now that I know what this is like, I'll protect me."

"Oh, Fel. Come on home."

"I can't, Daddy. I just wanted you to know I'm OK. Look, I'll call you later, all right? Sometime this afternoon."

He couldn't argue with her and win, he knew that. He'd started losing arguments with her when she was four. And she was a cop, she was trained for this.

"All right, Fel, all right. But, please, be careful. Be very careful, sweetie."

"Always, Dad, always. I love you."

And she hung up.

Stu tried to get back to sleep, but that was a joke, it was impossible. A couple of hours slipped by and he finally realized what he had to do. Hell, his father had seen this coming and was absolutely right. Stu had spent his life choosing the game over family and he'd paid a horrible price for that.

Stu used to read a lot, it helped keep him sane, and in one of those books somewhere along the line he'd read that the reason all the literary types liked

144

baseball so much was because it was a game where chaos did battle with order. Everything in the game moves along in a nice orderly fashion, batters up and down pitch after pitch, routine grounders and lazy flyballs and everyone makes the plays they're supposed to and all is right in the world. And then a ball hits a pebble; or your centerfielder loses one in a high summer sky, the tiny dot of white lost in the expanse of blue up there; or the ump just blows it on one call at first or at home and somehow that opens the door and the other guys score ten with two outs and you're clobbered when you thought you had it won. That's all it takes and suddenly there's chaos everywhere, everything gone to hell, nothing going like it should, situation hopeless, a manager's nightmare, the game as a lazy writer's metaphor for life.

Well, not this time, damnit. Baseball was not life. This was Fel, his little girl, the one person who mattered more to him to anything, more than life itself, and certainly more than any damn kid's game you play with a ball, a bat and a glove.

It didn't take him long to get ready: throw a couple of shirts, some underwear and socks and an extra pair of slacks into the duffle bag along with a pair of shorts and a toothbrush and a razor and that was good enough. He headed out to the Pathfinder, tossed the bag into the back seat, hit the button to open the garage door, and started backing out.

There was a car in the way, sitting in his driveway — a white Dodge, from what he could see in his rearview mirror. What the hell? He shoved the Pathfinder into park, and started to open his door just as the headlights of the car behind snapped on, the glare bouncing off his rearview mirror as he glanced into it.

Who the hell could that be? He was halfway out the door before it occurred to him that it might be someone dangerous. By then it was too late and he was standing there, slamming the car door shut behind him as the driver-side door of the Dodge opened and a shape — a fat shape — struggled to get out, finally getting loose from the tangle of seatbelt to stand there and look at him.

"Stu? Where you going this time of night?"

It was Nick Krusoe. Stu stood there for a moment, trying to figure out whether he was relieved or pissed off. Pissed off, in the end, won out. Not that it mattered much.

A half-hour later the two of them were at the airport, Krusoe about as easy to get rid of as a disease. Two hours after that they were both on the morning flight to Grand Cayman, Krusoe paying the extra so they could both sit in first class, since he couldn't fit his bulk into the seats back in economy class. Cayman Air flight 003, heading for Grand Cayman. Stu, in the window seat, asked the flight attendant for the first of a few Bloody Marys while he looked at Florida slide by below and tried to ignore Krusoe, who started snoring like a champ by the time they were at cruising altitude, needing to catch up on his sleep after sitting in his car all night outside Stu's place. The Bloody-damn-Marys tasted pretty good.

By ten-thirty, Stu figured as he sipped on the third one, calmer now, he'd be with his daughter and the hell with Nick Krusoe — he could sue him later for invasion of privacy or something. Right now all Stu wanted was to get down there, protect Felicity, not let anything happen to her, not like it had to Carmen. Not that. Not again. Not ever again.

THIRTY-EIGHT

Roberto watched the last four innings of Len's ballgame, the over-the-hill gang out there still playing hardball. Len was pitching and not doing too bad a job of it for a guy in his mid-forties, getting a strikeout here and there and generally keeping the ball down so there were a lot of groundballs his infield could handle.

Or not. It was obvious to Roberto that the St. Petersburg Over-40 Cubs were not, to put it kindly, the best defensive team in the world. There was an error or two an inning, and Len had obviously long ago accepted that it took four or five outs— or what should have been outs— to get out of every inning.

Roberto knew the game. He'd been a player himself in younger days back home in Cuba, before he'd drifted, literally, north to Key West and freedom, with all its costs. At seventeen, Roberto's pitching skills had him playing béisbol in Havana's Estadio Latinoamericano with the country's other all-stars from the National Series. He'd won that game, too. Later, sipping on those tiny cups of sweet Cuban coffee at the Pelota Café on 23rd Street, he'd thought he was on top of the world. Surely he'd be pitching for the national team, playing all over the world, be famous and rich and then maybe one day soon get away to the Estados Unidos and make millions, pitching for the Yanquis.

None of that had happened, of course. Only the escaping to the States part actually wound up being real, and he almost died in the doing of it. The boat wasn't much to start with, and was slowly falling apart as they struggled through the blue-green of the Gulf Stream. With the Florida Keys in sight it finally went down and they all had to swim for it. Twenty of them started the trip and they all would have made it; but eleven were still in the water when the Coast Guard pulled them up. They were shipped back home. Roberto was one of the nine who'd made it to shore, and policy said he got to stay, so stay he did. But not playing baseball. He put those dreams behind him when he faced reality and started trying to make a living. What a strange life that had turned out to be.

Len's game was a seven–five loss when it ended, and Roberto was smiling as Len, sweaty and tired, walked up to him to say hi after the game. "Hey, nice game, lawyer man. You got a hell of a slider there. You striking people out with that pitch, man. I saw it."

"Yeah, sometimes, Roberto. A few."

"But then you got the ball up to a couple of guys, too, and, whew..." Roberto laughed. "That one double off the wall, man. I didn't know people your age could hit a ball that hard."

"Thanks. I think."

Roberto wrapped his arm around Len. "No, man. I'm just joking. You pitched great, really. I didn't know you had that in you."

"What are you doing here, Roberto? I thought you said we shouldn't be seen together, that it was too dangerous for that."

"Yeah, well. Things change, lawyer man. We got to talk."

"You have some information for me?"

"Yeah, man. Something like that. We got to go for a drive, though. Something I got to show you."

Len didn't quite know what to make of that. Drive away with Roberto? That sounded maybe suicidal. But if there was something important, than maybe it could save Felicity's life. Did he have the courage to take that risk? He didn't know, really. "You can't just tell me, Roberto?"

"No, man. We got to drive there." He put up his hands, palms out. "I know, I know. But you got to trust me on this, OK? This is the only way, and it could make things a lot better for that girl cop."

Len looked at Roberto's face, stared at him. "I saved your ass, Roberto. I kept you out of jail."

Roberto stared back, smiling. "I know, man. I owe you." The smile faded. "And that's why we got to go, lawyer man. Now. You got to come with me. Only take a little while, so you just leave your car here, right?"

Oh, Jesus. It sure didn't smell good, not good at all.

"Lawyer man. Len. Look, man, you have to come, you know what I mean? There's people paying attention to this. You have to come with me."

People paying attention? Len started to look around, check in the row of cars parked by the picnic benches that lined the field. Maybe somebody up in the stands?

Roberto stopped him, hissing at him in a low voice. "Don't do that, man; you just make it worse. Look, just get in. Now. And come with me. You got to trust me, it's the right thing to do."

Oh, Jesus. Cut and run? Probably die trying that. No, there didn't seem to be much choice. "OK, Roberto. I'll come with you. I'm trusting you, Roberto. I have a family, you know. Sweet kids, a loving wife. You know what I mean?"

Robert just smiled, opened the passenger side door for him and Len climbed in. No waiting, no screwing around, they drove off, Roberto with a definite place in mind.

It wasn't the most pleasant drive Len had ever been on. Roberto constantly checked in the rearview mirror to see if they were being followed, which made Len nervous as hell. After awhile Roberto handed Len a pair of dark, wrap-around sunglasses. "Just wear them, OK?" Roberto told him. "Don't ask any questions, don't say nothing, man. Wear those and shut up." Len put them on and couldn't see a thing: they were totally black.

He tried one more time to ask Roberto what was going on, but the guy just shut him up, quietly driving until the pulled into a parking lot or driveway and Roberto killed the engine and said, simply, "Out. I'll walk you to the door."

Len got out, convinced he was a dead man. He stood there, blind, until Roberto took him by the elbow and steered him along, maybe sixty or seventy paces, that was all, and then they stopped. Roberto opened a door. They walked in. Roberto took off the blinders.

It was a small room with a big horizontal freezer, its top open, occupying most of the available space. Next to the freezer was a cot with a sleeping bag on it and that was it.

"Here, lawyer man. You got to drink this down." He was opening up the top lid on a small plastic bottle of Gatorade.

Len just stared. Roberto pushed the bottle toward him again and he took it.

"Just some Xannies in there man. They'll relax you. Gatorade gets it right into the bloodstream."

"Why are you doing this, Roberto?"

"Don't ask too many question, lawyer man. I got orders, you know, but I'm doing something special here, 'cause I owe you."

"Special?"

"Drink it man. Now." There was an edge to the voice.

Could he run? Fight him and get out of here, run like hell?

"Don't even think it, man," Roberto said, a tight smile on his face. "Just drink that shit down. Right now."

Len drank. Felt nothing.

"Now climb in there," Roberto said, nodding toward the open freezer.

"I don't want to, Roberto. I'm dead in there. No air."

"Just get in, lawyer man. You got to do it."

He turned to look at it, turned back to look at Roberto, who smiled, then reached out to shove him toward it. "You got to do this, man."

"'Trust me,' you said, Roberto."

"All right man, I'll say it again. Trust me. Now climb the fuck in there. I'm going to keep you out of trouble, that's all."

"In that?"

Roberto was done talking. Quickly, with a minimum of fuss, he grabbed Len's right arm — still sore from all the pitching — and pulled it behind him. He shoved him toward the freezer, so strong and moving so fast that Len couldn't do a damn thing about it, and then pushed him over the side and in, letting the arm loose as he did it.

"Goodnight, man," he said, and shoved the lid tight. Len could hear the latches being tightened down, heard the slaps on the lid before it went quiet. Then came the darkness, the total blank blackness. Then he felt the warm spreading through him as the Xanax hit. What a stupid way to die, what a completely stupid way to die. He wanted to fight it, but it felt so good, dying like this, Xanaxing your way into oblivion. Warm. Comfortable and warm. And then into the deep black, regretting, only, as he slipped away, that he didn't get to say goodbye to his family.

149

Driving away, Roberto figured he'd done the right thing. Hell, maybe Brooks was having him tailed, just to make sure it all went down like it was supposed to. This way, everything might work out OK. So now he'd done the clubhouse thing, and the thing with pobre niño Len Gold, and now there was this other thing Brooks wanted him to do, too. Take care of the nosy clubhouse boy, the retarded kid, Jimmy, Brooks had said on the plane. All right, he could do that, too. He shook his head. He was nice, that retarded kid — always with a smile and a hug. Too nice for his own good, that's all. Too damn nice for his own good.

THIRTY-NINE

The Reverend flat out didn't believe it. Not something like this. Not from Stu Lindsay. "There must be some mistake here, Barnett. I just can't believe that Stu Lindsay would ever do anything like that," he said to the chief of stadium security, and then pointed at the materials that Barnett had placed on his desk — a small glass pipe and a plastic baggie with five or six small stones in it the color of dirty snow. "It's just not possible that these kinds of things could possibly have been found in Stu Lindsay's desk."

"That's where they were, though, Reverend. Found them there myself, maybe an hour ago."

"You found them yourself? This morning? In his desk?" The Reverend struggled to stay focused, to hang onto the thought that came to him as he listened to Barnett. "Why were you looking in his desk, Barnett?"

"Mr. Brooks called me on my cell phone and asked me to find the keys to the training room, said they'd be in Lindsay's top drawer and that Lindsay never locked it. I was just supposed to get the keys and leave them on Mr. Brooks' desk. That was it."

"And?"

"And when I opened the drawer the keys weren't there, so I shuffled the papers around a bit in there, looking for them, you know, and this material was there in the back of the drawer. I knew you'd be here, Reverend, you're here early every morning, so I brought them to you. That's it, the whole story."

The Reverend shook his head. Good Lord, this was hard to accept. "All right then, Barnett. You've done the right thing bringing them to me. I'll have to take care of this. I'll take care of it right away. Thank you."

Barnett said OK and left. The Reverend almost expected a stiff salute from the man, who still walked and talked with that top sergeant demeanor though he'd been out of the Army for more than twenty years. It was funny how he could remember that about Barnett but couldn't remember what he'd eaten for breakfast this morning.

So now what? This was unbelievable. The Reverend picked up his pen, a cheap little plastic Bic, and shoved at the things. Surely not Stu, the Reverend couldn't believe that of him. So there must be some other explanation. He hit the intercom button. "Alice, could you please contact Stu Lindsay for me?"

She answered right back. "I'm trying, Reverend, you asked me to do that earlier. There's no answer at home, so I left a message on his answering machine and on his cell phone and reminded him to call your private office phone. And he's not at Ministry Field yet, either. I left messages there, too, of course."

The Reverend sat back in his chair and thought it through. Could Stu be involved in something like this? He picked up the phone. "Alice, would you please contact Stu Lindsay for me?"

Alice sounded like she was being patient. "Yes, Reverend, I'll reach him as soon as I can."

"Thank you, dear," the Reverend said and hung up. Then he pulled a large manila envelope out of his right-side file drawer and, again with the Bic, shoved the material into the envelope. He licked the envelope's seal, folded it shut and then pulled the tabs through and bent them out, as if he wanted to close this thing up forever, not just the half-hour it would take to get over to Stu's house. The phone rang, his private office phone. Who would be calling on that line? He forced himself to think on that — then it came, Stu Lindsay, of course. And there was some trouble with Stu, something with drugs. Maybe he could clear this up right now? He picked up the receiver, put it to his ear cautiously, afraid of what he might hear.

"Daddy? It's Cassidy."

Cassidy? Something was wrong, seriously wrong, or she wouldn't be calling him on this line.

"Sweetheart, what's wrong?"

"I'm all right, Daddy. I'm fine. But there's a lot going on and I thought I better tell you about it."

"Oh, my, there certainly is. What's on your mind?"

"I'm down in the Caymans, Daddy, with Felicity and her friend Michael. We flew down last night."

"Really? Why, dear?" The place in The Caymans. Why would she go there in such a rush?

"Well, we came because of Michael, really. He's Felicity's friend and he had to come down here right away because of his brother."

"His brother?"

"...and then once we got there, there was a break-in at the house, Daddy."

"What? A break-in? Have you called the police?"

"Everything's fine, Daddy. The alarm went off and they ran away. We're all fine. Everything's fine with us. But there's something else."

"Well, no doubt. Have you called the police, dear?"

"Daddy, I've been reading through some financial information I found on the computer out in the guesthouse and there are some things in there that worry me."

"Like what, Cassie?"

"Daddy, there's a lot of odd accounting in here, with money flowing through companies incorporated in the Caymans and people I've never heard of on the board. It's hard to tell what's really going on; it must all be in some kind of code. But it's not good, Daddy. It can't be good at all."

"So did you call the police, Cassidy?"

"Daddy, listen to me. I don't think calling the police is a great idea. All of this must have some connection to Craig Ministries, and if you don't know about all this, well then, something's very, very strange."

"I don't understand, Cassie. What do you mean they have something to do with the Ministry?"

"It's the Ministry's office, Daddy. And the Ministry's computer. And I'd guess it's the Ministry that's the cover, one way or another, for how and where the money goes. And there's a lot of money involved here, Daddy. A whole lot of money."

"A lot of money?"

"Millions, daddy. Tens of millions. Maybe more."

"Oh, my Lord, Cassidy. That much? And — what did you say? — you found this money in the guesthouse."

She sighed, got very patient with him. "Daddy, please listen to me. It's not cash, it's accounting. I think you need to see this, and we should talk about it."

"It's not cash? I don't understand. Why don't you catch the first flight back and get up here? Bring the money with you and I'll keep the afternoon wide open. We'll dig into this and find out what's happening."

"Daddy. I think maybe you should come down here for this. We should do this privately, you and me, away from Brooks and his people."

Away from Brooks? Why? Then he paused, thought about it for a moment. Wasn't there another problem he'd been dealing with? He couldn't remember. There was a manila envelope on his desk. Why was that sitting there? He set the phone down and opened it, struggling some to get the metal tabs opened and then pulling back the flap, which wasn't sealed very tightly. Inside, there was a little glass pipe and three tiny stones, the color of dirty snow. What was this?

He heard a voice in the distance. The phone was off the hook for some reason. Looking at the little pipe and the tiny stones he picked up the phone and put it to his ear.

"Daddy!" It was Cassidy.

"Cassidy, sweetheart. How are you?"

"Oh, Daddy," she said, then again, "Oh, Daddy."

"What's the problem, dear?"

"Listen to me, Daddy. You need to come down here to the house in the Caymans."

"Come down there? Why would I want to do that, dear?" he asked. "There's a big game tonight for the Crusaders, you know. A big, big game." Hadn't she been talking about something down there? Something serious. Something about money?

"Daddy. I'll talk to Alice and get it arranged. You just do what she says, all right?"

Alice. Ah, yes, he could trust Alice. "Certainly, dear. I'll let Alice handle it." Handle what, he wondered, as soon as he said it. Then, "I love you, dear," he said to Cassidy, and after that, tired, he hung up.

FORTY

George Brooks had been sitting here in Mackie's room for a couple of hours, chain-smoking, getting madder as each minute slowly rolled by, wondering where the friggin' guy was. Here he'd busted his butt to get down here, flown down here in the morning in that tiny friggin' little jet of Roberto's after getting all the things done that had to be done in St. Pete, from playing nice with the French doctors last night to swinging by the doc's first thing this morning to get the cough checked out; and then once he got here Mackie wasn't even in his room. Where the hell could he be?

Jesus, the whole thing was getting to be a mess. If that girl knew the details and told them to Cassidy, Felicity and the boy-wonder scientist, then it all might collapse, and that'd be too damn bad. But it wasn't a total disaster, not yet. He had Roberto—a guy he could trust — working on cleaning things up in St. Pete, taking care of a couple of problems there: the nosy lawyer friend of Lindsay's daughter that Roberto had told him about, and the retard clubhouse boy who'd seen too much when he'd walked into the clubhouse as Roberto was putting the stuff into Lindsay's desk. Take care of those two and things were pretty clean in St. Pete.

And if it really blew up on him, he could cut and run. He had millions put away in various accounts around the islands, here and in St. Kitts, and he knew where he could go to dodge the worst of the fallout. There were things you could get done these days in Russia, for instance — change of identity complete with a new nose, new papers, the rest. For under a million he would be a new man, live on one of the Leeward Islands where he had friends from the old days, retire from all this, entertain himself for a while, enjoy the profits of his labors.

But he'd rather not do that, not yet. He'd rather keep it going, make a little more, turn this whole operation into the huge enterprise it could be. There was a vacuum out there. Bogotá, Medellin, Cali — those beaners had screwed it up, let it get away from them. Typical beaners, all flash and tough talk, vicious when they needed to be, friggin' cruel sometimes; but not able to carry it through, keep it organized, keep it going for the long run.

That was his specialty, the long run. He'd been working on this thing for something like ten years now, count it all up, and had it really geared up from six years back, from the first time he'd met the Reverend at that political get-together, the one where everyone had their hands out. The Reverend, acting all squeaky clean and above it all, had given the invocation and then talked about his friggin' Ministry, talked about all the good they could do with enough money. And George Brooks had seen the light. The perfect little laundry. Crusader Retreat, the cover for the best little operation there'd been since the height of the Afghanistan thing, when he'd still been with the agency but couldn't help but see the potential for a little personal poppy profit. And this would be even bigger — a lot bigger — if a few more things fell into place. For one thing he wanted to outright own the planes and then hire better pilots— god knows he knew enough pilots, the very best of them, a lot of them running small charter companies like Roberto, guys running just enough drugs on the side to keep the ledgers in the black. Those guys would love to work for George Brooks again. It would be like the old days in Nicaragua with the stupid beaner Contras. Plenty of guys would jump at the chance to go one more round, make a pile of money while they were at it. Jesus, it was exciting back then.

But for all that to happen, for the thing to keep on growing and getting bigger and making them all bigger piles of cash, this little unraveling thing had to be stopped here. Now. Today, before it all exploded in their friggin' faces. And if that meant some bad news for Stu Lindsay's kid, well, then, that was too friggin' bad. He'd whack her himself at this point if he had to.

And Cassidy Craig: now that was the real problem. Nice girl. Bright. He liked her. And she was the Reverend's daughter. So it would have to look like an accident. Some diving thing, maybe. Or something on one of those jet-skis. Tragic, but an accident.

He smiled. Yes, that was it, a tragic jet-ski accident that killed all four of these kids. Couple of the things ram into each other, nobody wearing life vests, everybody bruised and broken up from the collision, the thing happening after sunset so nobody could find them in the dark. Perfect.

The Reverend would be in mourning, the faithful would send in millions to support him. It was perfect, would solve the problem and be a revenue producer at the same time. With the money from this they could start up the new system that ran through Honduras and then through Cuba and on into Florida. It was an expensive route, but solid, rock solid, with top politicians protecting it all the way, especially in Cuba.

OK, yes, that would do it. Just take some action, some firm action, and right away, tonight. So, OK, where the friggin' hell was Mackie?

There was a scratch at the door, one of those plastic ID keys being inserted. The door opened a bit, stopped, and then, with some huge friggin' Glock held out in front of him like a TV cop, Mackie came into the room, quickly scanned it, saw Brooks, lowered the cannon and stood there like a friggin' sick puppy. Oh, Christ, the things that Brooks put up with.

He shook his head, pointed toward the other chair, coughed hard once or twice to clear his throat, said: "Take a seat, Mackie. We got some things to talk over."

So Mackie sat.

FORTY-ONE

Stu had been to the Caribbean a few times, down to the Dominican twice in recent years to see kid shortstops. Good thing, too, since that meant he had a passport and he'd grabbed it before heading to the airport.

But the Dominican Republic hadn't prepared him for Grand Cayman. The Dominican was such a big place you didn't remember you were on an island most the time. Not here. Looking out the window at the island below as they circled over it to get lined up to land, he couldn't believe anybody would want to live on a place so small and so isolated.

On the way down he'd marveled at all the water, and found himself excited to see Cuba below when they crossed it, right over the Bay of Pigs. Incredible. Stu had been in elementary school when the Cuban Missile Crisis blew up in Kennedy's face. Living in Florida, his father a young professor and researcher then at the University of Florida, Stu remembered how tense it all was for everybody in Florida. Those missiles could hit anywhere in Florida, some of them probably aimed right at Gainesville, right at his school. They practiced hiding under the desks during twice-daily drills, as if that would help if a missile hit. And all that was because of the Bay of Pigs fiasco.

And now, down below, there it was, slipping away behind him as they started their descent into Grand Cayman, that little dot in the blue Caribbean. They landed at half past ten in the morning, the plane pulling up near the small terminal building and customs and then the ground crew rolling up the stairs—no jetways here.

Stu climbed down the steps onto the tarmac and felt the heat immediately. Hard to imagine that someplace could be even muggier than St. Pete, but it felt that way to him here, the heat oppressive and only going to get worse for the rest of the day. Stu shaded his eyes and looked up. Half the sky, mostly to the north and east so there was no shade here at the airport,

156

was covered with clouds, small thunderheads picking up the thermal heat off the land and building up to rain. One of them had a small funnel edging down from it, a waterspout out there over the bay, growing as he watched. It grew larger, darker, no more than maybe a half-mile away, and then, as Stu watched, it reached its saturation point, pulling up so much water from the bay that it cooled itself, self-destructing even as it reached its largest size, falling apart and scattering into gray broken shards of cloud and then, in moments, it was gone.

He headed into customs, and got lucky in the line, up near the front. Krusoe, who'd had trouble getting out of the plane, was ten or fifteen people behind him in line. Good, maybe he could shake the guy right here, just pretend not to notice that he was going on without him, grab a taxi and get out of sight before Krusoe even got through the customs. Customs was a breeze and then Stu walked outside the terminal building and looked around, trying to figure out where the taxi stand was. He saw it, a moment later, down at the end of the terminal building, empty for the moment.

A woman, attractive, thin, with dark hair tumbling down around her shoulders and beautiful wide-set, blue eyes, walked up to him. She was dressed in a breezy kind of summer shift, a flower-patterned thing that came up well past her knees. She wasn't wearing a bra. She had a hell of a smile. "Hi. Aren't you Stu Lindsay, the manager of the Crusaders?"

A fan then. Stu relaxed, nodded his head, said "Sure am," and smiled. He'd give her an autograph and they'd both be on their way.

"Could I bother you for a minute, Mr. Lindsay. My husband is over there with the car. He's just such a huge fan. If I could just go get him and bring him over here to meet you and shake your hand while I take a picture it would really mean a lot to him."

This wasn't the time for that, not while he was hurrying to see his daughter, but Stu's natural inclination was to take a few moments to sign, and there were no taxis at the stand right now anyway. So, "Sure," he said, "I'd be happy to, but we'll have to be quick, all right? I'm a little short on time." He tried to sound polite but firm about that, it was all too easy to get caught up in conversations with fans, little discussions of everything from trading deadlines to late-inning decisions on who to bring in for relief. He didn't have time for that, not with Pel in trouble.

The woman, who sure wasn't acting very married, so maybe she was a newlywed, waved to a car, a little Daihatsu parked up the road a block or so and that car jolted forward, the driver grinding it into first gear. Stu smiled, had to be a rental. Newlyweds, then, down here for a honeymoon. The car came up to where they stood and the driver, a real All-American lawyer type with short hair, horn-rimmed glasses, a loud flower-patterned shirt, leaned over to roll down the passenger side window. Stu leaned over, too, to reach in and shake hands.

And then he felt a hard jab in the kidneys, and the woman's voice, changed now from friendly and flirtatious to something harder, something dark and insistent. "Get in," she said. "Now. Quickly. I'd hate to have to kill you right here in front of all these people."

Kill him? Jesus. Stu went weak at the knees, could feel his bowels begin to loosen. Kill him? Christ. He froze.

"Now!" She was urgent, and when he couldn't move she grabbed him by the arm and started pushing him toward the car door. Her hand was on his left elbow, her grip so hard it hurt, the thumb pressing in against the tendons, a reminder of what she planned to do.

He finally got around to struggling, tried to pull away and found himself in an awkward embrace, the woman with her arms around him now trying to cram him into the little Daihatsu while he managed to free both hands and get them up against the sides of the door, shoving back, trying to save himself.

"Get in there!" she said, louder, and took her right arm back from around his chest and reached to grab his right hand, tugging it away from the door — she was stronger than she looked — and starting to pull it behind his back.

And then there was a yell, a loud scream of "aaaiiii!" like in a bad kung-fu movie, and a huge shape came flying by on the left. It was Nick Krusoe, all three-hundred-fifty pounds of him, sweeping in like a defensive tackle on the prowl for a quarterback, bowling into the woman so hard it ripped her away from Stu and sent her flying down hard onto the sidewalk. Krusoe, his momentum too much to control, went sailing right over her, landing in a heap beyond her, a loud oomph ending his screaming attack.

There was a still moment, everyone frozen in place by the craziness of it all. Then everything broke at once. The woman scrambled to her feet and dived into the open side door of the Daihatsu just as the driver jammed it noisily into gear and hit the gas. Stu started to grab her, to hang on, then thought better of it and, instead, had the sense to look for the license tag — CVQ-45W — as the car jerked away. Then he turned to help Krusoe, who lay there moaning, a beached whale of a man who'd just saved Stu from whatever danger that was heading toward: Death maybe? A kidnapping? Now, slowly, Krusoe was trying to roll over and sit up. He was not a pretty sight.

But a few minutes later he made it, standing there rubbing his elbows where they'd hit the pavement. He was moaning about the beating his body had taken while the local cops took notes from everyone who'd seen any of it happen. "It's a small island, sir," said the one cop after talking to Stu for five minutes. The cop was dressed in shorts, with a U.S. style police cap on and light-blue shirt with epaulets. "We'll have that car traced shortly and we'll contact you at the Craig house when we do."

So there was nothing else to do but wait and find out from the local cops what the hell this was all about. A few minutes later, finally in a taxi, Stu was on his way to the Craig house, on his way to see Felicity. Sitting next to him, occupying most of the back seat of the tiny taxi, was Nick Krusoe, still moaning, and still huge and annoying and still that hated breed, a sportswriter; but now a guy who'd earned Stu's thanks, and so he'd been invited along as Stu wondered what the hell was going on.

FORTY-TWO

Michael drove, sitting over on the right side, feeling weird but getting it done all right, happy the Camry was an automatic so he wouldn't have to shift with his left hand. Felicity, over on the left side, had a little map out, but Michael couldn't imagine they'd need it, the island was so small. How lost could they get, really? Parrot's Landing was just straight on down the coast, seven or eight miles, maybe less, and they'd be there.

West Bay Road was straight here, so he turned and snuck a quick look at Fel. She looked back, and smiled. He liked this girl. A lot. But how could he be thinking of her with any kind of romantic interest? How could he have made love to her last night? It was wonderful, fabulous, but how could he be thinking of anything else except Honker and whoever killed him? There was a kind of turmoil going on, emotions swirling around madly, out of control. Somehow he needed to grab hold of something solid and settle down, get the job done that Honker had asked him to do, keep it together for Honker's sake.

Then Felicity reached over to squeeze his hand and he squeezed back. Incredible. He'd made love with this girl last night. He was no great lover, that was for sure, and what little experience he had was with women as inexperienced as he was. And then, last night, he'd found himself lost in an act of transcendent wonder.

He'd been thinking that through last night, the craziness of it, lying there in a kind of sleepy daze wrestling with his own feelings, when he'd been damn near knocked off the bed by the screech of the burglar alarm and the madness that followed. The girl Robin again, and someone trying to break in but getting scared off by the alarm. Jesus, what a night. After the break-in attempt, Michael and Fel had sat up for the rest of the night, keeping an eye on things as Robin, exhausted, fell asleep on the couch in the living room and Cassidy, over in a big overstuffed chair, finally fell asleep, too.

They all figured that whoever had been chased off wouldn't come back, would figure they'd have called the cops by now and so would clear out and stay as far away as you could get on this tiny island. But, in fact, Felicity, Michael and Cassidy hadn't called the cops at all, despite what Michael had overheard Fel say in that phone call to her father. Cassidy begged them not to, said there was a lot of stuff going on and getting the cops involved right now might be a disaster for her dad, for the Ministry. One cop had come by to check on the alarm and Cassidy had gone out front and told him it was a false alarm and he'd smiled, said thanks, and gone on his way.

So they'd stayed up talking, the four of them, and then, later, just he and Fel after Cassidy and Robin went off to bed, Robin in Cassidy's bedroom with Cassidy in a couple of blankets on the floor.

Michael and Fel had talked about everything, about Honker and the murder and the stuff Cassidy said she was finding out about the Ministry. About themselves and their pasts. About the Crusaders and about her dad, who was drinking too hard and so stressed out he was hallucinating that he was getting phone calls from his long-dead father.

Eventually they'd both managed to doze for an hour or two, but then the bright Caymanian sunshine had brought back some clear realities for Michael and he'd been the one urging them to get things done. The plan now was to get to Parrot's Landing and ask around about Samantha, see if anyone knew anything. Cassidy was back at the house with Robin. The Reverend was coming down late today or maybe tomorrow morning — Cassidy would check with Alice in St. Pete on which flight — and Cassidy wanted

160

to find out as much as she could before he got in, have everything ready for him. Cassidy had found something really odd in the bookkeeping software out in the guesthouse, she said, and she wanted to work with it some more, something about cracking the code. So, as Michael had left with Fel, Cassie had gone back out there, taking Robin with her to keep an eye on her. She'd been buried in it out there, clicking away on her keyboard, as they'd left, barely having the time to wave.

"That's it, on the right," he heard Fel say, her voice cutting through his haze. There was a small parking area, maybe enough for four or five cars. He pulled the Camry in there next to an old Jeep Cherokee and a shiny new Suzuki Samurai. What could all these people want with four wheel drive here on this dot of an island where everything already looked paved over anyway? You could see the cars everywhere, most of them small but some of them the big behemoth sports-utilities from the States. They looked monstrous in this tiny place.

A nice-sized house sat on the backside of a small yard that ran right up to the edge of a coral wall that went straight down for ten or fifteen feet into the Caribbean. "Parrot's Landing," a nice-sized sign said in script, with a stylized head of a parrot right next to it in green, blue and gold.

You had to walk around the house and get into it from the seaside. There were scuba tanks everywhere, and a young fellow with blond hair and too many tattoos filling them with compressed air. A paving stone walk led down to a small dock that jutted out into the sea, and there was a cut made into the coral next to the dock where divers and boaters could clamber down a ladder and slide right into ten feet of water. Inside was a complete dive shop, with scuba and snorkeling gear of all sorts and the standard tourist fare of t-shirts, caps, and sunblock. The Parrot's Landing logo dominated everywhere.

"Can I help you?" the girl behind the tall, glass-covered counter asked. She, too, was a blonde; chewing gum, with a nice tan, perfect white teeth, a slim body that was, presumably, the standard Parrot's Landing look. It was a long way from Michael's own appearance, with a tan that ended where his t-shirt sleeves started, and baggy, worn shorts that had seen too many late-night beaches and turtle hatchlings and had earned, he had to admit, a graceful retirement. Felicity took Michael's hand and walked toward the counter. Fel had taken a couple of ibuprofen this morning to cut the soreness from her ribs, and she told Michael that they did feel a little better, though she'd struggled mightily getting in and out of the car. She seemed

OK when she was sitting or standing, but changing position obviously caused her a lot of pain.

"We're looking for a girl named Samantha," Felicity asked the girl. "She works here. She was his brother's girlfriend," and she nodded toward Michael and smiled gently.

The girl's eyes grew wide and she snapped a huge grin into place. "Oh," she said, "Yeah, sure, Sam. And you're, like, Honker's brother, right? That's so cool. We heard about you a lot. You're, like, the turtle scientist, right?"

Michael nodded.

"Listen, Honker's just the greatest guy. Sam's, like, so lucky. We all envy her. Can you imagine what it's like trying to find a nice guy around here? With all these scuba bums and bartenders. I mean, it's like all I can do to find a decent date a couple of times a week."

Michael realized she didn't know Honker was dead. He didn't know how to tell her, either, the way she was rambling on.

"Anyway, Sam is, like, so lucky. Your brother is a real gentleman and has that great job and all with the Turtle Farm. I mean, what a lifestyle he has."

"The Turtle Farm?"

"Sure. You don't know about that? For the last year he's been their, like, principal field worker person, you know, out checking on stuff like turtle populations, egg counts in nests, all that kind of stuff." She giggled. "I mean, I hear about it like constantly from Sam."

"Can we meet Sam?" Felicity asked again. "We just want to talk with her for a few minutes about Honker."

"Well, on a normal day you'd be, like, talking to her now. I mean, like, I'm on her shift, covering for her right now. But she hasn't been here for three days in a row, and, like, no one's sure where she's gone."

"She's sick, or out of town or something?"

"No, she's just gone. I mean, you know, maybe she's sick and, like, flew home to Chicago to be with her folks or something like that? We just don't know."

"Have you contacted the police about it?"

"About what? About her going home?"

"About Sam being missing."

"Oh, wow, no. If we contacted the police every time someone around here just, like, up and left for a few days or a week or two we'd be on the phone to the cops all the time. I mean, things don't work like that around here, you know what I mean? People come and go. I always just figure if I fill in for Sam now, she'll do the same for me later when some rich yacht-type wants to carry me off for a weekend of fun in the sun, you know?"

Felicity nodded. "Sure. It's just no big deal, right?"

"That's right," the girl said, snapping the gum again and flashing that white, toothy smile. "It's no big deal at all."

A few minutes later they checked with the owner of the place, another tanned blonde though a bit older, and he confirmed the story. Sam was gone but nobody was worried about it. She'd be back, and Honker with her, no doubt. That was when Felicity finally broke the news about Honker's murder in Rum Point. The owner seemed genuinely shocked, and the girl behind the counter, when she found out, burst into tears. She was still crying as Michael and Felicity left, not having learned a thing except that Samantha was gone. No one had any advice on finding Sam except for maybe checking the turtle farm. More likely, they thought, she'd left the island, headed back up to Chicago.

As they left, discouraged, Felicity shoved some coins into a soda machine just outside the building while Michael walked to the car and absentmindedly started to get into the left side, the driver's side back home, before he realized his mistake. Shaking his head, he opened the door and walked around and there, stuck into the driver's side wiper blade, was a tightly folded piece of paper. He was leaning over to grab it out from under the wiper blade when Felicity yelled at him as the machine clanked and delivered its soft drink. "What's up?"

He brought the note, showing it to her and then opening it up.

"Smith Cove," it said. "In one hour. Gear in boot."

And it was signed "Samantha."

FORTY-THREE

Goddamn Robert Mackie had walked in ready to shoot somebody. Here George Brooks had gone to all the trouble to fly down here with Roberto, just to meet with Mackie, calm him down, try to help him; the two of them had that history, so Mackie deserved that much, deserved some help in these troubled times. And in return Brooks had almost been killed right there, a bullet in the brain the way Mackie liked to do it when he could.

So Brooks calmed him down, got him to lower that Glock and put it away. Then he started working on fixing things.

"It's all falling apart on us here," he told him. "We got to stop it right here before it gets any worse. I got Roberto working on things up in St. Pete, and now you got to handle it all down here: the girl cop and her boyfriend, Honker's girl and that friend of hers, even the Reverend's daughter and Stu Lindsay. They're all getting too friggin' close to it."

"Yeah," Mackie agreed, calming down from his adrenaline rush when he'd opened the door and seen someone there, probably figured it had to be bad, had his Glock out and ready, had some pressure on the trigger, was ready, really, to let it rip, right here in the fucking hotel room, blood on the walls, blood and hair and gray brain from when you fire through the back of some guy's head so the last thing he sees, the eyes still working for that fraction of a second, is his own face blowing by.

"So we have to do something about them. We have to take care of this problem, now, before it gets any worse."

Mackie shook his head, seemed to understand, though there was a look in his eye, a crazed look that Brooks hadn't seen before in all the years they'd worked together.

"So, you have any ideas on what we could do?" Brooks asked.

"Maybe we could burn the Reverend's place down with all them in it? Make it look like an accident or something?"

Mackie was hesitant as he offered that idea, but it wasn't all that bad, thought Brooks, better than the jet-ski thing, in fact. "OK, all right, that sounds pretty close, Mackie. We certainly want to make it look like an accident, and the fire would probably work if we can get them all in there at the same time. But can you think of something else, something we can add to that to make sure it looks like an accident and incriminates all of them at the same time?"

Mackie thought about it, tightening his eyes in thought, working it through. Nothing came, though, and he stood there, helpless, no idea what to say.

"Well," said Brooks, "think of it this way. If we want them to look bad, really bad, when they find the bodies, what could we plant in there?"

It was funny to watch Mackie work this through. Brooks could almost see the little light bulb going on over Mackie's head. "Oh, yeah," he said. "Pipes, some rocks, maybe a little bottle of butane?"

"That's it, that's it exactly. We'll need to pick up some things to plant in there. We'll get them from Kelly and we'll figure out how to get the girl

cop and all the rest of them into the house at once while we get it organized. With a little hard work we can have this whole thing done by tonight,
and then we'll be clear again."

Mackie nodded, proud of himself for having come up with the right
plan. "Yeah, sure. This'll work. I already arranged for us to meet Kelly for
lunch, she's coming by here, OK?"

"You told her to come by here? While I'm here? In a friggin' public
place, Mackie?" Brooks shook his head, disappointed. "No, you get out and
talk to her, tell her what we need, and then we'll all meet later and get it
organized from there. I'll call you here about three o'clock. By then I'll have
the rest of this worked out and we'll do the thing tonight, around midnight.
We'll get it over with and fly out an hour or two later with Roberto, get back
to St. Pete and get back to work."

"OK, OK. I'll take care of it with Kelly."

"You know," mused Brooks, "this'll really screw up the Crusaders for
tonight's big game. Their manager and his kid, the Reverend's daughter;
all of them dead in a drug-related house fire." He chuckled. "But you know
what, baseball's a business. They'll postpone the game for a day or two,
have a little mourning period and then get on with it. All this will do is just
up the ante all the way around. Bigger TV audience. They'll have everybody wear black armbands or something. Hell, this'll be a great motivator,
probably send the Crusaders all the way into the Series. It's perfect. More
I think about it, Mackie, it's perfect."

"Yeah," Mackie agreed. "It's perfect, all right. We whack them and we
win all the way around, right?"

Brooks nodded. "Right. We win, all the way around." And he sat back
in the cheap-shit chair of the hotel room, relaxing for the first time in a
couple of days. This was all going to work out all right after all. He was
taking a gamble, for sure, playing both ends against the middle, but it was
going to work out just fine.

FORTY-FOUR

There was no car out front when Stu's taxi pulled him into the driveway in front of the Reverend's home. He'd tried his cell phone right after

they got the taxi, but it didn't work and a "no-service" message showed on the little screen. He felt isolated not being able to call her and figured getting to the Reverend's house as quickly as he could was the best thing to do. At least with the phone not working he didn't have to worry about his father calling.

Now, here in the driveway, he told Krusoe to sit tight, asked the driver to wait for a minute, then walked to the door and pushed hard on the bell, worried about what it might mean if they weren't there.

But within a few seconds he could hear some rustling behind the door, somebody looking through the peephole, then a latch being undone and a deadbolt being turned and then the door opened. It was Cassidy Craig.

"Stu?" She was looking at him in disbelief. Behind her stood someone else, a girl in her twenties, thin, nervous. "What in god's name are you doing here?"

He was awfully glad to see her, but uneasy, too. This was weird, seeing her under these circumstances, a long way from his nice, safe office at Ministry Field. There he could handle himself around Cassidy. There he was the manager of a baseball team and she was the owner's daughter. Here, somehow, that had all changed. Too young. Too damn pretty. The Reverend's daughter. That was three strikes, by his count. But he smiled at her, said "Hi, Cassidy. Can we come in?" and he pointed back toward the taxi. "Nick Krusoe is here, too."

"Stu?" she said again, so surprised to see him that she seemed to wrestle with the reality of it for a moment before smiling broadly back, adding, "Hi. I'm, I'm..." she fumbled for it a second, "I'm really glad you're here."

She turned to glance at the girl behind her, said "Stu, this is Robin, she's staying here at the moment. You're lucky you caught us, we were out back in the office and just walked in through the back door a few minutes ago to make some coffee. You want a cup?"

Stu turned to wave the taxi off while Krusoe shoved his way out of it and the driver popped open the trunk and hauled out their two bags. Krusoe handed the guy some U.S. dollars which seemed to work just fine. Cassidy smiled and said hi to the sportswriter as he walked up.

They went inside and Stu stood by the couch, the whole situation too weird to think on much as he looked for a moment out the big picture window and its view of the Caribbean and Seven Mile Beach. Quite a place here; the Lord had sure been good to the Reverend. He turned away from the view to look at Cassidy, beautiful in a t-shirt and shorts, barefoot, wearing reading glasses, her hair a mess. She was waiting for him to explain things, but having Krusoe around made things damn awkward.

He gave it a shot, glad to see that Krusoe wasn't taking notes, at least. "I just came down because Felicity called and she said there was some trouble down here last night and the more I thought about that the more I thought I should be here. So I caught the first flight down to see if I could help. Where's Felicity? And Michael?"

"They've gone into town, to a dive shop called Parrot's Landing, to look for a girl, a friend of Michael's brother. Don't you have a game tonight, Stu? Shouldn't you be at the ballpark right now?"

"A friend of Honker Kelsey, the murdered guy?"

She nodded, paused. "I'm not sure how much you know about all this, Stu. I know Fel didn't want to say too much while you were trying to get the Crusaders into the playoffs." She frowned, added, "I just got Internet access back and read on the Crusader website that we lost last night. I'm sorry. That makes tonight the big game. We have to win it."

He waved his hand, dismissive. "Where can I find them in town?"

"You know, they're probably done and on their way back by now, you'd miss them if you went. Who'd you leave in charge up there? Quent? And who's on the hill tonight? And what's the latest on Sonny?"

"You have a car around that I can borrow? I can at least get down to that dive shop and see if they're there. If they aren't, I'll come right back."

"And what's everyone saying in town if you're gone, Stu? Do they know yet? Have you told my father? Or Brooks? God, Brooks'll hit the roof. He's so mad he might fire you on the spot, Stu."

"Hell," he said, thinking out-loud, "I could always just get a taxi down there, probably just as quick. Where's the phone? And how come my cell phone doesn't work here?"

Krusoe was just staring at them both, wondering, probably, when the hell they'd get on the same page; but thinking, too, that this was great stuff for his big story for *SI*. He didn't quite get it, yet, what was happening here, but he knew interesting shit when he saw it.

Stu was heading for the phone on the little table over in the corner of the tiled living room. Cassidy walked over to head him off, took him by the arm. "Stu. Come out the porch with me and sit down and relax for a minute. I'll get some coffee and tell you everything I know, OK?" She smiled at him, "I'll even tell you why your cell doesn't work, and then you can use the house phone here to call the dive shop once you know a little more."

167

Stu bought the logic of that, and finally slowed himself down enough to take a deep breath while she went into the kitchen with Robin and then came back with some Jamaican Blue Mountain he could sip on. Robin stayed behind in the kitchen for another minute and then came back herself, holding a big mug of coffee.

What Stu really wanted was a little Scotch, truth be told, and there had to be some around here somewhere. But the Blue Mountain would do for the moment.

And then they sat, the four of them, while Cassidy brought Stu and Krusoe up to speed, telling them about the last couple of days, from sea turtles to Honker's note to Samantha to Robin. She even explained about GSM phones and why Stu's cell didn't work but Cassidy's and Fel's did. It took a while to get it all said, Cassidy winding it up with, "So Fel and Michael are following that little lead from the note right now, down at Parrot's Landing, seeing if Samantha is there."

"Doesn't sound very likely."

"No, it doesn't. But maybe someone there will know something? And if they don't, then at least Michael knows he tried and did his best, you know?"

Stu nodded. "Where's this parrot place?"

"It's a diver's hangout, Stu, with a reef offshore you can swim to. It's just down the beach, maybe six or seven miles, but I really do think we're better off just waiting here for a few minutes. They've been gone for nearly two hours. They'll be back soon. I'll call Fel in a minute or two and see how they're doing."

He nodded. "Where are the local cops? Did they just take a report and leave or something?"

Cassidy grabbed a wooden and canvas director's chair from the other side of the porch, the Australian pines of the beachfront rustling in the sea-breeze that came through the screens. She brought it over next to him, sat down, took a sip of her own coffee. She looked at Krusoe and he stared back.

"This is off the record — way off the record — OK?"

He nodded.

She turned to face Stu. "We didn't call the police, Stu."

"What? Why? I mean, why not? Someone tried to break in here last night, maybe meant to kill somebody, and you didn't call the police?"

"No, we didn't. One cop came by to check on the alarm and I said it was a false alarm and he left." She paused for a second to gather her thoughts.

"There's more to it than what I've told you, Stu. There are some things that have to do with the Reverend, and the Ministry, and the Crusaders. We're not sure what all is involved, and Felicity agreed to not call in the local police until we knew a little more, that's all."

Stu was frowning. "You know, when I got here there was a weird little run-in at the airport. This woman said she was a fan, asked me for an autograph for her husband, and then when this guy — her husband, I thought — drove up in his car, the two of them tried to shove me into the car, like they were maybe trying to kidnap me or something. Nick here broke it up."

Krusoe spoke for the first time: "No 'maybe' about it, Stu, they planned to kidnap you."

"And you broke it up?" Cassidy wanted to know.

Stu smiled. "He threw the best cross-body block I've seen in years; flattened the woman with it and that scared them both off. Damndest thing I've seen in a long, long time."

"And it hurt like hell," Krusoe added, rubbing his elbows; but Cassidy wasn't listening to him.

"Oh, my god, Stu. Were you hurt?"

"Me? No, it was nothing, a bruised elbow where she grabbed me, and I wrenched my knee a bit."

"Damn, it liked to killed me when I hit the pavement," Krusoe said.

"Stu, what were they trying to do? Why would anyone want to kidnap you?"

He shrugged. "No idea. But after Krusoe broke it up, we got the cops involved. We had the tag number of the car they tried to shove me into. The cops'll be calling me here once they find the car and track down who was in it. They said they knew your number here."

"It's a small island, I'm sure they *do* know the number."

"It was a good block," Krusoe was saying. "I haven't played football since high school, but it all came back."

Cassidy was shaking her head. "Stu, obviously this all fits together somehow. Honker's murder, the attack on Felicity, last night's trouble here, and now someone attacking you. Something's going on, something downright scary."

"All the more reason to call in the local police for the whole thing, seems to me. Let's let them know what happened here, and maybe they can fit it together with what happened to me this morning."

Cassidy looked at him. It almost unnerved him. Her face. Those eyes. "You know what," she said, suddenly standing. "I think you're right. I wanted to wait, to figure it out first, the things with the financial reports, the dummy corporations, the way the money flows, all of that. But this is just too dangerous, and it's dragging you into it, too, now. I'm going to call." She walked over to the phone that sat on the kitchen countertop as Stu rose from his chair to join her. She flipped to the front of the little island phone book, hesitated for a moment, gathering her thoughts, then picked up the receiver, brought it to her ear. There was a puzzled look on her face. "Stu," she said, "the line's dead."

Then they heard a sound, a crackling noise that filtered its way past the soft sloughing of the wind through the pines and the distant roar of the surf. A crackling, a pop.

"Holy shit!" yelled Krusoe, looking out the side window, "get out of here — now! — the whole goddamn place is on fire!"

FORTY-FIVE

It took them both a few minutes to figure out what "Gear in boot" meant, but then they realized the boot was the car's trunk, and they opened it to find a pair of snorkeling masks, some fins and two snorkels.

"Samantha wants us to go for a swim, Michael," Fel said, holding up a mask.

"But why?"

"Privacy, maybe? No one else will be out there. Maybe she'll swim out to us, or come in a small boat to meet us. Or maybe she has something else in mind. Hard to say.'"

"But we're going to do this?" Michael had his doubts.

"Absolutely, Michael. This is what we came for, to talk to this Samantha and find out what your brother needs us to do. If this is how she wants to run this little meeting, I don't see how we have much choice."

"I don't like it, Fel."

She smiled at him. "I don't like it much, either, Michael. But let's do what we have to do, OK?"

He looked at her, nodded his head. "OK. All right. Let's get to Smith Cove and get this done."

"Right," she said, "but if we're going to meet her in the water we have to do a little shopping first, and that's probably why she gave us an hour. Let's go back into town and buy a couple of swimsuits and some sandwiches and then get back here to Smith Cove and out into the water."

A half-hour later the two of them sat atop a picnic table underneath the shade of a broad almond tree and finished the lunch they'd bought from the Wholesome Bakery on Church Street—a chicken salad sandwich for Felicity and a spicy Scotch meat pie for Michael. While they washed it down with soft drinks, the family they'd been sharing the small beach with packed up their own picnic lunch and drove away in a tiny Toyota van. Perfect timing.

Smith Cove turned out to be a tiny sand beach in the middle of a rocky, raised shoreline. It looked like the only place that offered easy access to the water for a mile or so on either side.

"OK, it's a little early, but let's be ready, Michael." Felicity said. She was wearing her new swimsuit, an overpriced one-piece from a shop on Cardinal Avenue. It had taken her awhile to get past the pain of her ribs as she put the suit on back in the change-room at the shop. Over it she wore her blue Crusaders t-shirt to keep off the sun.

"How do you figure she's going to meet us in the water?"

"I don't know. Like I said, maybe she'll come on a small boat or a jet-ski or something. But now that I see how this shoreline is, maybe she'll just wave to us from the shoreline and there'll be some other place we can come ashore, with steps cut into the rock or something.

"We'll just have to see how it goes, OK? I'll head down the beach that way, maybe twenty or thirty yards offshore, and you head up. Take a look around the shore every few minutes and wave to me and I'll do the same for you. That ought to cover our bases, right?"

He hesitated. "Shouldn't we stick together?"

She smiled. He wasn't, perhaps, the most courageous guy in the world. "It'll be all right. We'll never be more than a hundred yards apart or so, and we'll keep waving to stay in touch. All right?" And she headed into the water.

Michael nodded. She was the boss in this kind of stuff, no question about it. Then he watched as she got knee deep in the water, sat down to slip on the fins, spit into her mask and then rubbed the spittle around on the glass and then put it on, and then slowly, carefully pushed herself into deeper water and in another few seconds was swimming away toward the open Caribbean, her Crusader t-shirt a darker blue moving through the water's robin's-egg beauty.

Watching her, he thought maybe there was less pain for her in the water; she was moving along pretty good. God, she was something; he was still getting used to her beauty — thin but muscular, small breasts, that wonderful face, those long legs, her black hair pulled back into a ponytail for her swim. He thought of what it had been like making love with her, recalling the perfection of her skin, the delight they'd found in each other, the pearls of sweat on her upper lip as she sat atop him at one point, riding him, smiling, eyes half-closed as he rose and fell with her, lost in that moment forever while outside the swoosh of the waves rolling onto the beach sang a kind of background harmony. How lucky he was, how incredibly lucky.

And then he thought of Honker and what somebody from this paradise had done to him. All the beauty here hid something awful and that something had killed his brother. He shook his head. He was here to do what he had to do, not to look at the scenery.

He watched Felicity snorkel out to the rock point that defined the north side of Smith Cove and disappear past the rocks. Then he walked on down to the water himself, waded in, spit in the mask and swished that around, then went out a little deeper to put on the fins.

It was a beautiful little cove. She was a beautiful, wonderful woman. It was incredible, the contrast between this and the horror of what had happened to Honker. Incredible. He shook his head, slipped on the mask and fins, and headed out.

Across the street, parked in the little lot for the First Scotia Bank of The Cayman Islands, Robert Mackie watched impatiently. He was getting fidgety and knew it, but what the fuck did Brooks expect? Watching these two play cootchie-coo wasn't going to get the job done, now was it? Jesus he was getting to really hate them, the girl cop and her boyfriend. It was unprofessional, and he knew it, but he was really getting to hate them. Every time he turned around they were in the way again, and, goddamn it, his head still hurt from the baseball bat she'd hit him with back in Rum Point.

He'd been following them since they left the Reverend's place, keeping an eye on them at Parrot's Landing. That's where the Samantha bitch worked, so that was trouble and he'd called Brooks with the cell phone from down the road where he'd parked.

"Just stay with them," Brooks had said. "See where they go. Honker's girlfriend is gone, right? I mean, you didn't whack her like you were supposed to, but she isn't there, right?"

"Yeah. Right. She's gone," he'd said to Brooks. "But maybe she told someone in there where she was going?"

"You didn't check that?" Disbelief in Brooks' voice.

"No, we figured we'd find out from the roommate, and then that got all screwed up when Kelly lost her cool. Hell, I can go in there right now and find out everything you want to know, Brooks. Just say so and I'm in there."

"No, don't be even more of an idiot, Mackie. There'd be local cops all over the place in minutes. Too many friggin' tourists in there."

"I thought you had an arrangement with one of the local cops."

"I do, I do." He'd paused, "but I think what you have in mind might be a little hard to cover up."

He smiled. "Yeah. It would be, at that."

"So here's what you do. Wait for them, then follow them and see where they go, see who they meet. If the opportunity looks right, and you can make it look like an accident, then take care of them. But listen, damnit. Call me first. You got that? Call me and get the OK before you do anything other than just follow them, right?"

"Yeah, right," he'd said and hung up on him.

So was this the right moment? Hell, they were just swimming out there, playing around in the water. They hadn't met a fuckin' soul yet. It would be so easy right here. Both of them would go down as drowning. The girl going under and the boyfriend tries to save her and they both drown. Even better, dispose of their bodies out over the shelf where the water goes from forty feet deep to one-thousand feet deep and they'd be listed as missing and presumed drowned. That would work fine.

He grinned. He liked that little scenario, no question about it. Clean. No loose ends. But it would piss Brooks the hell off, since they hadn't met anybody yet. He tried to think it through, follow through what would happen if he whacked the two of them and did it right so it came off as an accident; and it seemed workable and good. Brooks would be fine with it, damn it. These two would be dead, and whatever they were onto would die with them. Then they could take care of the others up at the Reverend's place, get them done and over with, just keep the one girl — the roommate of Sam's — alive long enough to get what they needed from her, and then, if it was needed, maybe take care of one or two back at that Parrot's Landing place.

It would be wet, that was for sure. Wet and hairy. But that was part of the joy of his work, and a man wants to be happy at work. Then it would be over. Done.

He nodded his head, like he was talking to somebody about it and agreeing. He laughed at himself for that, the first good chuckle he'd had in days. All right, then. All-fucking-right. Take care of this punk girl cop and her boyfriend and everything else would fall into place after that.

He watched through the windshield as the guy grabbed his mask and snorkel and fins and headed toward the water. OK, then, all the easier this way. Mackie smiled. He loved the water here, where everything was crystal clear. He snorkeled and scuba dived here every chance he got. He knew these reefs like the back of his hand. And he'd been trained in the water, had killed some people in the water in the Nam back when he was a teenager and then later in Nicaragua. He enjoyed it, enjoyed keeping them under until they got quiet and it was over. It was a very satisfying thing, really. Strength against strength and then very, very satisfying.

He got out, walked around to the trunk and opened it, pulled off his pants and shirt, slid a pair of swim trunks on over his undershorts, grabbed his snorkeling gear that he kept in the trunk, slammed the lid shut, then started walking over to Smith Cove.

His cell phone started ringing. He'd left it in the car, of course, and had to dig in his pocket for the car key, open the door and grab the phone.

It was Brooks, pissed as hell at Kelly Ennis and ready to get something done about it. Brooks had a new job for him. Something fun. Well, OK.

He hung up, tossed the phone into the car and locked the door. OK, Ennis: but first he had to deal with these two lovebirds. The guy was already out of sight, the girl with him somewhere out there, diving around looking at all the pretty brain coral and the parrotfish and the little angelfish. He sat down at the edge of the water, pulled on the fins, shoved himself into the water easily. He loved it here, the water as warm as blood. He loved it, and loved his work, looked forward to it as he pulled on the mask and snorkel, started swimming easily out into the deeper water, looking around. It was going to be an interesting afternoon. The visibility was great.

FORTY-SIX

George Brooks was thinking that change is good, change is necessary. It had been a really interesting last hour or two.

For starters, the guesthouse had burned like a son of a bitch. He hadn't seen a fire that satisfying since the eighties, in that little beaner village in Nicaragua — San Pedro del Something — when the whole place went up in flames to teach the locals a little lesson about how important it was to support their Contra freedom fighters.

The first change in plans had come to him a brilliant flash of genius when he'd been driving up West Bay Road. There was no need to wait until tonight and he didn't have to burn down the whole place, he could just torch the guesthouse. He chewed on the idea as he drove, thinking it through while cruising along like a friggin' tourist. In a good mood, he even left the windows down to enjoy the sea breeze, happy that things were breaking his way for a change. As long as the flash drive that Kelsey had stolen didn't show up, then burning down the guesthouse would get rid of all the hard proof about the whole project. The information on the guesthouse computer was all coded, but even without the flash drive's coding software he'd always have to worry about somebody getting that information and breaking the code on their own — there'd never been a code that somebody good couldn't break, that's what they always said at Langley. So the best thing to do was torch the guesthouse and everything would be fine — a few suspicions, maybe, but no paper trail. That would leave Kelsey's stolen flash drive as the only thing he had to worry about. He could stop and buy a ten gig flash drive at that computer store on West Bay, load that thing up himself from the computer's hard-drive, then melt the computer down by torching the guesthouse

Damn, but it had been a long, hard haul putting all this together — getting Sergei and his Russian pals together with Gabriel and his beaner amigos in Bogotá and Cali. Sergei had all that friggin' money and a nice distribution system in Europe. Gabriel had product, but he'd been losing his little war with the Nicaraguans, who wanted into the business themselves and were enjoying the luxury of all that old CIA-supplied armament, friggin' tanks for Christ's sake. Right time and right place for somebody who knew everybody in the business; friggin' everybody, on all sides. So he'd stepped in, offered his services to help them both out, helped ship product for arms and then even some Cuban mercs. Helped get the steady pipeline heading to Rotterdam and then, even better, to Tallin, gateway to Russian addiction and Rostock, up north of Hamburg. It didn't take long and there was money flowing every which way, and he could see the need for better ways to clean up all the profits. That, and once the Coast Guard put the pressure on the Eastern Caribbean he'd needed a place in the Western Caribbean to do all the grunt warehouse work. Enter the Reverend, and his minority interest in a failing baseball club after that strike about ruined everything in big-league baseball and the whole league was in the dumps. Plus, the Rev had the place in the Caymans. Plus, he was too simple a guy to have an inkling of what was really up.

Anyway you cut it, it was perfect. The Reverend got some needed cash and didn't ask any questions. Sergei and Gabriel needed a nice little laundry and a deepwater port not too far from Cuba and the Gulf basin. Perfect, perfect, perfect. And then with the final stroke of perfection: the deal with Kelly Ennis that turned the whole thing on its ear and got him out of it with a clean record and enough money to last a few lifetimes. It was too bad that he couldn't let Mackie in on all the details, but at some point in life you had to get a little selfish, and he could explain it to Mackie later, after the fact, when he paid him off. That'd be fun, to see how Mackie reacted when he found out the real story about Kelly Ennis.

It had been hard goddamn work, too, despite all the connections. There'd been a point in time, about three years ago, when he was starting to think it couldn't be done, despite all the people he knew and the people they knew and the people they knew. Frankly, they were all too friggin' greedy and self-centered. But that, in the end, was exactly why he'd managed to pull it together. He was the one guy in the right spot to be in the center of it all, tentacles out everywhere and not too greedy, let it trickle in from both directions—from all three directions when he played the company card with the agency, too. A million here, a few hundred thousand there, a couple of million over there.

In his first year with the Reverend, when he'd been building up this whole thing, the old guy had taken him over to the aquarium in St. Pete, showed him the place, stood there by the huge glass wall of the main tank when staff divers started feeding all the fish. The Reverend had gone on and on about fishes in the sea and tending his flock and how important the Ministry was to millions of people. What Brooks had seen in there were the sharks, who pretty much had it their way. Or even better, the octopus down in the bottom, hiding in the rocks, tentacles out where he wanted them, invisible but in touch with it all, safe and sound and very, very comfortable. That was the moment, looking at that octopus, when he knew that, eventually, it was all going to work.

When he'd gotten to the Reverend's place it didn't look like anyone was in there, but he couldn't be sure so he parked the car across the street and took a quick little walk around the place, checking it out, thinking about how there were enough records in that computer's hard-drive to put them all away forever, thick files of the stuff if someone got it and put it all together. He'd have to go live in friggin' Patagonia or somewhere if that got out before he was ready; just clear out the Swiss accounts and get lost in the Third World and if it comes to living like that, then it was all no use anyway. So, the hell with it, burn the guesthouse down along with the contents of the computer and the filing cabinet and there wouldn't be any proof of anything anywhere except on the flash drive he'd load up here and on his backup drive back in St. Pete, and he'd keep them safe enough. Once he was done with Kelly Ennis he'd keep his copy for some self-protection and kill everything else, wipe the computer's hard drive, delete the whole software package and all its documents. It would take five minutes, maybe, and that would be it. Done.

And the guesthouse was perfect for a fire. Wooden roof and concrete walls, it would chimney right up. This even solved the Honker Kelsey problem, since the codes Kelsey had put on that friggin' flash drive wouldn't matter if the coded data from the QuickBooks file wasn't around. Even better, the guesthouse was mostly hidden from view of the main house, tucked back behind a little garden, edged with casuarina trees and filled with a bunch of flowering hibiscus and a few palm trees. He'd be careful about getting back there. If Cassidy Craig saw him it might mean he'd have to get ugly with her, and he didn't want to do that until he had to. So he'd keep behind the bushes and edge along behind some low palms, and then work his way past the casuarinas and around to the back of the guesthouse, out of sight of the main house.

It all went fine; anyone who was around was in the main house. So once he was sure it was clear enough he got busy. The little maintenance shed was just on the other side of some trees. He walked through some more casuarinas over to it, got three of the five-gallon gas cans, brought them back, bitching to himself about how unexpectedly heavy they were. He opened the lock to the side door of the guesthouse with his key, got inside and sat down at the computer. It took him ten minutes, no more, to shove the flash drive into the port and drag everything into it. He shoved that into its little plastic case and put it into his right front pants pocket and then picked up the gas cans and got busy, pouring out the gasoline on the computer and all over the desk, splashing a lot of it on the wooden floor, the sidewalls, all of it in that one room. He wasn't too worried about arson investigations. If the locals thought something was up, he'd pay his way out of it — no problem, mon. The building would go up like a matchbox. Then he walked back to the door, turned around to take a look at things, liked what he saw, and lit a wadded-up ball of paper and tossed it in. The whoomph of the gas igniting was impressive as hell as he shut the door and walked briskly away, retracing his path.

Across the street was a little shopping center, with an upstairs cafe, the Pirate's Cove. He was up there sipping on an iced tea fifteen minutes later when the fire brigade arrived, and eating a grouper sandwich as they struggled to get the hoses connected and throw some water on it while the place went up like a torch.

He was on his second iced tea, smoking a cigarette and thinking about some dessert, when the second change of the afternoon appeared. He saw Cassidy Craig come out of the main house with a girl he didn't know, and then behind them came Stu Lindsay.

Lindsay? What the hell was he doing down here? The friggin' Crusaders had the most important game of the year starting in a few hours and their manager was down here in the islands hanging out with the boss' daughter? Didn't make any damn sense. Then he smiled, remembering. Hell, the drug goodies back at the ballpark must have been found — Roberto doing his job just like he was supposed to and then Sam Barnett, the old security guard, taking advice from his boss and checking out the manager's desk. And so the roof fell in on the Crusader manager and when the shit hit the fan he came running, down here with his new girlfriend, Cassidy Craig. It all fit together pretty good once you thought it through. He smiled. Lindsay and Cassidy Craig. He'd wondered a little bit about that, about how they looked at each other, how careful they were when they were together. So Stu Lindsay was so shook up by what they'd found that he'd come running to jump on young Cassidy's bones. Well, well. Interestinger and interestinger.

And then another change: a taxi showed up, weaving its way through the two trucks from the fire brigade and on toward the house. And god-friggin' damn if the Reverend himself didn't climb right out of the back seat, toss a few bucks toward the driver and then walk over to where Cassidy and Stu Lindsay stood, staring at the smoking remains of the guesthouse. Well goddamn. All the better, Brooks thought. All the friggin' better.

Then came the life-changer, the Big Change in Plans. His cell phone rang. Mackie again? Probably, since not many people had this GSM cell number, the one he kept private since it worked from here back to St. Pete. He pulled it out from his pocket, flipped it open, said "Yeah?"

"Mr. Brooks?"

"Yeah, Who's this?"

"It's Doctor Springler. We have the results from those X-rays."

Oh, Jesus. He'd managed to put that out of his mind since yesterday, when he'd stopped in at Springler's and had him check out the cough. The doc had insisted on the friggin' X-rays, just a precaution, he said, nothing to worry about, probably. Still, best to be on the safe side and all that. Yeah, yeah, Brooks had left him this number. Just in case. Nothing to worry about, but just in case.

"Mr. Brooks, there's no easy way to put this. The chest X-ray and blood tests do not look good."

"What do you mean they don't look good?"

There was a pause, Brooks could almost hear the doc sorting through how to say it, so, Christ, it had to be bad.

"Mr. Brooks, the chest x-ray shows a mass on the right side of your chest and a widened mediastinum. And your blood tests," there was another pause. "Your blood tests show elevated liver function studies."

"What's that mean, doc? That's cancer, right?"

Springler paused a third time, then "Yes. Yes, Mr. Brooks, I'm afraid that is probably the case. I think you have lung cancer that has spread to the lymph nodes and to the liver."

"OK, what do we do about this, doc?"

"First, you need to get back here so we can do a biopsy to determine what type of lung cancer you have. Once we know that then we can proceed with treatment, which will likely involve chemotherapy and perhaps radiation."

Jesus, he was a dead man, sounded like. God, the whole friggin' world was spinning on him. He grabbed the side of the table, thought about picking up the iced tea to take a sip but he'd probably just drop the damn thing

179

and call attention to himself, to the death sentence he was hearing over his goddamn cell phone.

He took a deep breath, steadied himself. "Doctor, can this thing be beat? Is there a cure?"

Another goddamn pause. "Well, there are some very promising new drugs coming on the market — they're called angiogenesis inhibitors and they work by cutting off the tumor's supply of oxygen and nutrients, and therefore its continued growth. These drugs have done very well in clinical trials."

"And I can get those drugs? They'll cure me?"

Springler had seemed to think that through. "These are very promising studies we're seeing, Mr. Brooks, but it's much too soon in their development to say very much for certain. The important thing is that we get you back here as soon as possible."

"So they won't cure me?"

"That's just not the sort of thing I can answer for you, Mr. Brooks. Every case is different. Cure of lung cancer is generally achieved only if the patient is a surgical candidate, and once the cancer has spread to the lymph nodes and the liver, surgery is really no longer an option. But with these promising new drugs..."

Oh Christ. That really was it, then.

The doc was still talking, "...but chemotherapy and radiation are fine for palliation — they should buy you some time, and then perhaps we'll find something effective for you from there."

"And it's spread to the nodes and the liver, like you say, right?"

"Yes, I think that's likely. The widened mediastinum on chest X-ray means it's virtually certain that the cancer has spread to lymph nodes in the central chest."

"And that's not good."

"Correct, it's not good. You really do need to get back into the office as quickly as you can, Mr. Brooks. I'd like to see you today or tomorrow, if that's possible."

Brooks had laughed. When it friggin' rains it surely does pour. "Sure, doc. Tomorrow. I'll be there in the afternoon, OK? I'm a little busy here right now and I'm not really able to get to your office, but tomorrow for sure." Not that it would do any friggin' good.

"Just come in anytime, Mr. Brooks and we'll get you right in. We can discuss all this in more detail then."

"Yeah, doc. I'll be there," he said, and clicked the phone off.

Well, shit. Lung cancer. A death sentence. Goddamn it.

He'd held up his cigarette, watched it smoking there in front of him. Finally got me, you son of a bitch. Oh, Jesus friggin' Christ.

Then he'd taken a long drag on it, his last, he figured, and then stubbed it out.

Well, Christ Almighty, this changed things, this really changed things. Change: that was the word for the day.

FORTY-SEVEN

Felicity had been snorkeling a few times in Florida, the first time in Homosassa Springs, the second time on a trip down to Marathon in the Keys. She'd been amazed then at what you could see — the turmoil at the bottom of the springs where the water came roiling up from the aquifer below, and then the coral and fish all over the reef a mile or two out from Marathon. There she'd seen a couple of big lobsters hiding down in the rocks and then, on her swim back to the dive-boat, she'd been tailed by a barracuda that was bigger than she was, drifting along behind her, keeping pace. It never came too close, but it'd sure made things interesting there for a while, adding a dark little edge to the beauty of the surroundings.

But even that was nothing like this. The water here was so clear, and so filled with tropical fish and huge mounds of coral, that it made her forget for a few moments why she'd come down here to the island, why she was swimming here at all. It was almost mystical, drifting through the warm water with just the barest flick of the ankles pushing the fins up and down to move her through the azure silence. On her right the rock wall that formed the northern edge of the cove cut straight down to the sea bottom, some fifteen feet down. The edge of the wall was alive with moving and swirling clouds of small blue and yellow fish. As she swam up to them the clouds broke and moved past her, reforming behind as she turned to watch. It was an amazing sight.

She realized that for the first time in two days her ribs didn't hurt. She'd gotten to where she wasn't paying much attention to the constant background pain of the ribs, just moving cautiously when she had to in order to avoid the sharp jolt of pain that could take her breath away. Now, with the water supporting her body, her breathing smooth and easy through the snorkel, and with the slight movement of her legs her only physical exertion, the pain was gone. She wanted to stay in here forever.

She moved away from the wall and out toward deeper water, where huge brain corals rose in isolated mounds from the sandy bottom. An unlikely pair of big stingrays swam by a coral mound off to her right, looking like they were flying, wings waving up and down as they cruised near the bottom. She heard they weren't dangerous, but decided not to get close enough to test that rumor. They were impressive as hell even from thirty yards away. And then, out where the water got really deep, she saw a movement, something big. She stopped, then peered ahead, trying to see what it was. A shark? Oh, hell, she hoped not. A barracuda? A lot less dangerous, everyone said, but still...

It was a sea turtle. It slowly swam toward her, a big one so not a Kemp's ridley she guessed from what Michael had told her. A greenback? Probably so. She'd seen a few of those on the beach up in Rum Point. She watched it approach, those big front flippers pulling it through the water, maybe twenty feet down but rising fast as it neared her, looking like it had a destination in mind, like it wasn't just drifting along aimlessly.

It kept coming toward her and she started backpedaling. They weren't dangerous, as far as she knew, but what was it doing coming right at her like this? It was within ten yards when it made a graceful angle to its left, pulled hard with those flippers, and arrowed toward the surface. There was a jellyfish there, a big round one, the kind they called moonjellies back home in Rum Point. She hadn't seen it, too busy looking down to notice the jellyfish so close to her. They had drifting stingers, those moonjellies, and in another few feet she would have found out about them, painfully. But not now. The greenback opened its large jaws and plowed right into the thing, flipping the head once to break the jellyfish apart and then, while she watched, gulping the parts down and then, without a backward glance, heading off back toward the deeper water. In a few seconds it was out of sight, into the deep, heading wherever greenbacks go.

She'd lost all track of time, she realized. Had she been in the water for five minutes? Twenty? She didn't know, and poor Michael was swimming around over there waiting for her to pop up and wave. She did that, and saw him in the distance waving. She waved back, which immediately brought back the pain, so much of it that she wished she hadn't promised him she'd keep waving. Still, everything was fine for the moment. She put her face back into the water, breathed through the snorkel, slowly headed north up the rock wall, thinking of Michael Kelsey. She was really falling for him, hard, and liked the thought of it. He was as kind and gentle a man as any she'd known — as gentle as her father, for that matter. She could see why he loved the sea and the things in it so much. He'd be terribly excited to hear about her encounter with the turtle and her sighting of the stingrays. He'd want to know all the details.

She surfaced, floated for a minute, took off her facemask to take a good look around and get her bearings. She was facing north, the rock wall to her right and the cove behind her maybe a hundred yards away. She grabbed the mask to pull it down onto her face and saw, over toward the rock wall, down at the bottom, some motion, like someone waving. The girl from the shop? Maybe, and she certainly had to find out so she headed that way, swimming as hard as she could. She tried using her arms, pushing them out in front together and then bringing them back to her side, helping increase her speed. It helped speed things up, but there was too much pain from the ribs to do it more than once. Instead, she just left her arms at her side and let the fins do the work. No pain that way and still pretty good speed.

She found, too, that it was easier to swim just under the water, keeping an eye out through the mask for whoever it was. Once or twice she paused, lifted her head to look, and then put her face back into the water and started kicking hard again, seeing nothing. It couldn't have been more than a minute or two and she was at the rock wall, but there was no one there, just the clouds of tropical fish and the translucent splash of the small waves against the wall, white bubbles tumbling through the water after each collision of water and rock.

Nothing. Where had she gone? Was it the girl or maybe someone else, maybe something else, a fish? She started to doubt herself, not sure she'd seen much of anything at all. Still, she swam along, heading slowly toward the cove but watching the wall all the while. No reason not to keep looking here. Then she saw a leg, right in the wall, a woman's leg with a huge fin on it. Then both legs, and the rest of the swimmer. She realized there was a little cave there, cut into the wall, half of it above water. The front edge of it had hidden most of the person from view.

The woman waved to her, gave her a thumbs up and then surfaced. Felicity surfaced, too. When they pulled their masks off Felicity could see it wasn't the girl from the shop, but some other woman, black-haired, pretty face, a little older, maybe thirty.

"Hey," the woman said, "I found you. Great."

"OK, you found me. Now who the hell are you?"

The woman smiled, said "Where's your boyfriend?"

"He's out there," she pointed out to the open water, "looking for whoever left us that note. I take it that's you?"

"Yep, I'm the one, Felicity," the woman said. "Look, I have a lot of answers for you, but we have to keep this very quiet, OK? You go get Michael and bring him here and I'll tell you all about it. There are some things about Honker's death that Michael needs to know."

Felicity didn't know if she could trust this woman, but she didn't see where she had a lot of choice if they were going to find out anything.

"You can get us to Samantha?" Felicity asked, and the woman smiled and nodded, said, "Sure can. And soon."

"All right, then, I'll go get Michael and we'll swim back this way. You keep an eye out for us and lead us back in here, right?"

The woman nodded, and Felicity slipped her mask on and disappeared under the water, out to find Michael. So maybe they would get some answers here after all. She didn't like all the mystery that seemed to be part of the package, but there didn't seem to be much she could do about that, and it did sound like this girl knew something, so that might make all this silliness worthwhile. All she needed to do was get out in the open a bit, away from the wall, and then surface and look for Michael. He'd be keeping an eye out for her, surely. She'd wave him over and then could get back there and find out what this woman had to say.

There was one big coral outcrop to get past, one so tall that it nearly broke the surface, surrounded by fish and covered with coral fans waving in the current. She headed around its right side and saw Michael swimming toward her, moving along pretty quickly, looking straight at her. He seemed to recognize her and waved. She waved back.

But there was another snorkeler out there, too, behind Michael. A good swimmer, judging by how hard he was pumping with those fins, coming their way. Felicity waved at Michael, pointed back toward the other snorkeler, and he stopped, turned to look, and then turned back to Felicity. He waved at her, his palm out as if shoving her away, telling her to get away.

And then she saw, as the other snorkeler got close, what he was carrying in his right hand. A barb, like a small harpoon, its arrowed front edge bright in the clear water.

He held it out in front of himself, turning himself into a kind of under-water missile, a torpedo, swimming right at Michael, pointed edge forward, no more than twenty yards separating the two of them. Felicity, too far away to help, could only watch as her lover turned to face his attacker.

FORTY-EIGHT

Stu kicked at a piece of black, carboned wood, knocking it a few feet toward the beach and the gentle sea. He shook his head. "Was it arson?" he asked the short, stocky guy in the shorts and a white, short-sleeved shirt that said "R. Retief, CFB Inspector" in two rows of small letters over the heart. He carried a metal clipboard, one of those with a cover on it, and was taking notes as he walked through, room to room.

"Too early to say, sir," the inspector said with that island lilt in his voice. It sounded odd, that island accent that you wanted to associate with rum drinks and sunshine and blue sea talking to you, coming to you from someone who was checking into whether someone had tried to burn a build-ing down around your ears.

The inspector had more to say. "I can't be certain yet, sir, but it cer-tainly does look suspicious. Here, I'll show you these scorch marks." He pulled Stu by the arm over to the door frame for the back door of the guest-house. All four walls, made from concrete block, still stood. The roof was gone and the inside of the guesthouse, most of it wood, was a blackened ruin.

"Here, see this?" the inspector was pointing at the inside of the back wall, where what had been a computer sat on the floor, melted and the hous-ing cracked open, wires everywhere, tilted against what was left of a desk. Behind it there were scorch marks climbing to where there had been a ceil-ing. "It looks like something flammable, gasoline I'd guess, got this fire going right in this spot." He looked around. "You know, sir, you're very fortunate that this didn't jump across the roof to the main house. A little later in the day, with the sea breeze blowing, and the main house might well have gone up, as well."

"And us in it."

"Well, I hope not that, sir" the inspector said with a slight smile, "and in any event, it didn't jump and you're fine." He shut the metal lid on his clipboard. "You can look around for a few minutes, but please be careful, right? Don't touch anything, let the investigation run its course."

The inspector walked back through the door frame and out as Stu stared at the devastation. He heard someone behind him, turned to see who it was, then offered a tired smile as Cassidy came up to put her arms around his waist and lean against him for a welcome hug.

"Stu, this is all so terrifying," she said. "This could have been the main house. This could have been us."

Stu nodded and held her tight. It felt very strange to do that with a woman, hold one tight like this. It felt strange and wonderful and now somehow dangerous. What the hell was going on? He didn't have any answers, and he didn't like that. He was a lot more comfortable when the questions were clear and the answers were available. On a ballfield he knew what to do. Here, now, there was no one in relief, no one to pinch hit for him.

Cassidy looked at the wreckage, murmured almost absentmindedly, "I left Robin inside with Krusoe. She's so terrified by all this that it hurts just to watch her, Stu. She's trembling." Then she shook her head, added, "And I'm not sure Krusoe is doing much better. For all the hot air and bombast he comes across with, he's no great superhero when it comes to the real thing. He looks as terrified as she does."

Stu managed a small smile. "He's got a right to be scared. Hell, I'm certainly scared, too." He held out his right hand in front of his face, palm down, rock steady. He hadn't lost it completely then, yet. And, he thought, he hadn't had a drink in several hours.

Cassidy was looking toward the far wall where the ruined computer sat. "Oh, Stu, look at that."

"Yeah, that computer's melted down to the metal. Whatever the hell this is about, that's where the real story was I bet, in that computer."

She left him, walked carefully over to the computer, stepping over the wet, black remnants of a chair, two of its legs jutting up from half-consumed bottom. She stared at the ruin. Nodded her head. "You're right, Stu. They burned this to wipe out the computer's memory." She looked at him, about to add something, then seemed to think better of it.

Stu nodded. "Makes sense. Burn this down and the proof is gone. Whatever's going on, no one can prove it now." He left unsaid the implications, about her father, about herself. Could she be in on this somehow? Was the Reverend in on it? He didn't think Cassidy could be. To be more truthful, he didn't want to think that. If she was, then he was in way, way over his head and he ought to leave right now, get his daughter, head back to St. Pete and the team and baseball, something he understood and could deal with. If she wasn't involved, OK, he had to help and do what he could. If she wasn't involved, then she and Fel were working on this with Fel's friend, Michael, and now Stu was here, had come on his own, and so was in on it, too.

He shook his head, puzzling it through. Too many possibilities. What was his father always talking about: multiverses, cosmic bubbles, quantum bouncing? A guy out at Stanford, Andre Linze, had been a doctoral student of his father's some fifteen years ago and wound up doing his research on those bubbles. The universe, our universe, our reality, is really nothing but a tiny part of one bubble, one reality, producing its own new bubbles even as it spins off from someone else's bubble, their reality, their universe. Every moment, every fraction of a moment, spins off its own possibilities.

A woman gets off a train and turns left and the Crusaders win the pennant. She turns right and the Crusaders don't even exist, or have another name and the city isn't St. Petersburg but something else in some other reality where the president isn't a woman and there are more than forty-seven states and there isn't a Cassidy Craig, and somewhere, somewhere, Carmen was still alive and that world was a little better place.

"That's it," he heard his father say, "You're beginning to get it, son. Now you're thinking."

Stu glanced around. He checked his left pocket. The cell phone was still there, and still turned off. He thought about turning it on, letting his father call and then talking it all through. But he didn't. That was the last damn thing he needed. But was he hearing the old man now without the phone being on? He shook his head. That couldn't be good.

"It's terrible," Cassidy was saying, misreading that head shake. "To think that someone could be doing this with Daddy's ministry? It's awful."

He looked at her. He hoped to god that the Reverend was somehow innocent in the middle of all this crap. Stu didn't know how that was possible; but please let it be that way, for Cassidy's sake, if nothing else.

The inspector came back in. "Someone here to see you two," he said, "and the chief inspector is here now, too. Time to get you out of here."

They followed him back outside, saying hello to the officious looking

187

chief inspector on his way past them, wearing a severe blue tie with his long-sleeved white shirt despite the heat. Then, coming around the corner of the building they saw, over by a taxi that must have just pulled up, the Reverend, standing there with one hand over his eyes as he squinted at them in the hard sunshine. "Cassie!" he yelled, waving his arm over his head. "Cassie, dear, over here!"

Cassidy ran to her father and the two hugged tightly. It was too real a moment, Stu thought, to be faked. Cassidy was either a hell of an actress or she genuinely wasn't involved and didn't think her father was involved, either — in cooking the books, in cooking this building *and* the books, in fact. Stu hoped she couldn't act worth a damn. The Reverend certainly didn't seem like the type, but could he be that ignorant of what was going on? Maybe, or maybe this was all part of some act he was putting on, some great deceit, something worth living a lie with your own daughter about.

"Good Lord," the Reverend said as Stu walked over to where father and daughter stood. "What has happened here? The guesthouse burned down? Are you two all right?"

"We're fine, Daddy," Cassidy said. "And there are two others in the main house — they're fine, too."

"Two others?" The Reverend, probably tired from the flight, seemed pretty confused. He stared at the ruined guesthouse, smoke and steam still rising from the ashes. "The guesthouse burned down? Are you two all right?" he asked again.

"We're fine, Daddy. We're fine," said Cassidy, putting her arm around his waist and trying to begin to tug him toward the main house and away from the scene.

But the Reverend resisted her pull. He looked at Stu. "The guesthouse burned down?" Then something clicked, his eyes narrowed. "I'm surprised to find you here, Stu."

"I'm surprised to see you here, too, Reverend."

The Reverend shrugged his shoulders. "My daughter needed me and I came, Stu. It's that simple."

Stu smiled at him. "Me, too, Reverend. Felicity is down here with Cassidy and she called me about this break-in thing. I came on the first flight I could catch this morning."

The Reverend looked surprised at that and then brightened. "That's right, the break-in. That's why I came. And now the guesthouse is burned down?"

"And they say it's probably arson, Daddy," Cassidy said.

"Arson? They burned it down on purpose? The guesthouse?" He was grappling with the whole idea. "Good Lord, why would someone...?" He couldn't finish the thought. He looked at Stu. "That's why you're here, Stu? I thought perhaps..." He let it trail off.

"Perhaps what, Reverend?"

The Reverend frowned, like he was working hard to stay locked into what he wanted to say. "I don't know, Stu. There was something ... some trouble..."

"Trouble?" Stu asked. "Something to do with Sonny Dickerson?" He shook his head. Violence? More drugs? It had to be something like that. Dickerson might have snapped, gone berserk. Maybe he tore up the club-house or maybe he overdosed and they found his body, nose full of powder. Had to be something terrible or the Reverend wouldn't have that look on his face.

But the Reverend couldn't come up with it. Instead, with pursed lips and a slight shake of his head, he reached into his pants pocket and pulled out a cell phone. He opened it, hit one button and put the phone to his ear, waited for a few seconds, then said with a voice that sounded pretty damn lost: "Alice?"

Alice must have answered, so the Reverend's phone worked here. Stu wondered how that was possible as the Reverend said, "Yes, Alice. I'm here in George Town with Stu Lindsay." He paused. "Yes, Stu is here. There was something I needed to tell him, wasn't there?" Another long pause. "Yes, yes, that's it. Of course that's it. Thank you, thank you, Alice."

He seemed about to hang up but stopped. "Really? Sonny Dickerson? Why would he want to do something like that?" Another pause. "Well, I don't know, Alice, I just don't know."

He paused again, frowning. Saw Stu watching him, seemed to recall something. "Alice, Stu Lindsay is here. Wasn't there something I needed to tell him?" He listened. Nodded. Listened again. He shut the phone.

"Stu," he said, "this is the sort of thing that's hard to believe."

Stu just stared back at the man, his imagination taking right off again, another rocket zooming up into outer space. Oh, shit. He'd been fired. That son-of-a-bitch Brooks must have fired his ass. That had to be it.

The Reverend's eyes narrowed. He was trying to remember something. This time it came to him. "They found things in your desk, Stu. Drug material. Some of that crack cocaine, they say. Awful things."

Stu's head was spinning. Drug material? Cocaine? "I don't understand, Reverend. In my desk? There's nothing in my desk but paperwork. And why was Security checking my desk, anyway?"

The Reverend focused, struggled to remember. What had Alice said? He couldn't quite pull it all in, but he remembered enough of it: "Security was checking in your office desk for the keys to the training room, and instead they found drugs, Stu. Cocaine, I think, and some other things. Drug things."

Oh, Christ almighty. It had to be a set-up, and now by leaving town to come down here it looked like he'd fled the country. What a damn mess. Stu shook his head. "You know better than that, Reverend. Listen, I found drugs the other day in the locker room, one of the players..."

But the Reverend wasn't listening. And what the hell had that been about Sonny Dickerson, Stu wondered. Well, no use asking about that now. The poor Reverend; his short-term memory seemed about a minute long, maybe less.

The Reverend was looking around, staring for a few seconds at the burned guesthouse. "What happened here? The guesthouse has burned?"

He turned to look at his daughter, reached out to sweep the hair from her forehead, the way he must have done when she was ten. "Are you two all right?" His hand shook some as he brushed her bangs back.

Cassidy just smiled at her father, realizing now completely what was happening to him. It was Alzheimer's, it had to be. And she realized, having that thought, that here at last was the thing she'd been looking for, the purpose to her life that she'd been seeking in drugs and men and everywhere else. Her whole life her father had been the unassailable moral force in her life, the perfect symbol of selfless love. She'd rebelled against that a hundred times, but now, here, this instant and moving forward until it was done, she could reject that rebellion. She could love him back at last. She could be the daughter she'd always meant to be.

"Stu," she said, turning to face him. She had to somehow explain this to him. She needed to tell someone of this revelation and he was the one person on the whole planet that she could actually talk to now. "Stu, I want you to know something..." But that was as far as she got, as the screen door of the Reverend's house slammed back behind him and Stu turned to look. It was Nick Krusoe rumbling through. Great. How long had he been there, inside, listening?

Krusoe walked the thirty feet over to where they stood. "Hi, Reverend. Saw you drive up. It's real interesting that you're here. It's real interesting, in fact, that we're all here."

"Who's this?" the Reverend wanted to know.

Krusoe looked at Stu. "So, Stu. You got big problems back home, pal. I was just on the phone to my editor. You know what they found in your office?"

"It was a plant, Krusoe. They're trying to set me up."

"So you do know." He looked at the Reverend, smiled at him. "You must have brought the news, Reverend. Seems pretty funny, wouldn't you say, you coming here to tell Stu they found all that stuff in his desk?"

"Who's this?" the Reverend asked again, looking to Cassidy for help. "And what's he talking about?"

"Nick Krusoe, Dad. He's a sportswriter, doing a piece on Stu."

The Reverend hung onto that for a moment, smiled at Cassidy, caught a fragment of memory that was sailing by and said "I'm here for my daughter, Mr. Krusoe. That's all. She called me and I'm here."

"Sure, Reverend, and Stu just happens to be here, too."

Krusoe ran his hand over his balding head — patting back into place the thin, wispy strands of brown hair that he combed over the top. He shook his head. "Damn thing is, I think you're probably telling me the truth, both of you. Hell, I've seen enough in the past few hours..."

"Reverend," Stu said, breaking into Krusoe's train of thought, "speaking of daughters, I still haven't found mine. She's on some wild goose chase with that Michael Kelsey kid, and they haven't come back yet. If you don't mind, I think I'll go look for those two and bring them back here." He looked at Cassidy. "You want to come along? You know this island a lot better than I do."

She wanted to come just as much as he wanted her to, but she was torn, he could see. "I think I'll hang around with the Reverend for a while, Stu. We've got some catching up to do." Which really meant, Stu knew, that she was so worried about her father that she didn't want to let him out of her sight. Not with all this stuff going on. Not with the way he was acting.

But the Reverend wouldn't hear of it, and even got angry. "I'll be fine, Cassidy," he insisted, his voice sharp with insistence. "You go with Stu and find those two and get them back here."

The Reverend looked at Nick Krusoe. "And you go with them, sir. I'll

191

be just fine here. I need a little time to sit and think all by myself, if you all don't mind."

"Daddy, are you sure?"

"Positive. You all clear out for a while, all right? Leave me be for a bit and then we'll all get everything sorted out when you get back."

"We'll take Robin along with us, Daddy. That'll give you a nice quiet house for a couple of hours."

"Who's Robin?"

"Someone we met here, Daddy. Someone in trouble. She was part of why that break-in happened last night, maybe the main part. She's staying with us for now."

"Well, take her with you, too," the Reverend said.

Stu could see what was going on. The Reverend was pretty shook up. Maybe a little alone time would help him. Stu looked at Cassidy and nodded. "All right. Your father will be fine here, I'm sure, Cassidy."

She nodded back. "I'll leave him my cell phone and check in with him every now and then, too." She smiled at Stu, "But only after I give him an hour or two for his daily nap, all right?"

The Reverend was shaking his head, the little flash of anger gone, buried beneath the confusion. "Burned down the Ministry's guesthouse?" It was hard for him to get his mind around that, apparently. Then he focused in again. "Are you two all right?" Then he looked at Krusoe. "And who are you?"

The chief investigator came over to them, wearing another of those long-sleeved white shirts with "S. Liburd, CFB" in two lines over the heart. "We'll be leaving for now," he said, "but we'll need statements from all of you in a couple of hours. I should warn you that arson investigations can take quite some time. You'll be free to leave the island after we get the statements, but you'll have to come back soon, I'm afraid."

The Reverend frowned, his mind backtracking again. "Arson? They burned it down on purpose? The guesthouse? Good Lord, why would someone..." One more time he couldn't even finish the thought.

"Daddy," Cassidy said, taking him by the elbow and slipping her cell phone into his pants pocket. "Let me walk you into the house, all right? I have a couple of things to tell you before I leave."

"Surely, dear," he said, and went along with her.

FORTY-NINE

The Reverend hadn't cried in fifteen years, not since Emily died. But here he was standing in the kitchen, looking out toward the still smoking ruins of the guesthouse, and the tears were streaming down his face. Lord, it's hard seeing the work of a lifetime in ruins.

He was seeing it clearly. He could feel it in his own mind, the fog clearing for the moment. This wasn't just the guesthouse burning down, it was the whole ministry. If Cassidy was right, this thing he'd built from nothing, this ministry that had started in a flimsy tent in an open field in Decatur, Georgia, a lifetime ago was in danger of being warped and bent and mutilated beyond all recognition. And he knew who was responsible. Cassidy was certain of it and he knew she was right. She couldn't prove it, not yet. But she was dead certain.

The Reverend walked to the kitchen door, out through the scorched garden and past the smoking ruin of the guesthouse out to the beach and its soft yellow sand and the blue Caribbean beyond. He felt a certain clarity of thought, something about the anger that coursed through him right now brought a focus, a purpose, he hadn't felt in a long time. It was George Brooks who'd done this to the ministry, who'd used it, raped it, for his own profit. It was the Devil's work. That was it, Brooks was in league with Old Scratch himself, and it looked like they'd won this round. They'd come in to this poor old preacher and offered something too good to be true, had offered salvation for the troubled Crusader Ministries. And Morrel Craig had been tempted and had succumbed, looking the other way when things didn't seem right, happy to see the money coming in and then going out to help the poor and the downtrodden.

He'd been a stupid man, a stupid, old man. And a sinner. He sighed, turned and walked back to the main house. He was alone, the others had gone to find Stu's daughter and her friend and he'd been happy to see them go. He needed to be alone with this for a while. He needed to keep his mind clear, to see all this and remember it. He looked out toward the distant horizon, then closed his eyes. He couldn't bear the sight of the water and God's glory reflected in it, couldn't stand the brightness of the day. He could only turn away, turn his back on it, walk back through the kitchen and into the darkened living room, the shades pulled tight. He sat in the old, comfortable chair and stared at the wall.

There was a scratch at the front door, somebody trying to open it, the investigators no doubt. The Reverend got up to walk over and help. They'd left and said they'd be back in an hour or two, hadn't they? This was early, but the sooner the better. He opened the door and standing there was the Devil Himself, George Brooks, a look of surprise on his face and then, in an instant, a worried look, full of concern.

Damnation.

"Reverend?" Brooks said, keys in his hand, ready to unlock the door and come in and commit more evil, no doubt. "Reverend, what are you doing here?"

And he remembered. "I'm here because my daughter called me, Brooks. Cassidy needed my help and I came."

Brooks walked by, into the faint pink of the foyer, turned to look at the Reverend, a frown creasing his broad forehead. "Is everything all right, Reverend? Cassidy is just such a wonderful young woman, I'd hate to think of anything bad happening to her again. Drugs. Those parties. Whatever." Brooks smiled slightly, added "You know, it's been two or three years since she had her little nose troubles, Reverend. I'm sure that's all over with. But you never know with drugs like cocaine, you know what I mean? You just never know. The need is always there in the background. It's easy to backslide."

The Reverend stood his ground, stared back at Brooks, and realized, as he looked at the man, that for the first time in his life he felt real hate toward someone. He could, the Reverend realized, attack this man. He wanted to harm him, he wanted to slap him in the face, take him by the shoulders and shake him. He wanted to hurt him.

There was a flush of blood to the Reverend's face, his heart pounded, its rate shooting up. He clinched his fists, could feel himself start to tremble.

"Reverend? Are you all right?" Brooks wanted to know, solicitous and friendly, that concerned expression hiding all the evil within. "Here, you better come over here and sit down. I'm sure she's fine, Reverend. And if there's been a little backsliding, like I said, we can get her into rehab, keep it quiet and everything and get her cleaned up and back on her feet again, no problem."

He came over to hold the Reverend's elbow and steer him toward the couch, and when he touched him, when his fingers first found contact with the Reverend's elbow — that was what set it off. The Reverend jerked his arm away and screamed "Brooks! You, you..." he lost it for a moment, then found his way, "...you're the Devil, the Beast."

"What? What the hell are you talking about Reverend? Calm the hell down, will you? Look, come over here and..."

The Reverend swung wildly at Brooks, missing him completely and throwing himself onto the floor in the process, so that he was on his hands and knees on the wooden floor.

"Jesus Christ, Reverend. What the hell?" Brooks, still played the role, reached down to help the Reverend try to rise.

The Reverend shoved Brooks' arm aside, struggled to his feet, faced him. "I know what's going on, Brooks. I know what you've done with the Ministry, you devil!"

So. Brooks smiled, nodded his head. No use playing anymore games, then. This was it.

"You've used the Ministry, you've used me, Brooks," the Reverend was crying now as he choked out the words. "You've perverted the Ministry for your own evil. Damn you!"

Brooks took out a cigarette, started to light it, paused, and then took it out of his mouth, looked at it, then shoved it back into the pack and shoved the pack back into his pocket. "Your goddamn Ministry is friggin' flush, Reverend, as a result of the organization I've put together. You like spending money all over everywhere on all this do-gooder crap, and now you can. Plus you own a goddamn baseball team, for Christ's sake, what more could you want?"

The Reverend was trembling, drew back his arm to strike again. Brooks took two steps toward him, reached out with his right hand and held the Reverend's clenched fist, then laughed at him. "You need to calm down, Reverend. You'll have a heart attack if you keep this up."

The Reverend's trembling just increased, like he was focusing all that energy, all the new-found hate, into his fist, trying to free it from Brooks' grip and use it on the man, pummel him, crush him into non-existence, exorcise him. A low moan came from behind the Reverend's closed lips as he stood there, shaking. His mouth opened and the moan grew, rising, growing louder still, turning into a scream as he finally moved his feet, twisted and turned his body, broke free from Brooks' grip and then flailed at the man, swinging wildly, blind with hate and fury.

Brooks just stepped back as the first two swings missed. "You sick old man," he said calmly, coldly, to the Reverend. "You're a stupid, sick old man, Reverend. You wanted me to save your ministry and I did. And, yeah, I did it with drug money. Lots of drug money."

Oh God, it was all true! And worse than he could ever have guessed! The Reverend swung wildly again with his right hand, then followed that with a swing from the left. Brooks, backed up against a corner cabinet filled with plaques attesting to the Reverend's successes in God's work, was hit by the left in his right ribs. The blow was just hard enough to really piss him off.

"Goddamn it, Reverend," Brooks was yelling, "you friggin' asked for this." And he struck back, a hard right to the Reverend's face that connected with a soft crack, like a hammer into an unripe melon. The Reverend's head shot back and he staggered a few steps back, blood splattering from his broken nose. But he gathered himself, came back for more.

Another right from Brooks, again to the face, breaking the jaw this time and sending several teeth flying, more blood spurting from the nose and now some from the mouth, too. Then a left to the chest, that fragile old chest, and the Reverend could hear his own ribs breaking. No pain, not yet, but the sound alone carried the news. The Reverend stopped, shocked by the blows, and stood there. Brooks hit him again, another hard right to the head, this one to the left ear. More blood as the Reverend's thin, frail skin opened at the front of the ear lobe. The Reverend fell to his knees.

"Goddamn it, Reverend. You friggin' asked for this," Brooks was saying, calmly. "I didn't want it to come to this, Reverend. I didn't want it to. But now I got to finish this thing. You stupid old man, I got to finish this thing."

He walked over to where the Reverend knelt and swung at him again, another right, this one crushing into the left temple. The Reverend, still conscious, knew there should be pain, a lot of pain, but there wasn't, there was just a warm, fuzzy glow over everything. None of this was real. He was distant from it, watching it all happen from somewhere up above as Brooks hit him again, and then again as he collapsed onto the floor. Then Brooks started kicking him, and the last thing the Reverend knew was the oddly soft thudding sound a leather shoe makes as it breaks ribs.

FIFTY

It started off looking pretty simple, just the one young guy, the one who'd blindsided him in the apartment, swimming around looking like he wanted to get waxed. Glad to oblige. And glad the spear was the same one he'd used to kill this kid's brother a few days ago. Nice sense of it all coming full circle.

So he came at the guy, holding the spear back a bit so maybe the guy wouldn't figure out what was going on at first. Then, when he was maybe fifteen feet from him he brought the spear out in front, pointed that wicked barb on its end right at the kid, and really started kicking with the fins. And then things got all sorts of complicated.

Suddenly the girl cop was there, too. Where the hell had she come from? Still, he knew he could handle things easily enough. It was, in fact, turning into his chance to get even with her the same way he was getting even with the kid. The two of them didn't have anything except their bare hands, so all he had to do was slash the guy to slow him down, then take-out the girl, then come back to the guy, who'd be swimming for shore by then. The trick would be to catch up with him before he could make the rock wall and start climbing out.

All this flashed through his mind in a second or two as the moment of that first impact slowly approached. God, he loved the way it was when it was face-to-face like this. Nothing sneaky, no figuring out ways to make it look like an accident or a suicide. No fucking pretense, just hand-to-hand and the best man wins.

There was always a dreamy quality to it. Back in 'Nam when he was just a kid, lying about his age so he could get into the action and kill a few gooks before the war ended; then later in Guatemala and El Salvador and Nicaragua: maybe two dozen times all told he'd faced it off like this and every time there'd been this slow-motion quality to it, this sense of every fraction of a second hanging out there, stretching out so that he was part of it and looking at it from outside at the same time as it slowly moved along. It was fantastic. No question about that. It was absolutely fucking fantastic.

He poked toward the Kelsey kid, expecting to reach him with that first jab. But he missed, the kid moving easily out of the way. He seemed to have more practice underwater than Mackie had expected. So he jabbed again, reaching out to make sure this time, swimming right at him, hard, at the same time as he shoved it toward the kid's gut. A stomach wound would do the job for sure.

But the kid dodged again, got out of the way pretty easily, really, just by turning sideways and watching the barb go by and then, son-of-a-bitch, kicking Mackie hard in the stomach with the heel of his right flipper for good measure, pushing him away and down toward the coral. Well, hell, that didn't go well. Getting too old for this, maybe.

Mackie turned and looked back up at the kid and then, from nowhere the damn girl was on him, coming up from behind and getting an arm around his neck and pulling his left arm behind him before he could react. A god-damn choke hold, and under fifteen feet of water. Jesus. He tried to elbow back with his right arm, but the water slowed things down and that didn't work at all. He needed some air, but she did, too, she had to. He tried to roll over, bringing her along, trying to shake her off, but as soon as he turned to the left and down the Kelsey kid was on him again, grabbing at his spear, try-ing to take it away from him. It was like there was six of them somehow, arms and legs everywhere closing in on him in the confusion. Had someone else joined the two of them? Damn it, it wasn't going right, that was for sure.

The choke hold hurt, and the girl seemed ready to break his left arm, the elbow flaming with pain while the kid grabbed at the spear and it was all going seriously fucking wrong, pain popping out everywhere and the two of them all the fuck over him as he tried to jab and slash. He reached back with his left hand to try and grab the girl but just got a handful of t-shirt, instead, tugging hard and ripping it off. That didn't accomplish much and he let it go. Then he thought maybe he got the Kelsey kid with one panicky slash of the spear, but he was so short of air he wasn't seeing things right. In fact, by then he thought maybe he saw two of them in front of him, but that couldn't be right because the girl was still behind him, putting on this damn choke hold.

He slashed again and then the spear was gone, yanked from his hand. He kicked out, hard, and felt his flipper connect with something, but all that did was push him down deeper. Then he felt a hard punch in the back, just inside the shoulder blade, and then another punch in the front, in the ribs just off center to the right. He put his left hand there to see what was up and damned if it wasn't his own fucking spear, the point of it coming right out of his chest.

There was no pain. It was comic, really, and he'd have been laughing at himself if he wasn't so damn deep under water. His own fucking spear. These two damns kids, no experience at all, neither one of the could even be thirty, and now they'd killed him with his own spear. He was looking up at the water's surface through a haze that seemed to cover his eyes. There was a bright, beckoning light up there. He wanted to head that way, he really did. He wanted to swim up there into the air and the sunshine, but he just couldn't get his body to do what his brain wanted. Funny, really.

Then there seemed to be someone else, someone swimming by him and then he felt the girl's choke hold ease at last and then let go of him entirely as he drifted down and then hit a coral outcrop, the sharp edges of it tearing into his back, shoving the back of the spear off in one direction and that son of a bitch sure did finally bring some pain. He could feel the skin letting go, knew there was a rush of blood coming from it, but couldn't seem to do anything about it, and he didn't seem to care somehow as he just lay there, staring blankly up to the bright, inviting surface, feeling strangely good about all this, feeling a nice glow despite the cuts and the pain in his back and his chest and his neck from that girl cop and her choke hold. Well, hell. She owed him. More than she knew, she owed him. He thought about that for a second, about the history he had with this girl over the years. There seemed to be plenty of time to think it all through, how it had all gone in his life from fighting with his drunk father to right here, right now. It was all very peaceful.

Someone was swimming toward him, maybe, a kind of apparition in the gray murk of his vision. Through the haze, he couldn't decide if it was really someone or not. Probably someone coming to finish him off. Well, that was all right. He felt very calm about the whole thing. He wondered, half-heartedly, if he should try and escape, put up a fight and then swim to the surface, get away from whoever it was coming his way.

But lying there on the coral outcrop seemed liked the easier thing to do, and so he just watched the form swim toward him and decided, in the end, that it made more sense to call it quits. Done. And so he floated there, peaceful, and let the gray go to a warm, comfortable black.

FIFTY-ONE

Stu, Cassidy, Krusoe and Robin had driven down West Bay Road in a little open-sided rental jeep, keeping an eye out for the Camry but mainly heading toward Parrot's Landing, where they could at least start tracking down Felicity and Michael.

Robin wore a wide-brimmed straw hat, sunglasses, and one of Cassidy's sundresses as a sort of camouflage, blending her in nicely with the tourists. Stu jammed a Crusader cap on his head and wore sunglasses as he drove. Cassidy, too, wore a Crusader baseball cap, a ponytail pulled through the opening in the back of the cap where the adjustable snaps were. Krusoe, weighing down the left side of the Jeep just by sitting there, had made them stop for five minutes at a little shop where he'd bought a tent-sized pair of shorts and a big floral print shirt. Very tropical, the all of them.

At Parrot's Landing, Krusoe kept an eye on Robin in the back seat of the Daihatsu while Stu and Cassidy went in. The people at the dive shop said it had been a couple of hours since they'd seen Felicity and Michael. The owner said he'd talked to the two of them himself, but had no idea where they'd gone since. Stu and Cassidy walked back to the Daihatsu and climbed in.

"Now what?" Stu asked.

"That way," said Robin, pointing toward the right.

"Why?" Cassidy wanted to know. "There's nothing down there. George Town is back the other way."

"One of Samantha's favorite spots on the whole island is just up that road," Robin said. "If they found out anything about her they'd go check it out, wouldn't they?"

"Why not?" said Stu, "I sure don't have a better idea."

So they'd driven that way, pulling out of the small gravel parking lot, and turning to the right. A half-mile mile or so down the road, driving along the shoreline, sure enough, they'd seen the Camry parked in a little park, next to a picnic table. There was a little tree-shaded sand beach there, then fifteen-foot high rock walls that curved to form a tiny bay.

"Smith Cove," Cassidy said as they pulled in, recognizing it. "The locals come here a lot. Nice quiet place for lunch, good snorkeling out there. I bet Felicity and Michael came here for lunch."

"And now?"

"Maybe they're out snorkeling together." She shaded her eyes and looked out to the Caribbean, "I don't see anybody out there right, but..." she shrugged her shoulders.

"So? Do we just wait there, then?"

"I suppose. We can't see past the rock walls, so they're probably just out of sight, up that way toward the big reefs. They might be back any time, Stu."

"Sure. But if they're not back soon?"

"Then I don't know. Trouble, maybe."

"Yeah," said Stu, shading his own eyes to look out toward the water. "Yeah, trouble maybe."

He couldn't stand just sitting there and waiting, though. "Look, I'm going to go walk along those rocks and look for them, OK?"

Cassidy nodded. "Sure, I'll come, too. From out there we'll get a wider view of the water. If they're in the water, we'll see them. But be careful, those rocks are limestone shards, they'll slice you up if you fall."

"I'll stay here in the shade," said Krusoe. "I could use the walk, but someone should stay here with Robin, right?"

"Sure enough," said Stu, and smiled. Then he and Cassidy climbed out and started walking along the sharp coral rock shore that bordered the Caribbean. The water was almost dead calm here, with only a slight swell from the open Caribbean slapping against the rocky shore. The footing was as tricky as Cassidy had promised, all sharp edges on the slick, salty lime-stone rock, so the two of them spent as much time looking down to where they were placing their feet as they did looking out toward the water, try-ing to spot any swimmers. They stopped twice to take a look, but saw noth-ing. There was an abandoned house up ahead, half wrecked from some storm, perched precariously on top of the rock, with a small dock cut into the stone. They decided to get to that spot and look around, and as they headed that way Stu's cell phone rang.

He pulled it out of his pocket, looked at the screen, opened the phone and said "Hello, Father."

"Did you read in this morning's *New York Times* what Tony Aguirre said about my work, Son?"

Stu stopped, smiled at Cassidy to let her know he had to take the call, then said "No, Father, I haven't had a chance to read the *Times* yet today. Aguirre's at Berkeley, right?"

His father sighed, Stu was wrong again. "He's a young gun at Cal–Santa Cruz, Son. He's quoted today saying that the collision of parallel universes might be visible. What poppycock! The very idea."

"Sounds really preposterous to me, Father."

"As it should son, as it should. And it's in direct conflict with things I explained quite well in *Physics Quarterly* nearly ten years ago."

"I remember that paper, Father. Brilliant work."

"It *was* well received, Son, as you'll recall."

"Yes, Father."

"Oh, and Son, be careful on those rocks there, if you break an ankle you'll be of no use to Felicity, and she's going to need you, she's going to need you very much. Several people are going to need you, in fact, Son."

And then there was a faint click and dead air. His father had hung up on him.

Stu shook his head, what the hell did that mean, Felicity and others needing him? Typical bullshit from his father. He shoved his phone back into his pocket and wished very much that he had a drink: a Macallan and a couple of ice cubes would be nice, but a beer would do nicely; anything to take the edge of this heat and the glare off the water.

Cassidy had walked on ahead as Stu talked on the phone. She reached the small dock first and, getting there, immediately yelled for Stu to hurry up, there was something caught on the wood pilings of the dock.

Cassidy had lowered herself into the water by the time Stu got there. He walked out onto the dock and watched as she grabbed it, something blue, and swam with it back to the side ladder. She tossed it up onto the dock before starting to climb up the ladder and there the thing lay, right at Stu's feet, a t-shirt, deep blue in color with the white script Crusaders written across the chest. The sleeves had been cut off it, someone had done that so the shirt would be cool when they exercised in it.

Stu knew that shirt, had seen it a hundred times. In fact, he'd been the one who bought it. For Felicity, on her birthday, not long after they'd first arrived in Rum Point.

FIFTY-TWO

The ring of a cell phone brought him awake from a kind of vague suspension where he'd been considering matters of life or death. Just let it go? Try to awaken? The phone, chiming "When the Saints Go Marching In," reminded him of Cassidy, his little girl, who needed him. He chose to wake up.

But when he opened his eyes it was to darkness and a stifling heat. It was hard to breathe and he was sweating. There was a dull ache that seemed to be everywhere in his body at once but mostly his nose, his mouth, his jaw and, oh my, his ribs. He heard a moaning, a low incessant groan that sounded a thousand miles away and right next to him at the same time. He was alive, or in Hell. Slowly emerging into consciousness, he decided it was life. Dark, cramped, stifling life: but life. The moaning was his own.

The phone stopped ringing and maybe, he thought, he'd imagined it anyway, but it was too late now to go back to that comfortable deepening gray place where he'd been. Had he been on his way to meet his maker? He thought maybe so, but now he was back. He couldn't move. He tried to move his legs, but they were bent at the knee and his feet were shoved up against his rear and he couldn't move them, the space was too confining. Hard edges everywhere. Where was he?

His arms were free, and he could move them a little. He managed to feel his face with his right hand. There were two huge swellings, one over the right eye, the other at the left temple. There were other, smaller swellings on the top, the left side, the chin, the jaw.

There was no pain. This was very strange. Why was there no pain? Shock, maybe. Later, there would be pain, plenty of it. And where was he? He asked himself that again, tried to think it through. He remembered the fight. He remembered being beaten and then nothing past that. But his mind felt strangely good. There was a kind of clarity he hadn't known in a while, hadn't even realized was gone. He focused on that. Brooks had shoved him into something, certainly. A trash bin? Could be. But there were too many edges around everywhere, there wouldn't be all those edges inside a trash bin, would there? The trunk of a car? Yes, probably, that was it. Hot, deadly hot and close in here. Brooks probably had stuffed him in here after knocking him out. Brooks probably thought he'd killed him, and had driven somewhere to get rid of the body. Funny to think of himself that way, as "the body."

Body of Christ, or, like the Jesuits he both hated and admired, the body and blood of Christ. Transubstantiation; that was him, dead and alive at the same time somehow. Ephemeral and real, alive and dead. But a lot closer to dead.

No. Don't start that way. Don't give in. Think instead of ways to escape, ways to get out of here. Assume it was a car trunk, a rental, not the Camry. The car wasn't moving, he'd be able to tell that. So, they were parked somewhere and Brooks might be back at any time, any second. When he found

his victim was still alive he'd just finish the job, certainly. So it was important to escape now. OK, fine. Escape now. But how? He moved his left arm.
Yes, it worked, and had a little room to maneuver. Both arms could do
things, then. He felt around behind his back, just feeling what was there.
Not much. Some wires. Some curved metal. Some cloth, rough, maybe a
towel.

The trunk latch. He found that, stuck his fingers into it, didn't have
the strength to move anything, didn't know what to move in any event.
Surely there was a safety device, some way to open the latch from the inside?
A plastic handle to pull or something. But maybe not. If there was, he
couldn't feel it. The metal, that must be the inside of the rear lights. He felt
it, tried to move it. Oh, thank Jesus, it was loose.

He wiggled it with wet, sweaty fingers. Looser, then looser still. Then
it came free, held only by the wires. Thank you, Jesus. He tugged, pulled,
the metal came loose. He shoved his hand into the opening and felt the
plastic housing of the outside of the rear lights. Have to break through that,
somehow. What was there to do that job with?

He felt around. Nothing. There was probably a tire tool and a jack
buried in this trunk somewhere, but they weren't where he could reach
them right now.

Felt around some more. There was a stick, no, a bat, a little baseball
bat. Souvenir bat day! Oh, Jesus, thank you for souvenir bat day. What was
this doing here? No. Don't worry about how, just use it. He grabbed it,
managed to wedge it into the plastic housing, pushed.

Nothing. Pushed harder. Still nothing.

He brought it back a few inches and jammed it hard against the plastic and there was a thin cracking sound. He brought it back and shoved
again, and then again, and then a third time and the cracking sound came
with each blow. Then a final time, shoving with all the strength he could
find, praying hard for more, begging the Lord for more.

And the housing gave. Light flooded in. And air. Warm air that felt
cool compared to the rancid air in the trunk. He felt back, found the towel.
Grabbed it, pushed it toward the broken housing, started shoving it out,
trying to attract attention, his only chance was someone would see it. Shoved
it more, then nearly all the way when there was a thunderous clatter from
above his head, another clang and bang and then the trunk yawned open,
someone had popped the latch and was looking down at him, turning him
over slowly.

A beautiful face. A mermaid, an angel, dripping wet in the hazy sunlight, looking down on him, concerned, reaching toward him, saying something about a good job of signaling, and how terrible this was, how wrong it was going, how it had to be stopped now. He was losing it, fading back to black, as she pulled him from the trunk and then picked him up, the angel of mercy, and carried him like a baby to her car.

FIFTY-THREE

Felicity remembered exactly the last time she'd been this glad to see her father, years back, in Detroit, after Mom's death. Dad had been there in the hospital when Felicity woke up.

Fel had been just a teenager then and fragile, shattering like thin glass from all the terror and fear of what was going on. She was stronger now, much stronger, and had just proven it. But she was still awfully glad to see him.

She stood on a narrow strip of sand beach that sheltered in the rock wall. Her right hand rested on Michael's head as he sat there on the sand, exhausted from the fight and the swim to shore. Her ribs hurt like hell. She hadn't even noticed the pain, really, during all the fighting, but she sure noticed it now. Slowly, she raised her left hand and waved at her father and Cassidy as they approached.

"Daddy, Cassidy. You're here! I am so glad to see you."

That sounded like she was eight years old, and surprised her as it came out. But it was exactly how she felt.

"Oh, Fel," her father said. He was almost in tears. "We found your shirt and thought that you..."

Felicity smiled. "It came off in the fight, Dad. Michael ripped it off to save me, actually, and then we were a little too busy to worry about getting it back."

"A fight? Out there?" He waved toward the peaceful Caribbean.

She nodded. "We were snorkeling, planning to meet someone, when this guy attacked us. He was the same one who attacked me back in Rum Point, Daddy, I'm sure of it. I mean, who else would do this?"

"And you two got away. Thank god for that."

She winced with pain from the ribs. "Actually, we may have killed the guy who attacked us. There was someone else who helped us, another snorkeler, and between the three of us, the last time I saw the guy he was lying on a coral outcrop at the bottom, bleeding. He's still out there, Dad. I'll have to tell the local police and they'll get some divers out there."

"He's dead?

"Pretty sure," she said as there was a rumble of thunder from the clouds building up inland. She looked that way along with everyone else. They could all see the rain falling a few miles away from the first dark clouds of an approaching squall line. It would be pouring here soon.

"It was him or us, Stu," Michael said. "I mean, the guy was definitely trying to kill me, kill us. Carrying a big spear, for Christ's sake. And he damn near succeeded."

"Well, thank god you're OK. Where's this other swimmer who helped out?"

"She had to be the one I met in the cave," Felicity said. "But then she disappeared when we came to the surface. Last I saw she was swimming away. I don't know why."

Stu shook his head. He felt as much as saw a distant bolt of lightning and heard, a few seconds later, a peal of thunder. He turned to look. That was a big storm building to the east.

Cassidy walked over to him, handed him back his cell phone that she'd borrowed to call the Reverend and check up on him. She was shaking her head. "Daddy didn't answer the phone, Stu, and I'm a little worried. I have to get back up to the house and check on him."

"The Reverend's here?" asked Felicity. "Why?" Then she laughed. "Come to think of it, Daddy. Why are you here? Don't you have a baseball game to worry about tonight back home?"

Then she looked at Cassidy. "You know, I really think we all should stay right here. I have to call this in, Cassidy. That was attempted murder out there, and I think there's a body floating on that reef."

Cassidy looked at Felicity. "I'm sorry, Felicity, I really am. But I *have* to go check on Daddy. Can you give me a little time? It's maybe a fifteen-minute drive to the house. I'll check on him, make sure he's safe and sound, and then drive back here. Forty-five minutes or an hour, tops. And then we can call in the local police, all right?"

Felicity looked at Cassidy, and then at Stu. He shrugged. What was Cassidy up to? He didn't know, but it had to be something more than checking on her father or she could just call the local police right now and have them check on him. She was stalling for something, no doubt something to do with the Ministry. How could she save it in an hour with her father? It wasn't adding up.

But then nothing else was adding up yet, either, and if they didn't stop yakking and get over to the cars in the distant little parking lot at the cove, they'd all be soaked, or struck my lightning.

Felicity offered a compromise. "My cell phone's in the car, Cassidy. Let's walk to the cove, get out of the rain, and then I'll loan you my phone. We'll get started with the police here while you're gone and you can get in touch with us to tell us your Dad is all right and then bring him back with you for safekeeping. I'll explain why you're not back if they get here before you do." Fel winced with pain again as she turned, the ribs reminding her with any sudden movement that they weren't over their beating. "That sound OK?" she managed to ask.

"That sounds fine, Felicity, thanks. And while we walk over there Stu and I can bring you up to speed, too. For starters, there was a fire at the house – someone burned down the guesthouse."

"A fire?" Fel's eyes widened. "It just gets worse and worse." But then she smiled and reached out to pat Cassidy on the arm, "I'm glad you're all right. And they think it's arson? Did they try to torch the house, too? Were there other threats?"

Stu shook his head. "Just the guesthouse, Fel."

Cassidy added, "That was about when Daddy showed up, too, Fel. He's back at the house now, waiting for us. I left him my phone but he didn't answer. He's just taking a nap I hope, but you can see why I have to go check on him."

Stu smiled. "And you can see why I'm here. I figured to fly back this afternoon for that ballgame." He looked at his watch, "but I've missed that flight now. Fel, I had to make sure you were OK."

"You flew down here for that? Left the team before the game that decides who plays for the pennant to come down here and check up on me?"

He smiled. "It's not as if you aren't in a little trouble, sweetie. I mean look at you. Your ribs are obviously really hurting..."

"I can take care of myself, Dad."

"I'll vouch for that," said Michael, standing there shaky but feeling better. "Without her, I'd be dead."

There was another sharp, bright flash of lightning and then a loud clap of thunder a few seconds later. There was a wooden walkway leading from the little beach some thirty yards over the rocks to the road. Felicity and Michael were barefoot, so though it would be a longer walk this way, they'd all taken that path to the road, then started walking down it toward the car park at Smith Cove. The extra distance was going to get them wet, they realized, as the first fat drops of rain and a strange, invigorating cool breeze from the storm hit them.

They didn't make it before the storm hit. There were two more thunderous cracks of lightning and then the downpour, drenching them in an instant with so blindingly hard a rain that they stumbled along the side of the road, unable to see more than a few feet ahead as they searched for the sandy driveway into the cove.

By the time they found the driveway the rain was easing and as they walked down it and up to the two cars, the sun was starting to re-emerge, the fifteen-minute deluge off to their right as the thunderstorm moved out to sea.

Krusoe and Robin got out of the little jeep as they approached and there were a few seconds of introduction and explanation as they all walked on over to the Camry, parked under the trees in the corner of the small parking lot.

Stu looked up to watch the storm pass by. They were in the eye of a circle of storms, and the one they'd just been through was only the beginning. To the east, that wall of cloud still looked ominous, tinged now with green. It didn't look like a great time to be out and about, but even as he had that thought he heard the squeal from the jeep's tires as Cassidy pulled it out of the little parking lot in a hurry and headed up the beach road to check on her father.

Felicity came up to him as he pulled the phone out of his pocket. "Why don't I make the call, Daddy? They'll keep a record of all calls. Let's keep you out of the record as much as we can, don't you think?"

He laughed. "You're forgetting my big shadow over there," and he pointed at Krusoe.

She shrugged. "Well, true enough. How much does he know?" And then it was her turn to laugh as she added, "Not that we know all that much ourselves."

"I don't think he knows a thing, really. Yet. He doesn't look it, Fel, but he's a pretty sharp guy, and he writes for the top magazine in the business. Anything that goes on here he'll be reporting on it."

She held the phone up. "So I should just go ahead and make the call? Get the police here?"

He shook his head. "Actually, I don't seem to be able to dial out, Fel, the phone tells me no service. But I've had a call come in, so that's odd."

"A call from grandpa, Daddy?" She sounded sad and disappointed and worried, all at once. "All right, no problems, we can use Michael's phone."

Stu shrugged his shoulders, this was not something he wanted to get into. "Look," he said, "Cassidy says this all connects up to the Ministry somehow. Something about money laundering, maybe."

"And murder, or attempted murder anyway."

He nodded. "Yes, murder, starting with your friend's brother, I guess, eh?"

She gave him a little half-smile. "The pieces are starting to come together, aren't they? Is Cassidy in on this, do you think? The Reverend?"

"I can't imagine that for either one of them. The Reverend is really slipping away on us for one thing and it's hard to picture him as a mastermind of anything criminal. And Cassidy..." he paused and thought that through. Could she be involved in something a whole hell of a lot darker than he'd like to think about? He thought he knew her pretty well, but what did he *really* know? Not much beyond some stories he'd heard about her past; troubles with drugs and bad boyfriends. Was that coming back to bite her now? Somebody she knew from those bad old days?"

"I don't know, Fel," was all he could manage to say. "I just don't know."

"Well, Daddy, we have to call the local police in on this, and now. I'm sorry if this is going to cause Cassidy some problems, I like her a lot. But..."

He nodded. "Go ahead, sweetie, make the call."

And she started to do just that, had asked Michael for his phone and was opening it up to start punching in the numbers, when her father grabbed her arm. "Look at that, Fel," he said, and she looked the way he was pointing.

There, big as life, was George Brooks, driving along on West Bay Road in a little rental jeep, smoking a cigarette like always, slowing down and coming to a stop in a row of cars working their way through the blinking red light that stopped traffic at the driveway entrance to Smith Cove.

Felicity closed the phone. "George Brooks?"

Stu was happy that a pair of scraggly, overgrown needle palms was between them and Brooks. They could see him all right through the fronds, but he wouldn't be able to see them. He wasn't looking anywhere but straight ahead anyway. What the hell was Brooks doing here?

"Daddy, we have to follow him. Come on," and she ran for the Camry as Brooks made his way to the light, slowed down to nearly a stop, and then accelerated away.

The others got the message as Stu and Felicity yelled at them, and within seconds they'd all piled into the Camry and Stu, behind the wheel, backed out of the parking spot, maneuvered his way around a couple of palm trees and two Australian pines, and headed toward the road. They were just emerging from behind the pines when Stu slammed on the brakes and held up his hand. They sat there for a moment and watched as another car pulled up at the light, just twenty yards away from them. Driving that car was Sonny Dickerson, a dazed look on his face, sitting still with his engine idling though the red traffic light was blinking and he was supposed to stop and then head on through.

FIFTY-FOUR

Where the hell had the body gone? It didn't' make any sense, and George Brooks was really tired of things not making sense. It was the cancer, that's what it was, messing with his mind; the news of it, at least, if not the snaky tendrils of it already wrapping around his mind. Shit.

He hadn't bothered much cleaning up the mess in the house; screw that, they'd all just think the Reverend had been kidnapped or something. By the time they figured anything else out — if they ever did — he'd be long gone. So he'd brought the rental car around to the back and thrown a big beach towel around the Reverend's body and then wrestled it outside and into the trunk, taking a couple of more good shots at the dead Reverend with that little baseball bat before tossing it into the trunk with the beach towel, slamming the trunk down, and then getting into the driver's seat and heading toward Mackie, who'd know how to dispose of the body quickly somewhere offshore.

Thinking it all through as he drove, Brooks smiled. The doc's news about the cancer had knocked him back, that's for sure: Jesus, he'd felt like shooting himself and getting it over with right on the spot. Truth was, he'd been sort of dizzy there for a while, his head spinning. Lung cancer. Those fucking cigarettes.

But after thinking about it for a while, he'd come to realize two very important things: First, if he was going to be able to do anything about this it wouldn't be through his friggin' health plan; no, it would be very, very expensive, the best doctors anywhere in the world, the best drugs, the best of everything. Second, if none of that worked, he was going to live the last months like a king. He owed himself that much after all this work, all these years of climbing the ladder. He'd go out on top, by god.

So he'd decided that it was time to cash in. Now. Today. And that had started with checking out the house to make sure there weren't any more flash drives in there, maybe one that Cassidy had brought into the house and plugged into a laptop she'd brought along or something. He hadn't even been thinking about the Reverend, but had just shoved his key into the locked front door and walked in to discover that the Reverend hadn't left with the others.

He'd tried to finesse it, really, but just didn't have the patience all of a sudden to bother with that kind of shit. So when the old man started to lose it, Brooks had just taken matters into his own hands, as it were, finishing the Reverend off with some quick shots to the head with a souvenir baseball bat from Ministry Field that he'd grabbed off the book shelves. Nice symbolism to that.

And, by god, it had felt good. In all his years in the business he'd never done that before, never killed a man with his bare hands. He'd forgotten for a few minutes about the cancer, about all the negatives that were flying around him every which way, and he'd just enjoyed it: it was honest and straightforward and it felt pretty good. Hell, it felt great. Hands on; that was the way he'd get things done from now on. Time to make some changes and enjoy what time he had left. Fuck Mackie and Kelly Ennis and Roberto and Sergei and Gabriel and all the fucking rest of them. From now on, George Brooks was in charge and fearless; he'd do it all by himself if that was what it took.

Lung cancer. Jesus H. Christ. All the work, all the years.

Then he'd driven to the friggin' hotel room where Mackie was supposed to be and the guy wasn't there. He'd even kicked the friggin' door in before he remembered he'd sent the guy to track the girl cop and her boyfriend. Jesus Christ, how could he forget something like that? Then he'd come back out of the hotel and the trunk of the car was popped and the Reverend's body was gone. How the hell had that happened? The son of a bitch was dead, damnit. He sure hadn't climbed out of there by himself; the stupid, frail old man was as dead as they get. Now Brooks couldn't figure out anything to do for the moment except stand there, dizzy with all the crap going on, all of it spinning out of control on him. Somehow he had to get a friggin' grip here, figure out what to do next.

There was the click of high heels on the pavement behind him. He turned, and it was more problems, in the form of Kelly Ennis, walking like she owned the whole damn world, and maybe, he thought, she did. With looks like that, and with who she was connected to, she might as well own it. She could get anything she wanted, anytime, so what was the difference?

He could see how Mackie would have the hots for her. She wore a swimming suit, a two-piece thing that showed off her tits and her tight, little ass. Her hair was wet, so she'd been swimming. She wore a tank top t-shirt over the suit, one of those Cayman Air tourist things with the blue and red turtle on it. It didn't hide a damn thing. Underneath all this, at the bottom of those perfect goddamn legs, were these kind of high-heel sandal things, kind of Roman looking with straps and the rest. Real come-fuck-me shoes.

And underneath all those looks and attitude was one sharp, tough-as-nails friggin' lady, able to handle working both sides of the street at once. He admired that about her. It's the way he liked to work, himself: work both ends against the middle and you come out ahead, way ahead.

"What the hell is this, Brooks?" she wanted to know, standing there, pissed off at him for something, hands on her hips, tossing that black hair back so her friggin' eyes could stare daggers at him.

"I just walked out and he's gone, something's gone. Somebody popped my friggin' trunk and he's gone."

"Who's gone?"

"The Reverend. We had a little trouble, the Reverend and me, and I had to take care of it. I shoved the body in there and was coming to get Mackie to help me get rid of it and now Mackie's not here and when I come out..."

"You whacked the Reverend? And now the body is gone, somebody stole it?" She laughed, walked over to the trunk, looked down into it, laughed again. "You are a fucking piece of work, Brooks. No question about it, a real fucking piece of work." She shook her head. "When we first started working together I thought you had all the right credentials, you know? I thought you were finally the right guy to work with. But lately," she stopped shaking her head, looked right at Brooks, staring at his right eye, focused on it, "lately I think you're losing it. You and fucking Mackie, both, losing it. What the hell is going on with you two? How am I supposed to count on you to get this done, when you pull shit like this?"

Brooks didn't need this. He had other things on his mind, the fucking cancer eating away at his patience, the clock ticking all the time now, tick tick tick, every second a moment closer to the end. He had to wrap this up and wanted to do with Kelly Ennis what he'd done with the Reverend, but she was way, way too important. She was the money girl and so he had to play nice for another hour or two.

"Look, it's Mackie," he said. "He botched the job on Honker, didn't get the flash drive when he whacked him, and then got into trouble trying to get it from the girl cop."

"She's the one who's the daughter of the baseball player?"

"He's the manager of the Crusaders. And, yeah, that's her. We figured she might know..."

"And you know she's down here, with Honker's brother and some local girl, too."

"Yeah, yeah, and Cassidy Craig, too, and then the Reverend shows up, the whole friggin' world down here at once."

"And all of them stumbling onto our little secrets, right Brooks?"

"Well, yeah. The Reverend's daughter, anyway, and I'm sure she told the Reverend but his mind is going — Alzheimer's or some shit — and I bet he doesn't remember a thing. She does, though. She pretty much has it figured out. None of the details, but she knows what's happening and she told her old man." Brooks shrugged his shoulders, "So, I did what I had to do with him to make sure he wouldn't ever remember, that's for fucking sure. And next I'll take care of her."

"And you brought the body here, and now it's gone."

"I swear to god he was dead, Kelly. I've seen a lot of dead men, and he was dead."

He could tell from the look of disgust on her face how disappointed she was in him, but, frankly, he didn't give a shit. Everything was different now. "Look, Kelly. Somebody broke into this trunk, probably just trying to steal some luggage, and found the goddamn Reverend's body and took off with it."

She laughed. Right in his face, she laughed. "George, you're a case. Sure, somebody broke in looking for a suitcase, found a body instead, and

213

so they stole that. Jesus Christ, George, get a grip." She got serious, switched tack. "Look, I don't suppose you have that thing with you now, do you? We could just do our business right here and be done with it."

He felt it in his pants pocket; could maybe do the deal right here. But what if she had someone with a Tango 51 aimed at him right now? That'd be like her, to have a sniper on backup. He looked around, thought maybe he saw a glint of sun off metal from the roof of the office building across the street. Hell, he'd hand it over and be dead on the spot. No. Do it right. "I'll get it. I need an hour, that's all."

She nodded. "Thought so. OK, then, the best we can hope for is that his body is in the infirmary's morgue and they don't know who he is. You didn't leave any ID on him, right?"

He nodded. He'd gotten that done, anyway, figuring on dumping the body at sea sometime soon and not wanting anything to wash up later.

"Well, that's good, George. All right, then. Let's take a look around and make sure he's not here in the bushes somewhere bleeding. If he isn't, it'll take them a day or so to figure out who he is, and by then it won't matter."

She was so friggin'—what was the word?—condescending. God, he'd about had it with this. She was asking for it, that was what she was doing. A whole scenario flashed through his mind, a delicious little fantasy where he teased her, got her to beg for mercy, and then whacked her. He could picture it in his mind: something with whips and black leather. God, would that feel good.

But he couldn't do it, of course, there was way too much money riding on her staying alive a little longer, just a couple of hours. Later, right after the transactions took place, he could get even for all this. He comforted himself with that thought for the next few minutes while they searched the parking lot and the bushes around it for the Reverend's body. They didn't find a thing. It occurred to Brooks, as they looked, that he needed a car without a popped trunk, so he used the cell to call the Cico guys. They gave him what they had—one of those stupid friggin' tourist Jeeps, canvas-roofed, open sides, stick shift. Not exactly his kind of wheels.

When it showed up—the one guy driving it and leaving it behind to drive off with his pal—Kelly Ennis found the whole thing real funny. The last sound he heard, driving off, grinding gears with the stick on the wrong side and all, was her laughing at him.

He got on the cell phone and got hold of Mackie. The guy was about to go snorkeling, he said, chasing after the girl cop and her boyfriend. Well it better not take long, since George Brooks had something else for him to do. One final Big Change. He had one last assignment for him, he told Robert Mackie over the phone, one final thing to wrap up. A little meeting in Hell with Kelly Ennis, get that done, and then he'd explain it all to him and make him rich. Mackie liked the idea.

Brooks shoved the stupid gear shift into third. Another hour or two, he thought, and it would all be done. Another hour, maybe two, and Kelly Ennis wouldn't be laughing anymore.

FIFTY-FIVE

He was Sonny Goddamn Dickerson and there was no way in the fucking world they were going to screw him over now. He was toasted, and almost started giggling as he realized it. Jesus, a bit too much there, Sonny, got to keep it together, pal. He focused harder on his driving.

It was hard, driving a rental — a little shitcan that was the only car they had available — down the wrong side of a road he'd never been on before. Hell, straight-up sober he'd have trouble with this, and now, tanked, it was a real challenge. But he was Sonny Goddamn Dickerson and he'd played outstanding ball when he was a whole lot more wasted than this. Just took a little focus that was all. Focus. Concentration. See the ball, hit the ball. Goddamned if he wasn't still the best hitter in the big leagues. Goddamned if Stu Lindsay or anyone else could take that away from him. And goddamned if he still didn't love playing that game, loved the sensation of the bat on the ball, watching it fly right out, up into the cheap seats in dead center. Seventeen years in the big leagues, MVP in the middle of it, that one great year with all those ribbies and fifty-three taters and wasn't he the greatest thing in the world? But never, ever, a pennant. All that time, all those games, and not one goddamn pennant. And now, lo and fucking behold, he could win one. If fucking Stu Lindsay would leave him fucking alone he could all by his fucking self win the division, win the NLCS, win the goddamn World Series.

Just leave me alone and let me play my game. That was all he ever

215

asked. But Lindsay couldn't do it. Typical manager, always sticking his nose in the wrong place, always getting in the way.

And now fucking Brooks was in on it, too, threatening to cut him off and all that shit.

A few hours before Sonny had been sitting in his beach house in Rum Point, up on the second-floor deck that looked out over the Gulf of Mexico, drinking Stoly and orange juice and then, fuck it, he'd come to the realization that he was, after all, Sonny Goddamn Dickerson, and they just couldn't do this to him. So he'd stumbled down the outside stairs and over to the Ferrari, cranked up all twelve cylinders, and driven his ass to the downtown Ministry Tower and demanded to see the Reverend. The Rev's secretary, a nice old gal, had been so calm and helpful that Sonny had lost his head of steam and listened to her. The Rev wasn't there, she'd said. The Rev was in Grand Cayman at his place down there.

And like a bolt of lightning, it had come to Sonny that what he should do—what he had to do—was get on a goddamn plane and get there himself. He'd had the secretary call US Airways for him while he motored over to the airport, left the Ferrari with the valet guys there, paid his eight-hundred dollars for first-class on a two-hour flight that was leaving in forty-five minutes, had a half-dozen rum punch drinks while he flirted with the flight attendants, and now here he was. Just like that. Four hours ago he'd been on his deck drinking Stoly and now he was driving on the wrong side of the road in Grand Cayman, on his way to see the Reverend.

The stoplight in front of him was blinking and he hadn't noticed. It turned red while he looked at it, then blinked off, then back to red. OK, OK, focus. No one behind him on the road so it didn't matter and he could go, right? Now: where the hell was he? Where was he going? He shut his eyes for second, opened them. Double-vision. OK, then, he shut the left eye, could see just fine out the right. He stepped on the gas, heading—yeah, that was it—to the Reverend's place, which was on this West Bay Road somewhere.

It dawned on him, through the haze, that he'd forgotten the fucking address, the one that secretary had written down for him. All right then, think it through: He'd written it down on a piece of paper and shoved that paper into his sportcoat pocket and then shoved that, in a blur, into the trunk when he'd rented this car. Jesus. Mad at himself he pulled off to the left into a little restaurant parking lot. He jammed the little Nissan into neutral, popped the trunk from inside, and got out to walk back and find the damn address. Jesus, he was really wasted, just standing up was something of a trick. Did it, though. And, sure enough, a minute later had found the piece of paper, and could read it perfectly fine with one eye closed. He walked back to the front, opened the door and slid in, only to realize he was on the wrong side —fucking cars here drove on the fucking left so the wheel was over there on the fucking right. Jesus, these fucking people.

He got out, walked around the front, and watched as George Brooks came toward him, driving a little rent-a-jeep with a canvas roof and open sides.

What the hell? Brooks? Driving by? And in that?

Sonny shook his heard to clear it. Had he hallucinated that? He looked again as the jeep zipped by and headed on down the road, back the way he'd just come, and swear to god it *was* Brooks, the son-of-a-bitch. Brooks hadn't even glanced Sonny's way, probably on fucking purpose. All right, then, this changed things. They had something to settle, him and Brooks. He could talk to the Reverend later, but right now he'd catch up with Brooks and let the bastard have it. Sonny found the steering wheel, got the engine started, wheeled the car around and got headed back down West Bay. Ahead, he could see the jeep stop at another blinking red light, then continue right on down the road. OK, no problem. He drove toward that same blinking red light, pulled up to it, lost his concentration for a minute and thought it was permanently red, then remembered himself and got the damn car into first gear again and headed on down the road. In the distance he still see the fringe top of the little tourist jeep that Brooks was driving. Pretty fucking funny, that car: Brooks and his Jaguar and his holier-than-thou attitude and all that. Well, all right, thought Sonny, he'd catch up with him, get him to pull over, explain things to him, maybe get a little blow from him, and they'd get it all straightened out. He'd been mad as a hornet at Brooks before, but a little blow and it would all be fine between them. Honest. It made perfectly good sense. It did. Really.

FIFTY-SIX

Surrounding Grand Cayman is a coastal limestone terrace called the Ironshore, a low rock bluff composed of coral, seashells and limestone compacted together during the Pleistocene period, some 120,000 years ago. In most places, like Smith Cove or on the south coast at the Blowholes, the Ironshore is at the water's edge, ten or fifteen feet above the waterline.

But in a few isolated pockets the Ironshore formations are a few hundred yards inland. The most famous of these is Hell, a bleak acre of rock sitting in the middle of the mangrove swamps that lie between the perfect manicure of the Hyatt Regency's golf course and the hard sand of Frank Sound's western shore.

You get there by walking down the marked path that winds its way between the twelfth green and the thirteenth tee and then onto an elevated boardwalk thoughtfully constructed by the Hyatt for its visitors who have an urge to go to Hell.

Hell is said to have received its name when a visiting British dignitary — on a typically hot day, no doubt — thought that Hell was exactly what it looked and felt like; dark, sharp-edged mounds of rock baking in the shadeless tropical sun, surrounded by mangrove swamps and filled with mosquitoes. The sharp rocks can slice into an unwary hand or sandaled-foot in a heartbeat, and the tourists from the hotels are warned about it — the cut can come so quickly and be so deep that you don't know you've been sliced into until the blood oozes — or, if you're very unlucky, spurts — out.

Kelly Ennis was early, figuring she had some things to do to be ready for the meet with George Brooks since she had to fly solo now.

She'd left the Reverend back at the infirmary. He was in pretty bad shape, but the docs thought he'd make it; he was a tough, old bird, addled brains and all. She'd left Thom Stephens back there with him to keep an eye on things, in case Brooks found out the Reverend was alive and came around to finish the job. That meant she had to do this without backup, but that shouldn't be a problem. It would have been nice, mind you, to have Thom back there with his Tango sniper rifle, ready to solve any problems; but it wasn't necessary. She and Brooks had a history, they understood each other, they were professionals. Or that's what she hoped.

The only real problem, in fact, was the weather. She could see another squall line, dark blues and greens in the clouds that rolled and swirled just a mile or two away. Weather forecasters were saying a tropical depression was building up, right over their heads. The squall line was a sign of things to come, she guessed. It might not get here for another half-hour or so. Time enough.

So, she thought, it had all come down to this. What a wild couple of

218

days, trying to keep it all from unraveling with the Reverend here and his daughter, and now this baseball manager and the chubby sportswriter. Jesus, a whole crowd of them, and her job was to try and keep the innocent ones alive while she got the job done.

It was a shame the baseball manager and his fat sidekick had gotten away back at the airport or they, at least, would be safely out of harm's way. Now all she could do was hope they'd keep their distance and not screw things up. God, it'd be awful if this got screwed up right at the last minute.

Three years of work, cultivating the relationship with Brooks and Mackie. Three years of living the lie you had to live to get the job done when you were undercover. Three years of feeding the monster until the day you finally got the chance to cut off its head. She couldn't believe how today had gone, from hauling the poor old Reverend out of the trunk of Brooks' car to saving Mackie's ass from the bottom of Parrot's reef. If ever there was a guy she wanted dead, it was Mackie, the murderous son-of-a-bitch. But there she'd been, hauling his ass up from the bottom and dragging him to shore after the girl cop and her boyfriend had done him in—couple of tough kids, those two. Last she'd seen, they'd been heading the other way—fast—as she dived down to get Mackie, that spear right through him.

He wasn't dead. Hell, she didn't know if he *could* be killed, the bastard. So she hauled him ashore, made sure he was still breathing and there was no ID on him and then called 991 on her cell phone and told them where to find him while she headed out to get her business done. Her cell phone was untraceable.

She hoped he was dead by now and her conscience would be clean on it; she'd done what she could. She had to hope, too, though, that Brooks hadn't found out about it one way or another. She didn't want this all to go bad on her at the last minute.

First, she took the repellent out of the backpack and slathered herself with it. The mosquitoes weren't too bad where you could feel a sea-breeze; but here, down in the mangroves and the sharp black-stained limestone rocks, if you stopped to listen you could hear their drone as they waited for you by the tens of thousands. She was in shorts and a knit shirt, so there were bare arms and legs to cover with the lotion, and then the neck and face.

Then, after wiping the lotion off her hands with the small hand towel, she started looking things over: where the boardwalk went, routes of egress should it come to that, places to find cover should it come that, making sure the satellite connection was working, running through it all once for practice. This had to be perfect.

It took a sweaty half-hour and she was starting to get nervous that Brooks would get here early, before she was ready. But no, George Brooks wasn't the early type.

She finished, then took out the cleaning wipes and gave herself a quick towel bath, getting rid of the sweat and then getting out of the now filthy shorts and shirt and into the sexy little shift and the come-fuck-me heels that were part of the job. More repellent, this time the spray that had the citrus smell to it. Didn't work as well as the good goop, but the smell was better and she was paying attention to details.

Got that done, looked at her watch. He'd be here in five or ten minutes. All right then. Ready. This was it. Five years of work and now the payoff.

A few long minutes passed and she heard his footsteps on the boardwalk and then he was there. "Hello, Kelly. Ready to do some business?"

"Yeah, Brooks, I'm ready," she said. And smiled.

FIFTY-SEVEN

Len Gold was relieved on two scores. First, he'd come awake, which meant he was still alive. Second, it wasn't completely dark in here after all; there was a little light on the sides, where someone had punched a couple of holes. When Roberto had first shoved him in here he'd thought it was pitch black. That, and the certain knowledge that Roberto was going to kill him, had him so terrified he'd wet his pants, whimpering like a baby as Roberto slammed the lid on him, slapped down a couple of latches, pounded on the closed lid a couple of times to tell Len to shut up, and then left.

It had been quiet then for a long few minutes and then the Xanax kicked in and he could feel himself losing it. He wanted to stay awake, he tried to stay awake; but there was nothing he could do about it, really, and he drifted off, angry at his own weakness but at peace with himself, too, right at the same time.

And now he was awake. How much time had passed? He had no idea. He took stock of things. He was alive. He had air to breathe, though it stank

220

of urine. Speaking of which, he had to piss again in the worst way. He thought about holding it while he tried to bang his way out, but then, hell, his pants were still damp from the first time, so why bother? He let it go, warm urine soaking his crotch. It felt awful and great at the same time. And then, he realized, it added to the odor. Man, the smell of it was overpowering in this small space.

Now he was thirsty, and so it dawned on him that being alive right now didn't mean he could stay alive long. Air, sure. But no water and no one to help. If someone didn't come let him out, he'd die in here sooner or later. That was a real comforting thought. Jesus, he couldn't decide whether he was really angry, or just terrified. Shout? Cry? He tried them both, but there was nothing and eventually, after ten exhausting minutes or so, he gave that up.

He pushed, shoved, tried to get a handhold in the cracks. But nothing. There was barely room to move his arms over his chest, much less get any leverage to pry the lid open. Hell, it was latched tight anyway. He'd heard Roberto, the son-of-a-bitch, clamping it down. So he was lying there, still, quiet, when he thought maybe he heard something, a sound coming in through one of the cracks. Somebody come to rescue him? Roberto back to finish the job? Jesus, it was terrifying. Should he just lie still? Shout and scream? He went for the latter, since he was dead either way if it was Roberto or some pal of Roberto's, and if it was rescue, they might not know he was in there if he didn't tell them.

So he pounded the best he could on the lid, shoving up with the top of his hands. And shouted help. And heard rustling noises, and then a clumsy effort to undo the latches. OK, then, this was it, rescue or death. One latch opened, a second, a third. One more to go, and whoever it was working on it was having trouble.

Then it came free, and in a wash of light from the ceiling bulb the lid opened. There was a round, confused face staring down at him, saying. "Hi. I know you."

It was Jimmy Smith, the clubhouse boy from the Crusaders, his round face filled with concern and then, when he recognized Len, a big smile. Len knew and liked the kid, who he'd met a half-dozen times through Felicity. "You help me, sir?" the kid asked again.

"Yeah, yeah," Len managed to croak, his throat dry. "Yeah, Jimmy. We'll help each other, OK?" And he reached up to take the hand of the Down syndrome kid who'd just saved his life.

FIFTY-EIGHT

Sonny had seen Brooks make the turn and so Sonny pulled his rental in, too, heading down the nice broad driveway, palm trees on both sides guiding you in like a plane on autopilot, which was, he thought with a giggle, actually a pretty good idea since he had to drive with one eye shut.

He drove down the half-mile of driveway on the wrong side, but, hell, at least he was getting there, right? Fucking right. He giggled again and kept driving and then, as he reached a parking lot up near the hotel's main entrance, he saw, sure enough, George Brooks, bigger than life, walking around the far edge of the main building, heading toward the back of the place. He beeped the horn but Brooks didn't turn to look.

OK, then, fine, Mohammed to the mountain. Sonny pulled the car over, half onto the shoulder and half still on the pavement. Jammed it into park, swung open the door, swiveled to get both feet on the ground, and hauled his ass out to stand up straight. Whew. Double-vision just standing there. No problem, though. A man's got to do what a man's got to do. One eye open, one eye shut, he headed after Brooks, hustling along pretty good, figuring he could catch up with Brooks no problem once he got around the corner of the building and could see which way he went.

But it turned out that once you rounded that corner there was a big pool surrounded by tourists, a golf course stretching off into the distance, and a mangrove swamp a hundred yards away or so on the far side of a fairway. Beyond the swamp was that storm headed their way, so dark it was starting to look green. So where the hell was Brooks?

Sonny was doing his best to stay focused — willing his eyeballs to work together for a few minutes so he could see his way around without that double vision. Jesus, he was really tanked. He checked the pool area first; thinking it wouldn't be hard to see Brooks in that bright blue Crusader knit shirt he was wearing. He walked down the length of the pool, everybody packing up their towels and sunblock as the storm approached. He was half relieved and mostly pissed-off that no one recognized him. Apparently no baseball fans in Grand-fucking-Cayman. Then he came back up the other side, smiling at one hell of a good-looking blonde who wasn't packing up a thing, lying there in the sun, oblivious to the dark clouds behind her. She reached up to tug down her sunglasses and give him a long stare before she smiled. He smiled back, on a what-the-hell basis.

"I know you," she said, "you're that baseball player."

Here we go, thought Sonny.

"I thought your team was in the playoffs or something. Shouldn't you be in New York?"

"St. Pete," he said. "I'm sort of taking the day off."

Her smile grew a little wider. "You must be hurt," she said, sitting up. There was a rumble of thunder behind them. She ignored it. "Is there anything I can do to help?"

Oh, man, thought Sonny, she was really something. A little old for him, now that he saw her up close, but those tits were just perfect, and that face. And it wasn't just the booze talking, she was really something. "Yeah," he said, sitting down on the lounge chair next to her. "I'm taking a day or two off for some R&R."

"I bet." And that smile flashed at him again, her teeth white, the lips full. "Well, me too. Maybe we could do a little R&R together, me and you?"

Too fucking easy. He smiled back, held out his hand. "I'm Sonny Dickerson."

She took his hand. "Danielle Abel. Dani to my friends"

"Hi, Dani." Jesus, his prick was firming up and that was great. He'd had a little trouble with that lately, to be honest; something to do with getting carried away with the Bolivian. But this was working, this was definitely working. And damned if he wasn't seeing things just fine at the moment, the double-vision gone. That was all he needed, a little something fun for a change.

"So, Sonny," she was saying. "Want to head inside before the rain gets here? Maybe relax in your room?"

Yeah, he thought, that sounded great. But wasn't he here for something? Oh, shit, that was right, Brooks.

"I'd love to Dani. But, you know, I just got here and I haven't checked in yet. And there's someone I have to chat with first. Business."

"And then pleasure?"

"Yeah, Dani. For sure, and then pleasure."

She stood up, started gathering her things, reaching into her purse to find a lipstick. She got that out, reached out to take Sonny's arm and used the lipstick to write "417" on the inside of his wrist. "That's my room number, Sonny. Get your business done and then come on up, all right?"

"All right," he said, and smiled while he let his eyes wander down from her face to that great chest and some truly inviting hips. He finished the visual

223

tour, knowing she was enjoying it, then leaned over and gave her a kiss on the cheek and whispered in her ear. "I'll be there soon, Dani, I certainly will."

She smiled, said "See you soon, then, Sonny," and turned to head inside. He watched her go. Damn. The day was looking up, for sure.

Fifty-Nine

Robert Mackie tried to kneel and aim, but even that was about more than he could do and he kept falling over to his right, up against the limestone outcrop that rose a good six feet from the shallow water. He was trying hard to do his job, trying to finish it, trying to be a professional; but it wasn't easy.

He'd come to his senses lying on his back in the sand down by Smith Cove, staring up a blue sky with a dark edge to it that was growing, overwhelming the blue as he watched.

It had taken him a few minutes to realize he wasn't dead, that the darkness encroaching wasn't Hell but just a squall line, that he was, in fact, alive and breathing. And in a lot of pain.

But the pain was good, the ache of it deep in his chest, the sharp tearing rip of it at the surface; these sensations convinced him it was worth trying to sit up, worth getting that done and then looking around.

There was an ambulance coming his way, he could see the flashing light and hear the siren. Well, he didn't want that, he had things to do.

He prioritized, just like Brooks was always telling him: first things first, think it through. OK, get out of here before that ambulance arrived.

And he did, rolling to his left so that he was on his hands and knees, noticing that his own diving spear was stuck in his chest, the front point of it emerging from the very center of his chest. It must have just missed his heart somehow, and missed everything else, too, or he'd be very, very dead.

He paused long enough to balance with his left hand down onto the sand while he reached up with his right hand to touch the spear. Amazing that it was there and he was able to move at all. Amazing, too, that there wasn't more blood. Why was that? Why wasn't the blood pouring out? He didn't know.

He started crawling, slowly at first and then faster, heading off the sand and into some scrub brush. He reached a fallen palm tree and paused there, decided to try and use the trunk to brace himself and see if could stand up.

And he managed it, a struggle for sure but then he was standing, and then walking, and then, a few minutes later crossing West Bay Road and walking into a small parking lot at an apartment complex. There was a little Hyundai there with the front door unlocked. Inside of two minutes he had the ignition wires pulled and was sparking them and had the car running. Two or three minutes after that he was driving up West Bay, heading toward the storage locker where he kept the sniper rifle, figuring he could get the rifle and get to Hell just about in time to do what Brooks had asked him to do, as long as he could stay conscious, stay awake, keep the car in its lane, be alert enough to put the scope on the rifle and get to that sandy side road along the far side of Hell and walk in from there. It was all doable and he got it done.

But at a price. He was so weak now he couldn't even kneel straight in the shallow water, even when leaning up against the limestone outcrop to his right while he braced the rifle on the mangrove root right in front.

He finished tightening the side screws on the scope and needed to sight it in. He managed to get back onto his knees and then lean forward, bracing the barrel of the rifle on the mangrove root and then leaning in to take a look.

Everything was murky and dark. Damn. He pulled back and wiped his face. He was covered in blood. How the hell had that happened?

He looked to his right and saw the blood on the limestone and realized what he'd done: the edges of the pitted limestone were razor sharp; every time he leaned against that rock he'd sliced his scalp. That had been a stupid thing to do, and even more stupid not to notice.

Slowly, clumsily, he used the cloth from the gun bag to wipe his face, his hands, the scope, and then tried it again, sighting on a distant tree, one-hundred-fifty meters away over by the boardwalk that ran from the hotel grounds out into the swamp and darkly stained limestone outcrops of Hell.

He heard voices, carrying over the water, and looked to his left. There was Kelly Ennis, doing a strip tease. He got the scope on her and she was just changing her shirt for some reason. The plan was for her to make the exchange with Brooks and then he'd waste her — one clean shot in the forehead if he could do it — and then Brooks would get back the flash drive from

225

her and then he and Brooks would meet in the parking lot out front of the hotel and get the hell out of Dodge.

All of which sounded fine a couple of hours ago. But now? He could barely keep it together, was fading in and out of consciousness as he kneeled in the warm water and tried to get his left eye onto the soft rubber socket of the scope so he could get the job done.

He looked again and Ennis was done changing. She was standing on the boardwalk and looked like she was talking to someone.

Damn. He came to with his face in the water. One second he's sighting in on Ennis and the next second he's waking up in the water. Part of his mind had a wonderful clarity right at the moment, and with that part he could tell that the rest of his mind was a fucking mess, and his body even worse. How much blood had he lost? Hard to say, but too much was an easy answer.

He struggled back into that same position, managed to get his eye into the scope's eyepiece, managed to find Ennis and watched for a few seconds as she stood there talking, holding something up in the air for someone — and that had to be Brooks — to see. The two of them were talking, so Mackie knew that all he had to do was wait until she had the flash drive — Brooks wouldn't hand it to her until she'd transferred the money into his account — and then squeeze the trigger.

Trouble was, he couldn't keep the scope on her, things drifting around on him, fading in and out. Damn.

He took a nice, deep breath, tried to steady himself, tried blinking and giving his head a little shake to clear it, tried another deep breath. It seemed to help, she was steady in the scope. OK, OK, get it done, get it done, get it done, he said to himself, trying to keep the scope from floating around too much. Focus. Focus. As ready as he could get, he watched, and waited, and got his finger onto the trigger. Any second now. Any fucking second now.

SIXTY

"You have it, George?"
"Yeah, Kelly, I have it."

"You look tired, George. Rough couple of days, I guess, with all these nasty surprises."

He raised his eyebrows at that, stared at her. How much did she know? "Yeah," he said. "Nasty surprises." Truth was, he'd hustled his ass out the damn boardwalk, trying to get here and get this done before that damn storm hit them. He could see it swirling around right behind Kelly.

Kelly Ennis frowned. He didn't mean the weather, though it was starting to get seriously darker now as the squall line approached. No, something was seriously wrong, but she couldn't pin it down, not yet. Her alarm bells were going off, though, and after fifteen years in this job she'd learned to listen to them.

"Something else come up, George? Something we need to deal with?"

He smiled at her. "Yeah, something came up, Kelly." But he didn't say what it was and she could see he wasn't going to. It was bad, whatever it was.

She pulled her data assistant out of her back pocket, held it out for him to see. "Deal was ten million, George. All I have to do is key it in and the transfer is done."

He smiled. Great thing about doing business on this little island was that the Bank of Cayman Brac, Ltd., where all this was taking place, was about a mile away in George Town, one of five-hundred banks floating serenely atop the river of money that flowed into and out of Grand Cayman every day. The island's total population was around twenty-thousand, so that meant either a lot of banking options for some curiously well-to-do fishermen, or a comfortable wash-and-dry laundry for those kinds of people who needed a certain level of discretion from their financial institutions. A thought occurred to him. What would a complete lung transplant cost? Could that save him? Could it buy him a few years, at least? Maybe that was it; a transplant and the new wonder drug that the doc talked about. Shit like that could buy him a few years, and he had the money now to buy whatever it took, goddamnit. It felt good just thinking like that. A few hours ago when he got the news from Springler he'd just given up, thinking it was the death penalty. Now, already, he was bouncing back. He'd always been able to bounce back. He was a friggin' survivor, goddamnit, and even this— elevated goddamn liver function or some shit—wasn't going to cut him down. He'd had plenty of close calls, plenty of tough spots, in his life and yet here he was, cashing in, still alive, still kicking right along. It wasn't over till it was goddamn over. He reached into his shirt pocket to grab for the Winstons, a reflex action, a habit built up over decades. He had his hand on the pack before he caught himself, smiled, took his hand out of there.

OK, then, this would take some more money, this little war he had to wage. That was no problem, though. Right here, right now, money was the least of his worries. He held the only card in the deck — not a bad way to say it, he thought, and chuckled down deep, felt a cough cropping up as he did it. He put his hand to his mouth to cover the cough. Got through it. Smiled again at her. "Thing is, Kelly, I've got some major expenses coming up, so I may need a little more."

She wasn't surprised. With Kelsey dead and his flash drive gone she knew she'd have to pay whatever he wanted for the codes. Well, hell, it wasn't her money, so screw it. The taxpayers — even the ones who enjoyed the products that Brooks and friends were shipping in by the ton every damn day — would just have to foot the bill. She'd negotiate some with him, but they both knew she'd pay what it took to get the information. With it, she could close down one of the two major cartels in the business. All the names, all the connections, all the whos and hows and wheres, all of it right there in Brooks' flash drive. Six years she'd been working toward this single moment, keeping her head straight through it all, taking the time to help Brooks feed the monster so it grew large and very hungry, pulling in the people they wanted with its success. A lot of people — some of them innocent — had paid with a lot of grief for her to be here, now, doing what she was doing. Time to close the deal.

She shrugged. "How much more, George?"

"Fifty."

"Fifty!" She laughed. "Jesus Christ, George, be realistic."

He shrugged, in control now. "Hell, I got ballplayers make that much just running around playing a kid's game in the dirt, Kelly. I've had a lot of risk getting this done — and like I said, I've got some expenses coming up." He smiled at her again, reached again for the Winston's, stopped, reached into his right front pants pocket, brought out the little plastic case that held the flash drive, held it up for her to see. "Plus, there's just one of these, and here it is."

"That's it?"

He opened the plastic case, tipped it upside down, shook it. Nothing came out. "You know better than that," he said, clicking the case shut. "But it's right where I can get it. Five minutes from here. And then all that information is yours. Put a lot of people away for a long time with that, Kelly, right? That's what it's all about, right?"

"Sure, George, that's what it's all about. How about ten more to make it twenty?"

"Fifty."

"Twenty, George. Twenty-five."

"Fifty, or I walk away and sell it elsewhere. Come on, Kelly, you know there are other markets for this. Certain people would spend a lot of money to get hold of this one little flash drive."

She sighed. "I'll have to check upstairs to get that OK'd, you know. That's a lot of money, George."

He laughed. "You don't have to check with anybody, Kelly. Jesus Christ, I worked there for twenty years. You can call Harry later and tell him to let the undersecretary know that this is what you paid and that's that."

He was right, of course, and she knew it. She smiled at him. "All right, George. Fifty it is."

"Fifty *more*, Kelly. Total of sixty."

"God damn it, George! Give me a fucking break here."

He turned to walk away, back up the wooden walkway to firmer ground.

"All right, all right, George. Sixty. Jesus."

He turned back, laughed once, a rattling dry chuckle, then pulled out his own data assistant, clicked on the readout. "Key it in, Kelly."

It was her turn to laugh. "The flash drive?"

"Well now, this is going to be a little tricky isn't it?"

"The drive, George."

"Key in half of it, Kelly, and then I'll walk you to the spot."

"You know you're dead if it isn't there, George, right?"

"You got a shooter ready?" He smiled, waved his right hand up and turned left and then right. "Sure you do, Kelly. And I got Mackie, with that Tango 51 rifle of his. You know that thing has a sub-1/4 minute of angle? Damndest thing to watch Mackie use it. He can put a three-shot group into a two-inch square at two-hundred yards. Hell, I've seen him do it. You want to wave hi to him, Kelly?"

She chuckled. Brooks was full of shit, of course. Mackie might still be alive, but he certainly was in no shape to be sitting out there in the coral and swamp with a sniper rifle. No reason to let Brooks know how much she knew, though. She wondered, briefly, if he knew she was bullshitting just as much as he was. She put her hand to her ear, pretended to hear a message from someone: "My guy says you can do that at one-hundred yards with the sound suppressor on, George, and two-hundred without it. He has the same rifle. So we're all up to speed here, right?"

She held up the data assistant, started punching in numbers. Bits of high-speed, encrypted data started flying around the planet, bouncing from Hell up to the NSA satellite and back through Switzerland to Grand Cayman. She finished, waited a few moments. "OK, George, take a look."

He dialed in, punching his own numbers then waiting, smiling. "Step one, Kelly. OK, here it is." And he reached one more time for the pack of Winstons, tugged them from the shirt pocket, poked one finger into the pack, got his thumb in there with it, and pulled out the flash drive — a little rectangle a quarter inch on the side and an inch long.

He held it up to the light from the sinking sun. "You know you can see right through it? Pretty damn amazing, isn't it? Fifty gigs in this tiny thing. Hell, pictures, videos, charts, graphs, spreadsheets..."

"And the codes?"

"Oh, yeah, and the codes." A coughing fit started, a hard, loose rattle that had him bending over with the spasm of it, then straightening back up. He spit toward the coral off to the side of the walkway, the spittle tinged with red.

"Ought to get that looked at George," Kelly said to him, realizing suddenly that maybe that was it, maybe the bastard was sick as hell. Cancer? Jesus, the way he smoked she wouldn't be surprised.

"Yeah," he said, just holding up the flash drive. "I'll get it taken care of. Now, transfer the other thirty."

"I need to see if it's all there, George. Give me the drive." She held out her hand.

He walked across to her, handed the drive to her, stepped back. "Just remember about Mackie," he said. Which was a helluva bluff, since he didn't know for sure that Mackie was actually there like they'd planned; but how could she know that?

"Sure," she said, and slid the flash drive into the side of the data assistant, took a look at the readout, tapping a few keys as she glanced through it. "Lots of shit here, George, but where are the codes?"

"Tap the little baseball bat down in the corner."

She shook her head, added "Real cute," and then tapped the icon of the baseball bat, watched for a few seconds, smiled. "This looks good, George." She tugged out the flash drive and shoved it into her pocket.

"Make the transfer, Kelly, and we can get out of here," he said, and she had just done that, had reached out to tap a few keys and in so doing had moved thirty million dollars around, when the sharp crack of a Federal Gold Medal 168-grain BTHP round breaking the sound barrier echoed through Hell as it left the muzzle of Mackie's Tango and headed her way.

Sixty-One

Cassidy had been in a hurry, driving crazy in the rental jeep, worried about her father. It was just four miles up the beach to the house, but there was a lot of traffic and it was just one lane headed each way and things were moving with agonizing slowness. She tried to hurry, passing on the left two different times when parking lots and bike lanes made it possible, running a couple of dubiously late yellow lights, and generally making a fool of herself trying to get there five minutes sooner, knowing that was a risk she shouldn't take and not caring about anyway.

And then she was there, wheeling into the driveway and slamming on the brakes, pulling up on the parking brake and turning off the engine and getting out of the car all in one mad rush.

She didn't run to the door; she walked, reached it, took a deep, calming breath, not wanting Daddy to see her flustered or worried, and then she put her key into the lock and discovered in doing it that the door was in fact unlocked and she could have just turned the knob and walked right in.

And there, in clear view on the far wall, was a splatter of something, a dark stain that ran from upper left to lower right. Blood, it had to be, a round circle of it where someone or something had struck the wall and then the trail, a smear, where they slide down the wall, from standing to sitting maybe.

Blood. Her father. It clicked.

She didn't panic. Instead, she found a dark, calm core that took over. Looking at the blood she pulled out Felicity's cell phone, dialed Stu's number. Nothing except a recorded message that the number could not be reached. OK, she tried again, dialing up Michael Kelsey's number.

He answered on the second ring. "Hello?"

"Michael, it's Cassidy. Is Stu there?"

"Sure," he said, "hang on."

There was a pause, then Stu said "Cassidy?"

"Stu, there's blood on the wall."

Silence for a moment at the other end for a long second, then Stu asked, "Where's the Reverend? Is he there? Is he OK?"

She hadn't even looked for him, she realized, and so started walking room to room, quickly, as she talked. Nothing in the front room, nothing in the dining room; she was talking as she walked, telling Stu. In a couple of minutes it was over. The Reverend wasn't there.

Stu had been listening to her talk her way through the house.

"Listen, Cassidy. I'm standing in the parking lot of the Hyatt. I'm just five minutes away from you. We've followed George Brooks and Sonny Dickerson and this is where they've led us."

"What?"

"Yeah, I know, it's crazy. But Brooks drove by and then, a few cars later, Dickerson. We've been behind them and now they've pulled into the Hyatt so we came behind them and let them get around the corner so they wouldn't see us. Now I'm going to try and keep an eye on them on foot."

"Brooks? Dickerson?"

"Yeah, George Brooks and Sonny damn Dickerson."

She knew, she was certain, what had happened. She was back in the front hallway, staring at the blood. "Brooks did this, Stu. I'm coming to meet with you. If I find Brooks I'll find my father."

Or his body, she thought with that cold, clear anger. But she didn't say that to Stu.

Instead, carefully keeping it all together and under control, she left the house, shutting and locking the door on the way out before she got back into the jeep and there, letting it go just a little, took a deep breath. Reality was catching up with her, the cold focus from the bloody wall slipping away as a wave of fear started rising. She felt isolated, alone, scared. It was the first time she'd felt this kind of scare in a long time and it reminded her of the old days: the bad old days. Back then she would have taken a little pop of courage, just one, to straighten her up. But there was none of that here and that was a good thing. She sat there, in the jeep, and took still another deep breath. Stay focused. No crying in baseball. Don't think about what it could be; think, instead, of finding her father alive. Find Brooks and

232

find her father, it was that simple. Save her father and maybe, in doing that, save herself.

Yet another deep breath. Daddy needed her. Stay on it. Stay in the game. Focus. She started up the jeep, jammed it into reverse, took off the parking brake and started backing up. She headed south on West Bay, hurrying but in control now, heading to Stu and the others, heading toward Brooks and some answers. Heading toward Daddy.

SIXTY-TWO

Stu had found it easy enough to keep an eye on Sonny Dickerson, who was weaving in and out of traffic and miraculously not banging into anything as he headed north on West Bay. Stu kept the Camry five or six cars behind Sonny, knowing he'd see him turn whenever that happened. The only real problem was the squall line from the looming storm that was north and east of them, a line of bruised-purple thunderstorms tinged with green at the bottom, marching toward them as they drove north on West Bay Road. When that hit he wouldn't be able to see much of the road, much less keep track of Sonny. But Stu figured he'd cross that bridge when it showed up. With any luck, Sonny would get wherever he was going before the downpour started, and maybe one little part of this whole puzzle would fit into place.

Next to Stu on the left, Michael was in the passenger seat. Behind them, Felicity, Robin and the huge bulk of Nick Krusoe were all crammed into the back seat. Nobody was saying much. The Caribbean evening — a lot darker than normal with the storm rolling in — was about ready to cover them.

The storm that was coming at them was curiously quiet; you'd think there'd be a lot of lightning and thunder from it. Instead, at the moment there was just the low swirl of blue-green clouds at the bottom as the squall line approached. Then Sonny Dickerson made a right turn into the long, opulent entry drive to the Hyatt Regency, where he and Brooks must be staying. OK, easy enough to follow him there without being noticed. Stu made the same right turn and headed that way down the long drive.

Sonny got close to the hotel and parked, then got out of his car and started walking fast around the side of the main building. Brooks had to be up ahead somewhere, waiting to meet him.

Stu pulled into a parking spot a couple of lanes away and then they all sat in the Camry and watched Dickerson walk away before they got out, the whole crowd of them, piling out one after the other — Keystone Kops, Stu thought.

What the hell were they doing? It made sense that he'd wonder about why Sonny Dickerson was here and if it had anything to do with all the rest of this craziness; but, hell, maybe the guy had quit the team and just come here to hide out from the media and drink some rum or something. But then what the hell was going on with Brooks: too many damn coincidences, that was for sure.

At any rate, he'd go — alone, damn it, no use anyone else doing anything stupidly dangerous — and find Sonny now and confront him and then he'd know if all this was just coincidence or if Sonny somehow connected up to the people who were trying to kill Felicity and Michael.

But alone, he needed to do this alone. He turned to tell the others that. "Look, this guy is my ballplayer and I'll go follow him and see where he's going. Fel, you stay here and keep an eye on things and I'll call you when I know what's up, all right?"

He didn't wait for her answer and Felicity, watching him go, just smiled. She was going to point out that she didn't even have her cell phone; she'd given that to Cassidy. But Dad wasn't listening. Which was OK. She waited a minute or so for him to get out of sight around the corner of the building and then turned to the others. "Stay here," she said, "while I go find a phone and call the local cops, all right?"

Krusoe nodded, happy to stand right there for the moment. Robin did the same. But Michael just shook his head no and started walking with her, strangely silent and determined. All right, then, fair enough. Off they went, the two of them, toward the hotel lobby and a telephone. Back by the Camry, the last time Felicity looked back, Krusoe had found a spot of grass with a little shade tree right in the middle of the lot and he'd taken a seat there. Robin stood next to him. That was all right, too; he and Robin were safer there than anywhere else around here, probably.

Stu had rounded the corner of the hotel and was nearly to the pool area when his cell phone rang. He assumed it was his father again and almost didn't even look at the call, but finally did on the fifth ring, and it was Cassidy and there was blood on the walls. He waited for her to look things over and tried to calm her down. That had to be the Reverend's blood, he knew, and the poor old guy was probably dead. It was time to call the cops. Now. He couldn't get that message through to Cassidy somehow, who was crying on the phone. He told her to get to the Hyatt lobby, just a couple of miles from the Reverend's house, and they'd work it all out from there. Then he hung up and tried calling 911. But that didn't work; he just got a canned voice telling him patiently to dial an area code and a number. And he had no idea what number to dial to get the local cops here.

OK, then, he would just walk into the Hyatt lobby and get the concierge to call the cops for him and he'd get them over here pronto before things got even more out of control.

He headed past the pool, figuring there had to be a door on the far side that led into the hotel lobby. Crazily, he noticed the landscaping, azaleas and palms and hibiscus flowering everywhere. Bright whites and reds and pinks, all of it very pretty. He could smell the flowers, too, like cheap perfume with a tang of chlorine from the pool. He felt a kind of hypersensitivity, all his senses on edge. Funny how the threat of death made you more alive.

Then he saw Sonny Dickerson sitting on the edge of a lounge chair talking to a blonde who barely fit into her swimsuit. She was up on one elbow, writing something on Sonny's arm; a phone number or room number, no doubt. There was no sign of Brooks.

Stu shook his head. His team was playing for the pennant in an hour or two, a thousand miles north of here, and Sonny was getting room numbers from women poolside in Grand Cayman. Typical Sonny Dickerson behavior, and Stu wanted to walk over there and make an appearance, see how Sonny reacted to having his manager show up.

But the manager was a thousand miles away from the big game, too, come to think of it, and there was a phone call that Stu had to make. People were dying around here, damn it, so talking to Sonny would just have to wait for a few minutes while Stu got into the lobby and got some help calling the cops.

Stu watched Sonny take a note from the blonde's hand and then get up to leave, no doubt for the lobby. Well, hell, better beat him to it, then, and Stu turned away from Sonny and headed through a little tropical garden, a cobblestone path weaving its way for thirty or forty feet before reaching the doors to the hotel lobby. He was just about through the garden when a shot — a single, loud report, came echoing from the swampy area on the far side of the pool.

Sixty-Three

Dani had finished getting her things together as Sonny stood up. She leaned over to whisper in his ear. "I've got some party powder in the room, Sonny. We'll have some fun. Call me."

And then she walked off, an absolutely perfect ass heading away from him and he debated whether or not he really needed to talk to Brooks right now. And then he wondered, wasn't it the Reverend he really needed to see? Shit, he couldn't remember. Oh, Christ Almighty. Well, hell, he was here and Brooks was around here somewhere, to he'd just go find him first, and then get around to seeing the Reverend if he needed to. He took a deep breath. Stay focused, Sonny.

He looked around; no Brooks by the pool. Nobody by the pool, in fact, everyone heading inside to get out of the rain. He started walking, trying to figure out which way it was to the lobby. The cobblestone path from the pool wound its way through some palms trees and huge hibiscus and damned it if didn't do a Y there. Which way to go, left or right? It was getting pretty goddamn dark out. There was a little roll of thunder. He was getting dizzy. Goddamn it, he was ripped. Shit.

And then he heard a loud bang from somewhere, hard to tell exactly where. It sounded like a damn gunshot.

Jesus, maybe he was hallucinating. Nothing seemed very damn clear, that was for sure. He looked again at the Y in the path, chose left, and headed down it. In fifty or sixty feet he came to a gate and another decision: go straight through the gate or take the path that went off to the right? What the hell was up with all these decisions? Hell, he opened the gate and kept walking as the path ended and he realized he was walking down a long wooden walkway that led into the mangroves. Up ahead, in the growing darkness, he could see yet another split, but this time at least there was a sign that would tell him where the hell the lobby was. He headed unsteadily down the path that led to god knows where.

236

A couple of minutes later he realized that all he was doing was walking deeper and deeper into the mangroves. Jesus, he thought, round one corner and you might as well be in the fucking Amazon or something, swampy water all around, mangrove trees rising on both sides, birds screeching into the air, a huge fucking parrot swooping by his head so close he had to duck. It was finally dawning on him that maybe this wasn't going to get him to the hotel lobby and he ought to turn around and head back, when he heard voices mumbling through a high-pitched background whine. The voices came from nowhere, from everywhere, drifting along through the goddamn swamps. The background whine grew louder, too, and then he felt a sharp bite on his neck, followed by another and then another. Jesus, mosquitoes, a thousand of them, a million. He swatted, swatted again, loud slaps in the stillness, the voices suddenly quiet. God, the bloodsuckers were draining him dry. He tried to run away from them, staggered, dizzy, and fell against the railing, toppled right over it, head over heels into the swamp, arms flailing as he fell, flat on his back, into a foot of water, enough to break his fall so he was conscious, peering up at the sky, a line of black clouds moving across the blue. He wished to god he was sober and could think straight. But he wasn't and he couldn't and he knew it. He did discover after a little trial and error though, that rolling over and getting to his hands and knees was doable, and so he did that, hands and knees into the water, splashing in the muck and mangroves. He stopped for a second to breathe and that, as it turned out, was a mistake.

"Stop right there, fuckhead," he heard. He looked up, and there was some kind of monster looking down at him, a guy, ugly as sin, with a huge jaw and — Jesus Christ — a spear point coming right out of his chest, right where his heart should be. The guy's shirt was covered in blood, his face splattered with that and the mud of the swamp. The guy was trembling.

And he held some huge high-tech rifle with a scope on it the size of a beer bottle. And the rifle was pointed at him, at innocent Sonny Dickerson, totally fucked up on girly rum drinks and oh shit all he'd come here to do was talk to the Reverend and Brooks, really, that was all, just a conversation to clear the air. And now this fucking monster was going to kill him — him, Sonny Dickerson, the best fucking hitter in the National League.

Sonny was on all fours, so, slowly, he sat back into a kneeling position, watching the guy stand there and tremble, his eyes slowly opening and closing like he was trying hard to focus. Sonny reached up and touched the muzzle of the rifle, tried to ease it aside.

All that did was wake the guy up, the eyes opening wide, staring at Sonny. Shit. Sonny started to back away, still on his knees, and the guy just staggered forward one step, and then another. At each step, the blood spurted from the guy's chest right where the point of the spear emerged. Sonny backed away again, slowly, and the guy came forward one more time, stumbled, fell to his knees, the blood pouring out of the chest in rhythmic spurts. How the hell was he still alive?

Time to go, Sonny figured, and started to rise, to run, to save his worthless life. He was, in fact, completely onto his feet and had turned and taken the first step before he heard the click of the bolt as the bullet fell into the chamber and he stopped and turned to see the madness in the monster's eyes and felt his bowels loosen as the monster, the blood spurting from his chest, squeezed the trigger.

SIXTY-FOUR

George Brooks hadn't had to move like that in twenty years, flying off the boardwalk and into the swamp and then beating it like hell for the cover of the mangroves. It all happened in a few seconds— though they seemed to take forever, waiting to feel a slug rip into him from behind as he splashed away from the boardwalk and slogged toward cover. He made it though, and fell down face first into the water on the far side, digging in to get away from the slug he knew had to be coming, but then didn't.

OK, then, he thought after a long minute's wait, lying there in the muck, what the hell had just happened? Was Mackie the shooter? Then why wasn't Kelly Ennis dead? Mackie would never have missed. But he hadn't been able to confirm with Mackie and wasn't even sure he was there, so if it wasn't him, who the hell was it? Some shooter for Kelly? Had to be, but those guys were professionals, too, and wouldn't have missed, either.

Which left no friggin' explanation that made any sense at all. Which meant, as he thought on it, that all he could do was clear out. He had the money, so why hang around?

He started crawling away on his hands and knees in the muck, aiming toward the golf course and from there he could scoot along the edge of the swamp back around toward the parking lot and his car and safety. He'd call Roberto and get that jet here, then get hold of Mackie if he could and get them both back to St. Pete where he could think it through, figure where to go for the cure, how to do whatever the hell had to be done to beat this goddamn cancer.

He had a half-hour, maybe less, before Ennis looked at the flash drive and then sent the data off to the agency and all hell broke loose — just enough time, maybe, to clean up his trail and disappear. Unless, of course, the shooter was sighting on him right now, in which case he'd be dead a lot sooner. Or, hell, sighting on Ennis, in which case he had a lot more time.

Problem was that he didn't know, and so the only thing to do was keep his head down and keep moving. At least the muck wasn't really that bad, he thought, still on his hands and knees, as he moved around another mangrove tree, roots arcing up out of the water turning the tree into a little island.

He heard another shot, this one very close, and he dived back into the water, putting his arms over his head to protect himself. This was it, then, the next shot would get him for sure.

But there was no next shot and long seconds passed. He rose up slowly from the watery muck and nothing happened. All right, then, that shot must not have been aimed at him, so it was Mackie pulling the trigger and right now Kelly Ennis was probably dead, a hole in that pretty forehead of hers.

He stood up, feeling safer, and started wading, hoping to find Mackie. A really large root was in his way, so he angled left to get around it, looking back once as he did it, keeping any eye out for trouble.

And when he turned again to look ahead as he maneuvered over yet another mangrove branch, he saw Sonny Dickerson — dead as a stone — lying there, his back against a mangrove root, his eyes open and blank, a nice, tight little hole right smack in the middle of his forehead, definitely Mackie's work, and definitely one of those recent two shots.

And there, oh Christ almighty, just a few yards away, around the side of a clump of mangrove roots, was Robert Mackie, on his back in the water, his face half under water in the swamp, the Tango 51 sniper rifle that must have done in Dickerson and missed on Kelly Ennis lying there next to him in the muck. There was, incredibly, a diver's spear coming a good ten inches right out of his chest. There was blood everywhere, dripping into the muck.

The two of them must have had a hell of a fight and now Robert Mackie, the best goddamn friend in the world, the only man George Brooks had ever loved — lay dead on his back, eyes staring up through six inches of water. Brooks reached down and pulled Mackie's head up from the water and placed it gently against the mangrove root, eyes still open, mouth open. Robert Mackie, whom Brooks had loved in a way that no one, ever, could understand, was dead.

Brooks was dizzy and the whole world spun. Mackie dead? No, that couldn't be true, there was no way it could possibly be true. But there it was. Jesus. He leaned forward, reached out to touch Mackie's face, not even cold yet. He was used to death, was George Brooks, but this was something closer, something more personal and awful. Jesus Christ. He'd never told Mackie the truth of it — never just said it out-loud.

Well, hell then. He bent forward and kissed Mackie on the lips, still warm, and then put his face to the dead man's cheek, whispered, softly, "I love you," and then took the Tango 51 from Mackie's hands, felt down into the dead man's pockets and found a few rounds, got one of them into the bolt action, and stood up, a vengeful angel.

Shit, he was going to die anyway. He'd just been kidding himself it could be any other way. So the money didn't matter, the whole thing didn't matter. He held the rifle up, screamed once in anguish and anger, and then turned back to run toward the boardwalk and goddamn Kelly Ennis. He'd kill her and then, come to think of it, he'd go find and kill friggin' Stu Lindsay and his cop daughter and her boyfriend. The daughter, Felicity, was the one who'd been the ruin of Mackie, goddamnit. She was the reason he was dead. It was way past time for her, especially, to die.

SIXTY-FIVE

Stu had stood there for a long moment after hearing that first shot fired. A handful of people came swirling past him from the pool area, including the blonde who'd been talking with Sonny Dickerson. They were hustling away from that sound and away from the dark line of cloud and rain that seemed about ready to hit. As they moved past him a flash of lightning and a quick crack of thunder — too damn close — lit the place up and then, suddenly, he was alone on the cobblestone path.

Had there really been the sound of a shot fired from a gun or had he misheard that? Was it just the storm? And did that sound come from the pool area? It sounded farther away than that, but with the wind swirling around and the rain about to fall, it was hard to tell where it came from. Oh, hell, he should just turn around and walk on into the lobby with the others and get the cops out here. And then he could get a drink while he waited for them. Or two drinks.

But it would only take a minute to get back to the pool and make sure Sonny Dickerson wasn't lying there with a bullet in him, shot by some angry husband for chatting up that blonde. Or, hell, shot by George Brooks: Sonny and Brooks obviously had something going that Stu only had an inkling of, and it couldn't possibly be anything good.

Damnit, he had to know, so he turned back and hustled through along the path between all the tropical foliage to get back to the pool. It took less than a minute and then there he was, looking out to a pool area that was completely cleared out: No dead bodies, thank god. No Sonny, no Brooks, no cops.

Where the hell was Dickerson? There was a Y in the path just behind him, maybe thirty feet or so, and that road not taken led off toward the mangroves, so that was the way Sonny must have gone. Stu headed that way just as his cell phone rang.

Cassidy wheeled the jeep into the Hyatt parking lot, almost running over a startled Nick Krusoe and Robin, who were standing under a tree. The squall line of the advancing storm was almost on them and they were glad to see her. She wasn't as happy to see them but shouted at them to come along as she ran for the lobby to find Stu. The first fat drops hit them as they made their way through the parked cars and got within sight of the sliding doors that led into the hotel.

Felicity was standing next to Michael and all she could do was shake her head as the three of them came through the door and headed toward her. The wind was really starting to whistle out there and the rain was almost on them, so she wasn't surprised to see Krusoe and Robin. But what was Cassidy doing here? Wasn't she at the house up on West Bay Road? She was about to ask Cassidy that very question but couldn't get a word in as Cassidy ran up to her, babbling, "My father's been hurt. He's missing. Maybe he's dead. Stu. Where's Stu?"

Cassidy was looking around, frantic. No Stu anywhere in the lobby.

"Cassidy, I think my dad is still outside, out back. He was following Sonny Dickerson and neither one of them has come in through those doors." She nodded at the wide glass doors that opened up to the back garden and pool area.

"Well, let's go. I have to find him. Now!" yelled Cassidy, and ran toward the doors, tugging on Felicity's arm as she ran. The tug was painful. Yanking on the arm sent a sharp wave of pain through Felicity's ribcage, reminding her of how sore she was, but she couldn't possibly let Cassidy go out there alone. So while she let go of Cassidy's hand, she also started running herself, staying right behind Cassidy as they headed toward the pool-area doorway.

When they got there it was a bit of a push to get the doors open against the hard, strangely cold downdraft from the squall line. Felicity's aching ribs complained, but she got the door open and they walked outside. She looked back when the door didn't slam like she expected it to and there was Michael, right behind her, and behind him were the others, all of them shoving their way through the onrushing wind, a Three Stooges routine almost, pushing and shoving with each other.

"Just stay behind me," she yelled at all of them, and then she heard a shot, a rifle she was sure, the sound coming from out in that swamp they called Hell. She wanted to turn around and tell them all to get back to safety in the hotel, but there was Cassidy running off down the path, heading out toward the mangroves, looking for one father or another out there. Felicity followed, and the rest followed her.

Sixty-Six

What the hell was going on? Kelly Ennis thought she'd had it figured right down to the minute. She'd meet Brooks, get the flash drive, get the money transferred and then send him on his way before getting back to help the poor Reverend and explain things to the others. Instead, Jesus, the sky was falling: Brooks holding her up for sixty million dollars and her stupidly paying and then, out of nowhere, a shot was fired and it certainly wasn't her guy who'd fired it, since there was no her guy to fire it, despite what she'd said to Brooks. She was flying solo here, like she'd done most of the damn time during this whole mess. So that meant Mackie was the shooter, despite the shape he was in when she left him lying there on the sand and hard rock north of Smith Cove.

Maybe, somehow, spear in his chest and all, he'd managed to get here. But why had he fired at her? And why had he missed? She didn't know, and she didn't like not knowing. Now, to top it off, that squall line was about to hit, huge raindrops splashing down like little bomblets into the water around her. She looked up into the twilight and saw the bottom of the squall line swirling and angry as it approached. It looked like a damn waterspout was starting: that'd just be great, get swept away like Dorothy in Kansas just as all this was coming down. She crouched in the muck under the raised boardwalk and just hoped to hell there wasn't some poisonous snake or some huge damn alligator floating around nearby while she took inventory.

Brooks was gone; he'd tumbled into the muddy flats and then run like hell past a stand of mangroves twenty or thirty yards away. He'd probably meet Mackie out there somewhere. Would the two of them leave without the flash drive that Kelly had in her pocket? Maybe. Or maybe not. Maybe Mackie was heading her way now to finish the job, get the flash drive back, and then leave with Brooks. The two of them could go with a clean slate, the only one who was witness to any of this— her — dead in the muck while they had sixty million dollars *and* the flash drive.

Still, for the moment she had the flash drive and she wasn't hurt, just a few scratches from crashing through the wooden railing and landing hard in the soft muck of the swamp. The drive was in her left front pocket — she checked there again to make sure. Problem was, she wasn't armed. Right after falling, rolling clear and coming up into a crouch, she'd reached for the little Glock 26 in the holster in the small of her back and it wasn't there. It must have come out as she fell, which meant it was here somewhere, in the gloom, in a foot or two of muddy water, somewhere nearby. So that was the first thing. Find the Glock. Keep quiet looking for it, but find it.

And she heard another shot, sounded like from the same weapon, with the same pitch and tone to the sound of it cracking out and echoing through the swamp. Who'd shot at whom, she wondered? Was that aimed at her? If it was, wouldn't the third one get her? Mackie, wounded or not, was a hell of a shot.

She started searching for the Glock, both hands into the murky water. It was getting dangerously dark out as the squall line hit, big fat drops of rain splashing into the water around her. She moved underneath the boardwalk as she searched along the edge of the walkway above. She couldn't see six inches into the water and so spent a couple of fruitless minutes at it. Nothing. Then she heard footsteps above her. Oh, Christ, that had to be Mackie, and she hadn't found it yet. She kept searching, trying to be quick and quiet at the same time as the footsteps went right over her head. She didn't want to go hand-to-hand with Mackie.

Then she felt the Glock, lying on the bottom on its side. It felt good; she loved the damn thing, so small and light they called it the baby Glock. A deadly little baby, it weighed just twenty-five ounces with a full clip and fit easily into the holster and then, comfortable as hell, in her hand. Damn accurate, too; she'd been in the black at thirty yards with all six rounds last time she'd tested on it.

And now here it was, thank god. She pulled it up from the water. Was it OK? Would it fire? Well, hell, she hoped so, because in a few seconds she was likely to need it in the worst way — live or die on whether it worked.

SIXTY-SEVEN

Stu had a headache and didn't want to answer that cell phone call. Instead, what he wanted was a drink, two drinks; and the only place to get those would be back at the hotel bar. Hell, Sonny Dickerson was long gone, no doubt, after taking another way back and sitting at the hotel's fancy indoor bar himself, probably, making good time with that blonde and working his way through a nice scotch or two. But Stu had gone past a couple of intersections on the boardwalk and lost track of exactly which way would take him back.

The phone rang again. Crap. He answered it. "Hello, Father."

"Son, you need to stay out there, all right? I wanted you to know that. Stay there, where you can help that granddaughter of mine."

"What do you mean, Father?

"Just stay there, Son."

"Why, Father?"

He could hear the old man sigh. "Because maybe Ashketar at Penn State is right. About multiverses, cosmic bubbles, quantum bouncing; all of that nonsense. Maybe, in fact, it isn't nonsense."

Was he hearing the old man right?

"Look son. Hang up and get busy. This is it, all right? I'm saying good-bye now."

"Sure, Father, goodbye."

"No, Son, I mean it. I'm saying goodbye. No more of these phone calls. You're going to do fine, Son."

"Do what fine, Father?"

But the call was over. His father had hung up on him.

The rain was getting serious, the few big fat drops of a few minutes ago getting a lot more frequent and coming with a strangely cold breeze. It would be pouring buckets in a minute or two. Stu stopped to look around in the darkness, and there ahead, at yet another intersection where two parts of this boardwalk met, was a little hut, a roof over a small bench. It would keep off some of the rain anyway. It wasn't more than twenty or thirty yards away. He headed down toward it and was almost there when a second shot banged out: a lot closer this one, just over in the swampy area somewhere, past that sharp-edged black coral to the right and the huge hunk of mangrove — like a little island — next to it.

Stu stood there for a minute. More than anything he wanted to get the hell out of here: who was shooting and why? Were they shooting at him? He didn't think so but it was hard to tell, damnit, in this stormy darkness and out on this isolated boardwalk, nothing around but coral rock and twisted mangrove roots.

He could turn around, but was that the best way to go? Jesus, he might walk right at whoever had that gun and was shooting it. Damn. And then there was that whole thing from his father. Damn again. OK, he'd stay.

He reached the little hut and the railing leading up to it was shattered, a brand new break by the look of it, a good ten-foot section of the wooden railing broken through at one end and hanging by a few slivers at the other end, so the long two-by-four of the railing led down into the shallow, dark water of the swamp. He had a bad feeling about this, a really bad feeling. And his head was pounding now like a son-of-a-bitch. Good god he needed a drink.

He heard noise, and felt it, too, a pounding on the boardwalk, someone coming his way, running toward him. Shit.

The break in the boardwalk beckoned to him. He could get the hell down off the thing before whoever was coming got here. He could hide underneath it, maybe, and wade over toward the mangroves and coral and hide out there. The pounding came closer, they'd be here in a few seconds. He started lowering himself down into the water, holding onto the broken railing as he did so, hearing the pounding behind him, scared as hell.

Kelly could hear the rustle up there as the guy sat down on the side of the boardwalk and lowered himself down, feet first. There was a pounding and a rattle, too, like someone else was running this way on the boardwalk. OK, then, now's the time. She moved, coming out the crouch and starting to stand as she came out from underneath, stood up quickly, holding the baby Glock out in front, both hands on it, finger on the trigger, left steadying the wrist. "Don't move!" she yelled, ready to shoot whatever target needed shooting.

But it was just Stu Lindsay, the poor, old alcoholic manager of the baseball team and the girl cop's father. How had he gotten himself out here in Hell? And why?

She didn't have time to mess with this, really. After only a moment's hesitation, she came out of the shadow and faced Lindsay as he dropped into the water and stood up, his back to her.

"All right, Mr. Lindsay, freeze. Hold it right there."

And freeze he did, a good little boy reacting to her voice just like she'd been told during her training at Quantico that most people would if the voice carried authority.

"Now turn this way," she said, letting the wet baby Glock drop down so that it pointed at the water. She didn't want any mistakes.

He slowly turned. She could see the relief in his face that the Glock wasn't pointed at him. All right, the first thing to do was keep this guy safe: he was just a bumbling innocent.

"Walk over this way, Mr. Lindsay and get underneath this boardwalk. I want you to keep your head down and try and stay behind these supports, OK?" And she patted the thick, wooden poles—the thickness of telephone poles—that held up the boardwalk. "Get in here, stay low and stay out of trouble. I have to do a little something and I'll be back in a few minutes. Got that?"

Eyes as big as a tumbler full of single malt, he nodded.

All right, then, she thought, that would have to do for the moment. He was as safe as she could make him, though god knows what kind of snakes or alligators might be in this water. At least this would keep him out of the line of fire which she figured was coming, and soon.

246

"What's going on?" he wanted to know as he moved underneath the boardwalk. He could tell she wasn't going to kill him, which seemed to make her one of the good guys.

And then, before Kelly had any chance at all to explain, there was a roar from behind them and a huge splash and she turned to see George Brooks, a rifle in his hands that was coming up to his shoulder to fire, screaming and bellowing and crashing through the water toward them from fifty yards away as he took clumsy, angry aim with the rifle.

SIXTY-EIGHT

They had heard gunfire off to the left, deep into the swamp and coral of Hell, just as they'd stepped onto the boardwalk. That had brought them to a halt. Then Felicity told them to wait for a few minutes while she checked it out and she'd slid down under the railing and out into the shallow water. If she wasn't back in ten minutes, she told them before going, they should get back into the lobby of the hotel and get the local cops out here, fast.

At first the water was only inches deep, the bottom more sand than mud, and so the going was pretty good. There were plenty of mangroves and huge outcrops of rock and coral, so she took advantage of that, hiding behind some of them as she worked her way toward where she thought the shot had come from. There was no sound coming from that direction now except for the whistle of the wind through the mangroves.

She turned to look back toward the approaching squall line, a dark blue-green line approaching them, minutes away. It had been ominously quiet until now but she'd seen enough of these storms in Rum Point to know that lightning could come flashing out there at any time. If she was going to find anything out there she needed to hurry. Sure enough, there was a quick, sudden brightness and a snap of thunder behind it as she waded past the next stand of mangroves, their roots up out of the water like the trees wanted to grow on stilts in the two feet of salt water. She ducked when the light flashed and then cringed at the thunder; that had been close, the light and sound only a second apart. A huge drop of rain splashed into the water ahead of her, big enough to raise a splash as it hit. Then another, then more. The squall line was almost on her. She turned to look at the group standing on the boardwalk, was going to wave that she was OK, but she couldn't see anything that way, all of it lost in the rain and the darkness.

Maybe she hadn't heard a shot fired at all? Maybe the sound was just a sharp crack of lightning? She was searching for reasons to give up this foolishness and head back toward the boardwalk, more little bomblets of raindrops hitting the water around her, then one hitting her on the shoulder, then another, hard enough she wondered if it was hail. One more look. She rounded the edge of the next group of mangroves and there, at the far edge, propped up against a rock outcrop and a mangrove's naked roots that arched out of the water, was a figure, someone sitting in the water, back against the root, a dirty white face just visible from this distance. She headed that way, careful with the approach, worried about who it might be, what they might be doing.

And damned if it wasn't Sonny Dickerson, the ballplayer for her dad. With a hole in his forehead where a slug had entered. Jesus Christ. She splashed over to him, knelt down in the water, reached out to feel for his pulse. As she touched the body it shifted left and she realized, as bits of bone and hair from the six-inch hole in the back of the head came loose and fell into the water, that Sonny was very dead, indeed. The slug had entered neatly and then tumbled through the skull. The brain would be a mess in there, the back of the skull a shattered shell barely holding in the dead tissue.

Her mind was roaring. What was Sonny Dickerson doing here, for Christ's sake? And why in god's name was he dead — murdered like this, a professional hit off in the mangrove swamps of Hell on the Cayman Islands? She wanted to check the body, but knew she shouldn't touch it, the local cops and their homicide people — she wondered if they even had a homicide department on this little bit of paradise — would want the scene as intact as it could be.

Which was a joke, since the squall line and its buckets of rain were just a minute or two behind her. All right, then, there was one more question, the big one: who'd done this, and was he still here?

She was still alive, so he most likely wasn't in the area. If he had been she'd have been shot, too, most likely, and this didn't look like the sort of work of someone who'd miss. She heard a noise, a mumble, from the other side of the big mass of root system. She stood, climbed over it, and there was another body — no, not a body, this one alive: barely.

Another victim? Most likely. He was a big man, tall and broad-shouldered, lying on his right side, one arm draped over a root just tall enough to keep his face out of the water. There was something coming out of his back. Oh, Christ, a spear from a spear-gun, the hard beveled edges of it shining in the next flash of lightning as she knelt down next to the guy. It was hard to see in the bad light, and the rain was coming down hard now, the real deluge about to start. She got to him, reached down to hold him, meaning to pull him up a bit and out of the water before he slipped all the way in and drowned in twenty inches of swamp. Incredibly, he reached back with his hand and tried to push her away. It didn't seem possible he could have the strength to do that, his back covered in blood from the wound where the spear came through, so much blood that it was dripping steadily into the saltwater, staining it a thin red and then pooling in a dark stain that didn't drift away here where there was no current.

But push he did, and then again. She started talking to him in the darkness, trying to calm him down, "Help is coming," she said, though she knew that wasn't true, at least not yet. "We'll get you some help, you just have to hang in there." And then he came free from the root and turned left, his head half in the water and only his face out in the clear. He saw her, eyes widening in surprise. "You?" he asked her.

And for one mad moment she had no idea what he was talking about. Then it dawned on her; this face, that big ornagnathic jaw, that black hair, those dark eyes. She knew that face. Behind the mask down on the reef, and in the shadows of her own apartment back in Rum Point. And now, seeing it here, the memory of it clicking fully into place, she knew it from the past, too. From a wet road over the Black River in Michigan, the stuff of a thousand nightmares, remembering how she'd scrambled free from the passenger side, forced open the door against the pressure of the freezing water, kicked her way free, rising to the surface, gasping with that first breath of air.

The face in the car window. That killing smile, driving by in the big sports-utility that had come up from behind, clipped them on the left rear, spun them over the low rail and into the river. That face, disappearing into the cold Michigan rain as Felicity had watched, then turned back to go for her mother, trapped on the driver's side, unable to get free, the mass of expended airbag and tangled seat belt and bent and torn steering while all too much to get free from in the cold and the rain and the rush of the winter river.

My god. This was the man who'd killed her mother and tried to kill her. He was dying, but not gone yet. "Help me," he said, and reached out toward her. It was a moment of clarity for her, time slowing so that she could patiently think it all through, think about all that had happened, how it had all led to this particular place and this particular moment and this particular confluence of people and events. That face, barely out of the water, just alive enough for her. Just enough. She reached out with both hands to touch him, to put both hands on his face. To push.

He struggled some, but weakly and the trembling was about done when Felicity heard some splashing from behind. She let go and turned. There, in the rain, walking toward her, was Cassidy Craig. Felicity raised her hand to stop Cassidy getting close enough to see, and then got up and walked toward her.

"It's Sonny. He's been shot," she told her. Cassidy put her hand to her mouth and he eyes widened. "He's dead?"

Felicity nodded. "And there's someone else, too. Dead." She reached out to take Cassidy's hand and lead her back to the boardwalk, away from the bodies. "Come on," she said, "let's get the others and get the police out here." Above them, starting to swirl down from the squall line, was a waterspout.

SIXTY-NINE

The squall line was on top of them, the huge scatter of raindrops suddenly thicker, fuller, harder — the front edge of a storm that would drop two inches of rain on them in fifteen minutes, blinding in its intensity. Felicity could barely see in the darkness and the wall of rain, but she slogged on through the water, Cassidy right behind.

It had taken her four or five minutes to realize she'd gotten herself completely turned around. Only when she went from calf-deep to ankle-deep water and then onto the perfect grass of the thirteenth fairway did she figure out that instead of heading toward the boardwalk she'd wound up back on firm ground. So she turned and ran toward the boardwalk's entrance. She'd left the others out there and she was the one with training, the one others depended on. She waved at Cassidy and pointing toward the hotel, trying to get her to go there. But Cassidy wanted to find Stu and her father, and so she shook her head no and stuck with Fel as they both ran out toward where the others were.

Felicity didn't want to take the time to argue with her. She had to get to the others and keep them safe. She had profound news for her father, too, about the man who'd murdered his wife. In another long minute she was there, hustling along, Cassidy right behind. Fel could see the group through the rain, huddled together near a small hut at an intersection of two main paths of the boardwalk. They were all looking out toward the same scene, their back to her.

As she came up toward them, the roar of the wind and the rain into the water drowned out her efforts to get anyone's attention. She could see, behind them, that the waterspout that had been up in the clouds a few minutes ago was now down touching the water, spinning up a huge swirling cloud of water and pieces of mangrove tree that was coming right toward them.

She'd thought waterspouts weren't too dangerous, but the thing looked nasty enough as it headed their way. She yelled again, but they couldn't hear her. And then, as she finally got up to them, grabbing at them and shouting, pointing toward the waterspout, she saw what they were all looking toward. George Brooks, crazed, covered in muck and screaming something about the man he loved, was running toward them through the swamp, carrying a sniper's rifle with a scope on it.

She got to them and they finally noticed she was there. The handrail was broken and trailing down into the swamp right where they all stood. Michael was there, and Krusoe, and Robin. But not her father. Was that good, that he wasn't there? She didn't know.

"Fel!" she heard from down in the water, and there he was, her father, down in the water, huddled behind one of the big supports that held up the boardwalk. He reached up toward her and she hopped down into the water and came to him, hugging him and pulling him down behind the support at the same time, out of the line of Brooks' fire that was sure to come.

She peeked out to take a look for Brooks, thinking she might get around him and tackle him from the side, god knows it was dark enough to get away with something like that in the blinding rain.

Stu tugged at her arm and when she looked at him he pointed behind her, toward the waterspout. It was fifty yards away now, maybe less. The others had finally seen it, too, and faced with that swirling mass on one side and Brooks on the other, they all hopped down from the boardwalk and climbed underneath it, scrambling for cover.

She helped them get down and then came another tug from her father. She looked and there, fifteen yards away but blocked from Fel's view by a wooden support was a woman, standing calf-deep in the water, taking aim at Brooks with a small handgun, a Glock.

Felicity looked out toward Brooks, who had stopped and was raising the rifle to his shoulder, clearly intending to shoot. Before Felicity could do anything to stop it, the woman squeezed the trigger of the Glock and fired off a round. And missed. Brooks still stood there, aiming. The woman squeezed the trigger again, but this time there was only a dull click, no crack of exploding gasses, no round screaming from the barrel.

There was no clip in the Glock. The first shot had come from the round in the chamber. Felicity and the woman realized it at the same time. "Shit!" the woman yelled and fell to her knees, searching with her hand for the clip. Fel went down, too, and as she did she heard the report of Brooks' rifle and saw chunks of wood from an upright no more than three feet away shatter where the round had hit it. She kept searching for the clip, realizing now it might keep them all alive. There was another muffled report from Brooks' direction and Felicity heard a sound from the woman standing down there in the mud, a dull oomph of surprise and pain as something spun her around and she fell back into the water, in a ludicrous sitting position, an expression of surprise on her face. Then, calmly, she held her Glock out to Felicity. Brooks was still coming at them, pulling the bolt open and dropping in another round as he splashed their way.

There was tap on her shoulder. It was her father.

SEVENTY

For all of his life that he could remember, starting with the very earliest childhood memories of swinging a baseball bat in a Little League game while his mother watched and his father stayed home, disappointed, Stu Lindsay had been part of baseball and baseball the greater part of him. He was so intimate with the game that he prospered in it through instincts, through guesses, that were grown and nurtured and informed by fifty years of knowledge. Cassidy called him courageous for these guesses. Sportswriters said he took risks and got away with it. Courage and risk.

But baseball, even professional baseball — especially professional baseball is a children's game played by grown men: Stu's father was quite right about that. Balls and bats and running and sliding and catching and throwing were a child's pleasures, meant to be played with cracked, taped bats and old balls with loose threads in the summer sunshine on a local playground with hats as bases and special rules because there's only five of you on each team.

A children's game takes no courage to play. Life, real life, takes courage. Being a father takes courage. Doing what parents do for their children takes courage.

All of this worked through Stu's mind in a long, slow, contemplative moment while the action all around him seemed achingly slow; Brooks slowly pulling the bolt open and ever so slowly dropping in another round, Felicity holding the Glock with no clip and slowly turning and leaning down to search for the clip in the shallow water, the other woman sitting there in the water, shocked disappointment on her face.

All of this in slow, slow motion while Stu had a world of time to think it all through and make his decision. No children's game: this, the real thing.

Stu moved. He ran, full tilt, through the water, dodging the sharp edges of the coral outcrops as best he could, splashing slowly for the first few steps and then he hit a dryer patch and moved faster as the water, now just ankle deep, hardly slowed him at all and the outcrops thinned. He moved at an angle at first, away from the group, away from Felicity, drawing Brooks attention as he ran, watching as Brooks turned to aim at him, diving as Brooks squeezed the trigger, then scrambling to his feet and getting back at it, running right at Brooks now, making Brooks shoot at him, buying Felicity the time to find the clip.

And it might have worked, too, if she'd found the clip.

But she didn't, and Brooks fired. Stu felt a thump in his left shoulder, like someone had punched him, hard. It spun him around and he stumbled and fell face first into the shallow swamp. There was no pain. There were no trumpets, either, and no Peter at Heaven's Gates. He was still alive. He put his hands down into the muck, pulled up his knees and tried to stand.

But his left arm didn't want to work for some reason. He could reach down but he couldn't push. Curious, he tried again and the arm gave way and he fell back in face first, which seemed very comfortable, actually, and he thought maybe he ought to stay there, face in the warm water and just relax some. He was very tired.

253

Then someone was helping him, reaching down to pull hold him by the sides of the face. Nice hands, the hands of salvation. He was able to look up and it was Cassidy. Wonderful Cassidy, here to save him. He came to his knees again as she gave him enough support to do that, then to rise, staggering with the effort to get to his feet. His back was to Brooks, Cassidy's face just a few inches away. A very beautiful face, really. He was thinking that it was a little confusing at the moment but he really did sort of like this girl.

She smiled at him. "Hey, Stu."

"Hey, Cassidy." There was a loud bang of thunder and an immediate bright flash of lightning. They both thought it was another shot by Brooks and it took them a second to realize he hadn't fired yet.

"C'mon, Stu," Cassidy said and got an arm around his left side to help him stagger along in the water. They aimed for a coral outcrop a ten yards away. Ten yards, a few seconds of struggling, and they'd have cover, they'd be safe.

SEVENTY-ONE

Felicity had watched for one horrified second as her father began to run. Then it dawned on her what he was doing. She dropped to her knees and ran her hands through the muck and sand of the bottom. Nothing. A long few seconds and still nothing. A shot was fired and at that same moment, too damn late, she felt the clip, half buried in the soft sand and sea grass. She grabbed it, wiped it quickly across her shirt and shoved it into the Glock. Would the gun fire? There was only one way to find out. She turned to see Brooks taking aim at her father again while he was struggling to get away, obviously hurt, and with someone there with him, holding him up. Oh, god, it was Cassidy, standing with Stu, tugging him along in the muck and the swamp, trying to reach some coral that might offer a little protection as lightning lit up the scene and there was an immediate crack of thunder.

Felicity turned back to Brooks, who was aiming at Stu and Cassidy. She steadied, had to take the fraction of a second to get this right, to bring Brooks down. She pulled the trigger and felt the recoil, saw the muzzle flash from the Glock. In that same instant she saw the flash from his rifle as Brooks got a shot off, too, all of this happening in the middle of the dark roar of the rain against the boardwalk.

Fel's shot hit Brooks in the chest. He stood there, frozen in the rain and the swamp and the mangroves, no more than twenty yards away. Then he dropped the rifle and, slowly, deliberately, like he was thinking it all through, he brought his right hand up to his chest, felt the hole there just as the blood began to spurt. A second passed, no more, and then, still touching his chest, he fell forward onto a narrow upright limestone outcrop that had compacted with seashells and limestone an ice age ago. His loose weight drove him hard enough onto the razor-sharp outcrop that it penetrated through the chest and emerged, nearly a foot of it, from his back as a peal of thunder roared around them all. Seconds later the waterspout ripped right through the boardwalk, no more than thirty feet from the group, tearing up the wooden planking and sending shards flying. It danced left and then right and then straight for Brooks, sucking up water and mangrove and muck and sand and, briefly, tugging at the body of the very dead George Brooks, who was brought upright for a second, yanked from the coral, spun around twice, a puppet pirouetting on god's dance floor, and then, dancing over, the spout moved on and the body of ambitious George Brooks fell forward into the shallow water.

Felicity's cell phone chimed "Take Me Out to the Ballgame." The noise of it was surreal, popping up in the sudden silence that followed the thunderclap, with Brooks' face down in the swamp in front of her, the hard rain easing off as the squall line passed, the waterspout retreating back into the clouds.

Her father was on his knees, holding Cassidy's head out of the water as best he could, his left shoulder slumping down. The woman who'd started this all was standing now, too, just a few feet away from Felicity. The woman was in a lot pain and there was blood at her hip, oozing through her pants. But she stood, and then she nodded at Felicity. "Nice shot, officer. Now let's go help your father."

And that's what they did.

SEVENTY-TWO

Cassidy Craig had been knowingly selfish her entire life. The only child of a famous man, she'd thought only of herself and had felt a kind of pride in that. And then had come this awful sequence of events that had brought her father, his ministry, and the one man she'd cared for in years: had brought it all to ruin.

Somewhere in there she'd come to realize that the world outside herself had its merits. She could care about others. She could save her father's life. And Stu's. And her own.

Now, as Felicity and the other woman and Stu all knelt in the shallow water with her, and as the sirens of the local police began to sound and then Dopplered nearer and nearer, she wondered if she was dying. It felt awfully peaceful, if that meant anything. And there was no pain, though she could tell she'd been shot in the chest, had felt the hard thump there like someone had punched her.

She felt pretty good, really. Kind of warm and good. She was sleepy. They were talking to her, trying to keep her awake, but that seemed a silly idea, since she was, in fact, very tired. She closed her eyes as the darkness settled in.

Felicity took charge when the woman who'd walked over there with her suddenly sat down, hard, into the swamp, overcome with pain in her hip.

Fel turned back to Stu, sat down next to him. In the distance, a siren was wailing, then another, even closer. She started looking at everyone, ignoring the cell phone until it stopped ringing. She kneeled next to Dad and Cassidy. Stu's wound looked pretty bad, but at least it was clean, both entry and exit holes so the round hadn't tumbled. The wound was bleeding but not pumping. He'd been lucky maybe.

Cassidy's luck was bad. Her chest was a mess and there wasn't anything Fel could do about at it the moment except wish her well and hope the locals got here soon and the EMTs were good.

"Hi, Sweetie," her dad said, as if nothing had happened. "I heard that last one go by my ear. Close, way too close."

"It got Cassidy, Daddy. Be still, help's on the way for both of you." He looked heartbroken when she said that.

She looked at the woman, the one who'd had the weapon and been trying to shoot at George Brooks. She was getting up to stand. She looked OK, too. She smiled at Felicity, began wading over to her through the muck, limping badly on her left leg, the hip bloodstained. "Nice job, Officer Lindsay," she said, holding out her hand to shake Felicity's. "I'm Agent Kelly Ennis. DEA."

256

Felicity's cell phone started ringing yet again. "Take Me Out to the Ballgame." Some other world, some other place, back up in St. Pete where they were playing baseball right now, where they had the time and energy to worry about whether one group of men playing a kids' game against another group of men would win a contest that had no bearing at all on life or death or who had murdered who and how and why they'd done it.

Still, it was chiming at her and it might matter. She pulled it from her pocket, hit the button. "Yes?"

"Felicity?"

"Yeah, it's me."

"Fel, this is Len, Len Gold."

"Hey, Len." What the hell was he doing calling?

"Listen. Alice, from the Reverand's office, told me you were down in the Caymans chasing down whoever it was that tried to hurt you. That right? You down there right now?"

"Yes. I'm sort of busy right now, Len, to tell you the truth."

"Well, I want to warn you. Be careful! There's some huge deal going down. I don't know all of it, but, Christ, it's drugs, for sure, and the feds are involved — god knows what all. It's dangerous shit, Felicity, really, really dangerous. They kidnapped me! Jesus, I'm lucky to be alive."

"What? Kidnapped you?" This had her attention now.

"Yeah, Fel. It was a guy I thought was a friend, an old client I got off. He took me at gunpoint, drugged me, and put me into some old food locker and latched it tight. Jesus, I thought I was dead for sure."

"But you're out now?"

"Yeah. Strangest damn thing. Jimmy Smith, the retarded kid from the Rays, you know?"

"The clubhouse boy? The one with Down syndrome?"

"Yeah, him. He just rescued me all by himself not ten minutes ago. He said Roberto Delgado, the same guy who put me in here, took him for a ride and he fell asleep — I know how that works, goddamn it — and when he woke up he was here, asleep on a cot, with a note pinned to his chest that said there was a prize in the freezer. The prize was me. Jimmy got the damn thing unlatched and got me out of there. I'm OK. I think I'm OK."

"Where are you now, Len?"

There was a pause at the other end. Len, still shook up no doubt, hadn't thought about it. "I'm in a bar," There was another pause while he looked around. "Extra Innings, that baseball bar maybe six blocks from Ministry Field, down under the Corey Bridge. You know it?"

"Sure. OK, Len. Listen, I'll have someone come there and get you both. Right now, you and Jimmy stay put, got it?"

"Yeah, yeah. Got it." He was scared to death. She couldn't blame him.

"I'll take care of it, Len. And thanks for the warning." No use trying to explain it all to him now, all the stuff that had gone down.

"OK, Fel. You take care of yourself down there, right?"

"Yeah, I will Len. You do the same."

Calmer, he said "Yeah, I will. Oh, and hey, you heard the news yet?"

"What news?"

"They got the game on here. First inning, Porters nothing in the top, Crusaders four runs in the bottom. We're looking good." There was a smile in his voice. He'd be euphoric soon, so glad to be alive.

"Dad's here, too, Len, and some others from the club. There's a lot going on. I'll let him know the score, OK? Got to go right now." And before Len could ask how and why Stu Lindsay was in Grand Cayman when his team was in the game of the year, she hung it up and clicked it off, smiling.

She turned to her father. "Four nothing after one."

He smiled at her, shook his head. He looked like that didn't matter much right now, but damned if it wasn't good to know.

The others had reached them as she hung up; they'd left the boardwalk and walked over through the shallow water. "But you're Sam!" Robin was saying to the woman, who was smiling through her pain. She reached into her left pocket, pulled out a shattered piece of plastic. Looked at it. Laughed. "Of course he'd shoot me right in the damn pocket." She shook her head, held it out to Felicity. "That held all the information we needed to nail all this down."

"Information?" She was starting to see how it all fit together, Cassidy and the Reverend, Brooks and that monster pal of his; all of it.

Ennis nodded. "All the details. Right here." She held her hand out, palm up, tiny bits of plastic and silicon lying in it. She wobbled a bit as she stood there.

The bloodstain on her hip was growing larger. The sirens had stopped and now there were people coming through the mangroves toward them — the cavalry, Felicity thought, arriving a bit late: island time at work.

"But Sam!" Robin was saying again. "But..."

Ennis smiled. "Yeah, I'm her, too, Robin. I'll tell you all about it, but you know what? Right now I'm really, really tired." And she collapsed, fainting into the muck, her fall broken only by Felicity reaching down to grab her and hang on, easing her down as the flash drive, the broken bits of it that had held the evidence she'd worked five years to get, fell from her hands down into the muck and brine of the saltwater marsh.

EPILOGUE

The Crusaders lost to the Porters, six to four in extra innings. Young Pete Macalaster struck out with two on, two out in the bottom of the eleventh and that was that.

The low-pressure gradient that spawned the squall line over Grand Cayman drifted west toward the Yucatan, picking up heat energy during that two-hundred mile passage. By the time it reached Cancun it was a tropical storm, passing overland into the Bay of Campeche where it regained strength, grew to hurricane status and headed north into the Gulf of Mexico. There, five days after the Crusaders' season ended, it gave St. Pete a scare before heading up the coast to the Florida Panhandle at Panama City. The waves it threw up onto the beach at Rum Point washed past the high-tide line and into the dunes, inundating for a day the nested eggs of the Kemp's ridley that started it all.

Stu Lindsay's wound was the result of penetration by a .308 millimeter sniping round. By far the most popular round in the nasty business of law-enforcement and military sniping, the .308 is known for its excellent terminal ballistics, its predictability in the wind and its overall consistency. Happily for Stu, it was fired by a man not particularly adept with the Tango 51 sniping rifle from which the round emerged, nor steady enough on his feet to aim well. Which is to say that George Brooks missed and so Stu was alive. The only round that found Stu entered at the anterior border of the acromioclavicular joint and exited at the posterior: through the shoulder and out the back, underneath the collarbone. On its way through his body, the .308 nicked the rotator cuff, and so during surgery at St. Petersburg's Baypoint Medical Center two days later Stu found himself going through a kind of inadvertent Tommy John surgery. The ligament resection went well and Stu healed nicely, the arm feeling good. The surgeon tells him he'll be throwing batting practice by mid-summer, perhaps.

Stu's other new doctor, a psychiatrist, is less sanguine about Stu's various kinds of health. After Felicity arranged the first visit to Dr. Conigliaro (the irony of that name escaped Felicity's attention but most certainly rang true for Stu), there have been six more and Stu is now seeing Conigliaro twice a week. They have a lot to talk about, starting with those worrisome phone calls from a dead father and going onward into murder and post-traumatic stress. Stu wants the phone calls to stop, or at least wants his father to accept who his son has become and be a little less abusive when he does call. Conigliaro wants to know why the calls started. The CAT scan, happily, came up empty; so the dead physicist didn't emerge from a tumor.

Stu tells the doc that he knows the phone calls were internal phantasms and he's enjoyed talking with Conigliaro about the origins of the bicameral mind. But when he's home drinking alone on the back deck of his house using that fine mind of his to read the *Journal of Cosmology* and thinking about the possibilities inherent in a multiverse reality, Stu does wonder from time to time how his ghostly father knew some of those things he warned Stu about.

Still, since that day in Hell the cell phone has been in his pocket and no one has called except Felicity a few times here and there. Stu hopes that's a good thing, and that his father is happy somewhere and is, at least a little, proud of his son.

Cassidy Craig died on the operating table in the emergency room of Grand Cayman's sixty-bed George Town Hospital. The resident in charge that evening didn't have a lot of experience with chest wounds caused by a tumbling .308 round that hit a rib on the way in and spun its way through. Cassidy didn't really have much of a chance.

Jimmy Smith, the clubhouse boy, spends his offseason working at the McDonald's on Thirty-fourth Street South and occasionally signing autographs for the baseball cognoscenti who come to visit. Every now and again Len Gold stops by and has lunch there so he can chat with Jimmy and shake the kid's hand. Len's pitching, hitting and divorce work prosper, and once or twice a month he also meets Roberto for a beer or two at the Wharf, where they talk about old times and Len repeatedly thanks Roberto for saving his life.

Nick Krusoe is a happy man. His piece for *Sports Illustrated* on Stu Lindsay and the Crusaders was changed somewhat by all the goings-on in Grand

260

Cayman, and he wrote it as he saw it, dead bodies and drug smugglers and the whole long thing. He's already written and sold the first draft of the follow-up book and got a nice advance. He's used part of that money to join a health club. He's on a diet.

The Reverend's Alzheimer's is confirmed. Joe Springler has him in a Phase III clinical trial for a drug called Mnemocept, which slows the memory loss. It's not a cure, but for now, it seems to be doing OK. Springler tells Alice, the Reverend's secretary and the one in charge of his life here toward the end just as she's been in charge for decades, that there are new drugs coming out all the time and maybe one of them will be the answer everyone's waiting for, hoping for.

For now, Alice has the Reverend in an assisted-living retirement center called The Fountains, over on Boca Ciega Bay. It's nice, but not too nice, as the Reverend says. He and Alice are struggling to do the best they can with the new accounting firm that's taken over the books. They're trying to straighten out the mess. The profit the Crusaders brought in with nearly three-million in attendance has helped, but the French doctors only got half of what they wanted for the Sahel project.

Alice is working hard with Major League Baseball to resolve the chaos around the ownership. She believes the commissioner and the ownership committee members to be honest, ethical men who will do the right thing for the Reverend and the Ministry. This belief will, in a few months, cost her dearly.

***

Now a good six weeks have passed since that day in Hell, and Felicity Lindsay stands on this beach with her father and Michael, waiting in the surprising warmth of a November night to see what might happen. It's her fourth night in a row, and if the hatchlings don't emerge this time around, she'll have to go dig for them. What she'll find in that case is probably a dead hatch, the eggs drowned by September's storm and crushed by the compressed sand.

Fel is in touch regularly with Kelly Ennis, who took a month off and then went back on assignment, again in the Caribbean. There's been a lot of death from all this: poor stupid Honker, in too deep and too slow to realize it; Cassidy, who'd been turning things around; George Brooks; Sonny Dickerson; Robert Mackie. That little twister that had ripped right through everything had picked up Mackie and Dickerson's bodies and shoved them

261

into the Hyatt's boat canal that ran past Hell about twenty yards beyond where they died. Dickerson's body floated into the Hyatt's marina just a day later. Mackie's body apparently washed out in Frank Sound and from there, the open Caribbean.

But for all that death there was still no final paper trail, no firm way to make the connections that the feds needed to go higher, to hit the home-run they'd spent five years prepping for. Kelly told Fel just the other day in a long, rambling e-mail from St. Kitts in the Leeward Islands that sometimes you get the bad guys and sometimes you don't. It wasn't a strikeout, really, just more of a double when they wanted that grand-slam.

Felicity looks out to the Gulf of Mexico; she's quiet and brooding in the darkness. She has the second watch today, so she'll be back here this afternoon, in uniform, watching it all, maybe handing out a speeding ticket or two on the beach road, maybe breaking up a fight at the Warehouse bar around the corner. It's not a tough job. She's starting to think, maybe, she's ready now for more, something a little more ambitious; the city of St. Petersburg's force, at least, where you can really do some good work now and then.

"Hey!" It's Michael, breaking into her thoughts. "Look, something's up."

She looks, and sure enough there's the slightest hint of something under the sand, a little poke from below, a tiny hole in the sand with grains tumbling into it and then, in a spray, some grains of sand flying out.

Then comes another poke, a little more sand flying, and then more and then, struggling, comes a tiny flipper, a half-inch of beaked head from the tiny hatchling, and then one quick glance around and it's pulling hard to escape the sand, pushing it back on the ones behind, struggling to get out, to get a firm footing and then head, quickly, for the sea.

As the whole gang starts to boil out of the loosening sand, Felicity and Michael and Stu get to work defending the path. It's a good twenty yards to the water and that's a risky trek for these little ones, but none of these hatchlings, not a single damn one, will be food for the screaming gulls that are gathering already. Michael owes that much to Honker.

It keeps them busy for a good half-hour, baby turtles by ones and twos scrambling hard for the water, that bright full moon calling to them, a beacon out over the Gulf for them to keep an eye on, to head toward as they start a life of wandering that might, just might, lead some of them back here to lay their own eggs in five or six years.

262

And then it's done, the last four of the hatchlings making a run for it together, side by side as if they'd planned it that way, a dead heat to the water and then, tiny flippers flailing away, they're into the Gulf and, moments later, gone.

"We better check up there in the nest, I guess," says Michael, smiling, glad to see that the hatchlings have made it. He counted sixty-three, pretty good numbers though sometimes there's one-hundred or more from a Kemp's nest. Still, he'll take it, and somewhere, he hopes, Honker was counting, too.

He walks up to the nest. Often there's a straggler or two, sometimes a weaker hatchling, sometimes one just caught in the sand or blocked by a stone or a buried piece of driftwood. It's always good to check, and sure enough, when he shines his flashlight down there he can see the top of a hatchling's shell, one of them caught on something in the bottom of the nest, trying hard to follow nature's dictates and get out of there, but held tight in the bottom by something.

Michael kneels down and then leans, reaching in to free it, sticking his finger down through the loose sand under the bottom of the hatchling. It's not a rock that has the hatchling's rear flippers trapped, it's a piece of plastic. Damn stuff, usually those six-pack plastic rings that traps them — hundreds of adult turtles die every year from those, a hatchling wouldn't have a chance.

He grabs the plastic, tugs. Felicity has caught up with him now and kneels beside him, watching, her hand on his shoulder as he tugs, figuring the whole strand of plastic is dug in down there and it will take a hefty pull to free it all.

But it pops free immediately and he tosses it aside as the hatchling, flippers freed, starts hurrying up the side of the nest. He gives it a boost, and Felicity grabs it, hands it to her father, who sets it down on the sand and walks along with it, managing this rookie's first moments as it finds the water.

Michael stands up, stretches, his work done. He flashes the light around for a last look and the beam catches the discarded plastic. It's a small, torn baggie, and inside is a piece of plastic a few inches long with a metal slot in one end. He bends down to get the baggie, holds it up to the light, pulls out the plastic flash drive with the metal end.

"It's a flash drive, Michael," says Felicity, "just like the one that was smashed. I'll be damned."

Michael nods and smiles. He looks at the tiny thing, a simple piece of plastic with a USB connection on one side. It looks cheap. It looks like no big deal.

This is what Honker buried here six long weeks ago. This is what he died for. This flash drive has the information that four governments want very badly and two drug cartels are willing to kill for. Codes for everything: names, dates, cash flows, profit and loss, liquidity. This is it, all of it. He looks at Felicity. She's smiling in wonderment. She must have been just a minute or two too late to see Honker bury it, back when this all got started. And now, here it is.

Stu Lindsay comes up. "Off and gone into the water, that last one," he says. He notices the flash drive in Michael's hand. "What's that?"

Felicity stands up, takes it from Michael, shows it to her father. "This, Dad?" she smiles, "This is a brand new ballgame." And she tucks the drive into her pocket and gets out her cell phone to call Kelly Ennis and share the good news.